Earthquake I.D.

Earthquake I.D.

a novel

by John Domini

 RED HEN PRESS | Los Angeles, California

Earthquake I.D.

Cover design: Mark Shepard
Book design: Stefanie Rosenblum

ISBN-10: 1-59709-076-X
ISBN-13: 978-1-59709-076-6
Library of Congress Catalog Card Number: 2006933035

Red Hen Press
www.redhen.org

The City of Los Angeles Department of Cultural Affairs, Los Angeles County Arts Commission and National Endowment for the Arts partially support Red Hen Press.

First Edition

Disclaimer: This book is a work of the imagination. Naturally the invention takes off from the facts, but any resemblance between the incidents and characters described here and actual events or actual persons, living or dead, is wholly coincidental.

Acknowledgements

No amount of thanks can begin to express how much the support of Kate Gale, Mark Cull, and Red Hen Press have meant to this book.

Lettie Prell, likewise—though I must mention her crucial late reading.

Mark Shepherd, thanks for another bracing splash of a book cover. Rick Lovett, Valerie Grey, Reg Gibbons, Faye Bender, Connie Fischbein, Alexander Hemon, Lex Runciman, and Roxanna Khosravi, thanks for early readings.

Financial support came from the Northwestern University Center for the Writing Arts, Drake University, and the Metropolitan Arts Commission of Portland, OR.

To write about Naples is to inscribe on a palimpsest. That very image is an older one, from Peter Gunn, a British lover of the city. My cityscape was scratched across his, and across other renderings by Shirley Hazzard and Frances Steegmuller, by John Horne Burns and Gustav Herling, by William Morris and Thomas Belmonte . . . and Goethe, and Shelley. . . . really, no book can complete the list, not even the heartrending *Naples: 44*, by Norman Lewis. To all I say *grazie*, and *bravo*.

Among my Naples friends, the essential connection was Ognissanti, a visionary in terracotta. Also see the dedication, and spare a thought as well for my late father, born Vincenzo Vicedomini by the Piazza della Borsa, also called Piazza Bovio.

Sorella, fratello,
e tutti i cugini

Earthquake I.D.

O heavens, that they were living both in Naples,
The King and Queen there!

—*The Tempest*

Chapter One

One good look at Naples on a map and Barbara began to wonder. This was weeks before the family got on a plane. Barb was still running the kids to springtime activities, and her husband, Jay, was tying up loose ends with Viccieco & Sons. One Friday her husband called from midtown to say he'd catch the later Bridgeport local, and when he did get home, Jay pulled from his ever-emptier briefcase a map big enough, unfolded, to cover the entire dining-room table. German make, the thing was four or five maps in one. You had inserts for the island of Capri and the excavations at Pompeii, for the inner city of first Greeks then Romans then, God knows, another ten ruling orders up through NATO. It was all Barbara could do to get her mind around the greater metropolitan semi-circle, the urban sprawl that curved around the Bay between volcanoes north and south. To the south was the more serious trouble, Vesuvius. The towns destroyed in the latest earthquake all lay near Vesuvius.

"We'll never be lost," the father announced over the gathered bent heads. "Hey. I mean, never."

But Barb had to wonder. For starters the thing was largely illegible, the distance key in kilometers and the indexes set up according to some obscure Teutonic notion of what a traveler needed to know. The only words she recognized were Italian. This confusion extended even to the coloring, since each of the maps-within-maps had a border on the Bay. The water was a brilliant ceramic blue, a color that attracted the twin eight-year-olds. The two girls had to touch, cooing, but meantime the mother's bewilderment gave way to worse. Against the ubiquitous sea the city center was always depicted in yellow, whether shown from a distance or in close up, and either way, to Barb it started to look like a gaping maw the color of pus. The few highways that threaded the area were blood red, and the metropolis itself presented lips spread wide for a love-bite. There was a bit of tongue, the peninsula on which stood the Castel Dell'Ovo. Barbara stood faced with a soul kiss full of disease.

And who was expected to return the kiss? The mother thought of her church work. Who was playing Jesus to this leper? She and the rest of her family, that's who. The husband she'd stood by for nearly twenty years and their five Lulucita children.

There at the dining-room table, tugging at the armpit and belt of a perfectly good spring dress, she managed eventually to wrestle down her worries. She convinced herself, by the time the map was put away, that the family wasn't in fact throwing itself into something grotesque and beyond diagnosis. What she just thought she'd seen must've had more to do, rather, with all the sore spots that preceded the move. Some of those spots weren't entirely free of infection themselves, yet. Barbara was still troubled by their failed attempt at adoption over the winter.

And anyone had to wonder, didn't they, about a longtime solid provider like her Jaybird abruptly quitting his vice-president's chair? About him accepting, instead, a position in the quake-relief effort, very much not-for-profit? Barb had agreed to the move, granted. Nonetheless she and Jay had hashed out their reasoning in yet another foreign language. They'd exchanged vague talk, vague and abortive, about how "a fresh perspective" might be good for them. This when, over in Naples, Jay would be working with the most volatile of the region's many quasi-legal populations. He'd been stationed at a facility for the people who were homeless before the quake. The boat people, most of them not long out of Africa.

Anyone would feel concerned. Anyone might see a horror show coming. And when Jay was hit and robbed their first day in the Mediterranean city—a quick mugging for such a big man, and a clean sweep of the family's contracts and credit cards and passports—Barb could only think: *I knew it.* The family could never survive such confusion. There in Naples, they'd come to the end of everything.

The muggers on the other hand had used the local scarring for camouflage. Their bike roared out of an alleyway, out from under the scaffolding of reconstruction, clearing a shot through the downtown crowd. Weekday crowd, early June, broad daylight. Somehow the thieves knew the exact moment and corner at which the family would present the easiest pickings. A number of streets in lower Naples remained walkable, if a person was willing to share space with jackhammers and power coils. This particular *vicolo* got a lot of foot traffic, and the intersection had forced Barbara's family to walk single file, with Jay and his refilled briefcase at the rear. You could swear the attackers knew precisely where and when.

They cleared a shot, the *motorino's* two riders, jammed together like lovers. Their closing in and gunning away might've been a single inhale and exhale.

No one saw what the crooks used to whack the man. There were two blows, the first with the full momentum of the bike behind it. But this was explained later, by doctors astounded at Jay's condition. At the time, Barb only heard a sound like clapping your hands around a soggy washcloth. What turned her to look was a stranger noise out of Jay's throat, a strangled shout and whimper the likes of which she hadn't heard since their first lovemaking.

She turned and took a blow herself, a hit to one breast. An elbow caught her, and as the cycle roared away the pain flared in her mind's eye in the shape of one attacker's kite-like blue bandanna—the lone bit of evidence the family would have for weeks to come. Barbara whirled in the eddy of the blow, that breast jarred out of its bra, so that her flag-bright pain was threaded with the shaming tickle of the nipple against her summer shirt, a shaming exposure; she saw the entire family half-naked and staggering here in the middle of a downtown crowd, under close-crowding palazzi. Then there was Jay, changing shape. Her husband shrank as if to fit the out-of-date street, as if finally and suddenly he'd lost the wide American back built up during varsity football and summer jobs on the highways. The hand that had held the briefcase began to purple, waggling, helpless, another bandanna aflutter above the thronging Smartcars and three-wheeled trucks, and all the other bikes, roaring but harmless.

"Mother of God!" she screamed. "*Mother* of God!"

Then: "No more. I can't. No way."

Meaning, no way things should have come to this, no way she could live with this—this had to be the end of everything. A shocking thought, far removed from the person she'd believed herself to be. Yet the idea took over even as Barb moved towards the shrinking male heap in its bright summer-weight clothes. The two of them could no longer share a life. They had to divorce.

She came close enough to glimpse the damage alongside Jay's ear, the blood down one twitching cheek. But she couldn't bring herself to touch him. She knelt as if protecting herself, bracing her hands on her legs, easing into the cobblestone grit. Every move gave shape to her cold new certainty: for years now she'd preferred the family over the marriage. For years she'd found it hard labor, harder every day, sorting out a household with this highhanded money-maker. In these recognitions, too, Barbara suffered a horror at what she needed to do next. A shame as bad as the scratching at her nipple, for this undeniable future set her apart from the good woman she'd been. A loving mother and a solid citizen, one of the faithful who put in hour after volunteer hour down at the Holy Name Samaritan Center—that person too was toppled and stripped.

On her knees, on the stones, Barbara sought her kids. She rediscovered her youngest first, the twins Dora and Sylvia. Before the attack she'd been warning the girls to stay close, and now in no time she had her fingers in their hair again. Wonderful, that elementary-school hair. As for Barb's two oldest, to find those she needed only look over her shoulder. John Junior, seventeen, had started elbowing through the sudden knot of onlookers after the thugs (but the boy was kidding himself, the thieves were gone for good: the bandanna had kited off, the briefcase was gone, and this was the end), while behind JJ trailed Chris. Her second-born was fifteen, less of a force at moving people out of his way but determined nonetheless. Like his big brother, though, Chris hadn't bothered to run.

So that was the youngest hugging her belly, the oldest not going far. Between these two pairs, Paul at first went overlooked. Didn't he always? Paul was the middle child, in middle years, eleven. Barb and Jay had fallen into nervous joking about how they'd done with him. "Guess we got Worst Parents of The Year on that one." "Worst Parents of the Millennium, I'd say." Now while the family fell apart, the end of the world on the first day of their new lives, Paul was the only child who'd kept his place. He remained on the sidewalk, the raised step that passed for a sidewalk, a block of stone that had once allowed a plebe to stand out of the way of a passing chariot. Maybe Barb had missed Paul because he stood against one of those parish posters that ask prayers for the recent dead. The poster colors matched the slim boy's perpetual outfit: white dress shirt, black permanent-press pants.

He was staring past Barb at his fallen father. Later the mother would ask herself if she'd noticed anything in Paul's face. The best she could recall, he looked the way he always did—barely with it. But it was after checking on the middle child that Barb at last took a moment for the man laid out before her. She got her hands on him.

The first shudder through her was the same chill of conviction she'd suffered the moment Jay was hit. She had to be rid of him. She'd been kidding herself, and so had he; by the time they'd boarded the flight to Naples, yesterday, they'd been dead and finished as a family for months at least. But then a different kind of trembling came over her. Barbara discovered her husband, her soon-to-be-ex-husband, was twitching under her hands. For the first time she saw how badly he'd been hurt.

Beside one ear blood was seeping so thickly that it had flowed uphill, into that eye-socket, as well as down across Jay's face and onto the hand-hacked stone. Barb might even have smelled the blood, through the pervading volcanic dust. Might've been the blood, might've been an unfamiliar sweat, dung-like, involuntary as the spasms that racked the man. Some serious head-bone had been broken, some connection in the motor control. At the center of the temple, where the muggers had hit first, a wedge of interior membrane bulged up, gray, blue-gray, not quite drowned in blood.

Jay twitched and Barbara too, another prickle through her unslung breast. Her husband's mouth was working, puckering, but Barb hadn't heard him make a sound since that first impossible, orgasmic cry.

"Mama?" asked one of the girls clinging to her. "Is Papa all right?"

"He doesn't look like Papa," said the other. "Mama, he isn't like Papa."

For Barb, simply bending over him took effort. Jay had always been the one looming over her. He was twitching so raggedly that she had to steady herself just to check his eyes. Rolling up into his head, these exposed an unblinking white too clean and sticky for the infected streets, and the corners of his mouth bubbled with foam. After that Barbara couldn't suppress another shudder all her own, another freezing touch of estrangement. The wife sagged on her haunches, astonished at herself. She should at least have pulled her bra back into place. But instead she went for her rosary, rummaging in her purse. A purse of some size and heft, now that she thought about it: a trip purse. You had to wonder why the thieves hadn't gone after her instead of the hunky Jaybird.

But she got her rosary and, crosscut by more contradictory impulses than she could name, lifted the beads to her lips. You never knew what a Hail Mary might accomplish. You never could predict when the Holy Ghost might rock her with one of Its untraceable tugs, welcome and clarifying, unlike any of her other shakes this morning.

But prayer, just now, only afforded her more of the same. She recalled that she was no doctor, and that for all she knew Jay would be up and filling out passport applications in no time. She recalled that strangers were looking on, and should the man come out of this, it might be hours before she found some quiet space in which to let him know the calamitous truth. Still Barbara ached for her husband, in the pit of her bruised chest—and still she was through with him. She could see the end of the marriage even in Jay's bloody face. If the man wore anything you could call a look, it suggested that the muggers' blow had brought home to him the same severe inevitability. The same change of life. He'd lost consciousness to a wake-up call.

"Jaybird," she found herself saying, lowering her rosary. "The Jaybird."

But she wasn't left alone with the runny unhappiness of his look, like a broken egg in which blood had spoiled the yolk. She enjoyed nothing like the Anglo notion of "personal boundaries." Over either shoulder Barb could make out handkerchiefs in the air, faces against cell phones, and already four or even five of the bystanders had butted into the hunched and quivering circle of Barb and Jay and the girls. Someone asked a question she didn't catch, someone touched her shoulder. And while the mother nodded over her rosary, nodded and murmured, there might even have been a bearded man beside her, extending a hand to Jay's thick neck.

It should never have come to this. "Jay, we should've known."

The husband had a position here: co-site-leader with the United Nations Earthquake Relief. The United Nations. But this morning was something else again, a cartoon, cannibals and missionaries. One young woman appeared to be getting the madness on video, an oblong black camcorder at her eye. Now Barb became aware of the cries for help: *Aiuto! Pronto soccorso!* She knew the language, sure, and the handkerchief trick. When Barbara was growing up, when her mom was still at home, the young mother had still spoken the slang of the Naples periphery. Torre del Greco, that's where Barbara's mother had come from. Whereas this oversized delusional case down on the cobblestones, the man who'd hauled the Lulucitas over here, he was only some fraction of an Italian. He was a saintly-come-lately.

Barb even understood one or two of the more complicated expressions. *Ma guarda, sta morendo!*—But look, he's dying!

Then there were the horns of the pint-sized autos, bleating and squawking. Cartoon punctuation. There was the woman scented with lavender who knelt at her ear, a hand between Barbara's shoulder blades. "Give him your love, *signora*," this visitor whispered, or stage-whispered. "Is your love now that will save him."

The woman disappeared with a rattle (bracelets? bones?) and Barbara slumped, whipsawed.

"Mother of God." She choked and tasted vomit. "Jay, this wasn't my idea. You can't say it was *my* idea."

The man's eyes showed only white. His twitching threw blood onto her hands. Barb didn't realize Dora and Sylvia had started to cry till she felt their faces against her hips, a smeary wet pressure right where Jay had always liked to squeeze. She recalled his current pet expression for her figure, "owl girl," as in, "Mine forever, forever, my owl girl." The phrase had been lifted from the twins, who a few years ago hadn't been able to pronounce "hourglass shape." The shape of a true Italian, the abundant body.

Then with her girls' pressure on her, with a fresh awareness of her body and its semi-exposure—with that Barb understood that the strangers in the street had put an end to their touching. The family huddle had become something to avoid. Not that the cacophony had let up, the Good Samaritan uproar, echoing round a well of medieval stonework. But a buffer space had developed around mother, father, and children, a bit of breathing room that made Barbara picture her downed group as Nativity figures, a Christmas crèche. Of course the Neapolitans were famous for these, every family had its *presepe*, terra cotta and balsa wood; maybe that's what brought the image to mind. Now when Chris and John Junior returned from their fruitless chase, the two teens were shepherds late to the manger, hanging back.

Paul however joined the Holy Family. The middle child found a stretch of Mom-space that Dora or Sylvia had left uncovered, perhaps pressing in on his knees, a penitent. The eleven-year-old was one more grinding discrepancy between what Barb needed to do and the way she must've looked. This mess was more like theater than ever.

But the boy went for Pop. Paul got hold of his father's twitching head.

Among the children Paul was the one who took after Mom, the most Italian, and not so much for the spongy silk of his hair or the glinty espresso of his eyes as for his hands: expressive hands, mindful. Since the trouble over this past winter, the boy's hands had been more articulate than whatever he'd had to say. And anyone with so close a view as Barbara's, here above Paulie and Jay, might've thought that, every day since last winter, the child had been working towards today's laying-on of hands. They spidered across Jay's dripping face as if each fingertip held a pair of kissing lips. When the boy reached under his father's chin the gesture recalled the bearded passer-by from a minute ago, the man who'd butted in to check the pulse. And when Paul began speaking, Barb at first only saw the lips moving. Subtle lips, feminine. Like he was the one whose mother had been born in Torre del Greco.

Yet if Paul looked like a local, he sounded like he came from the far side of the moon. Barb noticed the hitches in Jay's breathing, and she knew what they might mean, but she still couldn't begin to make out whatever it was that Paul had begun to murmur—though at the same time, his dreamer's babble struck the mother as familiar. Perfectly familiar: any stay-at-home parent would recognize the curve of her boy's preteen back, the spells he was casting. If this were all a Christmas *presepe*, nobody made it so more than Paul, because just then he was the only genuine kid on the scene, the only one who still could project a living mystery over Mother and Father and the rest. Paul was more the youngster than the immobilized girls at Barbara's hips. If you gave him balsa wood, he'd put up a whole metropolis.

"*Ma guarda*," someone declared behind her. "*Poverino. Pazzo.*"

Poor boy? Crazy? Maybe the middle child's response was the only one that made sense. Paul worked with his father's head in ways that seemed to encompass every fevered zig and zag of Barb's last few minutes. He'd slid unafraid into the epicenter, with soothing fingers. Keeping up his just-audible babytalk, the boy patted back and forth across the face, the gore. When a fresh trembling racked the head, Paul cradled the jaw and unhurt ear, surprisingly strong. At last he settled on a bizarre dual hold. One hand touched the center of the crushed temple, seeming to poke down the wedge of exposed membrane, while the other reached into the half-open mouth. All the way in, this child reached, prying apart the man's teeth until he could get a grip on the tongue. Barb couldn't miss it, Paul had the tongue, and she suffered another gag reflex. The image of the city as a diseased love-bite flared again in her mind's eye, and it paralyzed her, while at her hips the girls lifted their faces. Dora and Sylvia made small noises, disgusted, fascinated, like the neighborhood voices behind them.

Dio. . . . Ma che pazzo. . . .

Paul maintained his soggy two-handed grip for perhaps half a minute. His murmurs never let up, and finally Barbara picked out a few words.

"This, this is all he needs," Paul said. "J-Just a touch, that's all."

The boy sounded winded, but otherwise the same as he had for months now, his voice on the verge of breaking. Barbara's first response came in the wrong language, *"Poverino."* As Paul let go of his father's head, his small fingers glistening, she still couldn't move.

"Paul?" she managed. "Paul, I can't believe . . ."

"C'm, C'mon." He faced her. "What's everybody getting so, so, so upset about? Soon as Pop went down I could tell that this w-was a-all he needed."

Paul and she were so close that the boy's white shirtfront brushed against Barb's shaming nipple, and with that the mother regained her mobility and a sense of priorities. Lifting her hands from her husband was like lifting weights, but Barbara sat up and wrestled the cup of her bra back into place. She took her boy by the shoulders.

"Paul, we don't want to disturb him. Can't you see he's badly hurt?"

He was winded, gulping, lost. Barbara thought of her two older sons, their hopeless effort to follow the thieves.

"Badly hurt?" one of the girls asked.

And her two oldest, how were they doing? Barb found Chris and JJ hanging back as before, out of their depth on the first day in town.

"Mama, did you say Papa was badly *hurt*?"

Girls, Barbara thought, he could be dead already. At her knees the big body had gone slack.

"C'mon, guys," Paul said. "A-all he needed was a little touch. A little p-pep talk, maybe too."

"Paul, please." Her voice was a load likely to spill. "What's got into you?"

"But couldn't you tell that was, that was a-all he needed? Couldn't you just, just *feel* it?"

The crowd surrounding them remained subdued, keeping a distance.

"Badly hurt, Mama? Badly hurt?"

"I could feel it," Paul repeated. "I just knew."

"Hey," Jay said, sitting up. "What's all this on my *face*? Anybody got a mirror?"

He sat up, on the raised step that passed for a sidewalk. Frowning, swabbing his eyes, Jay propped his broad back against the palazzo wall and stretched out his hefty legs where he could, fitting them around the kneeling Barb, around the two erupting girls and out to the feet of the crowd. Everyone had been startled a step closer, maybe a couple of steps, just like that. Meanwhile grunting and frowning, a big American doing his best with aging joints and a spreading belly, Jay settled himself just in time for Syl and Dora to tumble hard into his lap. "*Papa!*"

They hit the man with such force that dried blood flaked off his face and spattered their tender hair.

"Hey," Jay said. "Easy there. Looks like Papa might be bleeding."

The crowd was noisy again, recharged. The family too was a different animal. Barb wobbled back onto her haunches, back until she would've fallen if her two oldest hadn't sunk down behind her, Chris and John Junior coming into the huddle with faces slack and wowed while the twins went on cuddling Pop. Only Paul didn't fit the pattern, Paul again, finding a place apart along the wall. Barb sank into the heavy smell of two teens who'd been up the block and back, of her own 360-degree whirling, while before them Jay fell into a scab-flicking match with two eight-year-olds. The impossible coagulation dotted the mother's kneecaps and skirt.

But Paul kept separate, rather prim on his knees. His shirt remained white except for street dust and his look was weary but serene. *Told you so.*

Barbara would've fallen if not for her two teenagers, and she couldn't seem to get a decent look at her husband's injury. Hadn't the thieves cracked his skull open? She had no trouble remembering the welling blood, the bulging viscera. Could a touch and a whisper really have fixed it? A touch and a dream? Certainly her Jaybird appeared, against the clean white mortar of the repaired lower wall, as handsome as ever. Jay's looks had if anything improved since he'd hit forty, his hair richly Mediterranean and his face flexibly Irish. At times his head suggested one of those noble and tragic officer's portraits from the Civil War.

But before Barbara could finish her examination, a local got in the way. The interloper might've been the same as before, he had the goatee. This time the mother could peg him as a professional type, and more than likely a doctor. With those glasses, those wattles beneath his beard, he looked to be pushing seventy. As he once more reached for Jay without asking, an old man with a task, his stare metallic, Barb had no choice but to acknowledge it had all taken place the way she remembered. The head-wound had been real, and divorce was the only solution. The blow could easily have killed her husband, or it could've left him strapped in a wheelchair and brain-damaged—all threats to which the Lulucitas should never have been exposed in the first place—all of it no less of an actual alternative life than her own twenty years as a good wife and mother.

Under the old man's spectacled stare, the twins broke off the scab fight. When he reached the father's neck, Jay tucked his chin. "Hey!"

He tucked his chin and hiked his shoulders. An owl, Barb thought blackly. You have the nerve to call *me* an owl.

"A moment please." The man's accent had a touch of the British. "A moment only, *signore*. I need the pulse."

"The pulse?" Jay got one arm around the girls. "What, like I'm dying?"

"Papa, don't joke." Sounded like Sylvia. "We were *worried*."

Jay let the man do as he wished, while what felt like everyone within walking distance leaned in for a closer look. Someone in the crowd said *"Miracolo,"* or perhaps four or five of them did, as the doctor probed the formerly broken temple and the woman with the video-camera bent in for a close-up. The girls in Jay's lap couldn't help but turn towards the whirring, and Barbara too, blinking back at the mechanical blink of the red recording light. A bloody electronic pulse as unrelenting as the anger that remained the closest thing to clarity she'd found.

Meanwhile however her husband had other worries. Jay had begun to run his hands over the stones nearby. In another half a minute, in spite of the doctor's ministrations, Jay was searching the area in earnest.

"Where's the bag?" he asked.

He shook off both the old man and the children and hopped up into a squat, agile enough to make the crowd shuffle back.

"The bag? The credit cards, all our ID? The *passports*—hey, Barb!"

Cocked as far from him as her knees would allow, she braced herself against his look. He wasn't an owl now, not up on all fours like this, his eyes rimmed in browned blood. Barb instead saw some earthbound nocturnal scavenger, a coon over garbage. And she was nothing but tooth and claw in return. Jay might still be confused but not her, no longer; she'd torn through to the end of everything. This morning she'd at last found the guts to admit how bad things had gotten back in Bridgeport.

If he'd asked her something, Barbara had forgotten the question. She'd lost the feeling below her knees.

"Barb?" he called. "Hey, where *is* it? What happened, anyway? Why is everyone staring at me?"

Wrong, Jay. Barb granted that she was staring at him, and the kids too. But otherwise he was woefully wrong, this man she needed to speak with in private, just as soon as possible. Everyone else in that close-packed block, both the gang down on the stones that smelled of manure and the stay-at-homes up in the windows flung open amid the morning laundry—everyone else, including the lucky one with the camera and the now-empty-handed doctor and a tall woman in too much jewelry who may have been Barbara's whispery love-angel (the mother caught glimpses of them all, in her antsy paralysis)—everyone else was looking at Paul.

Chapter Two

Whenever Barbara had imagined the end of her marriage—and today she was coming to realize how often she'd done it—she'd pictured it happening anywhere but Italy. Americans in Italy, that was a different story. A story with a happy ending, in which some tightly-wound Anglo arrives in this sultry country, more than halfway to Africa, and rediscovers the joy of sultry, of a steaming meal and an eventful bedtime. Barb had seen the movie a hundred times. The refinement of the French horns as the branches of the fig tree ripple before the Renaissance tower . . . the rekindling of an Iowan's kisses as the setting sun winks between the Roman brickwork. . . . Often the romance blossomed in some high-collared era a few earthquakes previous, Henry James, whatever. Or the chilly figure in need of a snuggler's renewal might be British, made no difference. Once they undid that first button, Italy was the opposite of divorce. It was a country, Barbara came to think, for someone like Jay's mother.

For Grandma Aurora, the love-tomato never lost its juice. The old bohemian had gone so far as to promise, as the family prepared for the journey, that she would "jet over soon." She wanted "a taste of that *dolce vita*."

Today as Barb cooled her heels in some sort of downtown health clinic, repeatedly failing to wangle so little as five minutes alone with her husband-for-now, she had time to understand his mother. Should Aurora Lulucita sashay into the examination rooms this very minute, she wouldn't even need to touch up her eyeliner and lipstick in order to vamp for someone like Dottore DiPio, here. DiPio was the one who'd put Jay though those hurried examinations out on the dusty cobblestone, and after that the old *medico* had taken over. He'd overridden any suggestions from the police who'd arrived on the scene, and cowed the ambulance drivers as well, showing such an eagerness for the case that Barb recalled her mother-in-law. Aurora too was seventy-something, yet still fired by a craving that blew past any notion of embarrassment.

The grandmother however was all about man-chasing; this doctor on the other hand wanted to track down a miracle. He'd had the Lulucitas brought to this—what would you call it? A palazzo put up a good two hundred years ago, converted now to slapdash cubicles and unexpected staircases. Here DiPio had proprietary rights. He made sure to get the family's local phone and address, by hand rather than on computer, using the long, whip-crack L of formal European penmanship. He asked again and again about the head wound, the exposed cerebral membrane. At times it seemed like the questions arose directly from the doctor's goatee, if not from a cluster of neckwear beneath that unruly salted bush. DiPio wore not only a crucifix, but also a medallion of the former saint Christopher. Whenever he wasn't touching somebody else the old man was fingering this bric-a-brac, though in time he impressed Barbara with a formality of bearing at odds with his free-handedness. After a couple of hours in the man's clinic, she had to conclude he had little in common with her sensualist in-law. He might be Neapolitan but he was no teeming Sophia Loren, nor any hot-lipped stud, aglow before a pizza oven. Rather, the family's new caregiver was so God-minded, he'd fingered his Mr. Christopher until it was flat and dark.

And Barbara couldn't help but think of the God she herself had in mind, her change of spirit, toughening now like the spatter from Jay's wound turned to scabs on her shirtfront. Her notion of the divine no longer seemed to dwell in high-minded and softhearted figures, the canon of saints she'd grown up with. Years ago, after her mother had run away, young Barbara had worked through a full five hundred rosaries each for Sister Teresa and Brother Francis. She'd kept the tally in her fifth-grade composition book. But this morning she'd seen such gentle profiles hacked off the church frieze. She'd hacked them off herself, with each blow of the hammer and chisel swearing allegiance instead to the sexed-up monster of the ancient temples. A god with lightning down his pants, and pitiless once he got started.

DiPio's beard, kinky, bobbing, presented a thousand miniature question marks. Herself, she no longer had the patience.

She didn't like the confusion about her name, either. Today everyone Barbara spoke with, not just the doctor but also the police, turned their

name into something she'd never heard before. In the States the word
tended to sound Hispanic, starting like Ricky Ricardo calling his wife
and then coming down hard on the next-to-last syllable, that lascivious
"*si*." Or you got something flat and Midwestern, cramming "lullaby"
and "cheetah" into a wet growl. In Naples however the name took the
emphasis on its second syllable, which sweetened and lengthened and
sang out from the whole mouth. Around DiPio's downtown clinic,
everyone used the new pronunciation, L'-*looo*-shee-tah.

To Barbara, it sounded like babytalk.

"Signora L'*looo*-shee-tah," asked a detective in plainclothes, "do you
know the word *scippatori*? Here in Naples it means a thief on the street.
Ship-pah-*torr* . . ."

The mother thought of slapping the man's solicitous face and
shouting the filthiest slang Italian she knew. She'd gone through six
time zones in two days. Anyway the whole point of the policeman's
patronizing blather was that the investigation would likely get
nowhere. The detective went on to say that the attackers must've been
rookies at this sort of thing. A job like this morning's would've been
too risky for anyone experienced at the smash-and-grab—anyone
connected to the *Camorra*.

"Here in Naples, do you know signora, the Mafia is the Camorra?"

"A professional," another cop put in, "a camorrista, he would never
have hit your husband so badly. You understand? He would not wish
a murder."

"And he would never be so stupid as to, to do injury an American."

Did Signora L'*loo*-she-tah understand that in Naples, a person can
see at once if you are American? "We can see it in the shoes or the
makeup, in the way you carry your hands." And did she understand
that, if an American is hurt, the NATO might get involved? The Sixth
Fleet is quartered here, signora. The NATO. Also these days we have
the UN Relief, more Americans . . .

John Junior, bless him, cut the man short. "So Pop was hit by
amateurs?"

The attack looked like the work of amateurs, yes, and therefore
the authorities couldn't count on their usual stool pigeons. "Also,
signora, think of it. In Naples now 15,000 are *terramotati*. They are
without homes, for the earthquake." With so many new hardscrabble
cases, the detective went on, the old mobster hegemony could no
longer claim a piece of every street hit.

"In other words," JJ said, "you're clueless."

The plainclothesman appeared to know the expression. His gaze hardened.

"It used to be," the big teen went on, "the police and the crooks were friends. Everybody got their coffee at the same place."

"JJ," Barbara said.

"That made it easier, back when you were all friends. In those days you guys would've had half a clue, when somebody nearly *kills my father.*"

The detective turned to the mother. His voice dropped to a murmur. You Americans must understand that an incident of this kind can be most difficult . . .

Babytalk, that's what they gave her. Meanwhile around Jay and Paul, everyone else appeared to be the babies, hanging on their every word. The father and middle child might've been a pair of CEO's, lording it over the damaged downtown, making promises of a thousand new jobs. When somebody carted in espresso, croissants, and lemonade, the mother got last dibs as the trays went around. A twenty-something with the clinic, an intern of some kind, ran a pretty finger along Jay's jaw-line. Meanwhile the wife couldn't get five minutes. More than once the mother had to un-stack a couple of plastic chairs for her and the girls, and settle in along a wall, uncomfortably aware of what the morning's banging around had done to her looks. Since she'd left off nursing the twins she'd made it a point to watch her appearance in public. She'd taken care to know what her hair was doing, and how her makeup was surviving.

Yet now, with all these men in her way. . . .

Signora, asked one of the younger doctors, you are certain you saw something from, ah, inside? Inside the head? Signora, ah, the blood on your dress . . .

This time Chris was the boy who gave her some relief: "Look, you know what we thought? We thought Pop was dead!"

The fifteen-year-old wheeled around in a squat. He'd been down between Dora's and Syl's chairs, reciting some toe-rhyme.

"Dead!" Chris repeated, shoving his glasses back up his nose. "*Morto!*"

Barbara blinked at the word, a one-two slap in her son's crash-course Italian. In another moment she'd heaved herself out of her chair and past the doctor. She headed for her husband, tugging at the armpit of her dress. Not that her clothing mattered; rather, she had to make room for the lightning underneath.

Jay understood that this was serious as soon as he saw her coming. It would've been twenty years for them this September, plus all the hugging and kissing beforehand, around Carroll Gardens or on the J train. DiPio picked up on her urgency as well, another case of the least she could expect, considering how often the *medico* had used the word "sympathy." He must've told them five times that "extra sympathy" had been the essential ingredient in what he termed "the healing episode." The mother wasn't entirely positive there'd been any actual healing—she recalled that seizures could follow a head-blow, and that these could end unexpectedly. But she was glad when the doctor proved his notion of sympathy extended to longtime wives. DiPio at once found a room for Barb and Jay, a nook typical of this ramshackle *ospedale*, practically tucked behind a secret panel. The mother kept her eyes on the old doctor until he shut the door.

"*Permesso. . . ?*"

They hadn't had long before DiPio returned. He came in with his crucifix in his beard, a miniature silver pick, and announced that Paul had started to cry.

"You will understand." He lowered his crucifix. "The healing episode is common associate with trauma."

Then the doctor spotted Jay, slumped over the table and massaging his face. You would've thought that he'd taken another hit. He went on groaning a single slow word.

"*Why?*"

Plenty of time for that, Jay. Plenty of time for the background behind the news flash. Or so Barbara stood thinking, falling into a more civilized meditation, as if she had to compensate for the growling and clawing she'd just let off its chain. The nasty business had her hurting too. Her blush burned up into ears and her breathing had gone tetchy. But the doctor didn't notice, bending instead to reexamine the Jaybird. The mother was left looking down at two bald spots, two scuffed ovals that looked a lot like the dirty-yellow tufa stone outside. And the stone wouldn't talk, she realized, or not about today's pounding. This new co-site-leader for the United Nations quake relief wouldn't tell anyone else what his wife had just told him. Jay's groaning had ended as soon as the doctor touched him.

The old *medico* wouldn't ask any difficult questions, either. With a scrubbed hand DiPio waved Paul into the hidden room. The boy at least had a moment for his mother, her mouth still ajar and her heat still visible. But Papa sat closer to the door, and he and Paul sank into a wordless hug.

The doctor went for the clutter around his neck. "Your husband, your son," he gushed at Barbara, "they have done something wonderful."

The Jaybird lifted his head. "You ask me," he said, "my whole family is wonderful."

The mother reminded herself that, to her and Jay, the tears of their eleven-year-old were in no way supernatural. She and Jay knew what they'd put Mr. Paul through, lately; this wasn't the first time he'd seen his parents upset. Besides, once Barbara and the others shuffled back out into the clinic corridor, it turned out she'd been right to speak up when she did. Her harsh words clanged around her head like a mugger's iron—but she'd been right to seize the moment. Out in the hallway she had to deal with NATO and the UN.

Both had sent a man, and each man wore a jacket and tie, severe for this weather. Talk about the opposite of an Italian romance.

Of course Barbara had seen the paperwork for Jay's appointment. The family could never have made this move without the presence of the Sixth Fleet and a half-dozen relief agencies headquartered at East Forty-forth and FDR Drive. Nonetheless, for most of her life NATO and the UN had existed only as acronyms stretching across a map, newsprint black on newsprint gray. She would never have imagined that they could appear as full-color guys in uncomfortable clothes, down at the same level as stackable plastic chairs. The UN representative at least looked something like what you would expect, unsmiling and some degree of Arabian, in banker's clothing. But the one who said he worked with NATO, he was an eyeful. This man had allowed himself a canary-colored jacket, Palm Beach, and he wore his blonde hair Botticelli-long. He wore it in an exaggerated flip, swept back from a fraying hairline that put him on the far side of thirty-five. Also this officer did most of the talking, if you could call it talking.

It's the understanding of our organizations that these American citizen volunteers have no compelling medical reason for staying on in this establishment . . . it's our belief that on their way home they could use a protected ride . . . it's our understanding that these citizen volunteers also have need of certain documents in our possession . . .

Barb had the thought that she'd gone from a closet full of whacking truths to a public square full of pillow-soft lies. Yet she couldn't be angry with these newcomers either. Queer as the NATO man came across, with that line of talk, he and the other allowed Barbara and her family to escape. They were even spared the usual release forms. The Palm Beach Botticelli took care of those, explaining that he and the other official would make the trip to the family's apartment with them, and along the way "address any pressing concerns."

The "protected ride" waited out front. It took up the entire medieval *via*, a cop at either end waving away traffic: a Humvee transport big enough to scare away even the rankest amateur of a *scippatoro*. Plus inside sat a soldier in Treaty Organization blues. Nordic, young, muscled enough to stretch the sleeves of his uniform, the GI held a small machine gun.

The weapon smelled of oil and was shaped like an H. H, Barb thought, for *What the Hell*?

But the police had no objections. DiPio too went along with the NATO request, though his wrinkled features showed a certain distaste, button-mouthed. The doctor lingered with the family in the cramped space between his doorway and the vehicle's, one last time touching a finger to Paul's chest.

"To heal is always good," he said. "One time, ten times, is always good."

Ten times? What the hell?

The family had been set up in an apartment on one of the hills overlooking the Bayfront. Now as the van began its climb out of the old city Barbara tried to focus on the practical. Child care was the first concern, now as ever; she needed someone reliable in place before she headed back to New York to draw up the papers. But the seat facing her, next to the gun, had been taken by the flamboyant NATO man. Not only was he intent on making conversation, but he used an entirely different voice than he had back in the clinic.

"Mn, *che casino*." A Southern tourist's voice, Dixie Italian. "No rest for the wandering Ulysses."

Was this public relations? Making nice for the injured homeboys?

"Ulysses," NATO repeated. "Except in this case, he's got the wife with him."

Barb shook her head. She tried to recall whether, from this end of the Atlantic, the airlines needed fourteen or twenty-one day notice.

"Mn. Doubt y'all've even had time to get over the jet lag."

Jay sighed stagily. "Murphy's Law."

NATO studied the husband as if waiting for more. Finally: "Tomorrow you've got to call the bank, one."

"The bank. Hey." Another extravagant exhale. "I don't think their switchboard has a number for this."

The official laughed again, thumb-stroking one bright lapel. But Jay never cracked a smile. Barb would've imagined that this kind of talk would feel familiar to him. The guy across the Humvee's aisle was a kind of executive, an Organization man. He might wear a nightclub hairdo or slip in a bit of Homer, but that didn't take the conversation out of shoptalk. Jay however wasn't looking at their host. Barb's husband kept his handsome head turned her way.

"No number for *this*," he said.

Her interior blade started cutting in a fresh direction.

"Mn," Dixie was saying. "Anyhow the worst is over, *grazia a dio*. And we've brought something that's going to help."

The UN rep nodded just visibly, adjusting the briefcase on his lap. The NATO man introduced himself. Kahlberg—Silky Kahlberg.

"Silky?" Barbara asked.

The Arab gave a snort. Kahlberg however kept smiling, his hand extended. His coloring was almost as Viking-pale as that of the soldier beside him, and the man's grip suggested he'd spent some time with a gun in his hands himself. His sleek blonde mop (okay, silky) must've been one of the privileges of rank: Kahlberg announced that he was a major. "Actually a Lieutenant-Major. Though I doubt y'all know the difference."

The man lost something off his smile. But he went on to declare, more or less cheerfully, that his job was "PR plain and simple. Public liaison, *capisce*? Events, communications, Jay here knows what I'm talking about."

He did? Barbara's Jaybird had worked in sales, not advertising. Kahlberg went on to explain that, since the quake, he'd also handled Public Affairs for the international relief efforts. "Working two jobs, see what I'm saying? The Organization and the UN, they've both got a piece of me."

"And you've got a piece of both payrolls," Jay said.

Kahlberg gave a shrug. "Jay, sounds to me like you don't understand. You don't know what we're up to, here. In Naples, anymore, it's not about worlds to conquer."

"I don't want worlds to conquer. All I want's right here in this van. My family."

"Touché, big shooter. Touché, but Jay—anymore, that's all we want too. The Organization and the UN, these days we're all about happy families, families like yours. That's quality of life, democracy on the march. That's the *Pax Americana*."

"Wait a second." This was Chris, who liked history. "*Pax. . .?*"

"Mn." The liaison officer tucked his hair behind one ear. "Got a bright kid here, Jay. Bright kid, he's thinking the Roman thing, *Pax Romana*. He's thinking, 'strength and honor.'" The man was good at *Gladiator*, too.

"Actually," Chris said, "the expression they used was a bit different."

"That's good, son. That's a bright boy. But the question is, what do we do about that? I mean, since it's our *Pax*, these days. What do we do with it?'"

Chris scratched an eyebrow.

"It's all on us now." Kahlberg went on. "Washington is the new Rome. That's the law of history, right?"

Barbara had to jump in. "Lieutenant, Major, whatever. Listen, the march of history, the triumph of NATO, that's not why this family came here."

"Mn, *triumph*? Ma'am, you don't understand. In this van, we're all on the. . . ."

"No, listen." It'd been too long a day. "I'm saying, Silky, you have no idea about this family. The sacrifices we made."

"I hear you, ma'am. I hear your pain."

Much too long a day. "Oh, give me a break."

"Barbara," Jay said.

"Jay, this bastard thinks we're playing some kind of *ballgame*."

"Settle down, Mrs. Lulucita." The officer used the Italian pronunciation. "Way I see it, this isn't about me. Isn't about *this bastard* at all. I can see that, what's bothering you, it's got nothing to do with me and everything to do with those old boys who just about took your husband's head off."

Barbara checked out the window. The shadows were unpredictable behind the tinted glass. And when had it gotten so late? Inside, Paul might've been napping in his seat, his head in his chest. Strange shadows played across the riot of his hair.

Kahlberg seemed to be saying the Organization had a heart of gold. "We're looking towards the *next* thousand years, you know what I'm saying? If history tells us we've got to be Rome, then it's on us to do Rome one better."

She couldn't just sit there stewing. "Lieutenant—"

"Silky, please."

"Silky, try this. Try looking out the window."

The van cruised along a wide and efficient city beltway, a road utterly unlike the medieval alleys where Jay had been hit.

"I'm saying," Barbara went on, "this is Rome too. I'm saying, let's get real, with the law of history. Naples is Rome too. Five minutes in the Internet Cafe, here, and I could have a ticket back to New York."

"*Brava, signora.*"

"Even the earthquake—that didn't really hurt the people in town, so much. The people Jay's going to be working with, they're something else, they're mostly refugees. The newcomers around here."

The officer went on nodding.

"And they came here to make money, most of these people."

"*Brava, signora. Complimenti.*"

What was that, a pat on the head? She didn't like hearing him use her title all the time either, not after "Jay" this and "Jay" that.

Chris had been trying for a while to get a word in. "Listen, if you're going to compare us to Rome, then like, what Pop's doing is more like, it's the aqueducts. Pop's helping to . . ."

JJ gave a laugh, scornful, and while Chris made some comeback Barbara turned again to the window. What had she been trying to accomplish, anyway? What did she have to prove? The van had climbed high enough that outside the reinforced glass, the color of a bruise, she could see the scabby and kiss-shaped downtown.

"That's pretty good, son," the PR man was saying. "Pretty good, actually, Chris. So, you're such a smart boy, tell me something. You ever read Vico?"

The teenager fingered his glasses, but Jay waved him silent.

"Anybody in this van ever read Giambattista Vico?"

"Silky," the father said. "The way I heard it, you had something for us. Documents, you said. Hey, that's what you told the cops."

"Yeah, the cops," John Junior said, "hey. When it comes to what happened to Pop, it sounds like you NATO guys're no more help than the police."

"Mn, son, you're barking up the wrong tree. The Organization, it's got no jurisdiction when it comes to a couple of junkies like the ones that laid out your Pop."

"Junkies?" John Junior pumped up his height advantage. "The cops only said they were *amateurs*."

Jay was frowning, troubled by the recollection. Barb looked to Kahlberg's partner, but the rep from the UN wore a fixed, cold smile.

"Junkies, amateurs, you can call those old boys whatever you want," the liaison was saying. "But I'll tell you what, they'll be tough to find. People like that, they kind of fall through the cracks."

"So you *are* as bad as the cops. You've got nothing for us."

The only person Barbara hadn't checked recently was Paul. She needed time with the boy soon. Time for his "eruption of need," and for her "core assurances," as they put it back at the Samaritan Center, at the Holy Name. But now the Lieutenant Major was spouting a jargon of his own, talking about "Earthquake I.D."

"The Organization arranged one for each family member." The man had also selected from another of his voices. "One for each, in keeping with the purpose of the document, and we worked hand in hand with the appropriate authorities, both local and international, in the kind of cooperation that has long distinguished our relationship."

The UN rep was thumbing the combination locks of his briefcase.

"In this way," Kalhlberg went on, "we ensured that this paper carries the full weight of law. For American citizens it possesses the value and function of a passport."

Chris remained the one who got the most out of this. Nodding, the boy shoved his glasses up his nose.

"You had an electromagnetic pulse," Chris said. "Yeah. I saw that."

The fifteen-year-old had his leg jigging. "An electromagnetic pulse," he repeated. "That happens sometimes with earthquakes. Computers crash big-time so, like, people lose their hard drives."

The NATO officer broke into a grin that constituted yet another change in tone.

"Plus you must've lost other records. In ordinary ways, ordinary for an *earthquake*. You had churches collapsing, and in Southern Italy, oh boy. Around here, when a church collapses, that's maybe a whole town just, like, *gone* . . ."

"Wow, Mr. Science," John Junior said. "I could listen to you all night."

"Oh, excuse me, Room Temperature. Room Temperature I.Q. Excuse me, I forgot to like, connect the dots. See, with the pulse and the rest, that meant there were, like, all these people who'd lost essential documents. . . ."

"Hey, Velma. Connect these dots."

Barb had put it together herself by now. The UN rep was pulling the goods from his briefcase, a sheaf of hand-sized pamphlets, and seeing those, she recalled that she'd read something about this. Maybe she'd heard about it on the good Fordham NPR. There'd been a similar crisis after the Christmas tsunami a few years back, over in Southeast Asia, and again down in New Orleans following the bad hurricane. The disaster had caught a number of victims with their pockets empty, their wallet lost somewhere along the way—without identification. The authorities had needed to go around making lists. Also they'd needed to come up with a substitute.

"Temporary papers," Kahlberg said, nodding towards his seat-partner.

The other coat-and-tie began handing them out: staple-bound pamphlets on some sort of specialty bond, light but tough and bearing a watermark. The paper had the roughage of an old scar.

"Earthquake I.D.," said the man from the UN.

"Temporary," repeated the NATO officer. "But for the time being, in certain cases, a lifesaver. You have to remember that the ones who lost the most tended to be the kind of hand-to-mouth old boys we were just talking about. The refugees."

As Barbara took her packet, couldn't help thinking that, in this van, she was the one who needed it most. She was the one headed for a scarifying new world. The paper before her, however, wasn't so out of the ordinary. It featured a well-scanned reproduction of her latest passport shot and long-familiar data entries: a birth-date from not quite forty-five years back, and the overformal "New York City" as place of birth. The document was like the terminology she'd just been running through her head, the therapeutic patois from the Samaritan Center; it was someone else's fancy vocabulary for an understanding that lay deeper than that, at the connection of spine and language. Indeed the words from the Sam Center, the syndromes she'd come to know thanks to her own family therapy, and to the work she'd done screening other potential clients—these would matter to her longer than the jerryrigged booklet in her lap. The NATO officer was making further explanations, but they sounded beside the point. Getting actual replacement passports from this side of the Atlantic, Kahlberg said, would take weeks. "For the real deal, y'all need to have your signature notarized." But there was no way Barbara would stick around Naples for weeks.

"One thing we had going for us this time," the liaison said, "we had all the S.S.N. Jay here's been great about that, keeping the Organization up to speed."

Jay, sure. This paperwork too was his doing, another container labeled *Mine forever, all mine*. The stuff even felt like packing material.

"You did move fast," Jay said.

"Well, back at you, Jay. You kept us up to speed."

The van slowed and came off the freeway. They shuddered once more onto cobblestone, the throat-clearing downshift of their combat transport echoing within the sudden steep folds of brick and plaster. The neighborhood scene, outside the broad and reinforced window, to Barbara recalled dog-day August back in Carroll Gardens. The trunks of the maples and beeches were blotchy from traffic (though here you also spotted a palm or two) and the stoops were full of troublemakers. Except tonight the real troublemaker sat in the van. As the mother folded away her Earthquake I.D., she reminded herself they were still in the first week of June. If she had the Connecticut divorce laws right, the worst would be over by the time the kids went back to school.

"Too much," Jay shouted, over the rattle and jounce. "We're too much for a place like this."

It came to Barbara that he was speaking of the vehicle. She checked the children, all likewise concerned with the scene on the streets, even Paul. He'd got his head up again, and with that, the family was home. Their apartment must've been selected American style, right off the freeway. Barb and Jay hadn't noticed last night, fried as they'd been from traveling. This morning they'd walked to the funiculare that had carried them down into the older city.

And tonight, they had a crowd waiting.

They had a crowd closing in, singles and twosomes and more, descending from the nearby stoops, or swinging off motorbikes and unfolding out of Fiats. Men and women, a handful of children too, nobody that caught the eye at first glance. Still, the way these folks came for the Humvee, Barb had to wonder about the thing's telltale markings, the wide NATO seal on the front and sides. She checked what people were wearing, out there—simple day-clothes, so far as she could see. No Hezbollah-style head-wraps, no ready-to-rumble jumpsuits. Nobody was waving around any protest signs either. Rather, this mob recalled the one this morning, by no means angry but awfully free with their hands. These people seemed to caress the van, reaching for it even as the NATO driver, turtling down over the wheel, restarted the engine and at once stalled it. Everyone inside hunkered down, their new paperwork rattling.

The UN rep looked so British in his alarm, Barb realized she hadn't noticed any accent when he'd spoken. She didn't know who she was riding with. Meantime across the windows dirty palms and fingers spread wide. A few in the crowd palmed the windshield too, never mind what the engine was doing. They didn't care if they got run over, this gang of strangers, with arms outstretched as if for a hug. It was yet another new signal-system for Barbara to make sense of. One old man pressed his face to the window beside her, kissing blue-black Plexiglas.

"Mary, mother of God," she murmured.

Across from her the young soldier shifted his grip on the gun.

"No way!" she shrieked. "This isn't a *movie!*"

Jay was speaking more calmly, Jay and Kahlberg both. One or the other made the point that the crowd seemed friendly. *Lighten up*, Barb heard, meantime, perhaps whispered in her ear. *The kids. . . .*

Kahlberg touched the shoulder of the Viking in uniform. "Son," he said, "you don't understand. Listen, can't you hear them?"

Hear what? The crowd wasn't making much noise. Outside Barbara's window, her Humvee fetishist kept repeating some phrase between each kiss, but he wasn't nearly loud enough to be heard inside. His lips, his whole unshaven lower face, hardly moved. He didn't look too scary, either, skinny and no longer young, white chest hairs showing beneath his half-open shirt. He only held his place at the car because a heaping earth-mother behind him blocked the way for anyone else. This woman might've been putting her shaggy armpits on display, reaching stiffly for the sky and mouthing some prolonged babble into the lingering evening light. But to judge from their looks, both these old people were glad about the Lulucitas' arrival. Elsewhere too, no one was screaming, no one was chanting, no one was pounding on the NATO steel. They only kept touching and, more and more, kissing.

Inside, John Junior crooned a single slow word, *Wee-irrd*. Both the older boys were straightening up, pulling their coolness back together. The mother, likewise: she needed to regain her gallows focus. Looking from one window to the other, she tried to get a more concrete sense of the carrying on. A crowd of twenty-five? Thirty? But when the Lieutenant Major took a phone from under his yellow top, for a moment she was sure it was another gun.

"Kahlberg," the man said into the phone. "That's right. Well, I thought we had this under control."

Jay was scowling at the officer. The girls kept asking, *what's happening*?

"It's a situation," the liaison said. "Definitely a situation."

Oh, don't panic, Officer. For now Barbara had seen something that, all at once, put a stop to her fretting. She'd recognized what some of the crowd were holding in their hands. No guns in their hands, no. No detonators, and no rope to sling over the nearest tree. Rather, the shifting gang outside the windows held up crucifixes, rosaries, medallions of a saint or the sacred heart. Everyone seemed to have an icon handy, even a pair of teenage girls in tie-dyed California tops.

Indeed all these day-clothes tended towards color, a midsummer palette, and this went well with the church bric-a-brac. A shift in Sicilian umber, a shirt in Neapolitan blue, these made a nice complement to the beads and miniatures in cream coral or soft carnelian. The pewter crosses might've been scraps of cloud. Meanwhile, too, these gewgaws became a part of the group hug. The way these people lay their pieces against the bulletproof windows, against the armored door panels, they might've been kissing in another form. Barbara saw believers who kissed three different ways, first putting their lips to their dangly charm and then planting a smooch on the NATO transport, while also, number three, touching the cross or beads or whatever to the van. At some point in there the mother began to laugh.

"It's Paul," she said. "It's about Paul."

Jay surprised her with his look, the gentlest she'd seen from him since they'd come out of their hiding place at DiPio's clinic.

"It's all about *Paul*," the father said. "These people, somehow they must've heard what happened. After I was hit."

"Big news." Evenly, she met his gaze. "You can't expect something that big to remain a secret."

With that, fumbling with one hand over the seat-back, the husband made an attempt at their private gesture. Reaching, probing through her skirt, he tried to pinch the waistband of her underwear. This was a line of communication established during their first meetings, when they'd cuddled beneath the bleachers alongside Jay's football practices. In those days it had thrilled her to be taken hold of so intimately, and she would give him back the same, her own fingers ducking beneath his padded shorts to tug lightly at his jockstrap. In those days they'd been twin Pinocchios, each finding the secret that turned the other to flesh and blood.

Tonight Barbara twisted out of reach, squeaking across the vinyl. She broke into the same laugh, harsh and dismissive, as before. "My mother used to tell me about Naples," she said. "She used to say that around here, sooner or later everybody knows your business."

As if she did it everyday, she hooked a couple of fingers over the gun barrel before her. She made the trooper lower his weapon.

"This kind of thing," she went on, "this tonight, I've seen it before. The church work I've done, I've seen it plenty of times. They think what Paul did was a. . . ."

Then Barbara noticed Kahlberg, the way he was looking her middle child. That shut her mouth, the calculation in the man's stare.

The officer never gave his phone a glance, as he folded it and slipped it back under his flaming jacket. "Apparently," he began, "there was a video."

Chapter Three

A lepers' city, a city full of crooks, a city for the end of everything . . . no. The Naples Barbara encountered over the next couple of days proved impossible to label and file away. At times it did seem a city of prayers. But more often she could be certain only of the appearance of prayers.

You knew the prayers by their empty husks, clinging to the walls of chapels and shrines. The things littered the old downtown churches, the ones that remained open. As soon as Barbara ducked into the sanctuary, navigating another doorway marbled with dust and braced by scaffolds, she'd spot the offerings on the walls, the *ojetti votivi*. Also hand-lettered notices lurked amid the ironworks of reconstruction: *OJETTI VOTIVI*. Where you found a church, you found a shop, supplies for the faithful. In there, among crucifixes and medallions, you could buy a piece to represent whatever prayer you had in mind: a miniature in low relief, plated with silver or gold. There were broken hearts, small as half a pinkie or as large as two spread hands, and sacred hearts crowned in flame. Also the heart as muscle, anatomically correct. Here was a leg, there a head, there a household animal, or (its lines as sharply drawn as if lifted from an ad for medical supplies) a syringe. Plus every shop offered the all-purpose clasped hands. These surrogates came with small hooks and nail holes, the better to be hung onto a reliquary, or tacked into the plaster of the chapel wall. The offering could linger for years, after that, growing as dirty as the streets outside. In the emptier chapels Barbara spotted graffiti too, beside these single-use icons. In one case she made out a date back in the previous century, scratched beside a few desperate words. The letters had gone black with accrued grime—something like the resentments built up over a long marriage.

The mother had good reason, over these few days, for going back into the breathless and rackety alleys down at sea level. She had obligations that got her out of her mansion on the hill. Now that was a puzzle, the Lulucitas' apartment, ten rooms and two balconies as a throw-in on her husband's deal with NATO and the UN. Plus anyone who'd gotten over the jetlag could see at once that the neighborhood was far better than the one in which the man had been hit. Barbara could see it the very next morning, as she fell into place among the commuters heading for the funicular. Nonetheless she rode down to the center, the original city. First she had her appointments with the bureaucracy, functionaries whose job it was to confirm that the face before them, flesh and powder, was the same as in the photo on the new I.D. Another day she had paperwork with an Italian bank and the American Consulate, and when she was done with those errands she could come up with something else. On one trip she went to the central police station and registered her picture and fingerprints, hers and the children's. This meant the kids were with her that time, down from the protected heights of the bourgeoisie, and so the family made only a single stop for prayers. A prominent cathedral lay a block from the station.

"You know Mama," John Junior explained to the girls, "she's always got to find the Duomo."

But when Mama descended into the *centro* alone, she had her choice of churches, outside of five or six that had been shuttered and padlocked following the quake. These always gave her pause, the edifice still consecrated and yet vacant. Their porticos were blocked with sawhorses, wood and iron both, then double-x'd with ribbons of orange plastic. The off-limits sign bore no church insignia but rather a government stamp, machine-black. Barbara suffered a chill the first time she faced one of those, during these confusing couple of days. She shivered, she blinked, and then she visited a travel office. She asked for the agent who spoke the best English.

The mother learned that the airlines preferred twenty-one day notice, in order to guarantee the best connections and a reasonable price. But on the other hand there were flights to New York every day.

Of course she couldn't make reservations till she had a better idea when Jay's mother was arriving. Grandma Aurora never gave a thought to the extra expense of last-minute travel, and there was always the chance that she'd wait till after Fourth of July. The old woman loved those fireworks. She would've flown all five kids in and out of Manhattan just for the night of the show, she was such a doting grandmother. Which was precisely what Barbara needed, while she left the country to make divorce arrangements. During recent Christmases and birthdays Barb had bit her tongue, fighting down the impulse to snap at Aurora over how she spoiled the children. But that same sort of lavish indulgence would be good for John Junior and the others, briefly, after Mom and Pop shared the bad news. Sure it would, briefly; Jay saw the logic too. The husband too felt that they should wait for his mother to join them, in these vast and airy new digs, before he and Barbara "hit," as he put it, "some kind of point of no return."

Husband and wife had had this conversation maybe an hour after the family at last clambered out of their NATO ride; it took that long for Jay and Barb to get some time alone. But Barbara had no trouble reiterating, quietly but firmly, what she'd announced at DiPio's clinic. The Jaybird took it with the same hurt as before, with the same question as before. "Why?" he asked. But as soon as Jay understood that Barbara intended to hold off taking action until Aurora arrived, he'd agreed. For a moment he'd been puzzled, fingering the gauze over his temple: "What does my Mom have to do with. . . ?" But then he'd clapped a hand across his mouth, audibly. He'd narrowed his eyes and nodded.

Besides that Jay heard her out closed-mouthed, except to say he loved her.

Now in the light of the Naples day, either the day after or the one after that, Jay's mother's daughter-in-law sat in a travel agency wondering just what she should say herself. Barbara came out of the place frowning. The vista before her turned out to be the prettiest she'd yet seen, outside her own neighborhood. A flower-bedecked piazza, it opened towards island ferries white as toothpaste, a high-shouldered castle the color of charcoal ash, and the up-shooting gem-glimmer of twinned fountains. Barb took it in and then turned away, once more heading for the deep urban shadows just upslope. She needed a church and prayer.

Yet whatever sanctuary the mother came to, while back on the cliff-top her older children watched the younger ones, the holy words to which she gave voice would turn to husks. She thought of the *ojetti*; she thought of the corpses from over in Pompeii, hollow and baked. It didn't help that at home she spent so much energy keeping up a front, likewise gold- or silver-plated, in order to evade the kids' radar.

These days their little emotional sensors kept picking up UFOs. Barbara could practically see the things herself, blobs that drifted across the screen out of an unknown quadrant. She had to keep smiling, up in her wide kitchen and out on her new balconies, and she had to pay their father a constant lip service. The effort left her tugging at her armpits and beltline.

And the morning she took the kids downtown, the playacting got that much worse. Barbara hadn't realized that, after the video on the evening news and the stories in the morning papers, she and Paul had become Madonna and Child. They could hardly go half a block without someone coming up for a blessing. Barb herself, the previous morning, had poked around incognito; she had the strong Campanian genes. But nobody could fail to recognize Paul. That day like every day, he wore the outfit that the locals had seen on TV: a starched white shirt and black perma-press pants.

At least down in the old city, amid the hawkers and masons and miracle-seekers, the middle child showed his mother something better than an obsessive-compulsive wardrobe. Paul revealed as well a mastery of street theater, acknowledging each new supplicant with a disarming hipshot posture, fey but friendly. The boy paced himself, taking neither too much time nor too little with the bric-a-brac offered, now a crucifix and now another of the votive bas-reliefs. He gave each a touch and a murmur, no more. Barbara was relieved by the child's command of the stage—you go, girl—but she still couldn't believe there was anything supernatural about it. Rather, what she saw was the wiles of a younger brother. Since coming off the plane Paul had kept an eye on his two elders, both of them loud and bumptious, obvious Americans.

So the kids were one burden. The Jaybird was another, in on the nasty secret and yet, these days, such a nice guy. When he complimented Barbara's looks, the man offered sweet nothings the likes of which she hadn't heard in years. Naturally she could see through his ploy, his own silver-tongued go at Paul's healing touch. But she couldn't begin to explain the slick and muscular way in which she'd repaid his kind words, two nights out of three. Two nights out of three, after they'd found themselves alone, she and Jay had tumbled into fucking. Fucking seemed to be the word for it, an angry business well-nigh impossible to make sense of. The grind and sigh were familiar, granted, as were the sensations of climax. These seemed to buck off her caked-on experience until Barbara was returned to layered glass, knitted and flexible, and between the glass gaps some other flesh-bound portion of her skied downward, hooting. Yet the need to come like that wasn't the same desire she used to know. Her greediness erupted in the middle of bedtime, it cut into her sleep, even as it set up a wholly unrecognizable counterpoint to the prayers that Barbara kept attempting during her days. Her downtown rosaries were supposed to offer Extreme Unction. At the end of everything, absolution.

The husband, beneath his bandages, must've suffered the same confusion. Like Barbara he couldn't think of anything sensible to say about their lovemaking. Rather, in the mornings as they shared a cappuccino, or in the evenings as he helped with the dishes, the Jaybird found other things to talk about. In particular, he was interested in Owl and the kids making a tour of his job site. He thought it would be good for the family to visit the Refugee Center.

"What we're doing up there," he said, "think about it. It's good work."

Was this was the second morning after the morning of the attack? Was it the third? In any case the man checked over his broad shoulder, in his white chef's top, making sure none of the children were in earshot. Then, just above a whisper:

"I mean, if it's over between us, okay. If that's what has to happen, okay. But you should at least get a good look at the kind of guy you're leaving."

Barbara knew this gambit too: calling the bluff.

"You should have a look, Owl. The kids too, the kids especially. Hey, you know Silky'll drive. You know he loves to take out that Humvee."

Barb shook her head, though she couldn't say just what she meant by it. She might've been declining a trip out to the Refugee Center, tomorrow or the next day, or she might've been shaking off the wild ride she'd taken in the bedroom down the hall, just the night before. Trying to understand, there at the table and later in the church, she recalled some of the seedier confessions she'd heard at the Samaritan Center. She remembered in particular an all-but-divorced couple who'd enjoyed a standup quickie on the way to their final mediation session. They'd done it in the elevator, those two, and now Barbara herself seemed none the wiser. Under her polished surface she seemed nothing but contradictory animal impulses: lick or destroy.

Which might be what she sensed, ultimately, in the pitch and rhythm of the original city. Downtown, everything revved with savage pretending. On all sides, even in streets jammed from wall to scaffold, hustling couples and threesomes kept up a baroque and airy masquerade. The performing style, the hands perpetually in the air, manifested itself in the hustlers and executive track alike, whether you were wearing a hand-me-down soccer shirt or a glittering silk tie. Even the people walking unattached made small gestures, the same sort of scene-stealing business Barbara had noticed in Mr. Paul. In particular these people had a shrug that was more than a shrug, an effort of the entire body, requiring a pause between strides. In the moment of that pause, fixed in place with shoulders hiked, a Neapolitan would look like one of the plated *ojetti*.

Barbara, taking it in, itched with a fresh doubt. Could she indeed trust the obliterating vision she'd had her first time through these spaces? Or had she become Italy-addled in spite of herself, bitten by some virus that incubated amid the clutter and breakage? For starters, it seemed unlikely she'd ever gone unnoticed. These mornings alone, as she'd dawdled on the Street of the Oil Cistern, or on the Street of Dried Grapes, the locals had known her, *la Mama Americana*, the one from the video. But they'd made believe otherwise.

Also the ruling color, other than the gray spectrum from sulfur dust to tufa stone, remained the same blue as had confounded Barbara when she'd first seen it on that map. *Napoli azzurra*, half the street vendors wore it, whatever their skin color. Nor did it matter whether their cart was chockablock with DVDs or piled with the kind of sea salad they'd been offering around here since Christ was a carpenter. The sea itself provided different colors, from scallop-white to squid-purple. Then the fish smell gave way to a citrus tang, the oranges and lemons like clowns hustling into the center ring before the elephant's out of the tent; then all the rest would be shot through by the acid stench of metalwork, another shop turning out the *ojetti*.

Even the commerce going on, the bills unfolding and changing hands, struck her as part of the show. Another flutter of gladrags. This even though Barbara knew how hard it could be to get by, around the ransacked Bay, and though she didn't fail to notice the ill-nourished Senegalese or Eritreans who manned the more decrepit of the open-air markets. Nevertheless, to her the Euros could look like Monopoly money. A tourist's delusion, this was, and stupid of her, and whenever Barbara scolded herself for it, she had the impression that she'd been deluded—infected—by history. She couldn't separate the buying and selling, and the false fronts that went with it, from the history. The displays shrieked for impulse buys, here as much as when she drove the Bridgeport bypass, but in so ancient a setting the pitch to feather your nest, your flimsy and rotting nest, looked inherently nutty. The very name of the city seemed at the same cross-purposes, an expression three thousand years old that meant, roughly, *New & Improved*! Barbara thought of a hustler working in a museum. In fact the Museo Nazionale was close by, with a thousand imitation antiquities on sale. She didn't need Chris to tell her that, under all the daily deal-making, the foundations went back long before Christ was a carpenter.

"This whole trip was an act," she told her chosen priest. "That's what I realized, that first day. It was the old shuck and jive, when we came to Naples."

"Really? And the refugees of the earthquake, the *terremotati*? They're children of God, don't you know, neglected children."

She shook her head. "I'm not saying it's not good work, what Jay came here to do." Back in Bridgeport, her husband had brought home a DVD put together by the relief agencies, a documentary on the quake damage. Some of the scenes had disturbed her as deeply as the materials from the Samaritan Center.

"Good work, well. God's work, rather."

"Yes, Father, but for Jay and me that was just the cover story."

"Cesare, please."

"Cesare, that was our *story*, doing God's work. But then came our first morning in Naples, our first time out in the sunlight. As soon as Jay went down, I saw this trip for the farce that it was."

The old priest eyed her, his mouth a red fold in a wall of limestone or chalk. Barbara had to remind herself that he had no trouble with her English; he'd done his seminary work in Dublin.

"Though the Jaybird," she went on, "he's sticking to the story. He keeps talking about the Refugee Center, saying the kids and I, we should visit."

"As indeed you ought," Cesare said, "if you do intend to stay."

Barbara's dress was binding under the arms again. She wished that she and this man were using the confession booth.

"If you do intend to stay . . ."

"Cesare, what am I telling you? I'm telling you, it's not so easy for me."

"No need to shout." He waved a heavy-nailed hand at the empty pews.

"I know what I need to do. I can feel it, Father, like I can feel a prayer. Like when the rosary's working, you understand? That's the way it came over me, my marriage is shot. But now what? The logistics, New York and a lawyer, it isn't easy."

There: her confession. The old man shifted closer, his crossed legs flopping like drumsticks inside a musician's black tote.

"I mean, Father, Cesare, what's it like for other people? When they've been married twenty years, is it just, boom, one day it's off?"

"Other people, oh my. You ask a priest about other people."

This visit was Barbara's third in as many days, but her first without the children.

"The will of God, don't you know, it's got nothing to do with the polls."

"Come on, what's so bad about looking for some kind of model, out there? I'm asking, just for example, what do other people do about the kids?"

A touch of self-consciousness softened his long face: you ask a priest about kids.

"I'm saying, the will of God, in my case that could cut either way. On the one hand, do I live a lie so that the Jaybird won't be disturbed, while he gives food and shelter to the *terramotati*? Or on the other hand, do I remain true to my conscience? The conscience that God gave me?"

Cesare turned thoughtful, putting the choice under the calipers of his Jesuit training. He must've spent a lot of time up in his head, or over in the library—like all Barb's favorite church people, over the years. The *Signore* must've turned so many pages, the paper had softened the edges of his testosterone. Not that Barbara was handling him gently, showing respect, the way she'd been raised. Her work at the Sam Center, she realized, had gotten her into the practice of being blunt. Especially the time one-on-one with Nettie, her mentor. A Bride of Christ, a Franciscan, Nettie had nonetheless taught Barbara not to pussyfoot around just because there was crucifix on the wall. Then too, when it came to Cesare here, one of the connections she'd felt from the first was his distaste for pat answers.

"Perhaps," he said finally, "it would help if you didn't always think in such personal terms. Try putting some distance between yourself and these vicissitudes. Imagine that it were some other family, in which a successful executive gives up all that he has, or he gives up a—"

"Come on, do you really believe it's that simple? Give up all your worldly goods, for the sake of the least among you? That's not my Jaybird, building the New Jerusalem."

"I should hope not. I'm rather a skeptic when it comes to New Jerusalems."

"Well, I'm saying it's not *about* a better world, or not only. Jay's got something else going, a private agenda." Her husband had brought the family here, Barb insisted, in an attempt to regain lost power. "He needed to run my life again."

The old man looked dubious.

"Listen, I realize I talk a good game. How do you think I know an act when I see one? But I'm telling you, Jay, he had the real power. He's always had it."

The old Dominican sat so still, his robes plainly laundered that morning, that he prompted the contrary image of Barbara's kids tearing around in a nearby soccer field, their shorts and sneakers smeared with grass. The place was open to the public most afternoons. Her chosen church wasn't down in the *vicoli*, but up in the family's part of town, where you found regularly groomed green-spaces and a responsible staff. The last she'd seen the children, the teenagers were playing goalie and the younger ones were sharing a pickup squad with a few locals. Paul had looked fine, just another kid with a ball, and Barb had no problem leaving to meet with Cesare, a couple of staircases farther uphill (in this city even the best neighborhoods presented an aerobic workout).

What did it matter that Barb had discovered this man uptown? Cesare wasn't defined by the parish assigned him any more than by Jesuit or Dominican. He'd committed his ministry to "the wretched of the earth," a phrase his new member from New York admired, though so far she'd avoided admitting that she didn't know the source. She knew enough, anyway. Barbara understood that though she liked the old man, there was chemistry, what she depended on in their give and take was his commitment to the opposing point of view: Jay's version of the Lulucitas' business in Naples. This made the Padre Superior a bracing corrective. Again, with him it was like with Nettie: if the wife could make her argument to this priest, then she might be frightened, she might be disappointed, but she wasn't merely whining. For Cesare hadn't needed an earthquake in order to do something for the non-Europeans, the people off the Italian books—the *clandestini*. Over the past couple of years, though it violated church policy, he'd allowed homeless blacks and Arabs a night or two of sanctuary. If they could make it up to Cesare's, these strays, they had an alternative to the lice-infested shelters in the old city, or the Camorra-run "squats" out by the mozzarella ranches.

Even now, the priest had two such lost souls camped in the church basement. The first time Barbara had spoken of the attack on her husband, Cesare had noted the date with interest; on her next visit, after he'd decided the American could be trusted, he'd revealed that he'd taken in "two poor creatures" that very same evening.

These two had been guests of the church for a week, Cesare reminded her now. "And it's obvious, don't you know," he went on, "that these young men have had some scrape with the law. See them flinch when they hear a siren, it's entirely obvious."

The mother wasn't sure what had brought this on.

"Well, one wonders, Mrs. Lulucita. These two in my care, one wonders if they weren't the same fellows as attacked your husband."

Barbara got a hand on her purse, a reflex.

"This husband who you claim had the power to drag you all the way across the Atlantic—well, two penniless beggars laid him low just like that."

"Mary, mother of God. What are—"

"Take care, Signora. That's a holy name you're using."

"But what are you *saying*?" She and the priest were alone. Between morning Mass and evening Mass, people in this neighborhood preferred to stay home with the appliances. Now Barb had the purse in her lap, her hands in fists around the handle. "Why are you telling me this?"

"Why are you complaining to me about some so-called power in a marriage? In this world, power is a piece of iron pipe. It's a wallet full of Euros."

"Oh, *Father*. The two that hit my Jaybird, that night they would've had the Euros. Now don't you think they would've taken the money and run? That's what the police think, they hightailed it for Norway or someplace that very night."

Cesare had kept his own arms down. In another moment, unflappable, he undid what he'd just done. He pointed out that Jay's attackers had had a motorcycle, which meant they must've worked with some under-the-table dealer out on the city's periphery. Out in a mob neighborhood like Secondigliano, for instance. The two men the priest was keeping in the cellar, on the contrary, had shown up on foot.

"One could see that they didn't even have 90 cents for the funicular."

Barbara hadn't quite shaken her panic, her blood-rush. "If you're saying there's no power dynamic in a marriage . . ." She tsked, irritated at her vocabulary, *power dynamic*. "If you're saying it wouldn't be about power out at the Refugee Center, the Glorious Jaybird Show, then you're the one who doesn't know how the world works."

"But think of the reason you couldn't stand to see him in power. If that man had power, signora, it was because you loved him."

Sighing, Barbara lifted her purse and set it back down.

"It was love between you two," the priest said.

At least she resisted the counseling-session response, *I acknowledge that*. She looked to the altar. A thing of glazed concrete, flecked with shards of glass in purple and green, it hardly seemed an Italian piece. It was New Age California.

"Well, and wouldn't that love be the reason you still find yourself making love, actually, Mrs. Lulucita?"

"Oh, so far as that goes, listen." Another reason she'd chosen this priest was how willing he was to talk about sex. "We can't be sure what's going on, so far as that goes. What does any of us know, honestly, when it come to the libido?"

"I suppose. But you are some years past forty."

"Some years. Some years, there's a nice way to put it."

Much as she preferred straight talk, Cesare's collar didn't give him the right to check her hormonal balances. Whatever menopause or its approach might have to do with Barbara's ongoing Neapolitan upheaval, she could handle that part of it herself. With Jay, she'd gone so far as to use the expression "change of life," just the night before. This was after another spasm of clutching and gasping, turning to glass and tumbling through glass; her energy had been up.

"But," the priest replied, "I'm not just talking about your body and its changes."

"Cesare, I had five children, you know what I'm saying?"

"Indeed I do, signora. Your body and its changes, that's your own affair, finally. What I'm trying to talk about is a long and happy marriage."

And faithful too, Father. Barb, nodding, sighing again, recalled in silence her lone suspicion of adultery. She'd suffered a wondering night or two early during her final pregnancy—and in the next minute, never mind that she and Cesare weren't in the confessional, she told him about it. "There were just two nights in twenty years," the mother said, "two nights of something Jay called a late inventory check, down at Viciecco & Sons." And whatever kind of inventory the man had been taking, it was over and done with by the time the twins had entered their third trimester.

The priest had come closer again. "You have your doubts, but you don't know for certain? You can't bring yourself to ask him?"

"But haven't you heard what I've been telling you, Father? Haven't I been saying, inside a marriage, power is just as real as out on the street?"

"Well, power of a kind, I suppose. But you made your own choices. Didn't you just see fit to remind me that you have five children?"

Do the math, Barbara. Three boys plus twin girls equals enough to keep you happy. Or it used to be enough, as she'd explained to the old Jesuit the last time.

"Oh listen," she reiterated now, "the mother scene, that's over for me."

Cesare folded his arms, more sticks in sacks. "Really, Mrs. Lulucita?" Barbara had told him how she used to thrive in parenting, its snot and intimacy. "I heard you say that even on your first morning in Naples, on the most bewildering streets in Europe, you were such a dedicated parent that you could enter the mind of an eleven-year-old boy."

"I know what I said, Father. Cesare. And I'll tell you something, I know the girls even better than I know Paul. But those girls are out of third grade now." Barbara faced the speckled altar wall again; she didn't want to whine. "After this, the way their social life takes over, it's as if they've gotten their driver's license. The best part of being a mother, that was over before I left Bridgeport."

Cesare might've shown some sympathy, a softening in his posture. But to hear him clear his throat, you would've thought he was grinding gears.

"Mrs. Lulucita." His tone frosted the name's musicality. "You know, Christ wasn't nailed to the cross for unhappy wives."

In his half-disgusted wave, Barb caught a glimpse of an alternative life. The man would've made a homosexual of the old school, courtly.

"In Dublin too, don't you know, the complaining was quite interminable. The song of the unhappy bourgeois."

"You're my priest," Barbara told him. "I have to ask again, do you want me to lie? To live in a lie?"

"Well, let's rehearse what we have here, shall we? Children grow up and leave home, isn't that a fact of our existence? And lovers lose their charms, inevitably."

Then with two knobby fingers still extended, Cesare reminded her that he went downtown three times a week, where he worked with people in real trouble. "The very sort of *clandestini* you'd find out at your husband's worksite."

"So. . . ." Barb needed another look around the church. "So what you're saying is, before I book a flight for New York, I should go see what he's up to."

"We live in a time of a great challenge, Mrs. Lulucita, one that seems to have come straight from Christ's teaching. This city, whether it can continue as a place of justice or not, seems now at the heart of that challenge."

When Barbara cast her eyes up, the stony heights tweaked her knees with vertigo. "You remember I worked with broken families, Father? I never got the credentials for actual counseling, but I've done some good for families. For children."

"But the effort Christ calls you to here in Naples, signora, requires no greater credential than a caring heart."

She went on staring at the ceiling, her head on the back of the pew.

"A caring heart, Mrs. Lulucita." The afternoon sun had sunk low enough to fill the stained-glass windows, and Cesare had leaned into a patch of these airborne colors. "When you adopted that girl, that time, what did you require, except—?"

"The adoption failed." Barbara sat up and heaved to her feet. "If you ask me, I required a whole lot more."

"Be that as it may, our *clandestini* brothers and sisters are lost children too." Cesare moved with her, the kaleidoscopic glimmer shifting down his robe. He asked whether Barbara knew that some of these outcasts had started a hunger strike.

"A hunger strike?"

"Mrs. Lulucita, what did you expect, coming to Naples? Better pizza? Kisses under the Moorish wall?"

"Moorish? A Moorish—what?"

But the old Jesuit appeared to think the conversation was over. Unfolding from the pew, he broke into an unexpected smile, wrinkle-lifting. He declared that she and her family too were "strangers at the door, don't you know." The culture might be different, he said, the skin color, "but Christ's challenge remains the same."

She had to laugh, and hearing herself, was surprised at the pleasure in it. You would've thought they'd had a reassuring heart-to-heart. Then back outside in the siesta quiet, the odor of volcano, Barb reconsidered the man. The old curmudgeon. He'd been forged by the preaching of John XXIII, the liberation theology and new liturgy, and he'd been taking shots at the bourgeois since he'd first heard a call.

Yet she was confused, no point denying, out under the maples blotched by a constant exposure to diesel exhaust. Estranged and confused, she stood dappled with shadow. Yet she'd found her Duomo, the place that afforded the shiver she needed. At Cesare's she'd felt her spirit flex, a muscle tremor hard to place but easy to recognize, if you're a believer. She couldn't say whether she'd chosen her church and her priest or they'd chosen her, but either way she'd been out of parochial school long enough to know that the movements of faith didn't always follow the syllabus—that confusion often played a part.

A car shrieked to a stop behind her. Naples traffic, typical.

It might be in keeping with her soul's exercise, she told herself, it might help strengthen her for life outside marriage to end the moping around and instead try something like Cesare suggested. . . .

Doors were slammed, above a couple of rough shouts, a man's voice. Barbara didn't give it a thought until one of the policemen took her arm. *Carabinieri*, this guy, not city police. He and the one with him wore braided hats and uniforms, like U.S. state troopers. They shuttled her into their sedan so expertly that at first Barbara had to marvel at it, Italian efficiency and a wide back seat. But then she recalled her kids. The thought branched at once down to the pit of her gut, spiky and cold. She couldn't be bothered with a seatbelt; she started shouting.

"*Sono sicuri.* Safe, safe." This was the officer in the passenger seat, shouting back. "*Tutti sicuri.*"

Barbara got her first decent look at the policemen, a handsome young duo. The one riding shotgun had lips as fine as John Junior's. Then by the time the mother could confirm that the problem had to do with her husband, not her children, she could see John Junior himself. The oldest, along with the other four, were in the precinct house. They were two minutes from the church, in a drab suite of offices that overlooked the funicular.

The kids had been put in some sort of holding cell, fronted by a broad window. It seemed to take longer to unlock the door than to drive here from the church. Barb could see at once, anyway, that they didn't share her anxiety. When she at last got into the cell, into the child-sweat, none of them made a fuss. The girls remained cross-legged on the linoleum floor, talking across a soccer ball. Paul and the two oldest had the three chairs in the room, and they'd set themselves in a row in front of the room's big window. Only the willowy eleven-year-old turned from the glass as Mom walked in, and then only for a glance. Barbara wound up checking the window herself. From this side, it turned out to be a mirror.

What was a mother supposed to do in here? "Your Pop's going to be fine," she said. "On the way over the cops told me it's not really a kidnapping. They told me it was more like a standoff."

John Junior didn't need the explanation. "They might take all of us out to the Center next."

"That's the way it works," Chris said. "They bring the family if they think it'll help negotiations."

"That's what they tell you," JJ said. "That's what they *tell* you, Crisco. But actually the plan is to give you to the bad guys instead."

"Uh-huh. Well you notice nobody's even talking about giving them you."

The boys were looking forward to the trip. Why had dumb old Mom and Pop dragged them off to a disaster area like this if it weren't going to be an adventure?

"*E un ostaggio, signore* Jay." This came from a trooper who'd moved into the holding cell with them. The scent of his gun oil cut through the closeness.

"*Che brutti, i poveri.*"

Barb looked up at their new protector, his uniform piping and chest strap. She concentrated on the translation: apparently the brutes, the poor out at Jay's Center, had made a move on the big American. As soon as the news had come from the camp, the law had rounded up the wife and children. They didn't want another *ostaggio*, a hostage; the quake had left desperate *animali* everywhere, even in this neighborhood.

"*Animali, i poveri.*"

The next to speak up was Dora, always the more adult of the girls. "Mister, hey. Nobody could possibly hurt our Papa."

The trooper in the room was the one with the great lips. But the smile he offered appeared so smudged and vacant, it could've have been one of the downtown prayer offerings, ten years after it was hung on the chapel wall.

"You don't know about this family," Dora said. "You don't know anything about Mama and Papa and us."

Barbara worked on her own smile.

"Mama is a very, very good person. You don't know, she works in a church."

Barbara stepped over beside the girls and put her fingers in that petal-soft hair. Now Sylvia had taken up the argument. "Mama works with *children*," she said. "Some children have been badly abused."

"Some children have been badly abused. Mama brought home a DVD."

The two eight-year-olds were possessed by such a dreamlike seriousness that they must have worked these ideas out at bedtime, after the adults had left them alone.

"That's why we moved to Italy."

"That's why we moved. Back in America, sometimes she even yelled at Papa about it. 'Don't you care about suffering children?' she yelled."

"All right," Barbara started, "all right now you two . . ."

"That's why," Sylvia said, "Paul was able to bring Papa back from the dead."

"That's why no one can ever hurt Papa now," Dora insisted, raising a finger. "Mama turned Papa into someone like her. Like, a saint."

Barbara seemed to choke on her objections, like Jay had choked a week ago—the last time he'd come up against the *poveri*. Once more she looked over her children, first the two big teenagers in primary-color soccer gear, then the two stocky fourth-graders-to-be in crayon-bright jumpers and tees (easy to spot in case they got separated), and last the odd, fragile, not quite adolescent boy in black and white. Paul was staring at the girls, thinking it over. The mother had by no means ignored the boy, these last few days; both she and the Jaybird had sat down with him, their riddle-some middle child. What's more, both had come away with the same understanding, on one point at least. They agreed that Paul didn't know what he'd accomplished over his father's choking body. But Mr. Paul needed better than that; if Mama was a saint, she had to do better.

The cell door opened, not far, not even halfway. Another *carabiniero* called the first into the hall. The two conferred in a whisper, but they couldn't hide anything from Barbara. She could read the pretty boy's smile, full Elvis all of a sudden.

"*E sicuro*, Jay?" she barked. "*Tutto sicuro?*"

The man who'd come to door met her look. He didn't smile, or not quite, but he gave a very different sort of shrug from what she'd seen downtown.

"Your father's safe, guys." Barb made it a point to catch Paul's eye first. "The man is safe."

Now both the policemen were nodding.

"And as soon as we can," she went on, "we are all of us going out to the Refugee Center. It could be tomorrow, it could be the next day, but we are going to get some backup from NATO and ride out to Papa's place."

The middle child was grinning more broadly than either of the carabinieri. He thrust a pair of fingers inside his open collar, exposing an inch more of hairless chest.

"It's time," Barbara went on, "we stop playing around."

Chapter Four

"Water buffalo?" Dora said. "Like in Africa?"

"This isn't Africa," Sylvia said, forcing a laugh. "This is Italy. Don't try to tell us they've got water buffalo."

JJ went on pointing out the Humvee window. "Guys, hey. Even I wouldn't try to confuse you about what continent we're on."

"Girls, look, what do you think those things are?" Chris was pointing too. "Moose? The mozzarella, like, the cheese? That's where it comes from."

Around them the landscape seesawed, here a scabbed, balsitic ridge and there the grass velvet of a creek plain. Across the more level areas sauntered the buffalo, hefty-shouldered and brick-brown, their horns like question marks. The NATO caravan had first taken the family through the Phlegrean Fields, north of the city—a low-rising outbreak of the same magma that underlay Vesuvius to the south. In the Fields the ground turned to dust around smoking fumaroles, mounds of pale flinders, like smoking dumps of extracted teeth. Two thousand, three thousand years ago, these badlands were said to house a gateway to the Underworld, the poisoned spring where Ulysses spoke with the dead. Yet soon enough the gravel and chalk gave way to actual fields, rippling with mid-June vitality. Low hillsides sprouted mixed greens in mouthwatering layers, while others flowered lavender, crimson, milk-white. Vest-pocket orchards and grape arbors cut rows and terraces across the flatter spaces, squeezing every workable inch of the nutrient-rich soil. Farther inland still, between the vine-rows and fruit trees, there began to appear the small herds of buffalo.

"Mozzarella?" Dora was asking.

"Best mozzarella in the world," Silky Kahlberg said. "*Da bufalo*, know what I mean? *Vera da bufalo*."

"Sure," said JJ. "The truth comes from buffalos. Old Neapolitan saying."

The NATO man chuckled, paternal, or the movie version.

"Yeah well," Chris said, "JJ, if the choice was between asking you and asking a water buffalo. . . ."

Kahlberg chuckled again, and Barbara allowed herself a laugh as well. She was going to have to learn to relax around the Lieutenant-Major. Certainly she enjoyed the benefits that came with having him somehow on call. She liked his van's state-of-the-art air conditioning, for starters, a terrific relief on a morning when she'd woken up itching. Last night Jay had put something extra into his thrusts; he'd wanted to kindle a special glow for today's visit. Then too, the mother was glad they didn't have to share the ride with a machine gun. Instead Kahlberg had arranged for a pair of soldiers in a second vehicle. This escort looked serious, bulked up in powder-blue helmets and vests, with a semi-automatic and a pistol each. But Barbara and the kids rode weapon-free. So it appeared, anyway; the mother couldn't help wondering about what the liaison man wore under his jacket. A white jacket, this time, and before the abbreviated caravan set off, as he'd huddled with the soldiers, he'd kept touching his lapel. His lapel or whatever he carried under it.

"Actually," the man was saying now, "out in your father's camp you'll find some folks believe that kind of thing. These people, they'll fall for every kind of superstition you could name."

These people? Barbara looked to Paul, but he'd cupped his eyes against the tinted window. Her Lakota child, following the buffalo.

"For this population," Kahlberg continued, "a lot of them anyway, the quake set off, mn, millennial fever. You understand?"

Chris turned from the window. "They thought it was like, The Rapture?"

"You got it, son. Some of these old boys, they figured it was the end of the world. That quake, it did leave them at the end of their ropes, anyhow."

Was that a reference to Jay's near-kidnap? A desperate stunt at the end of someone's rope, the day before yesterday?

Barb and Kahlberg had been circling the subject since she'd first gotten in touch to set up the visit. This morning too, though the mother had taken care not to sound nervous in front of the children, she'd fished for a guarantee that she wasn't exposing them to real danger. Give the liaison credit, he'd said all the right things. He'd echoed the children's father almost word for word.

Papa swore that the worst weapon brandished against him had been a piece of kitchenware. Also his would-be kidnappers never even got off the campgrounds, let alone came close to a getaway car—and not because the former Fordham lineman had put up much of a struggle, either. Rather, Jay explained, other Center refugees had stepped in. The people on the Jaybird's side had far outnumbered the troublemakers, a handful of *clandestini* only. Five or six young men, no more, claimed they acted out of solidarity with a downtown group on hunger strike.

Pretty strange, hey?, the father had said. *A hunger strike in Naples.*

Barbara, listening, sensed a different sort of urgency in her man's chatter. His hope for the marriage, that's what she heard, a hope bucked up by the mere mention of a family trip to the Center. So his storytelling came across as one part brag, one part gee-whiz, and overall nothing to be frightened of. During the brief struggle, he assured them, a crowd of refugees had surrounded the would-be abductors and made sure *il capo Americano* never suffered a scratch. By the time the carabinieri had picked up Barbara outside the church, the worst was over. By the time Jay was through talking, that night, the whole business had dwindled to nothing more than another story about Papa's job. And like all such stories it came with a moral.

My people in the tents, the husband declared, *they've seen enough destruction.*

At the opposite end of the table, Barbara drained her wine. She liked the taste anyway, a local vintage, the Tears of Christ.

Destruction, Jay went on, *that's never the answer.*

Yet here she was two mornings later, en route to her husband's worksite. It hadn't escaped Barbara's notice, either, that the Jaybird had traveled with an armed guard these last couple of mornings. His helmet-&-vest shared the same car. Plus what did it tell her when their NATO liaison suggested that the mother and the kids wait a couple of hours after the father left, before they headed to the camp themselves? Nevertheless here she sat, ignoring the itch between her legs, more of her husband's recklessness. She sat there and allowed the kids to ride out past the gate to Hades.

If she intended to destroy this family, she had to make the trip. She had to get a whiff of the air outside their cliff-top bubble.

But how was Barbara going to clear her head here at the Refugee Center? At this a lake of rippling nylon, spread across one of the broader hollows in the landscape—nylon or some other faded synthetic, all of it rippling from the neediness beneath the fabric? Again a crowd greeted the van. Again the gang gathered with hands in the air, waving, seeking, and one or two thumped the vehicle's windows and panels. There were shouts, too, rough open syllables, vaguely Italian. Barb couldn't pick out the words at first. Faced with a crowd like this, it took an effort just to realize that no one held up any bits or pieces for Paul to bless. No one carried church bric-a-brac. Yet the *terremotati* filled the parking lot, a patch of flattened grass. From there the tent city ran down-slope, here and there revealing a nylon cord or an aluminum pole, or a scrap of ground the color of driftwood, or—something else again—a flutter of laundry in party colors. Barbara thought of the old-city warrens in which she'd spent her mornings, this past week. From an occasional tent-corner there trailed a few bright ribbons, as colorful as the laundry. The mother even spotted something like one of the prayer *ojetti*, perhaps halfway downhill. This appeared to be a group photograph, a collage in an ornate frame, under a corrugated plastic rain cover of dirty turquoise.

Also here and there played shadows, children still intent on their games. The ones who'd climbed into the sunlight, the flat space surrounding the van, tended to be the parents or grandparents. Their crumpled faces came in a dozen shades of black, under unkempt Afros or wobbly dreadlocks.

The mother had a question. "These are mostly illegals, right?" She looked to Kahlberg. "I'm saying, do they even have a work visa?"

The officer went on checking the crowd. "The epicenter was outside the city, in the periphery. That's where you get the more transient population."

"And the—the radicals? On the hunger strike?"

The liaison shot her a glance. "One has to expect," he said slowly, "a certain amount of political tension in marginalized populations. One has to consider, as well, that many of these people arrive on these shores with criminal intent. Their sole purpose for being in Italy is to generate as much income as they can. Chris, big shooter. You know what the old Silk-man's talking about, don't you?"

The shifts of tone sounded doubly spooky under the blurred shouts from outside.

"Libya used to be an Italian colony," Chris said. "Ethiopia too."

"And Ethiopia—" Barbara began.

"See," Chris said. "Mussolini was all fired up about a new Roman Empire."

"Chris, Ethiopia is *starving*." Barbara tried not to glare.

"A seriously depressed economy, big shooter, over a disturbingly long term."

"That's what I'm saying." She concentrated on the Lieutenant-Major. "So far as the folks outside are concerned, Naples is the land of milk and honey."

Kahlberg stared back mildly.

"You know," John Junior said, "when Mom was a kid, she couldn't tell the difference between the pictures of Jesus and the pictures of Che Guevara."

"Stop it, *stop* it." Barbara whipped around; the teens were grinning, slapping hands. "If I hear one more stupid sarky remark—"

"There's Papa!" shouted Sylvia. "Papa, right there!"

Right there. Jay changed the whole shape of the scene beyond the windows. The man had his vice-president's swagger even here, and as he approached the Humvee you could see he was bigger than nine tenths of the brown crowd around him. Plus he wore a chef's baggy dress whites and a white long-visored cap, an outfit more bright and bleached and complete than anything among the faded dashikis and tourist T-shirts surrounding him. The *terremotati* appeared happy to see the Jaybird, including a few lighter-skinned folk Barb spotted now. Italians, these might have been, but more likely they'd drifted here out of the jigsaw nationalities across the Adriatic. A face or two out there looked Arab, as well. In any case everyone smiled as they made way for the *capo*. One of the blackest of the refugees, a man whose seamy face called to mind the folds in Father Cesare's robe, mouthed what must've been some sort of wisecrack. His eyes, though they were hardly more than glints in a cracked rock, glowed with obvious warmth. Barb's husband matched joke for joke, meantime. He shot a smirk one way and, glancing the other direction, tapped the peeling brim of a baseball cap. This was a person who would do nothing rash, a person with no hard feelings.

Barbara on the other hand was startled just to see her husband slide open the van's door. She hadn't known they were unlocked.

"Hey," Jay said. "Have I been looking forward to *this*."

"Papa," Dora said, "you look so sharp!"

"Well I feel sharp. Feel real good, baby doll. Feel good all the time, because I know I'm helping people."

The father tugged the long bill of his cap. Barbara looked over the bandage by his ear. Jay's bruise had faded, the scar had shrunk, but he was careful about keeping the spot protected. Now he found her eyes.

"We're helping a lot of kids here, too," he said. "A lot of these boys and girls, without us they'd have no chance."

Around his gleaming bulk came the smell of the crowd, unwashed and sun-blasted. The family stepped out into chock-full air, as much as into the flap of tenting, the creak of plank pathways, or the singing of the aluminum poles each time the breeze picked up. Jay led the group down through the jumble to his central tent-offices, stopping several times for introductions and more banter. He took into account, as well, how the NATO guardsmen affected the refugees. The *poveri* hadn't even had time to grow accustomed to his own armed tagalong, and now the family had arrived with two more. The campers who were made the most nervous appeared to be the most African, with tribal scarring and brimless sequined caps. Their steep-cheeked faces fell, when these men and women spotted the extra brace of gunslingers, both of them blonde and pale to boot, down from the European North. The tent-dwellers from the deepest South gave the troopers the widest berth, backing into the mud that bordered the plank byways, never mind that they were barefoot or, at best, in plastic flip-flops. Everyone in camp, really, backed away from the pair in uniform. The mother was grateful that the soldiers had slipped off their padded bulletproofing, and grateful too that Jay adjusted his patter. The man started to sound like a schoolteacher. He made it clear that he would never have brought his family to the camp if he believed there were any possibility of trouble.

"The heavy artillery," he said, "that wasn't my idea."

As they went, Barbara and the kids also learned about the camp's layout, a wider semi-circle that sloped down to a smaller one. It was an amphitheater, and down at the stage lay the important setups, including Jay's beloved kitchens. Papa directed a staff of twenty-plus, something else the wife hadn't realized. Besides that, the Jaybird was the lone worker from the U.S. He had his Coordinator's work cut out for him, needing to communicate across several varieties of anti-American resentment. Barb thought of the electronic misunderstandings that JJ and Chris got into over the internet.

Yet she alone seemed to understand the difficulty, and to see through the upbeat charade. Barbara alone, the half-out-the-door wife, seemed to be the only one who worried for the *capo*, even as he struck poses that implied he was everybody's friend. But how could these *poveri* connect finally with this transplanted food-industry exec? Most of them spoke a mangled Italian, and more than once she heard them break down into pidgin French or a sub-Saharan patter. From underfoot, meanwhile, came the suck and pop of the walkway boards in pockets of mud. Not that it had rained, out here; the water was the run-off from the hose-and-coat-hanger showers—if not from some less sanitary facility. Plus chalky clouds of pesticide would waft across the family's path every now and then. Lice powder, Jay explained. The Site had a doctor come in and dispense a fresh dose every week. But for Barbara the acid-flavored dust only reinforced her unhappy take on the place, as bad as that first day down in the original city, a reeking underworld in which you could barely speak with the ghosts.

After the group reached the center of the camp, the mother tried twice to point the way back to the parking area. Wrong each time. The Jaybird corrected her, stepping in front of her and thrusting out his chest.

"Listen," Barb said, "I'm not sure the kids can—"

"Kids," Jay said, "I'll tell you what to look for. If you're ever lost in here, just look for your family."

He pointed at something closer by. At the corner of a broad tent hung a wide and ornately framed photograph, another group shot, a rough match to the one up by the parking area. The portrait itself, now that Barbara looked at it, held several heads in the surreal fixity of the Sears Roebuck studio. One of those heads however was impossibly enlarged, some kind of trick with the copier. For this was a copy, a doctored full-color scan of a shot Barb had seen before. This was her and the children, in a free portrait she'd won at a church raffle a year ago. The enlarged head was her own, mushrooming above the kids' as if she were the family Vesuvius.

"I don't ask this guy about the technology," Jay announced, waving a hand at Silky Kahlberg. "I don't want to know."

"No," the Lieutenant-Major said. "You don't want to know."

He was fluttering his lapels, getting some air under his pretty jacket. Not that you could see what he might have in the armpit.

Jay went on with the story. A number of the refugee families, he explained, had arrived at the site with, of all things, a hefty self-portrait. "Hey," the father said, "everybody wants a picture of themselves. Think about it, it's like I.D." In the camp, however, the ungainly squares and ovals took up space in tents already crowded. In a couple of cases, the odd item of salvage made the neighbors jealous. So after a few days of getting to know his site, The Boss had hit on a plan for community building.

"It was time," Jay said, "we had some *signage.*"

Circulating with his least-busy staff members, he'd labeled and cataloged all the larger, more garish frames—and Barb for one realized what that part of the process was about, community building among his colleagues, tunneling through their built-up suspicions when it came to Americans. Jay had insisted, too, that the records be kept in English, Italian, and French. Then he'd rounded up volunteers from around the camp.

"Oh," Barbara said, "I get it. You—"

"Now this next part," Kahlberg said, "this is the miracle part, if you ask me."

Jay's volunteer homeless had gone around collecting the catalogued pieces. The families had let Barbara's smiling but still-unknown husband remove their family photos and take the fittings, though often it was their sole possession of any value. The Center took them away peaceably, with nothing but a piece of paper in return.

"I just figured," Jay said, "the Site could be a city and a nation. A nation, it says somewhere, is just the same people living in the same place."

Again, Barb understood better. She could appreciate how the *Americano's* fair business practices had mattered less to the people in camp than the picture of his family. At the same time as he'd asked for their frames, he'd shown them what he had at stake, in Naples: his own little band of runaways, smiling and airbrushed. He'd shown them what he'd given up.

The mother tried to explain. "These *clandestini*, for them it's probably been years since they saw anything like this."

"That's just technology," Jay said. "Silky does it in the NATO shop."

"No, I'm saying, the way we look, it must've seemed like we come from—"

"The liaison officer," Silky said, "has access to all document functions."

He went on smiling, between the tips of his hair, tucked back and poking from under his ears. Meanwhile, Jay pointed towards the reshaped portrait overhead. Even the NATO guards looked up at it, letting their rifles hang slack.

"Signage," Jay said. "Now everybody's got an *address*."

The light through the blue plastic visor made the mother's mushroomed head all the stranger. Barb recalled that she'd been a nervous wreck on the day of the shot, still been trying to make a go of it with Maria Elena, their Mexican ward. At least she'd known better than to spring that girl on the folks at the photo studio.

"We-ird," Sylvia said. "It's like the stuff Chris shows us on the web."

"But that's so we can *find* it," Dora said. "Right Papa? If we're lost, we just look for the weird stuff."

"Hey, you got it," Jay said. "Smart girls. You got it." Then as he gave the photo another look, did Barbara see him shake off a chill?

The way Jay put it was, so long as he had the extra hands, he was going to put them to work. Kitchen duties for the girls, carpentry assignments for the boys. But when Barb asked where she fit in, her husband dropped his eyes. *Wherever you like*, he said, scrubbing his forehead with a calloused palm. The wife, aware she was under NATO scrutiny, briskly declared she'd make herself useful in the camp chapel.

Good thing, too. Best to look busy when, it turns out, the family's Public Relations Department has arranged for the media. The reporters joined them after the Lulucitas moved into the community kitchen. Cooking took place in an open-sided tent, where standing fans whirred between the ropes, but even so a patch of heat-fog lay between the broad steel stoves. Jay handed out smocks and gloves, and the girls fitted on each other's hairnets, refusing Mama's help. Then the air got closer still. Along one open wall gathered another knot of visitors, white folks.

"Well, *meno male*," said Silky. "*Meno male*."

Chris was the first to translate: "less bad," acceptable. Among the new arrivals, a couple of the men were getting out notepads, and the lone woman clicked on her video-camera. Five reporters, altogether, everyone wearing the Southern Italian version of business casual, a lightweight dress shirt. They all knew Silky and seemed comfortable with his Dixiefied Italian. Indeed as the liaison made the introductions, including the names of the newspapers and the TV stations, he might've laid on the cornpone more thickly than usual. Might've played to the stereotype, keeping the press comfortable.

Not that the refugees trusted the man, whatever his accent. Barbara, checking around the kitchen, realized that the campers tended to allow Kahlberg the same space as they gave his gunmen. But the *poveri* at once proved great fans of the press, especially the two with cameras. Several crowded in behind the reporters, and beyond the kitchen's floor-fans, outside, you saw fresh clusters of naked feet. Inside, the posing quickly turned shameless, the Africans even popping their eyes. The most animated cluster gathered around the woman, a young woman, good-looking. She was new at TV work, if her gloves were any indication. Fingerless thoroughbred leather protected the girl's hands, and she kept adjusting her grip.

Barb, for her part, hid her face. She fussed with her hairnet. Anyway the NATO liaison was directing the media elsewhere, towards *"il famoso Paul."*

Here amid the stainless steel, however, Mr. Paul didn't appear particularly famous. Jay had made the boy strap on a carpenter's tool belt, breaking up his stark color scheme, and the work-gloves muted his hands. As he nodded under the cameras, he seemed merely young and clumsy. The belt's hammer-holster hung to his knee. Barbara gathered herself and stepped in beside him, deflecting the reporters' attention. The eleven-year-old put a gloved hand on her back.

Then the mother found herself fielding a question from out of left field: "How many years are you married?"

"Twenty years," she said, working up a smile.

"It will be twenty years this September," Jay said.

This reporter was a man, his shirt-cuffs folded back from the wrist Italian-style. He looked from wife to husband. "How much time do you stay in Naples?"

"Uh, all right," Barbara began. "The kids start school again—"

"We're in it for the long haul," Jay said. "The long haul, *capisce*? Today, hey. You'll see. This is my family."

The husband kept up the stage business even when he put his back to the reporters. As he gave the children their assignments, he loudly threw in additional tidbits, anything the press might find useful. He reiterated what he'd done with the frames and photos—a thumbnail version, *meno male*. He mentioned the camp's specialty meals based on country of origin. Barb had caught the act before, after all she'd married a salesman, but today the pitch wasn't just Jay. This was Jay morphed, Jay after he'd learned a few things about the "printing facility" from Lieutenant-Major Kahlberg. She couldn't see a decent way to stop it. When her husband asked if she wanted to say anything about what she might do in the chapel, Barbara only shook her head.

He continued quietly. "Church work, guys. You know. It's private. My Barbara, she's always done church work."

Catching her reflection in a steel stovetop, she tried not to scowl. But in another minute, give the man credit, the Jaybird again diverted the reporters' attention. He had them taking pictures. First group shots, sentimental as Sears Roebuck, and then the photographers singled out Dora and Sylvia and put them together with the kitchen crew. Peach-fleshed blond schoolgirls with rope-sinewed black laborers.

The Africans spoiled the effect somewhat, saying cheese. Seeing their gap-toothed smiles, one with a fat gold insert, Barbara again wondered at how little fuss these *clandestini* were making over Paul. When the family had pulled into the parking lot, the refugees had acted the same as they would have for any drop-ins from the white world. They'd come to say hello, they'd given the van a rap or two, but they'd acted like the middle child was just another well-meaning ofay. This when they must've heard of the boy. The communications network that began down in the *centro storico*, the exclusive Neapolitan wireless network, surely had a relay station up in this *Centro*. Besides, here and there among the tents, you caught the blather of radio or TV. But these musclemen in the kitchen would rather pose with the girls, and Barbara began to think that, here under the doctored photos, the faithful prayed to another miracle-man—not the son, but the father. Jay had named the roads, Jay provided the manna. Even to the Catholics in camp, then, the Band-Aid on the *capo's* temple might be just one more piece of proof that he was extraordinary. Just, the rich get richer.

Then too, it'd been more than a week since the healing. A week was a long time in a place like this. The aborted kidnap, just day before yesterday, must've gotten hashed over a thousand times by now. In camp, no doubt, every morning hatched a fresh crop of rumors. Everyone was so willing to clutch at a wild hair.

Before leaving the girls, Jay looked to Kahlberg. The officer shot a glance at his soldiers, and the blue-shirts slung off their semi-automatics. With the guns at their feet, the troopers settled into the coolest corner of the kitchen they could find. Then the father took Barb and the boys over to the infirmary in the adjacent Big Top, accompanied by the press and fifteen or twenty *clandestini* still hopeful of getting on the news. These strays thinned out further once the group reached the hospital and everyone went to work. Paul was put on the same detail as John Junior and Chris, fitting together beds and shelving. At that point a couple of the reporters decided they had enough, and a couple others elected to stay with Jay and the boys. When the mother set off to find the chapel, only the woman with the half-gloves followed.

Barbara believed she recognized the woman, but she wasn't going to say anything. The reporter was busy anyway, checking a light-meter and then switching on her spot. The chapel tent ran longer than broad, with rows of dull folding chairs facing a riser on which stood a low table. The walls were strung with wraps and scarves, from blush-purple to grape-blue, polyester or even silk. What with the heat, the flutter, the color, a visitor seemed to have arrived at the sacred campsite of God's chosen refugees. It seemed like sunset, time for worship, so much so that Barbara enjoyed a mild wave of spirit-tension, a tremor or two. Ahead, front and center, a low table held a burning oil lamp, a willowy flame that sweetened the camp's dank and sent glimmers along the first row of chairs. Before this makeshift altar sat a dark girl in a wheelchair.

Dark, but not African. A gypsy, rather, the girl had features of a near-Asian sleekness, and her skin matched the color of the heavy liquid in the lamp. Someone had fitted her legs into limp black jeans, and topped these with a flamboyant wrap, its indigo flecked with tassels and in-sewn coins. The wheelchair itself was a one-woman gypsy caravan, draped along the arms with gilded velvet.

In the next minute the camerawoman was asking for a shot of Barb and the girl together. The invalid made excellent copy, a pretty face and a crumpled body.

Barbara ignored the request. If she started striking poses she'd be no better than Kahlberg back in his print facility, gussying up the family photos. Anyway the press would have a Suzy Spotlight soon enough, after Jay's mother arrived. The wife, with her back to the camera, fished her rosary out of her purse. Propping herself against one of the locked chair wheels, she went down on one knee. From that angle, in the false twilight, the eyes of the cripple beside her appeared almost supernatural. The eyes of a Mongol goddess. *La Mama Americana* kissed her beads and began—but how could she have failed to realize that prayers made terrific television? While she worked through the first Hail Mary, trying to get to the bottom of her rage, the camerawoman went into a crouch and began looking for the best angle, spider-legging now left and now right in glamour jeans. She paused only to gesture *go on*. Barbara got the picture, another Nativity scene, even as she kept up her murmuring. She was never comfortable stopping mid-rosary. Her mind's eye however returned to profane business. Wasn't this young woman with a camera a ghost from that first dusty morning downtown? Wasn't she the one who'd taped the attack and the healing? The camera had been a smaller model, that morning, but this was the woman, all Cher-hair and bold moves.

Barbara finished her *Ave* and stumbled back, up then down, seating herself with a thump on the riser. The curve of her spine brushed the rim of the coffee-table altar. When the reporter lowered her camera, for a moment Barb couldn't distinguish between the two flashy younger women. Then the reporter started to ask questions. Had Mrs. Lulucita always known such faith? What sort of a churchgoer was her mother?

Barbara eyed the gloves, accessories of a career girl. "I don't know how to talk to you," she said.

"Tell me about Paul, signora. A woman of the Church, you must wonder about Paul. What do you make of him, the miracle?"

"Make of him . . ." Barbara tugged at a seam.

"Is it a miracle, do you think? What do you think?"

"Oh, listen. If you learn anything as a mother, you learn that once a kid gets out of the house, sooner or later they're going places you never dreamed of."

Tough Mama. Barb let her dress alone and sighed.

"I know you," she said. "You were there that first morning."

The woman's smile was the last thing Barbara expected, a grin straight off the playground. "Yes, *si*." Her nod came from the waist. "I was there, I was. After that I am having this new position."

She hoisted the camera, the light briefly blinding. "Yes," she went on, "your son does good for many people that day." And she introduced herself, Maddalena.

"Really? You're saying, you got this job because. . . ?"

"Oh yes. Before then I am always looking, looking, with my little camera. But that morning, *colpo d'oro*."

A stroke of gold. And if anyone seemed made for media work it was Maddalena, chic and electric right down to her cobalt fingernails. "*Beato lei*," Barbara said, blessed are you. Blessed was any woman who knew what she wanted.

"*Beato lei, Madonna Americana*."

Barbara wasn't that bewildered. "The American Madonna," she said evenly, "is someone else. She's a pop star."

Maddalena showed she deserved her job, recovering fast. "But the mother of Jesus," she declared, "she too is a pop star. The American Madonna, she takes for herself what is already for a pop star. *La Madonna di Jesu*, for two thousand years she has all the songs. She has the merchandise. In Naples you see her *ojetti votivi*."

Barbara dropped her gaze. "Listen, all right but . . . listen. I can't do this, all right? I didn't come here for an interview."

"*Per carita*. You didn't come here simply to pray."

What's your answer to that, Owl Girl? As Barbara slid her beads over her open palm, she was relieved to hear a different voice in the tent.

"*C'e qualcuno?* Is there someone to help the girl?"

The voice was a man's, vaguely familiar, but the mother couldn't see through the light from the video-cam.

"To help the girl, someone?"

It was a pair of men, coming around the rows of chairs. One wore a coat and tie, he had a goatee, and the other wore all-purpose khakis and revealed a shiny bald dome. After a moment Barbara recognized *Dottore* DiPio.

"Please," the doctor said, "wait for me for the girl." Then, blinking at Barbara blinking at him: "*Ma si!* Signora Lulucita. Where else would I find you?"

The other man was the first to extend a hand. Still young for someone so hairless, he had a German name, something like Interstate, and he served as the Center's chaplain. "Well," he said, "chaplain, schoolteacher, bookkeeper, *and* general errand boy for that force of nature you call a husband."

His English smacked of Middle America. Around his neck hung the Franciscan T, the italicized wooden capital, very different from the doctor's elaborate silver clatter. Also the chaplain kept calling everyone a saint, first the Jaybird, "a saint of energy," and then DiPio, "very generous, a saint."

The doctor bent over the girl, shining a penlight into her black eyes.

Interstate went on, "If I weren't able to stay with the doctor here, who knows? I might be living in a tent myself."

He was setting up the altar, lifting the oil lamp, tossing a purple cloth across the tabletop. There didn't appear to be a cross. Maddalena withdrew up the aisle between the chairs, trying to get a shot of the group. Barbara closed in on the chaplain.

"You live with him?" she asked. "With DiPio?"

"Yeah. He's got a big old place up on the hill, in the Vomero. You know the neighborhood?"

"I—know it, yes."

"Yeah, you take the funiculare. The doctor's family has lived up there for a hundred years. He's got a garden out back, a veritable hermitage."

But Barb didn't want to hear any more about saints. "The Vomero, this was the doctor's idea? It was him who set it up?"

"Sure it was him." The chaplain circled the altar, adjusting the cloth cover. "Who else could've arranged something so comfy?"

"But there's the UN relief—"

"Oh, the UN, Lord no. That housing stipend of theirs, huh. Most of the staff live two to a room."

"*Niente*," the doctor said, pocketing his light.

"Housing stipend?" Barbara asked.

Behind the altar, the riser, Interstate squatted to unlock a trunk full of Bibles. "It's peanuts I know, but then, after all." His long face regained its smile. "None of us came to Naples for the money."

His arms full of the floppy black books, he strode back past Barbara. He lay one on every fourth or fifth chair. "This isn't about having a nice apartment."

As he angled between the rows of chairs, in limp khakis, his body language seemed to call the Center's flock to worship. Refugees began to duck in under the far tent flap. They came in respectfully, buttoning their thin shirts or pulling off their spangled caps. A couple stopped to brush daubs of the reeking pesticide out of their Afros. Barbara hadn't expected this, and there in Maddalena's spotlight she couldn't do anything about the sham of her good dress and morning makeup, settled and bourgeois. A Vomero mother. Under the surface of course she remained another business altogether, a feral clawing for scraps. She wondered how much she should tell the chaplain about his Saint of Energy.

"Signora Lulucita?"

This was DiPio, fingering his neckwear. "Signora, perhaps the sympathy of a mother. Perhaps if you held her hand for the, the *messa*."

It came to Barbara that he was speaking about the crippled gypsy.

"Well," the chaplain put in, "it's not a Mass, strictly speaking."

"But for the service," DiPio said. "Would you come hold the girl's hand?"

Interstate (was his accent from Missouri?) had no objection. He handed a Bible to a refugee woman a good three times his size, an African Fat Venus, tucked sausage-tight into a t-shirt that bore the words *Lido Parthenope*. She had a chest scar—though nothing ritual, no mark of initiation. The wound on this obese *clandestina* had left a ridge of tissue clearly visible under the fabric, a line that cut down one breast in a jug-handle curve. It crossed and dented the nipple.

"Signora," the doctor said. "You may help."

Per carita, she hadn't come simply to pray. Certainly the need in this crowd had touched her, chilled her; that dented nipple reappeared each time she blinked. But Barb doubted that she could deliver much at today's service. The tent was filling, a sensation like children clustering under a beach umbrella, and she could feel already how distant the German's prayers would seem. She'd have to squeeze into a packed row of folding chairs, and there wouldn't be room for the spirit-muscle. There'd be nothing like that, the flex out of nowhere, despite the tremor Barbara had felt when she first stepped into this artificial twilight. There wasn't even a crucifix.

But the doctor was only asking for, what, half an hour? DiPio wasn't the one suggesting she spend the rest of her life in a lie. Besides, who could say what else Barbara might discover during the service? Interstate might poke another glowing peephole in Jay's high moral screen.

The mother sidled past a few of the seated worshippers, holding her breath against the worst of the pesticide. She settled into the chair the doctor had pulled up beside the gypsy. But when Barbara took the girl's hand, the invalid responded with a squeeze. Her fingers found a good fit. Barb looked up startled, and the gypsy's lashes fluttered.

DiPio didn't miss a moment of it. "Yes," he said. "Sympathy."

Whatever that meant. The man had his crucifix in his goatee, picking, scratching, and Barb shifted her attention back to the chaplain. Pacing the riser, Interstate looked eager to start. The voices behind Barbara's back sounded the same, and judging from the air the place was nearly full. For something like the fifth time the German adjusted the purple throw across his knee-high altar, then returned to the box that held the Bibles. He fished up a scarf, striking, Prussian blue.

She had to ask. "So what happens now?"

The chaplain kissed the silk and hung it around his neck, evening its ends around his dangling T, and explained that he worked freeform. "As far as I'm concerned, the *terremotati* can do anything this side of animal sacrifice."

"What? What are you saying? Is this a church service or not?"

"Mrs. Lulucita. In here, it's new heaven, new earth. If someone's in the camp, that means they've seen their world destroyed twice over."

"But, seems to me, that's why they need something reliable. If you show them one God one day and another the next, you'll only confuse them."

Somebody laughed, somebody American. American, with an accent more Southern than the minister's. Silky Kahlberg, sure, and Barb couldn't suppress a scowl. She hadn't been joking. She wondered whether, just by coming to the Center, she'd *asked* for everything and the kitchen sink.

The NATO liaison had already worked his way to the front of the tent. He'd made it through the congregation even though he was walking backwards, cupping to his stomach one end of some long stick of furniture. In his ice-cream suit, and still chuckling, he backed past Barb. Behind him, carrying the other end of the piece, came Paul. The boy acted on the officer like an anchor, stumbling, never knowing where to put his feet. As his mother watched, the eleven-year-old had to stop and hike up his carpenter's belt. Yet Barb remained where she was, her hand in the gypsy's. When she wasn't watching Paul, she eyed the two reporters who trailed him.

Of course Silky had brought along the remaining media. He and the *Americanino* toted a great visual, a freshly constructed cross. Freshly treated pine on a simple box stand, it went up tall and bare as chaplain Interstate.

"We heard you could use one of these," the liaison announced.

Barb looked the thing over. Insta-Icon, the cross revealed uneven stain along its upright and furred sanding at the corners. Then there was her child, his face drained, his gaze intent. He wasn't two feet from his mother and her quake victim, yet he squinted at the two women as if trying to make out some distant temple frieze.

Kahlberg turned and squatted beside Barbara, finger-combing his hair. "A little lay ministry?"

Barb made no answer. Paul too ignored everyone other than her and the invalid. The boy hardly gave a jiggle when Interstate opened the service by clapping him on the shoulder and loudly giving thanks.

"You don't *know* the good you do," the chaplain declaimed. "You and this gift from God you call a family."

"Mn," the Lieutenant-Major whispered, "if I were you, Ma'am, I'd be careful about the way Paul's looking at that girl."

What? Barbara's grip on the gypsy's hand retightened.

"A girl like her, you'd never find her in church before the quake, know what I mean? Not unless there were a hundred Euro in it."

Now the mother was angry plain and simple—her first entirely clear and justifiable emotion all morning.

"Fact is, anybody who comes to church in this place, he's playing catch-up ball. These people're nothing but lowlife."

Another word and she would've clawed out the man's eyes right there before the altar. But in the next moment Paul stepped away from the cross and the coffee table, away from the preacher. Interstate had let go of him and launched into some swaying prayer, and as the man's arms rose the boy went down. He knelt between the girl's useless legs. Clumsy preadolescent though he was, Paul managed this without interference from his tool belt, his movement in fact appeared seamless, and he tugged off his heavy gloves too, he flung them aside, all nothing like the hobbled mess he'd made of coming in. Also he was talking, Barbara's middle child, though she couldn't hear what he was saying, muttering, since to see him like this, easing himself between those young legs, mounting the helpless girl—to see Mr. Paul like this sent the mother's emotions into whistling new cartwheels, and she herself began to speak.

"Honey," Barb groaned. "No, no, honey . . ."

She needed to jump in and she couldn't even get her hand free. Barbara remained in the gypsy's grip as she jerked off her chair, or half off, tottering into the NATO man's cologne. The scent made her eyes prickle.

"The chaplain can handle it," Kahlberg was saying. "He gets a lot of holy rolling at these things."

"Mr. Paul." Barbara touched a hand to the boy's back, a white slab against the girl's spangled upper body. "Baby, I'm sorry . . ."

The hundred-throated prayer around them drowned her out. Not that these strangers needed to hear about it anyway, the trouble Barb recalled, seeing her youngest boy in so nasty an embrace.

"Just a touch," Paul might've said. "A-all she needs is a touch."

The same as he'd said over his father, a week ago down by the Naples waterfront. But Barbara was thinking of other trouble, worse, back outside New York.

"C-can't you feel it?" Paul might've said. "Can't you just tell?"

There was also the reek of carpentry, another reminder of downtown. Every alleyway in the *centro* had some kind of construction going, and with that thought the mother staggered at last off her chair, away from Silky's cologne. The change in perspective gave her a moment's relief, she no longer saw her child as a rapist, but on second look Paul's body-length embrace began to seem, if anything, even more of a nightmare. Barbara glanced at Maddalena, the only other person here who'd been present at Jay's healing. What had she heard last time, and what did she think now?

The camerawoman was merely doing her job, swinging this way and that under the fluttering purple and lavender. Now she took in the pileup around the wheelchair, now the crowd's reaction. And DiPio too, though he was a part of the pileup, didn't seem to realize what the boy could be up to. The doctor showed more concern for the girl, saying something like *Easy, please,* and nudging the liaison man aside in order to reach towards Paul. When the black-and-white child straightened for a moment to undo the work belt, DiPio caught hold of one narrow shoulder; when Paul pulled free Barbara felt pride. They couldn't stop her boy. A mother's pride, fond and blushy, how about that, on top of fear on top of rage on top of guilt—all slashing back and forth under her breastbone, along with thoughts of the other kids, the boys in the hospital and the girls in the kitchen—how about that, a mother's bedlam?

Around the cross-clutching over the wheelchair the dim tent had grown louder. The foreigners buzzed and the cameras went *click*, while the preacher had started bawling in mixed languages.

Guarda! Look! L'amore di Dio, sempre nuova! God's love, forever new!

Well, maybe new, but certainly strange. Once Paul got his shoulder free, he wedged his small hips more deeply between the gypsy's thighs. He actually pawed the girl. One hand worked around her waist, clutching her unresponsive body up into his, while the other traveled over shawl and neck to face. The doctor bent closer, his own odors tickling Barbara's nose; his soap had a hint of rose. The more Paul manhandled the girl, the farther stretched the wrinkles on the old man's face. Then DiPio's voice started to rise, yet another strain of frenzy in the tent.

"*E possibile?*" he yelped. "*Possibile?*"

In Barbara's hand the gypsy's grip likewise revealed mixed emotions, shifting and sweating. Her sideways glance, however, revealed something more sophisticated. The eyes remained angular and warlike as ever, but they suggested a touch of amusement, like *Somebody get a leash for this puppy*. As Paul gripped her you couldn't help but notice her young breasts, too, her sweetly tapered midsection, and Barbara had to wonder about the wheelchair's decoration. What was the point of all this tasseled party drapery, all but leopard-skin? And how could the girl within find the fun in today's muttering assault? Yet Paul did look a little like a puppy, at play across the gypsy's body. A boy at a game, again. With the hand around the gypsy's waist he searched for some spot between spine and wheelchair, pulling at her bohemian swaddling.

"Son," Kahlberg stage-whispered, "you don't know what you're messing with."

Talk about a boy playing a game . . . by now even the Lieutenant Major could see that whatever was going on, it wasn't about sex. What kind of sex involved one partner taking hold of the other's tongue?

"Mrs. Lulucita," the liaison said, "aren't you the parent in charge around here?"

"Mary, mother of God."

"Never mind her. Think about the Siren on the rocks, the devil in a woman. Think about where that tongue has been—"

Or maybe that was what the officer said; Barbara tuned him out, looking instead to the chaplain. Interstate had been silenced with mouth open. One thin arm held a Bible overhead, and his un-sleeved elbow revealed what was either a fresh bruise or more purple shadow. DiPio meantime had clamped one hand around his neck-stuff, the crucifix and Mr. Christopher, and his stare looked likewise clenched. He was rooting for the miracle so openly that Barb had to look away. She had to avert her gaze from all three of these looming full-grown white guys, casting her eyes across the congregation, dun-brown to domino-black, layered in castoff exotic colors (fig-blue to mirror-silver) and quieted for the moment. But the scene the mother had to deal with remained right in front of her, the willowy boy with his hand sunk to the knuckle between the girl's lips.

At least this time the love-bite hadn't drawn blood.

Again the cripple's hand fluttered in Barbara's. Already Paul was withdrawing his fingers from her mouth, releasing her to an involuntary birdlike moan. And when the gypsy arched her upper body after his retreating spit-slick touch, it seemed natural, a spasm. Certainly she didn't mean to show off her figure, curving up from where the boy's other hand still cupped her spine.

"All, all she needed was s-someone to hold her." Barb heard him clearly that time. "Couldn't you just f-feel it?"

Mr. Paul let go altogether, sinking onto his haunches, folding backwards from between the girl's legs. The quake victim collapsed too, dropping into her chair, and Barb found herself thrown into yet another brand of confusion. She suffered a letdown. She didn't want the girl to collapse. She'd brought everyone out to the chapel, and she wanted something to come of it.

But then the gypsy gathered herself and stood. At that the reporters and the congregation went berserk—erupting, attacking—and Barbara and the others in charge were left looking stupid.

They were left helpless, as the crowd's toy-store colors flared up everywhere, erupting, smothering. The mother was knocked onto all fours. The wheelchair somersaulted over her back, a stab in the back, an end to her dithering. How could she have been so stupid? How could she never have realized what Paul's magic would mean for people like these? How many of their barrel-bottom tatters did they need to wave in her face, and how loudly did they need to raise their searching prayers? Now as she lay beside the altar's riser, at first she couldn't tell if she were seeing stars or only the dots and dashes that decorated their t-shirts and dashikis. Anyway the view from the floor called to mind something else as well, the slash and blot of cave paintings, lit by dancing torches. Stick-figures agitated the air and the noise wasn't anything Barb recognized either. She couldn't tell whether the mob was calling on God or her husband or, in some third or fourth language, somebody else again. She only understood the clang and rattle of chairs toppling over, the whisper of blood-dark tent-hangings spiralling down. The reporters were in it too, shouting and elbowing over her head, fighting for a decent camera angle on Paul and the gypsy.

The resurrected girl had taken Barbara's youngest boy in a deep embrace. A standing embrace, both on their own feet, though the gypsy had wrapped herself around Paul from neck to ankle. Their hug might've been the riot in microcosm, a starved and ferocious response to a child who had no idea what he'd meant when he first held out his offering. Paul's own arms hung at his sides. He searched beyond the head that lay on his shoulder till his eyes fell on his mother's, at his feet. He went on mouthing his bewildered denials: *Just a touch, th-that's all.*

Well, what was she doing down there? Her legs were fine, her elbows sharp, and in another moment Barb was back on her feet and between the boy and girl. She was bracing herself for a tussle. But the gypsy let go at once, moving out of reach with a toss of her lank hair, a spatter of miracle-sweat. The mother had figured the girl wrong, the girl too. The gypsy's look might've been flinty, almost an accusation. But that was the way a lot of young people appeared to Barbara. Her son was the one she had to worry about, and now she wrapped her arms around his undersized chest and began to haul him backwards. Behind the tumbled coffee-table she shuffled, and her heel caught briefly on the altarcloth, sticky with lamp-oil. The flame had been snuffed, at least, in the fall, and the mother had gotten some breathing room for herself and the boy just by pulling him away from the girl. That dark and attractive stranger was, for a moment, the one drawing a crowd, the reporters in particular. The camerawoman Maddalena already had attached herself to the gypsy. Barbara meantime discovered a protected space, a corner of the tent, loosely walled off by the doctor, the chaplain, and the liaison. All three of the men had regrouped behind the fallen wheelchair and the cross.

It was Interstate who'd taken up the cross, brandishing it like a quarterstaff. With this barricade before him, he began shouting again, throwing some French into the mix. The meaning was as clear as DiPio's hand signals, palms out, arms out. Calm down, *calmavi, calmez vous*. A step apart from those two Kahlberg stood relatively unruffled. Relatively—the mother didn't like the way he fingered his jacket.

Nonetheless in back of these three, in back of the wheelchair and chapel's storage trunk, Barbara found a moment's safety for herself and her boy. She shuttled Paul around behind her, one last barricade, and in the process she bumped a hip against the tent's corner pole. The upright wobbled, the nylon rattled around her ears. With one backwards-reaching hand she discovered a seam was torn.

A torn seam, the least she could expect, in a place like this. Then it occurred to Barbara that she could tell the boy to run. He could duck out through the seam.

Mr. Paul could do it, looked like. Whatever this child's prodigies took out of him, they left him nowhere near so rattled as Barb. Her own clothes were soaked through, jammed up, and yet while the mother had been pressed against her boy, one hand at his neck and the other across his lightly-downed chest, she'd found Paul's pulse only a few ticks fast and his muscles just lightly trembling. He still had that carpenter smell, but his skin was dry.

She thought of heatstroke, of shock. One push would put him out in the fresh air. What would other people do?

But both of Paul's cures had been miracles in an inferno. Today, even if the boy escaped this particular volcanic circle, this bruising ritual of the hunt, he'd still be in the Underworld. He'd have to move through poison clouds. The family portraits overhead were supposed to guide him, but their deformed and colorized smiles had been fake to begin with. The whole camp would be on the child before he'd cleared the central amphitheater, and then there were the infantrymen from NATO. God knows what they might do. So Barb kept her boy with her, crooking one arm around him, and as she eyed the oncoming crowd she set herself the way Jay used to at the scrimmage line.

Hadn't there been a lot of brave talk about the end of everything? Well what would she call this, out beyond a crucifix turned sideways? The crowd had kicked aside the fallen coffee-table, and behind the people who'd come for the service, others were rushing into the tent. Others wanted to see what the fuss was about, they'd heard something and they'd wanted to see, and more of the chairs went over. There was bawling across the steam and the language of metal. Barb had to worry again about her girls and their guards, about Jay and the boys and the agitators in the camp, the ones in league with the hunger strikers. Not all the refugees would get excited over this, a scrap from the table of the white man's God.

But then too, Maddalena and the born-again gypsy had found a quiet spot at the other end of the tent. Among toppled chairs and fallen drapes, they were doing an interview. The older woman gestured conversationally, with her free hand. Her subject had struck a pose, hand on hip, camera-friendly.

They were doing an interview. Still the mother was clenching her jaw, bent and sweating. Hardly five feet from her face a gang of refugees clamored against the chaplain's jerryrigged barricade. They waved and bellowed as if they didn't have any words, let alone whole questions. Nor did they look anything like a movement with a plan, a political organization or some sharp *cosa nostra*. Rather the mother faced an addled and hollering urge to grab, the fireworks of their shirts and caps not nearly enough madness for them. Now the obese Venus in the Parthenope shirt had grabbed one of the smallest new arrivals, a boy with half a face. The rest of the kid's face was a crumpled gray-green smear, maybe a birthmark but more likely a scar. The color didn't match his own pink palms, nor his mother's either.

She was his mother, surely, this screaming mound of flesh. "*Ancora!*" Again. "*Ancora, questo!*" Again, this one.

Did this woman honestly expect another healing? On demand, just like that?

"*Ancora!*" the mother screamed. "*Per l'amore di Dio!*"

By now Interstate and the doctor had backed almost off the riser. Silky Kahlberg had eased sideways, but he was at Barbara's shoulder, and the trunk that had held the Bibles nudged her toes. Meanwhile the scarred mother and her scarred child slammed against the chaplain's crossbar, the woman's pleading gone raw. What did she expect, once she got their hands on Paul? But what had Barbara expected, what simple international exit symbol, when she'd come to the Center?

Then Kahlberg pulled a pistol from under his jacket and fired into the air.

One shot: consummate PR. One shot and the tent went silent, other than the clatter of the falling cross. The thing must've hit someone in the facing crowd, it must've bounced and caught someone's shin or toes, but nobody made a peep. Parthenope the Earth Mother whipped around, putting her bulk between Silky and her damaged boy. A few of the refugees threw up their arms or ducked their heads. But by and large the crowd went catatonic and baby-faced. The chill even dropped over the plank walkway outside. From beyond the purple nylon came a creak of wood under pressure, someone shifting their weight. Barbara herself had to remember to breathe. She recalled the wide leeway given her bodyguards as the family had descended into the camp. "These people" had long since learned what to do when The Man pulls a gun.

The liaison ran the muzzle along the tent-top, as if cocking a tennis racquet for a serve. The fabric buzzed against the steel.

"*Terremoto?*" the officer asked. "*Sono io il terremoto.*"

Barb realized she hated the man. Whatever name she'd given her feelings before this, it hadn't been nearly strong enough.

"Y'all want an earthquake?" Kahlberg went on—the dandy, the power freak. "You don't understand, *I'm* the earthquake." He stepped around the startled chaplain. "I'll bury y'all so deep your Mama won't know where to look."

DiPio was the first to move, scuttling back into the corner beside the mother and Paul. The doctor held his neckwear as he went; he didn't want it to rattle. Nonetheless by the time he reached Barbara, a white man in motion, the refugees had begun to allow themselves the same. The mountain-woman with the scarred chest eased herself and her discolored child back down off the riser, away from the weapon, and with her shifted the crowd's center of gravity. The cave-dancers turned to sleepwalkers. Arms down and eyes averted, they backed around fallen chairs and reporters pushing forward.

Barbara hated this Lieutenant Major—now the creep would say he'd rescued her—but she had better things to worry about. One of the reporters had stepped between her and Kahlberg, raising a camera. These digital models made everyone an expert, and the PR man didn't mind having his picture taken with a gun in his hand. Barb retightened her hold on her boy, not yet Paulie, and she tried to think. She remembered Silky's huddle with his troops, before they'd left the Vomero; more than likely the blue-shirts were on their way already. The cavalry was coming, and the *clandestini* were running off. The congregants found ways out all over the tent, their splashy outfits turning to shadows beyond the synthetic walls. The space grew airy and the bunting that hadn't fallen dangled freely again. In five minutes the scene had changed from Armageddon to the End of the Prom.

Behind her the boy began to speak: Mom, come, come on, l-let me go.

Then Jay showed up, bear-like and ready for trouble, under the far flap. Barbara made sure he had the kids with him, the girls in particular. The youngest in fact appeared to be the safest, bracketed between both their own older brothers and the NATO gunmen. Not that Dora and Syl took any time for Mama. For them, slack and moon-eyed, this was all about Paul. They'd heard what their brother had done, of course they had. The whole camp was on the network, no-secrets-dot-com. Barb's husband however took in the scene more carefully. He looked over the puddles of torn and bunched drapery and the naked metal branches of the upended chairs. The wheelchair had wound up face-down against one nylon wall and the gypsy girl, up on her feet, kept whispering to the camerawoman. Finally, for a long, crook-necked moment, the Jaybird stared across the tent at his wife and middle child. When he at last spoke, he gave orders.

"Silky, hey. Lose the gun. Come on, man. Nothing happens till that happens."

"You know the drill, big shooter." The liaison sounded conversational. "Escalating situation."

But he was already lowering the gun. After the iron was hidden once more under Kahlberg's jacket, Barbara realized how her shoulders were aching. She didn't know how much longer she could keep her arm around Paul.

Jay carried his arms loose at his sides, his chest up. A polar bear, in those whites. "Silky," he said, "translate for me."

Barb tugged her dress more into place. Why should the NATO man translate?

"Help me, Silky. You know the drill."

What drill, and why Kahlberg? Barbara could handle the Italian for whatever the *capo* had to say. Then there was the chaplain, hardly brainless, though a little shaky still. His purple stole had somehow gotten knotted around his wrist.

Once the Jaybird began to speak, Barb didn't catch every word. She needed to concentrate elsewhere, on the upheaval of her interior strata, the outrage and lingering panic and fresh suspicions. Jay's voice came across the wrecked chapel as if via a transatlantic relay.

Hear me, my people! You know you can trust the Boss.

Around the still-steamy tent, the refugees turned towards the husband. Never mind that it was Kahlberg who spoke the language most of them understood. Here and there members of the congregation found a chair, almost reverent in how they looked up at Jay. The gypsy cut off her interview, shaking a finger.

With the Boss, there can be no question. And now you know his family.

Barbara's only distraction was the doctor at her side, asking if there was pain.

Now you know about the Boss and you know his family. Everything is clear, and everything is good.

Chapter Five

"Signora, I do realize, your life seems to have confronted you with nothing but strangers. As if the very image in the mirror were a stranger."

Seductively, or almost, the priest cocked an eyebrow.

"But at the head of the host," he went on, "there's Paul."

"Yes." She began to nod. "Paul."

Cesare's look turned sober again, and the mother stopped nodding. God knows, today's visit must seem strange. It wasn't a week yet since the Refugee Center, the second "healing episode," and every evening before dinner Barbara had arranged for time with the old man. Today they occupied their usual pew, a couple of rows back from the altar to the New Age, and the priest lounged as comfortably as his robes allowed. Nonetheless this must've seemed like something different. Barb had come poking at the front intercom during the afternoon *riposo*, when even a rabble-rouser like Cesare shut up shop for a couple of hours. By the time the father answered the buzz she'd actually pulled off one of her flats, preparing to rap the heel on a window somewhere, and—a stranger to herself—she'd found herself leaking tears too.

She must've been a sight, through the viewing slot. She had to wonder, was this menopause? Was it time she took a serious look at the possibility?

What had brought her to the church today, wet-eyed and unshod and flushed from climbing, was hardly a tragedy. Her family excursion had been cut short, that's all. In the morning Barb and the kids had headed out with the Lieutenant Major, him and his army, and then they'd come back early and liaison-free.

Cesare returned to his point. "I do realize that what I've asked of you and Paul, it might seem like overmuch, just now. The straw that broke the owl's back."

She reached to tug an armpit, then let her hand drop. "Oh, listen. The least I could expect was that you'd try to enlist us in your cause."

"Well I won't withdraw my request. I want you to stay on in Naples."

Through the thin leather of her purse, she could feel the vertebra of her rosary.

"Forgive me for saying so, but I believe it's what Christ wants too."

"All right. I told you already, when I ask myself what I'm still doing here, that's always one of the answers I come up with. We can do a lot of good in this city."

"Indeed yes, but it may be that you've already done enough. You speak of my 'cause,' now. Yet as for that, hasn't your husband already done enough? Just the other day, didn't he minister to the lost sheep down in Castel dell'Ovo?"

The hunger strikers, the old man's pet project. As for Jay's visit down to the security ward, a new holding pen in an old waterfront castle, the most Barb felt she could offer was a Neapolitan shrug.

"Signora, I do recognize, even I, that what's good for the starving *protesti* may not be good for you. As you say, you're the one who's had five children."

"Is that how you'd prefer me?" Barbara asked, "Just another unhappy wife?"

The lines around his squint lengthened.

"Cesare, am I saying anything about what Jay did, down at dell'Ovo the other day? Today is about today. That's what I'm here for, today and this girl again, this gypsy. She doesn't take Kahlberg's shit. Excuse me, but I have to call a spade a—"

"It's as clear as the cross on the wall, Mrs. Lulucita. Quite brilliantly clear, don't you know. You feel as if, yourself, day after day you swallow that man's shite."

"Well he's my Lieutenant Major, isn't he? My tax dollars at work."

"And you swallow any disgusting business he slaps on your plate, while this girl picks it up and heaves it back in his face."

"You've got it, that's what I'm saying. Romy, this teenager, this orphan, a week ago she was a quadriplegic. Still she's got Kahlberg looking over his shoulder. Today, you should've seen what she did. She comes out of nowhere and in another minute . . ."

"Oh now, signora, you know where Romy came from. You know perfectly well where she gets her information. '*Na clandestina*, that one."

Barbara shook her head. Not that she denied the allegations about Gypsy Romy, especially not when it was the good Father who brought them. The girl must've had criminal contacts, going back to a criminal past—the poor girl. And wasn't that a good reason for a mother to shake her head?

"Of course," the priest went on, "these days it's no great a challenge to find you, signora. You're a regular traveling circus, the Flying Lulucitas."

That stiffened her neck. Barbara pointed out that the resurrected gypsy did more than merely catch up with the family entourage, once they all arrived somewhere. "The girl's always there first. She's waiting for us."

"Quite right. We must assume she has her spies."

But Barb didn't like to think about spies, either. Spies and spying—the cloak-and-dagger which must've been some part of Jay's and Silky's arrangement—that was more or less why she kept rushing back to this Dominican Jesuit. Everybody around her seemed to have made a place for that arrangement, in their new Mediterranean lives. And Barbara knew what she'd seen out at the *Centro Rifugiati*. She had evidence enough to show the same backbone, to take her own life back to Long Island Sound. But here she sat, Mother Maybe-Maybe-Not.

Whenever she thought about her terrible hour or so at Jay's worksite—the family had actually spent more time at the hospital afterwards, with DiPio and a fresh wave of media—some new uncertainty started sawing at her backbone. The idea that Jay and the NATO man were trading favors had started to seem dubious as soon as Barbara had stumbled out of the chapel shadows. The camp plank-way beneath their feet revealed splinters, mud, blotches of pesticide. The stink had gotten worse as the sun rose higher, and the campers who lined the walk remained battered, hand-to-mouth, and impossible to talk to. What sort of a *favor* was this?

Later she reminded herself that the job wasn't the favor—the family's cushy Vomero setup was the favor. But then she had to ask another question. Just what sort of service, she had to wonder, could the Jaybird provide for Kahlberg? What names could the husband have heard, through the nylon walls? Any criminal activity in the camp had to be nickel and dime. Nobody was scheming to tunnel into Langley, Virginia. Nobody had any way to hijack the next trainload of Euros down from Milan. Jay had Muslims in the camp, to be sure, but not nearly room enough for a madrassa, nor anything like weapons either. Spoons and brooms, that's what they had, like the *clandestini* who'd tried to kidnap the American Boss. And as for that ragtag group, a four- or five-some, they posed no threat to international security.

Really, what could Barbara's husband do for NATO? Kahlberg's people must've had plenty of stool pigeons already.

She knew better than to expect answers from her husband, anyway. The wife watched what he said, closely; she flipped over every evasion and poked at its underbelly. The day Jay paid a visit to the strikers down in Castel dell'Ovo, though she didn't know what she might be looking for, she'd scrutinized the clips on the TV news. Over the past week, though, Barbara found herself looking more and more for help from the Samaritan Center. Not that she sent an email, much less made a phone call. She felt too shaken for actual contact, too much in the wrong. But the mother went back to her web research, the sites where she'd learned a thing or two about screening cases for counseling. Library work always had a calming effect, for Barbara. More soothing still was the file folder she'd insisted on bringing from Bridgeport, the one labeled *Sam C//Nettie*, which held printouts and clippings marked up by her mentor. Every line highlighted in orange, every backwards jotting and five-pointed star, seemed to strengthen Barb's better judgment. She paid special attention to the verbal cues or body language that might reveal what a person had on her mind. On his mind, rather—the Jaybird's mind.

Meantime, Silky Kahlberg took over the family arrangements so smoothly you would've thought he'd been expecting the job. The morning after the second "episode," at the same time as Jay and his guard set off once more for the Refugee Center, the Lieutenant Major arrived at the palazzo with a couple more blueboys and a day's itinerary on NATO letterhead. *Heard you tell DiPio at the hospital y'all weren't gonna let this run you off . . .* Also the liaison accompanied the family on every trip, with the obvious exception of the day he joined the husband down in the waterfront security ward. Whatever other business Kahlberg had, he ran it from his cell phone. This morning too, he'd started out with Barbara and the kids.

This morning too, she'd gone along with it. Her energy felt tied in slipknots, now wound around Jay at midnight, now bunched before her file folder or computer screen, now unraveled in single file behind the Lieutenant Major. She'd taken the man's printout, the itinerary of their NATO-approved Tour of Campania, and gone along.

The liaison had scheduled them into the coming weeks, a trip every day almost till the end of June. And wouldn't you know it, he proved an excellent guide, thoroughly boned up on local arcana. For every trip Kahlberg arranged a professor's worth of paperwork, in a fuddy-duddy accordion satchel. From this he would hoist up whole chapters copied from guidebooks and histories. Of course, he handed the same materials to Dora and Sylvia as he did to their mother; he hadn't thought of everything. But then the man wasn't a professor. Rather, you saw him in his element when it came time to deal with Italian bureaucracy. The Lieutenant Major's baggy carryall also held, for every trip, a sheaf of documents that granted high-level clearance at the site. The liaison would climb out of the van first in order to get these papers approved, while the family and driver and guards watched through tinted windows. The transaction always required a meeting with at least two others, once there'd been three, but in every case the NATO man handled the process with as much efficiency as the system allowed. He ignored the men who were there for protection, bull-bodied and cow-faced. He went straight to the actual gatekeeper, and as that man looked over the authorizations, the liaison officer fielded any questions with a smile sweet as a Georgia peach.

As for the factotum whose job it was to approve or reject the family's clearance, to say yea or nay to Kahlberg's paperwork, he tended to take his sweet bureaucratic time. Those guys would pore over the stuff, testing it between finger and thumb. Only after the documents had gone into their bag (the Italians tended to carry the classic bureaucrat's attaché) would Barb and the others be allowed out of the vehicle.

Once that was over with, however, everyone onsite would act as if they and the Lulucitas had been friends since confirmation class. The family was allowed to linger as long as they liked, and no matter how busy the place might get, Barb and the kids were kept separate from other tourists by yards of gunswept space. Restricted areas were unlocked for them and additional guides provided. It could all seem like too much, in fact. Whenever Barbara succeeded at approximating tough-mindedness and clarity, for a moment, she would wonder at all the fuss. The very slickness of what this officer arranged for the family reinforced her suspicions that he'd finagled something with Jay. Yet even at moments like these, the mother had to admit that Silky offered valuable fun. The past as he presented it came in rich package deals—why not think of Neapolitan ice cream, its layers of flavors? Also Barbara liked to see her kids fascinated by history, an exception to the American-clod stereotype. She liked better still the emotional repairs that took place among the children. A stay-at-home mother noticed at once: as they poked around the region's stony hands-on classroom, Paul and the others recovered from the strains of the previous days. You could see it in their faces, Paul's in particular, as his eyes regained their glitter and his curiosity overcame his stutter. Naturally Barb had thought of Chris as the museum buff, the one who'd get the most out of what she'd come to call "the educational aspects of the trip." But in the younger brother too, this week, there burgeoned the same affinity. Nothing like your mainstream clod.

The black-and-white child was intrigued most of all by Pompeii's Villa of the Mysteries. The Villa frescos portrayed, room-by-room, a young woman's sexual initiation; the presiding god was Dionysius, and the process was largely unclothed and touched by frenzy. As the Lulucitas circulated the rooms, Paul pumped the guide for ever-more-uncomfortable details. In the final room of the sequence, the initiate reaches for the drape that veils an immense erection. The shape is unmistakable, shroom-like, and in that room Paul asked questions that left their guide speechless, staring at the mother. Signora, what. . . ?

Barb knew she only had to wait.

"Paulie," Chris said after a moment, "duh."

The mother would've preferred something less harsh. "Easy, Chris . . ."

"You remember," the older brother went on, "crazy Maria Elena? The girl Mom brought home. Like, what do you think *she* went through back in Mexico?"

She would've preferred something else altogether. Barbara was left with mouth ajar, and when she cast around for help she felt as flat and out of touch as the initiate on the walls. The mother's first clear thought was of a question she had to ask Cesare, *Am I a good person?*—a question she never did put to the old cleric, not in so many words, though she could feel its weight bearing down on their give and take inside the Vomero church. In the Villa of Mysteries, same thing, Barbara couldn't find her voice before her fifteen-year-old finished his explanations. Her second-born loved to play the professor, during these day-trips. How often, for instance, had they heard his lecture about the bricks and stones? *If it's bricks it's Roman, guys, and if it's stones it's Greek.* Also the excursions under the NATO flag allowed Chris to develop a broader expertise, not limited to the empires before Christ. The family and their escort also vanpooled east to Nola, where a fifth-century saint had hung the original rack of church bells and so provided their name: campanile, after Campania. *It's like, every time you hear a church bell, you're hearing Naples.*

On another day the boy and his students, plus of course their bodyguards, rode out to Caserta. They toured a behemoth of a palace, eleganza, the country estate of the Borbon king. Chris delighted in pointing out that it had been put up during the same years when Americans were throwing out their own king. The boy loved his parallels, his ironies. Outside the windows sculpted waterfalls sparkled, notched like silverwork into terraced gardens, while between those vistas wall-wide portraits linked the dynasty to Old Testament heroes. Chris had something to say about those as well, explaining for instance why the monster Leviathan kept turning up. But his sisters were barely paying attention by this point, distracted by the bed curtains. These were tasseled velvet, more eleganza, drapery strung from canopy bedposts, along doorways and windows and even as a curtain on the occasional armoire. Dora and Syl, thanks to Kalhberg's paper-trading on arrival, were allowed to fiddle with the stuff. Hands-on classroom, emotional repair. In the biggest of the royal bedrooms, Barb's two youngest claimed the tassels and drapes recalled the decorations that, up in Papa's worksite, used to hang along the wheelchair of the injured gypsy.

The girl herself—without ID, she preferred the name Romy—smiled with an uncharacteristic shyness. She let Paul do the talking; he agreed with Dora and Syl.

"In a, in another life," he said, "you must've been Qu-Qu-Queen of Naples."

John Junior looked at him sharply, mock-sharply, cutting off the girls' laughter. "What do you mean," he asked, *"another life?"*

He took Romy's chin and, right there in front of his Mom and siblings and their official escort, he kissed her.

The two kept their mouths shut, *meno male*. The girl's lipstick, though thick and showy, didn't leave a mark. Barbara noted every detail, even as she was astonished again at her lack of response. Things would never have gone this far between Romy and her oldest if the mother had been anything like her old self. These daytrips themselves would never have gone so far, even with the pressure from her seventeen-year-old. JJ appeared to be the child who'd gotten the most out of these five or six days since Romy's healing. The boy's internal repairs might seem small, on the one hand an easy-going acceptance of his younger brother's lectures, and on the other a kiss with a PG rating. Indeed, Barbara felt confident that a peck on the lips remained the extent of John Junior's sex life, in Naples at least. In Naples, her sense of the big teen didn't depend on snooping around his desk or listening outside his door; on top of that, she had NATO surveillance.

No, JJ and the former paraplegic didn't appear to have much going on. Yet it was he, the oldest, who'd announced one evening over salad with lemon and pasta *con vongole* that it would be "better for everything" if the family stayed in Naples.

"Hey." His face set, JJ looked every inch the co-captain of varsity soccer. "I'm with doctor DiPio. DiPio and your priest there, Mom."

What kind of Christians were they, he went on, what kind of good works did they have in mind, if they turned tail and ran as soon as things got a little strange?

Then the second-oldest fell in behind his brother, quick to take advantage of the parents' silence. *That's the pattern here, you know. The rich and powerful, they like, jet in and jet out. Make a mess and goodbye.*

"The rich and powerful," Barbara repeated now for Cesare, alone with him in the still-locked church. "My Chris, he believes that's us."

"But the boy has a good point, don't you know. So far as the history's concerned, I admire his thinking."

Barbara gave her head another ambiguous shake. She might've had no answer for the Father, just now, no more than for her two oldest that night at dinner, but she knew the person in her house who came closest to rich and powerful. She'd kept up her scrutiny of the American Boss. She'd made sure to let Jay know what she thought of his act out at the Center—"act" was just the word. She'd chosen a time to tell him when the news packed a wallop, just after they'd finished their latest roughhouse. She and the Jaybird had shared kisses a lot hotter than JJ's and Romy's, and afterwards, as her climax cooled, Barbara had realized: now was the time. Their skin and hormones could confuse them; she had to clarify. She'd removed his hand from her breast and declared she didn't trust him. She believed he was some kind of liar, she'd said, a bad person.

"Which leaves me with no choice," she concluded. "It's got to be divorce, starting as soon as Aurora gets here."

Actually, this conversation had taken place the night before. Hardly fifteen hours before Barbara's mid-siesta visit with the priest, she'd left her Jaybird grumbling and rubbing his face.

"I got to point out," the husband had said, "we don't even know when Mom's going to arrive. She'll just drop in without warning like always."

"A man on her arm, too. That's Aurora."

"Maybe, maybe. But think about this, hey. You're going to let my *mother* take over the kids? My mother who you've never trusted?"

"What are you saying, take over the kids? Aurora's only going to do the kind of thing she's done before. Short-term care."

"Jesus, Owl. You've got it all worked out."

"Well, would *you* be available? Won't Kahlberg need you on the job?"

"Hey, whatever I'm doing, whatever I'm—I mean, it's for the family. Jesus, Barbara! You want to leave just when things get tough?"

"So you admit you're doing something for Kahlberg?"

Jay had exhaled slowly and fingered her hipline. But the private gesture didn't work; they were already naked.

"Jay, you say you're doing it for the family. But don't you see, when you're hooked up with a man like that you're bound to put the family in harm's way?"

The husband had taken his hands off her and returned to his fallback argument. "Hey, I'm doing a lot of good." He'd brought up his visit to the hunger strikers, "Down there with the strikers, I mean, there was your priest there. Your priest, Barb." But Barbara was tired of hearing about it, the Jaybird as angel of mercy. Not only had the story dragged on throughout kids' time and dinnertime, that evening, but also the visit had been on the news and then, the following day inside the NATO caravan, the liaison officer had taken time to buff up the husband's saintliness further.

Through it all, the wife couldn't help but see her husband's dell'Ovo visit as a deliberate counterpoint to her own earlier visit out to the Refugee Center. After the Refugee Center, the struggle in the Jaybird's heart had needed to breach the surface in the same way, with a big whoop-de-doo. He'd needed to send his wife a message by way of the Church and the TV. In the process Jay again proved that his spiffy new friend, the officer in charge of PR, had taught him something. The care unit for the hunger strikers had been set up as maximum security, but the Jaybird had wangled the clearance for a pair of camera crews. The *Capo Americano* had even brought mail for the strikers, and in one case a couple of handicrafts from a tribesman back at the center.

"Your priest," he'd repeated finally, last night as he'd climbed back into bed. "The old man, he was there. You think he's in on Silky's scam too?"

"Jay, what kind of a question is that? Is that going to get us anywhere?"

"Get us anywhere," Jay said.

"Jaybird, there's got to be something going on. Just this place—how could the UN afford a place in the Vomero?"

"Hey. You think I ever in a million years expected something like this?" With the heel of his hand he'd massaged his forehead. "Accommodations like this?"

As Barbara watched, her sympathies had unclenched within her. She'd suffered for the man again, as she had on and off since she'd first become the apostle knocked from her horse, blasted by her vision of a new and marriage-free heaven and earth. Some of her husband's motives for visiting the downtown castle, after all, had been genuine. Some part of the Jaybird, separate from NATO influence, had nurtured a good-faith wish to turn the Africans in dell'Ovo away from their slow suicide.

If only he'd gone down there alone, as Cesare did, without TV or NATO. If only it hadn't looked, as he pawed at his big head, as if he were trying to hide his eyes.

Jay didn't much snore, last night no more than any other during the week, and so after he dropped off Barbara she could hear, two floors below their balcony, the NATO guardsmen practicing their English. *Excuse me please, please could you tell me where to find the cathedral of this city?* In Europe too the foot soldiers tended to be the boys without better options, the working poor. The mother also enjoyed the grind and bleat of the traffic beneath these Vomero heights, a hundred thousand machines probing the alleys or shaving the Bay, a vast ecosystem crackling with tenor horns and basso transmissions, the turbulence widening her perspective until Barbara would shed the anxiety that had mounted during the day, and come to understand that she wasn't so confused. She wasn't a mad housewife. She was only exercising a quality control, like the experts that even now might be running a forth or fifth scan on her new I.D. Sooner or later Jay or his liaison would expose their dirty dealings, and she would have the glaring betrayal she needed in order to dump the man. The certainty of it buoyed her up, and she spun slowly on a chuckling surface tension, all foreign voices and invisible travelers. As she drifted towards sleep, Barbara even felt comfortable about the puppy love that had sprung up between her oldest boy and gypsy Romy.

If the girl were bad for the family, then she would be good for the liaison officer. She'd strengthen Silky's manipulations, somehow, and the Lieutenant Major would act accordingly. He'd treat the doll-face as an ally. But so far as Barbara could see, Kahlberg never missed an opportunity to attack the girl.

"Romy," he would say, sneering, "Romy, or whatever she's calling herself now."

He remained blunt and nasty about how she'd made a living before the quake. "That girl didn't care if you were American, Italian, Somali, whatever. All she cared about was what was in your wallet."

On top of that, whenever the liaison had some more shit in his pocket to throw, he made sure that he and the mother were alone. He didn't want any of the kids to butt in, to undermine his slander, because of course his filthy talk was all about control. About maintaining his Svengali hand. The Lieutenant Major was trying to forge a secret bond with the person he took to be the second most powerful on the scene. But then too, the way Silky whispered, he had to be worried about the gypsy herself, her calling his bluff somehow. The man was the closest Barb had come to James Bond, but he was afraid of a former wheelchair case.

Anyway, no matter how dirty the brush with which the NATO man tried to tar the girl, in one respect she remained spotless. A few hours after her healing, in the hospital closest to the Refugee Center, *dottore* DiPio had put Romy through a battery of tests. He'd checked everything from her muscle responses to her blood, and he'd checked her again in his downtown clinic the following evening (the following *morning*, of course, the girl had had a conflicting appointment, a surprise meeting with the Flying Lulucitas). The gypsy had come through every exam as clean as a whistle. Was she merely lucky, or had she been more careful than the NATO liaison would like to have everyone believe? Had she been, perhaps, no whore to begin with? DiPio's tests didn't reveal anything conclusive about the young woman's history, and Romy herself wasn't saying. For all Barbara knew, the family's new companion might've had all her sins washed clean at once, as soon as Mr. Paul had touched her.

Nevertheless the mother didn't believe Romy had lived a life of purity. In the years before the gypsy had spent two and a half days trapped beneath a collapsed apartment building, out on the city's *periferia*, she must've made her living as a shady operator of one kind or another. And it didn't help, so far as Barbara's suspicions were concerned, that Romy bore an eerie resemblance to the bad girls of her un-gentrified childhood Brooklyn. If the estranged wife had any image for the toughness she wanted to achieve, she'd picked it up from the skanks in Carroll Gardens. The dropouts from Sacred Heart. The sluts always had a mongrel quality, as if their clothes were so skimpy because they fell between types, as if they needed all that makeup to pull the eyes and mouth into their assigned places. Romy's eyes still seemed like something off the far Asian steppes, and her complexion remained unfiltered honey, and this much together suggested Baghdad or Tel Aviv. But her sharp brow and nose, her tight and uplifted shape, these suggested London or St. Tropez. Granted, the gypsy's legs would grow stubby in another fifteen or twenty years. They weren't so shapely just now, either, still recovering bulk and muscle. But at Romy's age—perhaps within a year of John Junior's age—she turned everything to teasy combinations. Even in this skin-full corner of Italy, among the low-rise Capris and the billboards full of breasts, she had men gazing sidelong and puckering in thought.

But it wasn't just the gypsy's looks that made Barbara believe she used to be a criminal. It wasn't anything Silky Kahlberg had to say either. The evidence that mattered was the way that, no matter where the family's excursions took them, Romy was always waiting when they arrived. She was there before they set up the Big Top, and she did it her first day out of the chair.

That morning Kahlberg had begun trying to create the illusion that Barbara's family was no different from the other Americans in Italy. They were bonding amid the ruins, he'd wanted them to think, just like everyone else. And by the end of the trip the Lulucitas had also attracted the usual cluster of supplicants, with their martyrs and rosaries. But the gypsy had been there waiting for them. She'd tuned into a different information system, side of the mouth.

Back on the day she was healed, the girl had pretty much dropped off Barbara's radar once everyone got to the hospital. Rather the mother had paid attention to Paul, on whom DiPio of course ran the same tests as he did on Romy, plus a couple more. As the stunned afternoon wore on into evening, too, the doctor more than once pulled Jay and Barbara aside with beard-scratching requests "not to do nothing all of a suddenly." He clutched his neckwear and pleaded with her "to stay in this place where the child demonstrates this power, and where we have him under observation from the first." Meanwhile the boy was passing all his tests and looking fresh. He caught a cat-nap during the ride from the camp. He suffered no crying episodes, either, not even when Jay and Barb ducked into a storage room for a quick hissy fit. Mother and father worked through a bout of mutual recriminations, their words barely emerging from the backs of their throats, and then they'd stepped out from the closet to confront a blasé boy in re-tucked black and white. Mr. Paul was unfazed. What was the big deal, if he'd become a child saint? He knew the drill by now, the role was a Mediterranean classic anyway, and it hadn't escaped his notice that the fast-rising Maddalena had made another video. He knew about the crowds, the competing packs of TV units and miracle-seekers, first outside the hospital and later in the Vomero. He didn't see what Mama was so worried about, keeping a hand on his head—her fingers actually threaded through his hair—till they were back inside the apartment. He didn't see why she had to keep his big brothers breathing down his neck, one at each shoulder.

No, Barbara hadn't given the gypsy a second glance, that afternoon at the hospital. Nor Kahlberg either; she'd tuned the officer out as he began to make arrangements for the morning. He started right in working the cell phone, and he did quite a job, the mother had to admit. Apparently the Lieutenant Major had pull with the Consulate. Between sunset and breakfast he got his entire North American et cetera to put pressure on the editors and producers of the local and national news, reining in the media a bit, allowing the family some recovery space in the coming days. Barbara didn't want to think about the quid pro quo. Rather she pictured Kahlberg's arrangements as a wrestling match between titans. The aging but powerful Captain Red White & Blue took down, with effort, the young but dangerous Mass Communication, Master of Disaster. She pictured it as a comics panel, a fairy tale—the sort of thing she'd read to Paul that very night, once she got him into bed. She sat down beside the boy with the anthology on her lap, the big book of fairy tales she'd brought from Bridgeport. She'd known he'd want to hear them sometime, her Mr. Paul, her fairy child.

The mother could still play Mother Goose. That night she picked a favorite from a land far away, the story of the Irish Queen Bab.

As for the Gypsy Queen, the dark young lovely restored to her feet, who could say when John Junior had noticed her? Perhaps it had happened up in the Center's chapel, in the sweltering purple aftermath of the riot. His Michelangelo lips had taken on a fresh shape, as he looked the girl over. Then the next morning Kahlberg had taken the family far away. They'd gone out to Capua, due north.

The liaison showed shrewdness, typical, in his choice for their first daytrip. They began at the beginning, on a site where Etruscan war parties had taken over an earlier settlement still, Neolithic. Though Chris nitpicked about the choice. That was another shred in the moil of this past near-week; the officer and the fifteen-year-old couldn't get onto the highway without a disagreement. On this first day following the second healing, Silky pointed out the castle at the highest point in the Vomero, Castel Sant'Elmo. Next thing he knew, he was in an argument over something called "St. Elmo's fire." Chris insisted that the stuff wasn't actually fire and Elmo wasn't the saint's real name.

"Now son," the Lieutenant Major said, "I don't know as there's any place in Naples that has what you'd call its real name."

Yeah, okay. But Chris went on to claim that around here, recorded history didn't begin out at Capua, in the foothills of the Appenines. Rather things had started along the coast, at Cumae. There the Greeks had set up their first temples and shops.

"Mn," the liaison replied, "you know a hundred years before *that*, the Greeks were out on the islands."

"Sure, the islands," Chris said. "The Sirens."

But what Barbara wanted to hear about, once the family reached their destination, was the time-blackened artifact known as *arrangiarsi*, making arrangements—a business less than legal and yet embedded all over greater Naples. Anyone who stuck a hand under the table, in this city, could always find another one down there. There was always somebody who'd read the day's Duty Roster, willing to swap a secret for one of the prettier banknotes. How else could Romy have wound up here beneath the Capua Duomo? How except by Camorra-dot-com?

She lounged against a church pillar that had gone up well before Christ was a carpenter, a column left over from an Etruscan temple that had first occupied this ground. Sunlight glinted off her gypsy array, the bracelets of tarnished silver and sparkle-dusted plastic, and the sequins sewn into her halter top. The outfit revealed so much olive-dark midriff that at first Barbara thought, with relief, the priests wouldn't let Romy in the church. But then as soon as Kahlberg had finished his transactions over the documents and satchels, John Junior had jumped out in front of the family's little crowd (from the first, the NATO man never brought along fewer than three bodyguards). Romeo had offered Juliet the long-sleeved windbreaker he always kept knotted, *moda Americana*, around his slim midfielder's hips.

So never mind that Barb had deprived the priest of his nap. She brought the subject back to this girl and today. "I should take her for an enemy, shouldn't I? An enemy or an accident waiting to happen. Her looks alone, that should—"

"Beh, don't exaggerate." Cesare crossed his arms and knees the other way. "Don't talk like a bourgeois. What worries you about that girl is, you don't actually worry about her. 'Should,' you say, 'should.' You believe you *should* worry."

Barb started to nod, almost getting it.

"You believe this—what would we call it, espionage? Espionage, the way the girl keeps sussing out your daily rounds? You believe this should worry you, but in fact it leaves you entirely impressed."

The mother tried for more solid ground. "There's also what's happened with John Junior, don't forget. It's puppy love at full yap."

Romy and JJ generated waves of attraction that Barbara could swear rustled the petals of any flowers nearby. There was a breeze even in the heat of mid-June, the most breathless urban canyon. The lovebirds rode the air currents with acrobatic balance, without so much as a glance at Silky's gunmen. They had the mother trying to pull off the same, for a moment or two; they set her cuddling up with Paul or one of the girls and drifting off into Dimension Infatuation. But Barb was too much the adult to get so carried away, to believe herself beyond the reach of a stray bullet or a secret she'd rather leave buried.

"Full yap," she repeated, as Cesare broke into a smile. "It doesn't matter that JJ hasn't gotten under her clothes."

The old man gave her the eyebrow again. Earlier that week he'd let Barbara know that, as part of his ministry among the displaced and the *clandestini*, he carried a secret stash of condoms.

"Father, Cesare, those two, there's no way they've gotten that far. Ask our friend the Lieutenant Major, you think he isn't watching? So far as that guy's concerned, the kissy-face stuff is bad enough." Once more she massaged the beads through her purse-leather, settling into confession. "Myself, the truth is—I am impressed with her, aren't I?" And she added, halting, each word another bead, that she believed it was good for the kids to have the distraction.

"I know, I know," she went on, "where do I get off, worrying that the kids might get hurt? It's tangled logic, I realize. But, tangled, Father, that's where I live."

Anyway she was glad the children had something else to occupy their wondering heads. During these five or six days since the Refugee Center, Barbara imagined, the last thing on the kids' minds had been whatever trouble they sensed between the two ends of the dinner table. To them the 'rents must've always seemed on the prickly side. Jay and Barb must've seemed like another part of the Greater New York Immigrant Bicker, the spectrum from Lucy and Desi to Tony and Carmela. And now that Barbara was through with the role, she was sick of it, she'd come to notice that there'd been a few advance indicators. There'd been a significant disturbance or two over the past year, and the kids had picked up on these, the way they made the family gyro wobble. Back in Bridgeport, in the months before the trip, everyone from JJ down to the twins had preferred to hole up at home. In the case of the oldest boy, this had put a dent in his social life; the girls at his high school used to come up with all sorts of ideas for a Saturday night. But these days, in Naples, what JJ felt for Romy was much more of a show than the varsity co-captain had ever put on in the States. With no more than a hug and a bit of a backrub, he and the gypsy could send tremors through the thick camellias of mid-June. A valuable distraction.

Cesare yawned, flagrantly. "Well, is that it? You came banging at my door to tell me you're tangled? Tell me in rather a tangled fashion, I might add."

"I'm saying it's been that way for years. Everybody else, they've been free."

"Don't exaggerate, signora. Don't talk to me about lack of freedom until you come down to dell'Ovo. Down in the castle, don't you know Mrs. Lulucita, you might well find the fulfillment you seek. I daresay Christ is there."

"Maybe," Barb said. "But so's our busy Lieutenant Major."

"Well, when your husband came . . ."

"Tell me, at some point or another, did Kahlberg and Jay go off somewhere? Somewhere alone, behind closed doors? I bet they did."

Cesare lifted his chin, his wattles. "Signora, I ask you formally. Have you any proof that your husband is involved in some secret arrangement with NATO?"

She didn't bother shaking her head. "Listen, whatever's going on between those two, what it's saying for me is, God didn't send me the hunger strikers. He sent me this girl, Romy. He sent me Romy and whatever she has to tell me about my family and the weirdo in the ice-cream suits."

"The girl is simply a lost sheep. She was lost and now she is found."

"All right, but after that, why'd she turn around and find us?"

"Signora, you see the hand of God in this? You're the mother of a healthy young man, one who finds himself in southern Italy in springtime. You should be grateful it's a girl such as this, a girl of some shall we say *practicality*. Heaven help your Junior if he'd fallen instead for one of the pampered rich kids around this neighborhood. One of Berlusconi's Army, don't you know."

She took the man in, his black and gray itself a penance, on a hot afternoon. Nettie had taught Barbara a thing or two about Cesare's order; she'd taken vows with the Maryknoll Sisters before coming out of the closet. The brotherhood was one of the most orthodox. You weren't supposed to find a Dominican carrying condoms. On top of that he had the Dublin schooling, Jesuit, steel-trap.

"Listen," she said evenly, "here's the news. Kahlberg's not content with spreading nasty rumors, anymore. He wants me to put my foot down."

The priest's narrowing eyes revealed a new set of crow's feet.

"That was today, I'm saying. Mr. Lieutenant Major Mojo gave me an order. 'Tell that boy the little whore has got to go.'"

This morning's visit had been to the ruins under San Lorenzo Maggiore, one of the foremost downtown churches, with at least five layers of edifice on the same spot: Postwar on Baroque on Gothic on Roman on Greek. The liaison man had used the word "palimpsest," dropping his Southern accent in order to enunciate precisely, then pausing to eyeball Chris. But the second-oldest had wanted to see the place, and Barbara too. It was jam-packed yet vaulted stone like that, temple on church mounting far over her head, that tended to exercise her God-muscle.

"But," she said now, "this morning Romy told us there's neater stuff right across the piazza. *Napoli Sotterraneo*, there."

"Neater stuff? The *Sotterraneo's* been closed since the quake, Mrs. Lulucita. Closed for good reason."

"Yeah, but can you imagine how it sounded to my kids? All these caverns and cisterns and tiny passageways. Romy said it's like Indiana Jones down there."

"Please. The figure who comes to my mind is Dante."

"Well, Father, give or take an obscenity or two, that's just what Kahlberg said."

At some point her gaze had shifted to the po-mo altar. The red flecks of stone or ceramic recalled the NATO man's aggravated face. "The only people who'd been down there lately, he kept saying—well I believe he called them lowlife scum." Shouting and gesticulating, Kahlberg had let his jacket fly open. He hadn't cared if anyone saw his shoulder holster. Barbara, even after he'd punched the remote to open the van doors, could only sit and stare for a minute or so. She took in his carrying on, strange as it seems, with a distinct touch of envy. She could've used a tantrum herself.

"He said that the girl was scum too," she went on, turning again to the priest, "scum lowlife and a born crook. And a menace, he said. The man put his finger in her face and screamed that she was trying to lure us into a, a compromising situation."

The liaison had fallen into Orgspeak, the final elastic binder on his self-control. Barbara had to wonder what would've happened if there hadn't been an audience. Various non-combatants had gathered at the bottom of San Lorenzo's steps, jogging up behind the NATO van (a smaller model, a Fiat, for the trip into the old downtown). The usual needy ten or a dozen, with their medallions—but if there hadn't been so many witnesses, would the family have seen some gunplay?

"You know," she added after a moment, "it's strange that Jay should wind up working with a guy like that. Because Jay's your basic open book. I'm saying, when the Jaybird's upset, he might not come up with the right words, but you always know pretty much how he's feeling."

The priest went on frowning.

"But don't you see, our friend from NATO, he's just the opposite, he's got a ton of talk but zero information. Don't you see he's been a spook, for two weeks now? I'm saying, that girl, this morning, she got the closest I've ever seen anybody get to the naked truth about Officer Kahlberg. And all she did was, she surprised him."

The girl had popped up beside the liaison man before he'd finished handing over the day's papers. "The rest of us were still in the van. Chris makes some crack to JJ, 'where's your girlfriend?' And then like that, there she is, right there next to our NATO mojo. Can you believe she jumped right in there between the guys who have to check Silky's papers? That gypsy, she must've known one of those two Italians is there for protection. One of 'em's got to have a gun, you know? But she jumps right in."

"Are you suggesting, do you mean . . ." The old man's eyebrows, white and fluttering, might've been another variety of Naples tassel. "Was this espionage again, Mrs. Lulucita? The girl was trying to catch the officer off guard, so that she might discover something?"

Now there was a question. The morning's uproar, for Barbara, had concerned other sorts of secrets, the personalities in play. Now the old Jesuit had to wait while she tugged at an armpit. Finally: "I can say this, the two Italians there, the ones that had to check our authorization, they didn't like the girl either."

The Italians might've come here from the Office of Antiquities, but they lost control as badly as the Lieutenant Major. Angrily they'd shoved her away, and for a moment Romy had somebody's hand at her throat. A minute or so later, after Silky had popped the van doors—he'd wanted the family to know what he thought of the girl—the Neapolitans were still shouting at her in dialect, threats or obscenities or both.

"I'm telling you, Father, Cesare, I thought we were going to see gunplay."

Eventually the bureaucrat on the scene, along with his security man, had disappeared back into San Lorenzo. Before they had, however, they'd scowled blackly down the steps at the folks waiting for Paul. Now that Barbara thought about it, she might even have seen the American officer restrain the two. This had happened earlier, just after Romy had taken the men by surprise. Barb might've seen Kahlberg slap an extended arm across his cohorts.

Her chosen priest, meanwhile, took care to raise a different possibility. Kahlberg and his fellow-officials might've had reason to keep the gypsy at a distance. "If the girl is indeed some sort of crook, they had good reason. Since the *terremoto*, don't you know, there's been no hotter contraband than stolen or forged papers."

"I realize that, Cesare. Don't you think that's what Kahlberg said?"

Using his position at the top of the stairs to face down John Junior—the boy had leapt from the van—the liaison had loudly reiterated what everyone knew already. The quake had left a lot of people without documents, important documents. *And don't you think*, he'd gone on, *a known criminal associate like this would love to procure some fresh papers for her friends?* With one hand he'd swept back his fallen hair, and with the other he'd stabbed a finger at the gypsy. *Fresh documents, easy to fix?* Barbara, for her part, had preferred to look at Romy. Once she'd recovered from getting flung across the church fronting, the gypsy had sneered and stiffened her back like the Goddess of War. On your knees, puny NATO Man.

"I know what I saw," Barbara told the priest. "And if that girl was trying to catch Silky at something, she did it."

On top of that, Romy had seemed determined to rub it in. The first time the Lieutenant Major paused for breath, the girl had cut off any retort from JJ's with a sweeping gesture, almost the pose of a model, tossing her head and extending one arm. She pointed across the piazza to the boarded-up entrance of *Napoli Sotterraneo*. When she spoke, she addressed the youngest on the scene, the twins, all the while acting as if Kahlberg weren't standing within reach of her frail throat. *Oh, there's a place you girls really want to see.* Romy dropped her warrior look, too; she put on a wide smile. *Napoli Sotterraneo, totally neat stuff, not another dumb old church. Like, all these caves and secret passageways . . .*

The gypsy might've fallen in love, the kind of love an adult had to stand back and envy, a thing of the spirit and yet powerful enough to raise blisters. But she hadn't forgotten how to tease.

Like, who needs all this dumb old paperwork.

"This morning," Barbara told Cesare, "that girl, whatever else she was up to, she had her fun. She made a game of it, Freak Out the White Man."

"And you admire her."

She laughed, briefly. If she couldn't have a tantrum, if she couldn't do whatever it was Romy had done—whatever—she might as well laugh. When she let her head drop back against the pew, the small thump felt good, actually. A reality check. "Cesare, that girl, this morning, you'd have admired her too. Don't you see how it helps to talk about it? Don't you see how much you help? I'm saying, she got to that man so bad, he stormed off."

"Stormed off? The officer left you?"

"Well, first, he gave me an earful." *The little whore has got to go.* "An ultimatum, is that what you'd call it? Kahlberg told me, if Romy was part of the deal," *if you insist on treating this trash like a member of the family,* "then he wasn't going to arrange any more excursions. The Lulucitas, he said, we'd have to do without, what was it? 'The benefits that the Organization offers.'"

"The . . . benefits? The obscene cornucopia of Empire, he intends to cut you off?"

"That was today, Cesare. He said it was the Organization or the girl."

"Oh, the fellow's a Master of the Universe." The lines on the priest's face deepened. "The rest of us, all the children of God, we're cast out of the garden."

"But you hear what I'm saying? We stayed there, the rest of us, in San Lorenzo."

"Yes, and good for you, Mrs. Lulucita. Furthermore, let me assure you, I appreciate that you came here and told me. I understand your irritation with this, this Lieutenant Major."

"Well, we stayed, we had Chris. We had the girl too, she knows a lot . . ."

Barbara let the story drop, losing herself at the wooden ceiling, a classic ceiling for any church without a dome. Slat-thin panels, railroad-tie rafters. In her mind's eye lingered other sets of lines, the stone fittings where the roof of one ancient sanctuary, beneath San Lorenzo, met the floor of the next generation above it. Then there were the seams across Cesare's face. The man's voice sounded seamy too. He was repeating himself, prompting the mother: "The girl, you admire her."

There was some echo she hadn't noticed before. She thought of the strays Cesare had taken in, the two *clandestini* camped out in his church cellar, a simple hollow compared to what she'd seen downtown. Then with her next blink all today's lines came together, they knotted so that their ends stretched off to the echoing cool corners of the stone. And Barb had an idea. The notion triggered a flashing along her spine, a trembling, yet at the same time it cleared away the fog or whatever it was that had clogged her spirit since Paul's second miracle. Yes, and she'd needed a church in order to get to this point, never mind whether it had a dome or not. Yes—she knew what she had to do in order to prove that Silky and Jay had a deal.

"You wish you could be like that girl." The priest knew her better than anyone in Naples but he hadn't noticed the change. "Young again and stronger than you ever dreamed."

The gypsy had shown her the way, no point denying it. Even Barbara's disrespectful posture, slumped in the pew with her dress above her knees, seemed like something Romy had taught her. The girl couldn't so much as shift her weight without exposing some hot flesh.

"Like Samson among the Philistines, don't you know."

The mother had a different image for what the girl had taught her. She pictured a kiss full of disease, a nasty surprise for an unfaithful lover. Surprise, that was the key.

"Mrs. Lulucita, are you there? First you wake me up and then you take a *riposo*?"

Barb shook her head, rolled her shoulders, pulled an apologetic smile. But she sat up knowing what she was doing next, holding down the hem of her dress. Also she got her bearings from the old man's strong eyebrows and nose. His looks remained potent, a good front for a protest poster or a call to the people. Now Barbara had joined him in the revolution. Telling Jay that they were through, that had been just for starters. Today the gypsy had carried her to the next level, where every action would cast enormous shadows against antique pale stone. And the kids would be safe, sure. The place was wall-to-wall security, the kids would be fine, and the fact that the mother needed them along actually bore out the seriousness of what she was up to. The children proved again and better that she was no mad housewife.

"Is that it, then, signora? Is your soul at rest concerning today, the choice you made?"

"Well." She gave another breathless laugh. "Well, my soul!"

Chapter Six

This morning, the Lieutenant Major wouldn't be joining them. His absence made it happen, Barbara's plan, her revolution. After all, yesterday she'd heard the man loud and clear: him or Romy. Today then the officer would follow through. But on the other hand he'd set up the day's itinerary a week ago now; everyone in the family had gotten the printout. The liaison man couldn't go breaking those arrangements out of the clear blue, not while he still had others to answer to. But he could refuse to go along, depriving the Lulucitas of his "benefits." So Barb had her opportunity, her surprise.

Silky Kahlberg would learn what she'd done via the city's murmurous website—the *ojetti* on the chapel walls, the bulging hammered metal, could all be receiver units. And when the officer did get the news, it would shake him up worse than Romy had on the steps of San Lorenzo. The mother would loom like a whole new ferocity, out of nowhere. Barbarian.

Though she wasn't about to dip her hair in blood, nothing like that. The kids would be safe. Under Cesare's church ceiling, her inspiration had amounted to nothing more than the right place at the right time. If it worked, she would rip off all the Lieutenant Major's masks at once, and Jay's too. And if it didn't? Naturally the mother had her doubts, those moments when her breasts felt as heavy and as roughly packaged as groceries for two teenage boys and three other kids besides. After she'd left the Vomero church, after one of the NATO farm-boys had as always walked her down to her home palazzo and checked out the lobby and elevator, Barbara was grateful for the few moments alone in the creaking lift. She spent the time studying herself in the mirrored door. Had the woman in the reflection in fact developed new muscles of the spirit? Strength enough to trip up the overgrown tennis brat who'd been swatting her family all over town?

Or was this afternoon only another pivot of the inner whipsaw? Barbara might've been fooled by how tough her skin had grown, leathery, after twenty days in the *Mezzogiorno*. The country of permanent noon. Local women resorted to cosmetics she'd never heard of, and there were mineral baths out on the islands.

The lift stopped and her reflection split apart. In another ten minutes Barbara was planting her idea in her children's heads.

Not that she had to force anything. She wasn't the first to bring up the hunger strikers, not by a long chalk. While Barbara took the chair by the door and swapped her street shoes for house slippers, Chris sat just beyond the entry's archway, before an IBM clone out of some valley up by the Alps—a machine provided free of charge, along with a fat and speedy internet connection. The boy had pulled up a page about the castles of Naples, and he went straight into an announcement about dell'Ovo. He knew his brothers and sisters would want to hear it. Loudly Chris explained that what was going on down by the waterfront was history in action; it was the first time in hundreds of years they'd kept prisoners in the old safe-house.

Barbara had already heard as much from her priest. Most convicts did their time in another penitentiary, inland, a complex a mere couple of centuries old. But these strikers had set themselves apart, defining themselves as a group, The Shell of the Hermit Crab. They proudly claimed a Catholic heritage, the same liberation theology as Cesare, and their published statements set forth twin goals: "*Unum*, a fixed European identity; *Duo*, the opportunity for individual potential." The particulars of that agenda remained murky, as near as Barbara could tell, as did its connection to hermit crabs. Also the size of the Shell's membership hadn't been perfectly ascertained, as yet. But the core group remained small, clearly, and likewise anyone could understand that what they sought was better legal standing in Italy—and that they made the authorities nervous. They'd come under police scrutiny, this little crew, before they'd begun to refuse food. Unlike the vast majority of illegal aliens in-country, members in the Shell didn't just take their under-the-table payout and keep quiet about it. Rather they shared Cesare's fervor to speak out, to make others notice, bred in the neglected missions of upriver Africa or the isolated parishes of the Balkan hills.

In one demonstration, inside the Archeological Museum, the Shells had posed themselves beside the plaster-cast corpses of Pompeii. The next month they'd chained themselves to the statues of the kings of Naples, in the alcoves that lined the Royal Palace. That case, following their arrest, had been the first when the Shell were kept separate from other prisoners. The police pretext for this was the same as used in Guantanamo and other such places: suspicion of terrorism. And after the group—just five scrawny young men, it appeared—had been let go, in another week they lined up in the largest piazza in town. They pulled from under their battered denim jackets a full-size cardboard cutout of the Sword of Islam. These weapons were decorated oddly, in purple, with patterns of lines that didn't make sense, but the Shell five-some had waved their swords overhead, showing their teeth and crying *Allah akbar.* Then once they'd drawn a crowd, including puzzled police and a few cameras, with a practiced and video-ready movement each man had folded his sword origami-style so that it formed, instead, the harmless purple rectangle that was the Italian passport.

If you asked Barb, that last public action sounded like a good one, an easy one to understand. But once more the cops had pulled out the handcuffs. As the Shell Five were hauled away, the noisiest of the bunch, a sub-Saharan runaway who might've been the leader, had explained at the top of his lungs: *But that's your choice, the sword or the paperwork! That's your only choice!* Fresh charges against the group had taken a couple of days to draw up, and according to Barbara's chosen priest, they "weren't worth the letterhead they'd been printed on." Nonetheless the Shell of the Hermit Crab still had neither proper representation nor a trial date set, their case had gotten hung up in Parliament, when they starting doing without food.

A holding cell hadn't been easy to come by, in a close-packed metropolis riddled, *soterraneo,* by tunnels. Then too, the recent quake had registered near seven on the Richter. So the most intact and manageable penal alternative in town turned out to be the oldest, Castel dell'Ovo, a hulking keep from the era of Robin Hood. This stood on a promontory in the Bay—the peninsular spot of tongue at the center of the map's sickbed kiss. The narrow quay between fortress and mainland made policing easy.

Also anyone visiting would be perfectly safe. All in all Barbara had an easy time planting the idea. She needed no manipulations, only a word or two while watching the news with Chris and JJ, waiting for Jay's little armada to rumble back home. A couple of hours later she mentioned something as she folded back the pima coverlets on the girls' beds. Then again at breakfast, after Papa went to work, she spoke of the starving *clandestini* while she opened the doors to the dining-room balcony. When she turned to face the children, she found them all looking up, thoughtful, not even wrinkling their noses at the morning scent of sulfur.

Paul too. The boy had been gooping up his grapefruit juice with DiPio's prescribed daily protein packet, but now he stared somewhere over her shoulder, his long-lashed eyes narrowing. Barb turned away quickly. Laundry.

Then the Hummer in the piazza, Kahlberg-free. The driver made the explanations, unnecessary explanations, as everyone slid into the air conditioning. The *tenente* had many important duties; the *tenente* wouldn't be coming.

But the Lulucitas could see what was on the itinerary: a trip down the coast to the town where Barbara's mother had been born. "Torre del Greco," the driver announced. "Where they make the cameos."

The man's smile was pretty puny. He didn't use the vehicle sound-system, instead turning to face the family without undoing his seatbelt. Barb shot a look at JJ; he was the one to get things started.

"Hey," the boy said. "Who needs the ten-*nenn*-tay? Only reason I'll go where he has in mind is, I know my girl'll find us."

The mother didn't much care for that *My girl*, but never mind.

JJ went on, "Hey, we could go wherever we wanted, and she'll find us."

The driver was too much of a flunky to drop his smile, but he turned away and geared up. Barbara reminded herself: right time, right place. "Dora, Syl," she began, "I just can't stop thinking about those men on their hunger strike. Down in the castle."

"Yeah," Dora said. "That's sad."

"Sad," said Syl. "Some people have been badly abused."

"I can't stop wishing we could do more for them," Barb said. "You know, something like what Papa did."

"That's what I've been wishing too, Mama."

"Last night we lay in bed wishing," Sylvia said. "It's like Jesus."

Barbara wasn't sure what that meant, but she knew what would happen once Dora and Sylvia came up with questions. Already her second oldest was taking on his lecturer's look, avid, almost charismatic. Chris's eyes were his best feature, no bookworm's goggle. In another minute you would've thought he'd taken over the Humvee's address system.

"Guys, can you imagine the scene down there? Incredible, I mean like, *totally*."

His body English set the vinyl squeaking beneath him. "I mean, on the one hand it's up to the minute. It's satellite feeds and state-of-the-art machine guns."

"Okay, bro." JJ didn't sound like he was making a crack. "Rock'n'roll."

"Yeah but, on the other hand, all this is happening in a castle that's a thousand years old. Like, from the Crusades."

"Rock'n'*roll*," the older brother repeated. "Next stop, dell'Ovo."

Barb was getting so good at insinuation, she was practically Neapolitan. "Now wait a minute, you two. I realize we've been talking about this, but, wait a minute." Careful of her tone. "But I've got to say, down there, with men in their condition, it won't be pretty. Are you sure you want to . . ."

The kids came back like something out of a Jell-O commercial. Yeah please, come on please. Yeah!

"Mom," Chris said, "where else could we do good like we'd do there? Have you thought about that? Torre del Greco, that would be like, merely personal."

"Where your Mom grew up," JJ said, "that's totally personal. Hey, none of us ever knew her."

Careful of her frown, her posture.

"Plus, I mean. Where does it say we have to obey the *tenente*?"

"Ten and—" said Syl—"ten antennas? What?"

"It's not ten antennas," Dora whispered loudly. "The most anybody ever had was one antenna. Or maybe two."

"Plus," Chris said, "back in Bridgeport, like, you took us to the nursing home."

JJ was wagging a couple of fingers at the NATO tag-alongs, two in the seats farthest back and one riding shotgun. "I'd say we're safer here than in Bridgeport."

"I hear you," Barbara said. "But what about Paul?" If this was a commercial, the stage blocking called for her to face the boy. "Mr. Paul, honey, how do you feel?"

He shrugged, the Italian child. "I'm, I'm tired of doing what K-Kahlberg says."

Barb went on: "You know there'll be sick people there? Like in the hospitals?"

When the boy waved a hand, the gesture looked decidedly more effeminate than JJ's. Mr. Paul remained unfazed: hospitals, whatever. Barb realized, too, that one reason her middle child could take the possibility in stride was that, in so far as she could, she'd kept him out of the sick wards and the trauma centers. Taking the children to visit St. Anthony's Rest back in Bridgeport had been one thing, a learning experience and a Christian duty. They'd brought flowers, and once Paul and the girls had performed a St. Patrick's Day number. But here, both she and Jay had figured Paul didn't need any additional exposure to the halt and the sick. They'd got that much right. For instance on the afternoon following the second episode, Romy's episode, Dr. DiPio had steered the slender eleven-year-old into a room with a couple of bad cases from the quake. The old *medico* had laid the boy's hand on one of the patient's heads, so swaddled in gauze you couldn't tell whether this was a man or a woman. But that was as far as the little experiment went. In the next moment Barb and Jay had spotted DiPio and the boy, and they'd come barreling into the room, barking at the man (yes, the Jaybird had been barking too; give him credit).

The evening after that, the evening of the Capua trip, the doctor had made a formal proposal. He'd showed up at the Lulucitas' palazzo—only a few blocks from his own, it turned out—and asked if he could take Paul to a nearby center for physical therapy. This time the father had almost knocked his handsome head against DiPio's, he had to say no so often and so emphatically. The old doctor was in the grip of a vision; he saw the lame throwing off their crutches all over Naples.

Barbara, for her part, had done some research into faith healing. An easy business so long as she was on the web anyway, a matter of half an hour's extra trolling. But what she read in those sites and downloads seemed like another sequence of mental slipknots. Nobody had reliable conclusions. Also the mother took one or two of her visits with Cesare as an opportunity to discuss Paul's case. She was working up to complete honesty about the boy, she thought she would tell the priest everything, but on the day she'd come closest there were others in the sanctuary. The old Jesuit hadn't paid her much attention, confining his responses to monosyllables, and Barbara understood that these visitors might be the *clandestini*. There were two of them, actually prostrated before the altar, their faces on a bandanna spread across the floor. The dark couldn't hide the shabbiness of their sandals.

Anyway, this morning Paul no longer looked like a kid who required extra research or outside counseling. "I'm with, with them." To see him nod towards his brothers, you would've thought he was a normal bubbly inarticulate American preteen. "Like, wh-who needs all this dumb, dumb old p-paperwork?"

Chris again: "Guys, it's like, unreal, down there. Everything's way up to date and way old at the same time."

John Junior undid his seatbelt and leaned close to the driver. When he spoke, he was the man of the house. "Castel dell Huevos."

"Guys, it's like, the only thing of its kind on the planet."

"Like Jesus," said Dora.

"Like Jesus," said Sylvia. "This whole family is very good."

The first to acquiesce was the soldier nearest Barb. He gave a slow nod, a stolid bit of body-talk typical of the Organization's Dutchboys. Barbara could read his Teutonic mind, though. He had to be giving himself the same reassurances as she did: the castle was crawling with cops. Dell'Ovo, more than likely, offered tighter security than the hometown of Barbara's runaway mom.

And this soldier appeared to hold rank. Following his wordless okay, the other two nodded as well, nodded and shrugged. Then there was the driver. This man waved John Junior off his shoulder and, at the next clutch of traffic, he found Barbara in his rear-view mirror.

"We change, signora . . . we don't the *itinerario*?"

Barbara gave him a frown: What part of this don't you understand?

"The *tenente*, Kahlberg . . . he doesn't know."

"Castel dell'Ovo," she snapped.

"I am never without orders from the—"

"The hunger strike. Right this minute."

The driver went so far as to pick up his cell phone. But the Lieutenant Major couldn't be reached just now—wasn't that the point of today's arrangements? Meantime the wild young Americans had broken into a war chant: *Dell-oh-voh! Dell-oh-voh!* The man at the wheel slapped down the phone, perhaps he left a page, and then he wrenched the van into a U-turn. The chant was joined by the squawks of car-horns.

Barb didn't waste her energy on celebration. Her opening had proved a winner, yes, but now she'd better brace herself. She might accomplish nothing more than jerking the liaison man around a bit. She might leave him a little sore, *e basta*. Yet wouldn't that alone be worth it? To make this unsought Wizard rush out from behind the curtain, like the lying slob he was, wouldn't that be worth the effort? As for the gashes of guilt, Barbara would've had to endure those anyway. Anyway, bottom line, she couldn't help but believe that with today's surprise, she'd do better. She'd startle the PR man into showing her the smoking gun, and establish once and for all that the marriage was dead. The mother studied herself in the tinted window, putting on her game face. Beyond her reflection she enjoyed the 180-degree whirl of one cliff-side switchback after another. The driver didn't need the beltway to get down to the Bay, and here and there Barbara caught glimpses of the age-old market theater, the hawkers in the museum.

The drive bottomed out onto the harbor straightaway, along breakwaters of heaped stone. Moored to iron hoops sat fat low boats, wooden boats mostly, brightly trimmed. Motionless, they made you think the weather was off the Sahara. But once everyone piled out, the two girls started cooing at the breeze. Dora and Sylvia liked the whole scene: the waddly fisher-craft, the strings of plastic pennants above them, the flags' goo-goo colors in constant flutter. The eight-year-olds were too quick for Barbara, rushing out onto one of the plank walkways over the breakwaters. The girls hopscotched along the bouncy flats, giggling and delighted till they were quieted by their first good look at the castle.

Dell'Ovo rose like some outgrowth of the stones beneath the twins' feet. It seemed like base material, a heap of pockmarked sand, and at first you didn't notice the windows and doorways. There were only the elephantine walls, rough-cut manmade cliffs, ugly dirt-yellow, the whole effect so spongy you got the impression it could swallow incoming cannonballs. The stronghold looked nothing like an egg. The name had to do with something else, a story Chris started to tell as the group approached the quay's security gate. The boy launched into "the earliest story, anyway," one with Virgil in it. Here the Roman poet, under a full moon, had seen a mystic vision: an immense egg rising from the sea, and in it a new epic, a new life.

"Though the egg just turned out to be a big rock," Chris said. "Maybe this rock. The kind of rock where you could put up buildings and people could live."

Dora pouted. "Buildings and people? What's so magic about that?"

"Dora, the guy was a poet."

John Junior let his brother talk. Barbara knew there was more to the castle's name, a story about an egg hidden inside somewhere; so long as the egg remained un-cracked, Naples would never fall to pieces. But she didn't interrupt her second-oldest, and the rangy oldest couldn't be bothered either, turning this way and that to search the marina. By the time the family and their gunmen reached the castle quay, JJ lagged several steps behind. When he craned his neck, Barbara could see where his beard had begun to come in. And even with her subterfuge underway, moving along nicely, she felt sorry for the boy. Mama understands, *Primo*. Mama made this happen, a trip where your girl couldn't find us.

Barbara had worried about the gypsy's interference, in fact. She'd worried even more about how far she'd get without the liaison and his papers. Yet the castle's first checkpoint turned out to pose no problem. The police in the booth seemed, if anything, as if they'd been expecting the family: first the father had come, and now the rest. The troopers, as for them, were colleagues in the law-and-order business, never mind that they wore helmets rather than caps. Once the gatekeepers on the mainland end of the castle pier got busy on their walkie-talkies, it was less than ten minutes before they were passing the clipboard for sign-ins. Just the kind of improvisation Barb had hoped would come into play: more *arrangiarsi*. She did have to deal with one delay, brief but troubling, though it had nothing to do with getting security clearance. She had to wait while a policeman asked for Paul's blessing. One of the cops never got off the phone, but the other went down on one knee, stripping off his semi-automatic and pulling out, from between the buttons of his uniform, one of those Franciscan T's.

With that the check-in felt dangerous. The family was exposed; the cops were neglecting their weapons. Barb saw terrorists roaring out of the closest alleyway, the Sword of Islam in the hands of *scippatori*. She had to be out of her mind to pull a stunt like this, counter-espionage.

Yet once again Paul handled it without a ruffle. The boy broke into a smile at the familiar slant T, the wood pale with use. Paul pushed back the crisp cuffs of his white shirt and gave the icon a spirited two-handed clasp. He and the cop could've been two Little Leaguers doing a pre-game touch-and-go. And around the middle child, the others appeared likewise pumped up. John Junior, after he stopped expecting the impossible of Romy, pressed quickly to the front of the group. The way he was bouncing in his cross-trainers, how could his Mama be out of her mind? What was it with her zigs and zags, now dread, now confidence? The castle was locked down tight and the kids were having a ball. Dora and Syl, next on the sign-in sheet, were trying their hand at cursive.

"Everybody's having a ball," Barbara said.

The girls needed some time, over the clipboard, and as they worked a TV broadcast unit pulled to a screeching halt on the marina boulevard. One of the news programs must've had a stringer posted by the castle. The first out of the vehicle was a woman, limber and young with a lot of hair—who else but Maddalena? She hoisted a camera to one shoulder, in fingerless gloves. Barbara didn't need to think about it. As Maddalena approached the checkpoint, the mother huddled with the Franciscan cop, making sure the camerawoman too would be allowed inside. When the twins started prodding Mama with the clipboard, she made sure to sign on-camera.

"Also NATO needs to know," Barbara told the cops loudly, while passing the board to the reporter. "You be sure to call NATO."

"*Si, certo.*" The policeman was trying for eye contact with Maddalena. "Don't worry, *signora*. There is nothing inside that can harm you."

Easy for him to say, out here in the sun. Once the family was past the security gate, dell'Ovo appeared gloomier than ever. For the last two or three hundred years the castle had been a husk, little more than a postcard backdrop, but still it cast an oppressive shadow. The walk into the fortress gate took Barb and the others between dingy guardhouse rooks that bristled up top with guns. Their footsteps echoed beneath the twitter of radiophones. Farther on, even with a policeman leading the way, the castle passages kept forcing John Junior to duck and Maddelena to protect her camera. Also the place gave off a stink, now sulfur, now sea-sewage, now the sweat of unhealthy bodies. The holding cell for the strikers was up on the second floor, or maybe the third.

Or maybe—where? The mother should've gotten used to this by now, the sensation that she was starting over, taking her first steps into the city. Was dell'Ovo the third recurrence of the nightmare? The fifth? Barbara hardly seemed able to count, as she stood before the ward's metal detector. She tumbled back into muzzy jetlag and all she could be sure of was that she'd found the source of the castle's stink, the gates of a plague-ridden city.

In time it occurred to her that the smell might've triggered her flashback. That first day, there'd been Jay's spatter and drool, his exposed brain. She blinked, she spoke up. "Maybe the girls, my little girls . . . they should wait outside?"

Her answer came from within the ward, people she couldn't see, with accents she couldn't place. Men, men's voices. They were saying something about therapy.

"Please," she said. "One thing at a time."

Therapy, they replied. *Grief management*: the men beyond the metal detectors had the same vocabulary as Barbara had picked up at the Sam Center. She caught the phrase "International Red Cross," then "interaction with children." Maybe she recalled hearing that nothing helped to keep up a person's spirits so much as playing with children, or maybe she heard it now, from the Shell of the Hermit Crab. Dogs were also good, and items from home, the kind of souvenirs these guys had received from her husband. Barbara didn't so much nod as try to shake off the déjà vu, the wrinkles in her thinking, and she couldn't fail to notice the mini-cam at her shoulder. The oblong silver box whirred in her ear.

Maddalena remained quick on the uptake as ever, and the hunger strikers were eager for attention. What better press than pictures with children? Now too Barbara felt additional pressure, a jostling from behind the camerawoman. Felt like John Junior, poking her shoulder blade.

"Hey," he said. "Chris and me, we got the girls."

Barb gathered herself and moved in, noticing first the rigging underfoot, the floor pads and extension cords. As for the layout of the kitchen-sink hospice, that eluded her a while. The gray prison blankets turned the beds to *ojetti votivi*, though in their case the point of the praying was hard to decipher. The IV units seemed more of the same, dangling shapes that might be hearts, might be mittens, might be masks. Also the mother's revived bewilderment called up images of the Underworld, a catacomb beneath the Roman Naples. One of the strikers had his bed set high, like a head of household front and center in the family crypt.

Later Barbara wondered about how quickly she'd headed for that raised bed. She wondered how her urgency had affected the children. Paul and the others had hesitated, once they got inside the metal detector. She could understand that she'd wanted to get away from the cops and the camera. As for the doctors, she hardly saw them; she'd come to the castle to make things happen. Still she wondered at how quick she was to lay hands on an unconscious African who looked half mummified.

The man must've started starving before the others. The apocalyptic reek came worst from him, and Barb recalled something out of her schoolgirl reading about missionary work, something about how the glands broke down as the body lost fuel. She could feel the patient's breaking down when she took his hand. The palm was moist but cool, and up at the elbows the skin bunched like the sleeves of a long john. His hospital shirt couldn't hide the fence-lines of ribs and shoulder, and the bones of the face were prominent as well. He might've been handsome a week ago. Now his features had darkened like a gum-caked penny and, even as he took this morning *riposo*, his scooped cheeks stretched his lips to the point of exposing his teeth. And there was another pressure on his face too, a stranger business. Fist-sized packs of cotton had been taped against the corners of the striker's eyes.

Barbara bent nurse-like. She cradled the hand, a lone sandal found rotting by some Congo roadside, and touched his eye-sockets' padding.

"Mom, careful." Chris stood at the foot of the bed. "That stuff, he needs that."

Barbara put a finger on the dreaming face.

"You remember," Chris said. "That cotton, that's so he can see."

Himself more than arm's length from her, Chris was the only child to have ventured in. Beside him stood Maddalena, with her camera at her eye.

"Mom, don't you remember? They explained it on the news."

What Barb remembered came, again, out of her schoolgirl preparations for becoming a saint. The African's cottony blinders were to help with double vision, one of the symptoms of starvation. But was this any way for a woman to visit such a needy place? Knowing next to nothing? Could that have been why she'd lunged so eagerly to this poor man's side, that same half-baked Samaritan impulse?

Now a doctor approached, his white wrap suggesting a toga. He too had something to say about striker's head. *Signora, gli prego. . . .* The formal third-person pronoun straightened Barbara up.

Five patients, men, occupied beds set in two rows. Also she spied a kind of fortified stretcher, with padding and straps, standing against the wide room's second door. Not that this exit needed additional protection. The door was bolted and padlocked, and an armed guard sat beside it in a mammoth chair. A cop on a throne, he made three altogether in the ward. The other two were at the detector. Thanks to them, the NATO Vikings had seen no point crowding into the ward. They remained out beyond the archway, slouched against the cool tufa of the corridor, their helmets off and their semis at their feet. Closer to the mother roved a pair of medical staff, checking either the IV's or a flat-screen monitor hooked to one wall. Barbara felt chagrined to see all the technology, nothing like a chapel full of *ojetti* and even less like a catacomb. But on the other hand there were the figures in the beds, flesh and blood and nearly naked. Smaller guys, like a lot undocumented immigrants, they could've worked as galley slaves or salt miners. Everyone had some icon around his neck, finger-polished and wafer-thin. Then too, while none of the other strikers were so far gone as Barbara's, they all had that twitchy underfed quality she'd seen in a number of *clandestini*. Certainly it was neediness that linked these members of the Shell, not race. Only Barbara's man and one other came from south of the Sahara, and one was something like Macedonian or Kosovar; he passed for white.

As she watched, the protesters kept breaking into smiles. Spooky smiles, really: their cheeks were already going slack. They grinned for Maddalena's camera, of course, and out of the giddiness of malnutrition. Then too, they must've been enjoying the pick-me-up that their Red Cross inspectors had mentioned, the pleasure of the family's company. That much the mother could understand, but there remained bewildering business everywhere, such as this IV at her elbow. What good would it do to give this man fluids? Also she couldn't tell what sort of scars those were across the sleeper's cheek. Could've been a ritual marking, the crescent moons of initiation.

If she could be sure of anything here, it was the effect on her children. They'd fallen in behind Chris, breathless and slack-faced between the rows of beds. John Junior had buttonholed one of the doctors, but Barb couldn't hear him. His voice was as small as the creak of the cops' leather.

Dora was the first to move closer. "Mama? Is he dead?"

Barb lost the girl in the mini-cam's spotlight.

"That, that guy. Is he dead?"

"Honey," the mother managed, "you all told me, dell'Ovo, you told the driver too. This place, it's like—don't you remember St. Anthony's Rest? I warned you, don't you remember? It's like at St. Anthony's."

"Like at St. Anthony's." Sylvia tiptoed up behind her sister. "Some people are very sick."

"You all said, all of you." She focused on a point between the two girls. "You knew what was going on in here, but you all kept saying you wanted to."

The girls didn't quite nod.

"I can't tell you everything," Barb said, "about what's going on."

Chris joined his sisters, sidling past the camerawoman. "But like, come on, you know what's going on here." The boy had taken on a different voice, non-professorial. "Dora, Sylvia, you remember, like, the bad Italian laws? How hard it can be when people come to a new country?"

Barbara let the fifteen-year-old explain, figuring the one she had to worry about was Paul. The younger boy stood between two hospital beds, and after Barbara's first look, for a shivery moment she thought she should turn everyone around and march them out. It was one thing to have the children visit the sick and aged. Barbara had been raised that way, talking about her schoolwork with a bedridden aunt, or taking the chair beside her father's mother at the Sunday table, though the old woman couldn't do more than blink and mutter over her plate. But the way Paul was looking just now, here on the second story of Castel dell'Ovo, that shook her. He'd lost his American-Kidness, his elbows tucked, his torso clenched. His clothing turned him into an undertaker. Like that, the mother started thinking of alternatives, get 'em out, Torre del Greco. Except—she'd seen the boy that way so often, these days. Lately he'd shown his mother a look like that, what? Twenty times? Twenty-five? Her Mr. Paul had tensed up and zoned out even while he lay listening to fairytales. And what was Barbara doing here if she was going to get all timid and cross-wired again? Why had she gone visiting Cesare everyday and having revelations under his ceiling if it wasn't to wangle precisely this detour and assert her new power?

With her free hand, she dug in her purse and fingered up her rosary. She kissed the big central bead and then bent once more over the raised bed beside her, the slow suicide. No sooner had she started, of course, than Maddalena closed in.

"Oh, you are so good," said the younger woman, behind her camera. "*La Mama Americana*, so very good."

Was she talking morals or mediagenics? Barbara huddled close enough to gag briefly on the smell, the dysfunctional sweat. She could see, too, that the man's cotton headgear had gone snot-yellow where it touched his cheekbone. The doctors needed to change the dressing. Meanwhile Maddalena's spotlight stayed with her; the newswoman found the best angle, on the opposite side of the bed. How was Barbara supposed to pray under these conditions? How could a rosary make things better, anyway? Again the dell'Ovo venture felt nutty or worse, even as she noticed the awe in her two youngest, visible out of the corner her eye. If Chris weren't with them, Barb realized, Dora and Syl would be hanging on to Mama's dress. They'd probably start praying along. Back in Bridgeport, they'd helped a couple of old-timers sing a round of *Dona Nobis Pacem*. And the twins weren't the only ones moved, just now, by Barbara's hesitant Hail Mary. Also the African's papery lips began twitching. The mother realized this might be delirium, but she tried to make a connection, to restore the strength in her spirit muscle, bending even closer. Yet this only left her aware of her cleavage. Maddalena had the front of Barbara's summer dress squarely in the middle of her frame. All around her, *La Mama Americana* confronted a perverse mirror image. She was the one who needed to pack her eyes in cotton.

She kept at it, be-with-us-now-and—and close enough to give the leper a kiss.

So another brand of hypocrisy began to gnaw at her: the way the African was dying. He'd been at his physical peak, a warrior, and his collapse had nothing to do with a gunshot or a virus, nor even the earthquake. Rather the owner of this human engine, fully operational as recently as when the Lulucitas had landed in Naples, had willed its breakdown. And wasn't that how a person became a saint? They renounced the world and denied their own flesh? Barbara was holding the sweaty hand of a saint. Every time he gave a labored exhale, she shared his breath.

She'd blundered in here fuming over her family's comforts, but these young radicals in the old castle, they were the ones who truly rejected the comforts. They embraced the end of everything.

"Some people set an example," Dora said. "We should pay attention."

"There are lots of people," Sylvia said, "who don't have our advantages."

Chris, beside the girls, made some hushed reply. But what could the mother tell them, with this mocking skull-face beneath her? The African was himself what her prayer should be, and what's more, the opposite of whatever Jay and Kahlberg were up to. Whatever those two had going, it was about good meals and the sweet life.

What could Barbara tell anyone? She straightened up, coiling her rosary.

She would've abandoned the young man faster—she needed time to herself, out of the ward—except as the mother lay the African's hand back on his institutional blanket, he gripped her. The dreamer took hold with surprising force, the tendons popping along his shrunken wrist, the muddy sweat grinding into her palms. He never seemed to wake, exactly, but all at once he had her hand cinched tight.

What? How. . . ? Barb was left with pinched knuckles, backing away. She stumbled past her children, towards the metal detectors.

Maddalena was the first to speak. "Signora Lulucita?"

Flexing her fingers, Barb hoped there wasn't some sort of exit procedure.

"How are you, signora? You can talk to me. How do you feeling?"

And what was she going to do about the girls? Dora and Syl would want to come with. "I don't know," Barbara said, "I don't know what to do about the girls." She faced the camera, blinding herself again in the spotlight.

"Can you, Maddalena—would you watch them? My girls, that equipment of yours, who don't you show them what you do with that, just for a minute or two?"

Barb didn't look for the others. "Just, all of you—Paul, everyone. Please, could you give me a couple of minutes? I'm just saying, Mama needs a little time."

The girls may have had questions: Mom? She couldn't be sure, the way this sob gathered in her throat and clogged up her ears. Some third party may have put in a word, one of the patients maybe, encouraging the kids to stay. If Barbara heard the voice, it sounded the way her man's last grip had felt.

John Junior was next. "Dora, Syl, hey. You know Mama. She's got to find the Duomo and she's got to have her Mama-time."

JJ, lighthearted and able to deal. No wonder Romy had fallen for him. Still Barbara saw only glare-shadows, the same brown as the stains on the starving man's cotton. She didn't stop moving till the detectors' tin skeleton loomed from the blur.

A chill, a hesitation. "I'll be back soon," she croaked. "You know Mama."

Then she was into the hallway. She kept moving until all she could hear was the echo of her own gagging and spluttering, her moans and whimpers. The grief mounted from the gut and insofar as Barbara chose a direction, it was uphill, the opposite of the way they'd come. She needed unknown passageways and a place to cry. When at last she broke stride, she all but collapsed onto her knees. She slumped into a wall scrubbing her tears into her face, massaging her sockets and brows the way Jay did. God knows how long it took before the air tasted less of suicide and failure.

Eventually all she smelled was the tufa stone, and her head felt likewise porous. The building material, a thousand years old, in fact gave her a kind of comfort. It reminded her that she wasn't the first woman to start with decent impulses and wind up in a mess. What she'd done by coming to the castle, lying the way she had, acting so selfish, was like having an affair. And back at the Sam Center she'd heard about more than a few affairs, always full of bruises.

Her eyes drying, clearing, Barb spotted an occasional cop on patrol. They weren't letting l'Americana run around unwatched. A couple of times she caught the shout of an excited eight-year-old ("Wow, try wide angle!"), not far off. She reached overhead, giving a lengthy, sighing stretch, then got her clothes adjusted and poked along the corridors, trying to think again through the morning's plan. A couple of times she came up against a barred hallway or padlocked door. These gave her a pick-me-up, a touch of ordinary iron, suggesting she might not be a saint but possessed some reliable backbone herself. She still had strength enough to confront the tenente, Barbara. The scene in the ward—Mary, Mother of God—that would've upset anyone. But Kahlberg was bound to bust in any moment now, and she'd still gotten him at a disadvantage.

When she heard Jay, she couldn't miss it.

From the first chewy syllable, more Queens than Brooklyn, she couldn't miss it. She'd need to be a lot more lost than this not to recognize that voice. Barbara pulled up short on the poorly-matched flagstones, outside the room in which his complaining squawked and seesawed. She knew he was complaining too, she couldn't mistake that either, after so many evenings spent nodding along with as much sympathy as she could muster. Her husband was talking in a small space, a room without an echo. He'd actually left the door ajar, behind him. From what Barb could see, peeking crook-necked, the Jaybird and whoever he was talking to had squeezed into a cubicle, a nook for a Norman archer. She saw too that she hadn't escaped the castle's surveillance grid: a video camera hung in a hallway corner.

"I *know* it's partly my fault," Jay said, more loudly. "I know. Hey, why else would I ask for confession?"

There was a reply, quiet, the accent very different.

"Well, I have sinned," Barbara's husband went on. "I've lied, number one."

The confessor's response again eluded her, sounding almost like a musical phrase. But her nerves enjoyed a dual awakening, from exercise and from amazement. In another moment she'd understood who the priest was too.

"I've lied," Jay repeated, "but not that way. There's been no adultery, father."

"Cesare, please."

Cesare, who else? Judging from what he'd told Barb, the priest would've preferred having his ministry down here, within wafer's reach of the strikers.

"A couple of times," Jay went on, "I've talked to women more than I should've. One woman anyway. But, hey. Barb knows all about it."

Fresh heat rose in her face. For a moment she might've had Maddalena's spotlight back in her eyes.

"She knows, it's in the past. Happened when she was pregnant with the twins."

The priest put in a word, again inaudible.

"Yeah, three kids and I wasn't much past thirty. But that, hey, that was the idea. That sounded right to me."

Another scrap of Irish melody.

"Yeah Paul was an accident. Came out of the blue, Mr. Paul. Still."

Cesare, thought the wife, stop interrupting. Let me hear about his late inventory.

"Now that woman that time, I mean the other time, with the twins on the way. My hand on the Bible, on the eyes of my children, that was just talking."

Barbara got a decent breath, her circulation settling.

"The wrong kind of talking, okay, sometimes. Inappropriate, okay. But I never touched her, and you ask me, hey. It was talking to myself. I had to. I had to hear somebody say, out loud, how I could do this. Twins on the way, Cesare, I mean. Old Jay had to turn himself into something new. New man, new kind of husband and father."

The priest changed his tone, probing.

"Well, I went to confession. Sure. That kind of thing. I, I had people. I had Barbara too. Barb and me, we've always talked. But I mean, two more kids, just like that. Girls at last, okay, that's nice, but, hey, who's the breadwinner? Who's bringing home the bacon? First the baby food and then the bacon. It's all part of the package, Father, Cesare. And in the back of mind, the whole time, I'm thinking, my Barbara, my wife—she lied to me. About her cycle. My wife lied to me. I had condoms, I mean."

Barb suffered a spasm of embarrassment, so absurd under the circumstances that it had her checking up-corridor and down.

"No, no, no way," her husband went on. "With the girls, that wasn't an accident. Barb admitted it."

Admitted it more or less. She'd fudged the truth about her ovulation, before the girls came along, but she'd also told him what she wanted. More or less.

"She told me, 'Paul's never home. It's like he's got his driver's license.'"

A long marriage was another no-secrets-dot-com, everything came to light in time, but the code could be hard to decipher. Barbara missed Cesare's next question.

"Yeah yeah," Jay replied, "a house full of men, that must've been hard for her. The Owl, she wanted some girls around. Okay. That—I've got a handle on that. Hey, I'm kind of more-the-merrier, myself. You can probably tell the kind of Pop I am, can't you, Cesare? Soccer with ten kids at once, you can see that. So, having a couple more, that's not what's so aggravating. That's not what's making me lie to Barb. What's aggravating is, that Owl Girl, these days. The woman just doesn't *understand*."

She reached for her elbows. Here it came: the cost of everything and the sacrifices a man had to make. "She just—it's like she can't do the math. I mean, the extra bedroom we had to have, Father, five months they were working on that. Five months, and after the first month, forget about it. They throw the bid out the window."

A confessor couldn't tell a sinner to shut up, but the priest's interruptions started to sound irritated. Once, the priest spoke with force enough for Barb to hear: "Well, cheating on a contract, in Naples too that kind of thing has been known to happen." Still Jay poured out his woes. "But it's not just the money, Cesare, can't you see that? It's about respect." Then in the next breath he was back to money. "Single-salary household, you know? And there's swimming lessons, there's play shoes and there's church shoes. Plus, hey. Can't take 'em to school unless the minivan's still on warranty."

The wife was backing away from the door, thinking she wouldn't learn anything new here. When she looked down the sloping hallway, however, she faced a policeman at the next corner. He had a phone to his ear and his eyes on *l'Americana*.

Cesare at last managed to shift the subject.

"Then, I mean. When Barb started to look into those abuse cases, from the Center. You have no idea. The worst."

The priest spoke more sharply.

"No." Jay's tone softened. "I'm not, not sick of her. No, Father. Cesare. I'm still in love with Barbara. Pushing forty-five, going through the change now maybe—what do I care? That woman, I don't want to lose her."

Again the wife crept towards the makeshift confessional.

"No, it's not just the family. Don't give me that, the 'investment.' The family thing, sure, I love it. But, I mean. First it's Barbara herself. My Owl Girl."

Down the corridor, the cop strode out of sight.

"Okay, that girl she brought home last winter. Okay, that was terrible. That was a nightmare. If we're going to talk about that."

Through the few inches of open door, Barb could make out the curve of her husband's back. He must've been rubbing his face.

"I mean, I had to be the bad guy. I had to be the one, send Maria Elena back to Children's Services. But, still. Hey. I'm the injured party, after that, but still, I didn't want a divorce. No way."

The Jaybird sounded as if he'd gotten his head out of his hands. He acknowledged that, after Maria Elena, he understood there needed to be some changes made. "I mean, the way things were going, forget about it. My Barbara, she needed meaning, you know? Meaning. But then I found it for her, didn't I? The work I found in this city, hey. Brought Barb a lot farther than just across an ocean. Brought her some meaning, big time, and that proves, that fucking proves—excuse me. Forgive me, Father, but still. What I did coming to Naples, it proves divorce is not for me. Hey? It's not for Jay, the end of the family. Jay, his family, he'll go halfway around the world to save it. He'll take risks. He'll fight, he'll lie and, and he'll . . ."

Then a silence, surprising. Barb had thought that Jay was going to lapse once more into complaining, but now the priest had to prompt him, twice.

"Bless me, Father," the husband said, "for I have sinned. I have lied to my wife. I love her, but. I have lied to her. I've lied about what I'm doing here in Naples, and she's starting to figure it out, and still. I go on lying. I'm not telling her the truth, anyway. What I'm doing, it's—I make reports to NATO, Father. To one man at NATO. An officer, you figure it out. He says he needs to know about the refugee underground. The big dark hairy-scary so-called underground."

In the hallway the mother had drawn up straight, no lazy Franciscan T.

"I *mean*. Kind of people you've got downstairs, what's so scary about them? But. I hear a name in a tent, I tell my guy. I keep my ears out, Papa the Spy. Because what I hear, it could be serious, according to my friend. My NATO contact. Serious, what 'these people' could do.

"And, hey. This guy, why shouldn't I make him happy? I make him happy, that's money. That's money there, that's benefits. The man can do things, Father. Cesare. For my family, he can do a lot. You figure it out."

She'd been right to come. This was something she could offer even the starving creatures downstairs.

"But, I mean. This so-called radical underground, *what* is the big deal? The big hairy-scary . . . Father, we're not talking Al-Qaeda out at the Center. Back in New York, for instance, that memorial at Ground Zero? Hey, that place has got nothing to worry about from Naples. I mean, Muslims in Italy, you know what? Muslims tend to go for the boom towns, up north. Milan, they go for. Follow the money, right? But down here, the *clandestini* I've got, forget about it. The one time they tried anything—what? They grabbed the cook. The cook, and he never even got his hat off. He never even left the kitchen. That's the kind of hard core I've got out at the Center."

Jay might've laughed. "NATO, I mean. Your tax dollars at work. Lately, now, you know who Kahlberg keeps asking about?"

Speaking of names. Barb pictured Lieutenant Major Kahlberg poring over a list, a schoolboy over a skin mag.

"That gypsy girl, Romy. The Lieutenant keeps asking if I've heard anything about Romy. I mean, what's he want? We all know what Romy had to do, back before Paul. It wasn't about national security, what she had to do. So what's he want, the Lieutenant Major? Especially since the girl has changed. Since Paul, she's changed. Nowadays, national security, anything like that, it's a joke for Romy. Kahlberg—she tells me to say hi to Kahlberg. Just last night she told me. She's still got friends out at the Center, people she used to run with, and last night she tells me to say hi to Kahlberg. 'Mr. Kahlberg your NATO contact,' she tells me. Forget about it, Cesare. For that girl, that whole thing's a joke. She knows my arrangement's supposed to be a secret."

Both men needed a long moment, enough time for Barbara to notice a bit of a commotion farther off. A shout or two perhaps. Then, Jay:

"The lying, Father. The lying to Barb, it hurts me. It's—I have sinned, Father. Thanks for meeting me like this, too. I know what it's like to have to make arrangements on the fly, so thanks, really. And bless me, for I have sinned. But then there's Barbara, Cesare. Her with her I-want-a-divorce, but nothing happens. I mean, waiting around for my crazy Mom? Plus, the sex? A lot of sex, you ask me. Multiple orgasms—Father, I have to tell somebody.

"Okay, maybe it's all part of the confusion. Part of the pain, okay. But. She keeps going back to you, too, Cesare. There's that too. I mean, with whom am I speaking, when it comes to my Barbara? What's she want?"

Barb had come her closest yet to the stony closet. She was squaring herself away, preparing to step in and speak up. She and Jay needed to talk.

"Does she really want," Jay repeated, "to grow old alone?"

Barb could see that the Jaybird had started massaging his face again. She thought that she heard him fighting tears, choking, but now there was new noise in the halls. A fresh commotion, substantial, from a group of some size.

"Bad enough," Jay was saying, "how lonely I am already."

A group was coming this way, uphill, with scraping footfalls and sharp but indistinct jabber. They moved in bursts, now striding along swiftly and now slowing down. Barbara backed away from her unsuspecting husband. She had the thought that she didn't want to be spotted, and she fretted about the camera over her head. A foolish thought—wasn't she planning to tell Jay exactly what she'd heard? Wasn't she going to throw it in Kahlberg's face too?

Her husband's voice had regained its strength. "What is that?" he was asking. "That out in the hall, you hear it?"

The cubicle's door, sluggish with age, creaked wide. Jay emerged looking down-ramp, his back to Barbara. When the oncoming crowd appeared at the bottom of the hallway, at first she didn't see them. Instead she studied her husband's head and shoulders, his hair improbably full despite the bald spot.

"Pop?" asked John Junior. "What are you doing here?"

"Jay?" asked Silky Kahlberg. "Jay, my man? This is a surprise."

The voices came from opposite ends of the crowd. The liaison officer stood at the front, the farthest uphill, while Barbara's oldest was among those at the rear, almost out of sight down around the corridor's corner. The gang presented an unlikely mix, altogether. The mother needed a few moments to sort everyone out, kids and guards and Silky and, about the middle of the group, gypsy Romy in full makeup. The girl in fact looked better than the Lieutenant Major. Kahlberg's blazer hung lopsided, revealing a corner of his holster strap, and a swatch of long hair was sweat-stuck across his forehead. Barb enjoyed a surge of triumph: gotcha. She'd caught the officer with his silk down. But this exhilaration dwindled quickly when she got her first decent look at John Junior. After all, her seventeen-year-old could move faster than anyone in the crowd, and yet he was the last up the hallway. There had to be a reason—like his younger brother Paul, looking drained, hanging by his spread arms between JJ and Chris. The two older brothers weren't quite carrying Paul, he still had his feet on the ground, but Barbara's middle child was clearly bushed. He had trouble keeping his head up, now hiding and now revealing his neatly done collar button.

Beside the boys stood a group arranged in the same fashion, with the two on the outside propping up the one in the center. These were two policemen flanking a handsome African. The black wore serious shackles, wrist to waist to leg. Nevertheless he showed Barbara a smile unlike any she'd seen before, a glowing surprise of a reminder, in pink and gold and weathered ivory, that she had come to this city and castle knowing next to nothing about what she was getting into. Even his cheeks seemed to glow, and one of these was scarred with a pair of crescent moons.

"What is this?" asked Jay. "What are you guys doing here?"

Chris and JJ shared a look, across their sagging brother. It was Dora and Syl who said it first.

Chapter Seven

The days that followed, the days and the nights, had Barbara thinking often of her childhood visits to Manhattan. Bedtime had felt different over at her mother's cousins' place off Lafayette. That branch of the family lived with another world of night noise. Little Barba-bella had come across the East River before her mother ran away, but it was after the disappearance that Barb had spent the nights that now came back to her with the greatest intensity. On those nights she'd been hustled over to the old Little Italy because there'd been word of a lead, a possibility. And in the second-story front space of the cousins' brownstone, formerly her Mama's bedroom, the traffic spoke to the visiting girl. Barbara would notice the heart-of-the-borough rumble when she was left alone to slip into her nightshirt, that tender cotton, and her eyes would follow the pattern of the headlights coming through the blinds, a yellow surf across ceiling and wall. She'd pick up the noise in the morning too, before her cousin poked her head into the room and began to wheedle, like the soothing fussbudget she was, about getting dressed for Sunday Mass. During the night, in the streets towards Roosevelt Park, the machinery sometimes offered a bit that she could identify. There might be a horn going off, a truck gearing up, or the squawk and clomp of a dented door. But Barba-bella could hear that sort of thing over in Carroll Gardens. Around her mother's former home, rather, the night growled through risings and fallings that the daughter couldn't understand, and she loved the sound precisely for that, because she could never get her mind around it all, because it contained the ignition, transmission, and brake of too, too many others to know. In that motor noise beyond the narrow brick-framed windows, there resided possibilities so wild that her preteen self could no more limit them to particular car parts than she could tuck her fertile visitor's dreams into neat stories over the morning orange juice. Rather the whole overnight sequence, the horsepower coil that wheeled her into sleep and the sapphire glints left behind when she woke—all this she could only give the shape of hope itself. In the city she heard so much energy at work, at large, that she had to believe some part of it would complete its trek. Some part of that mumbling runaround always made it the entire long way out wherever it had to go and then back again; it returned to the girl, to the pillow-space beside her, chuckling in an accent and smelling faintly of cheese and olives.

The Manhattan traffic had done more for her than any other night-time soundtrack, including that of the good Bridgeport neighborhood where she'd lived as a five-star Mom. She had to admit, too, that the intervening years had hardly felt devoid of happiness. She'd even taken the same fractious reassurance in the stories at the Samaritan Center, the uproar of guilts and resentments that always somewhere revealed, improbably, and if only they could see it, fulfillment for the people involved. Also there were evenings when Barbara found the same comfort in Naples. The Vomero wasn't so bourgeois that you didn't get people driving at night. Even after the uproar at Castel dell'Ovo, and even with the chatter of the troops beneath her balcony, she had sleepy moments carried along within the infinite circumnavigations of a vast motor-driven flock, the same as had cradled her ear and spirit years ago in Lower Manhattan. Buildings and people. Downtown palaver without end, forever making the rounds.

Not that, now as they came up on three weeks in the city, the mother could forget the trouble she'd seen the first time she looked at a map. Whatever good she might get from the night traffic, in daylight Barbara was barely coping. Five days after dell'Ovo, her counterespionage, she found herself once more trailing behind the Lieutenant-Major. She'd discovered his secret, his and Jay's and yet nearly a week had gone by with her doing next to nothing about it. This morning again, she followed the NATO plan.

And her children too. The family, minus Jay and plus Kahlberg, were all getting their photograph taken on the steps of the *Museo Archeologico Nazionale*.

They were tourists again. As the group posed for the papers, to either side waited day-trippers in loose bright nylon and shelf-like waist-packs. The museum overlooked the original downtown and dominated the guidebooks. Chris had read from the *Blue Guide*: "of prime importance." Then there was the tourist pitch, *Vedi Napoli e mouri*, see the Nazionale and die. That was the translation, right? The museum was the only reason most Americans came to town, right? Its exhibits gleaned from the entire ruin-speckled lower peninsula, greater metropolitan Siren-land. As Silky's choice for the first family excursion since dell'Ovo, it seemed a no-brainer.

Barbara went along.

This was after five days of recovery. Five days she'd hesitated, before heading to the Nazionale or anywhere else, instead shaping her time around the family's eleven-year-old question mark. These were five days without talking to the media, number one, and without fighting over what she'd overheard in the castle hallway, number two. Of course she'd told her husband, the very night, and Jay had understood what the discovery meant. As the week went on, he'd arranged to stay home more than half the time. Once or twice when he and Barb were alone together, he'd felt for the band of her underwear, but even then she'd found his expression wary. Still, what was there to fight about, once the wife made clear that her worst fears had been confirmed? What was the point of yelling and banging? What mattered was telling the kids, finding the moment.

The Jaybird had his testy moments, his fully loaded stares, but by and large he too had kept their dealings mild. As Barb and he stretched out on the bed he would agree, in a conversational rumble, that she needed to leave for America and find a good legal mediator the moment his mother arrived. Indeed the big man's self-restraint left the wife that much more committed to silence and withdrawal herself, during these days at home. To see the husband this way triggered, in her, her worst cross-the-heart zigzags yet. At her most confused, Barbara suffered the impression that the things she and Jay spoke of weren't actually going to take place, but had only been given voice as a shared penance. A two-person rosary.

These were five days of many an unsettling sensation, with the girls endlessly underfoot and Silky watching the family's every move. Sometimes the officer stopped in at the apartment and sometimes he used his cell, but either way he felt like a burden. After all, DiPio too dropped in for his checkups, AM and PM. Then there was Romy and JJ, finagling moments for their puppy love, for hugging and kissing out back by the palazzo dumpster, while the mother waited in the doorway to the alley but made it a point not to watch, like the NATO gunman who'd also been party to arranging the tryst, averting his eyes at the alley entrance. The kids' make-out sessions went on for a couple-three days before the Lieutenant-Major heard about them, of course he heard, and of course he called to object even as he was on the way up to the Vomero to make certain the teen sweethearts wouldn't get together again—fat chance of that, Silky, but Barb had to deal with the man's call as soon as she and her oldest returned to the apartment from their latest trip down to the alley. Barbara had to deal with it all these days, plus she always had to work in an hour or so of reading aloud to Paul, no matter what else was going on. Also she chose the DVDs for the evenings. Among them were a couple in Italian, made in Hollywood but dubbed in Italian, because she'd noticed how all her boys liked to laugh at what became of the dialog. Likewise after she saw how Paul enjoyed a certain flaked ricotta pastry, nuggeted with fruit bits, she arranged for the *pasticceria* to send over two a day, and when she saw him dig into the pizza from Acunzo, the following night she had them deliver a selection of their best. The day after dell'Ovo she'd announced to the kids that no one besides their father was allowed on the street until further notice, but then that very afternoon, following a call in Dick-&-Jane English from one of the NATO boys stationed at the stoop, she'd allowed the first of JJ's conjugal visits down in the alley. And the next day there'd been the first of her renewed sessions with Cesare (and Barbara had the NATO van take her those few blocks, and she ignored the supplicant or two who always came to her, unless they reached her on the steps of her church, in which case she allowed herself a touch of their upraised Catholic doodads), and then the third day, gutting her stay-at-home rule altogether, she arranged an afternoon soccer scrimmage for JJ and Chris with the girls and Paul as cheerleaders. This was the middle child's suggestion. His demand, rather, and he wouldn't allow Mama to park him in a wheelchair, either. The family *miracolino*, it turned out, was the one for yelling and banging, so stir-crazy and over-examined by the third day that he waved his girlish hand in Mama's face and hollered he wasn't some kinda in, in, *invalid* for God's sake! These dumb he, he, *healing* episodes weren't that h-hard on him! As the boy carried on, rising to a full-blown preadolescent tantrum, he provided Barbara a contradictory reassurance; he reminded her of anger plain and simple, something she herself didn't seem able to manage these days. Later, during the scrimmage itself, Paul spent most of his time jumping up and down along the sidelines, stippling the cuffs of his black pants with snippets of new-mown grass.

These were five days complicated further by a media circus, in which some cameraman was set up under the balcony every time the mother looked and newspaper stringers appeared never to need so much as a coffee break (anyway, in the Vomero you didn't need to go far to find a good café). The ringmaster, however, wasn't any journalist or production chief. Rather it was the revived African hunger striker who dominated the scene on the piazza out front of the family's place, a young man still little more than skin and bone but nonetheless capable of such intensity that Barbara could feel his staring from five floors up. And soon enough, beside the not-so-*clandestino*, there appeared the enterprising Maddalena. The woman might've been a rookie reporter, but she'd learned long ago what it meant to have youth and good looks. At once she grasped the advantage in coming round to the front of the camera, especially buddied up beside a young man who'd been pretty lucky himself when it came to lips and eyes and bone structure. The would-be suicide, as he returned to his natural physical bearing, turned out to be a stirring package of lightsome and hard-packed, a coppery spokesmodel for The South. His color fell midway between the dun of Maddalena's skin and the black of her hair, and this range of tones made them all the more eye-catching. Cuter still was the way they would help each other with their English, as they went on the air with repeated thanks to "these so special Americans who reach out to the poor and hopeless." These video clips were replayed a hundred times, and every day either Barbara or Jay had to stand up against the photogenic young couple's pressure for some sort of a press event with Paul. Either Barb or the Jaybird had to repeatedly refuse, while a small but respectable fraction of the world's attention was drawn to this "refugee Lazarus" (the headline writers had a great time). By the end of his third day back on his feet the former illegal alien regained, with the help of Amnesty International and the Italian Green Party and the rock star Sting, his right to walk the streets.

At the same time, too, his colleagues in the Shell of the Hermit Crab were let out of the castle's security ward, and none showed the least compunction about tearing into the local mozzarella, or a sprightly octopus salad. Apparently Maddalena's pretty African, this man Barbara had tried to pray over, held some sort of command status. And on that same third day MTV Europe threw its weight behind the evanescent brown star, not sixty hours removed from almost dying in prison without a trial. Via a notarized and certified letter to the Lulucitas, the network promised the children new CDs, DVDs, X-box goodies and jeanswear, plus full-access passes to a half-dozen upcoming concerts in Rome and Milan and Florence, including travel, lodging, and two meals a day. All the family had to do in return was grant the station's local affiliate an exclusive interview with Paul and an on-air meeting between him and the African, now going by the name Fond (the word tended to get the English pronunciation on TV and the radio, but the young man himself preferred the French).

The parents held firm: No. No new denim, no hanging out with the rock stars. No way. But the very next morning that champion wrestler Mass Media, the Mangler, the Murgatroyd, threw a new move at the family. The mother had to contend with MTV on the phone, a VJ calling her at home, thanks to the old technology, hand-to-pocket and mouth-to-ear. Barbara picked up the receiver only to get her ear split by a moaning dual-speaker feedback, a warped girlish chirping—because the call was live and on the air, from Rome, and Chris and JJ, desperate for something to do after breakfast, had tuned in the webcast. The MTV-ette who'd made the call looked like an ice princess, her hair as bleached as bone, and after Barbara got the boys to mute the computer, she found the VJ's tone unnervingly cheerful. The girl sounded far too bubbly for the way she was putting on the pressure: *Why do you stay there in Naples if you don't want the good things you can get from staying? All we want to do is give you more of the good sweet things you have already, like this nice big apartment in which to live and . . .*

These were five days with one moment of doubt on top of another. The midnight traffic offered its relief, now and again, and before going to bed Barbara always got her hour or so of reading aloud. The daily down time allowed her to take a certain pride in how she'd protected the kids. She could see herself like an angel in one of the fairy tales, skating her children safely across the swarming Neapolitan surface tension, and motherly pride would shroom up in her chest. Once she even felt confident enough to shoo Chris and JJ off the computer and compose an email for Nettie, back at the Samaritan Center.

Barbara's mentor from the Holy Name was conscientious as ever about getting back, and she didn't seem at all disturbed by the mother's questions—on the contrary, Nettie had studied cases like Paul's. While pursuing her Master's, her email explained, the former nun had written a paper on healing episodes. Research had established that the phenomena occurred most commonly in children entering puberty, and the counselor listed a handful of informational websites, "reliable scientific sites, none of that Christian balderdash." She mentioned a couple of books too, and summarized what she recalled from her Master's work, saying that healing such as Paul's tended to be "situational"—that is, the "acting out" was rooted in earlier trauma—and "its incidence is never defined geographically." That last left Barbara frowning at the screen, recalling other times when her guru had slipped into a koan, too much Zen and not enough plain English. The mother sent a follow-up and Nettie proved to be still online. Briskly she clarified: miracle cures, "so-called," were never limited to a particular place. A child might begin laying on hands in the middle of Kansas, but after that he or she could do it over any rainbow and down any yellow brick road; "what matters isn't the physical environment, but rather the continuing vulnerability to the root psychosis." So whatever energy was at work in Paul, these days, it would travel with him. Barbara nodded at the screen, and yet after a moment the voice in her head wasn't Nettie's but Jay's. Barb could hear her soon-to-be-ex as clearly as if he were crouched beside her, reading the mail. *Owl Girl, hey. This means New York would be worse, for Mr. Paul. If he's still going to be doing this kind of thing, back in New York? In the media capital? Forget about it . . .*

These were her five days, plus a transatlantic call on Father's Day. Her quiet Dad had a one-bedroom in Boca Raton. Then Barbara went meekly to the *Museo Nazionale*.

Not the boys, though. Paul wasn't the only one who'd gotten a little stir-crazy. Before the family went down to the Humvee, while Barbara was setting out the laundry on the balcony, John Junior had claimed he didn't want to be seen with the PR man. The big teen claimed he'd "almost rather stay home" than follow Kahlberg around again.

"I mean," JJ had said, gulping down his second orange juice, "after what my girl told me." *My girl.* As for Chris, he'd come out spoiling for a fight. Once the press gathered round, out on the museum steps, Barb's second-oldest began to pick at Silky.

"The Borbons were monsters," Chris insisted, there in front of the cameras. In another moment he and the officer were squabbling over kings and queens dead and gone for nearly two hundred years. The Borbon dynasty seemed admirable to Kahlberg; he waved his fat briefcase at the front pillars, braced by scaffolding, and reiterated that the museum was a Borbon legacy from the eighteenth century. In those days Naples had been the most dazzling stop on the Grand Tour. "Goethe came to visit, you heard of him? Mozart, he wrote some of his greatest—"

"Yeah yeah," Chris said. "But for the average person, what good did that do? Like, so what if they had a few celebrities at the palace?"

Silky played his annoyance for laughs. "If I *may* continue. The present structure, as you see, is painted Pompeiian red—"

"Exactly. The new monsters imitated the old monsters."

Barbara tried to follow, anything to distract her from the spineless way she held her place in the photo lineup. Chris argued that the Nazionale didn't fit the standard notion of a major museum, since it had only a few major pieces. "There's like, for instance, the Farnese Bull." Rather Naples offered a slice of life, two- and three-thousand-year-old life, thanks to an unmatched collection of kitchenware and bedroom accessories, sifted from the buried homes at the foot of Vesuvius. Barbara gave a nod, thoughtful. What she was trying to think of, however, was something else again: how to escape at last, and for good, from her own time-worn kitchen and bedroom. Her fifteen-year-old had mentioned a bull, and some big creature like that, a monster really, had been clomping around her home for almost a month now. But the mother still hadn't figured out how to harness the beast. This morning she could see that her hard feelings had rubbed off on Chris and John Junior, and even with all the bedtime reading, the aggravation must be getting to the others as well. But when was she going to tell them the truth? Just tell her children and get the awful business underway?

Here on the steps of the Nazionale, in full view of the press and the suppliants and assorted tourists, Chris was the one upsetting the applecart. The boy fingered his glasses up his nose and claimed that the best pieces from Pompeii and Herculaneum, "like, the five-star items," had been stolen by the British or the French.

"Mn," said Kahlberg. "I see where you're going, big shooter. This is all about those big nasty-damn superpowers, pushing around the poor and the helpless."

"Sure." Chris explained that the nasty-damn powers of the eighteenth and nineteenth centuries had raped the newly unearthed ruins. "They took the major items. They took the emperor's head." But the Naples collection represented a kind of revenge. Once the foreigners had hauled off their booty, locals had a free hand with the smaller stuff.

"The real stuff," Chris said. "The collection here, it isn't about the emperor's head. It's a slice of life. Like, the toolshed, the table arrangements."

"Arrangements," Romy put in. "This sounds like Naples for sure."

Romy, for sure. Ignoring the hoots of the construction workers, she'd been waiting on the steps when the family arrived. Her wisecrack drew a terrific laugh from JJ, rocking him out of the family lineup, freeing him from the need to come up with some sarky remark of his own. The older boy and the gypsy shared a soft kiss.

Once more the workers hooted and the cameras went off. What Barb noticed was how Kahlberg's pale face grew heavy, and she knew how the man felt. The idea made the mother slip her fingers through Dora's hair, at her hip, but there was no denying it: she had a pretty good idea what this officer was feeling. He had to stand there bombarded by static when the whole time the Off switch lay in easy reach. About the dell'Ovo escapade, too, Kahlberg had had to remain polite and aboveboard. He'd said no more than the obvious. *We can't have that, Mrs. Lulucita. Mrs. Lulucita, I've been assigned to this family by my superiors, and your safety is my first concern.* Then too, the mother had to admit that, insofar as anyone had kept the attentions of the press under control, it had been Captain America.

Besides, this morning Kahlberg had no objection to Romy tagging along. You would've thought that his screaming fit outside San Lorenzo had never happened. Not that the liaison didn't find a moment to slip in a nasty word about John Junior's exotic crush. As the family climbed out of the van, Silky muttered to Barbara: "Knew that little skank wouldn't have any trouble finding *this* place." But otherwise he ignored the girl. On the museum steps, Chris and the Lieutenant Major jawed back and forth as though Romy weren't there. Barb wondered if, by setting up a visit at the best-known tourist destination in town, the PR man were offering a truce.

Maybe the man was making changes. Actual changes . . .

Also the Lieutenant Major didn't try to keep the gypsy from coming in, and once the little group was into the cool of old marble and high ceilings, Barbara's concern shifted to Paul. She laid her fingers against his cheek, his neck, before he nudged away and a woman from the museum staff stepped forward with two photos to bless. Baby photos, these were, a little girl to judge from the color of her pj's. One was for Barb and the other for the *miracolino*. Both Mother and Child were in demand now. Believers hadn't failed to notice—of course they hadn't—that before each healing *la Mama Americana* had said a prayer. Supplicants had reached out to Barbara outside her church and, after Paul got through shouting at her, along the sidelines of the children's soccer outing up in the Vomero.

Now Paul handled the baby's photo with the same efficient goodwill he'd shown since the first. The mother gave the quiet blessing she'd come up with: *Una preghiera.*

Meanwhile Kahlberg was handing over today's documents, the authorizations signed off by officials from NATO and the UN relief. Checking the papers was a member of the security, in the standard grey blazer and red tie—though on second glance this rent-a-cop revealed a touch of the bad boy. The man had a stringy mustache and a jaunty set to his hips; he might've been a lounge singer. After he slipped the documents into his attaché (what else?), he put on a cheesy grin while Kahlberg introduced him, Umberto. After that the officer turned to Chris.

"Big shooter, Umberto here, he knows what's in all the closets. He knows where the Nazionale keeps the bodies buried."

The liaison was talking as if cameras had followed them inside. "You want to know what's in the closet, around here? You want to, son?"

Kahlberg was sounding bad-boy himself, but he passed out the usual handful of study aides, and Umberto took one too. The NATO trooper who'd accompanied the family inside, off the steps, was left posted by the entryway. The family moved into the galleries with only plainclothes protection, and either Kahlberg or Umberto would offer occasional explanation among the initial ranks of statuary. Neither had much to say, in any case, and the visit felt more restrained, more subdued, than any the family had made before. This was one corner of Naples where people had something like American notions of personal space. Not that everyone was from the U.S. (though you saw the Stateside lumpiness, the go-to-hell vacation duds), and not that the other museum-goers could resist staring, what with the gypsy in her clingy pastel Capris, the Lieutenant Major in his dandy's whites. The morning crowd also included four or five who approached Barbara and Paul. But by and large the Lulucitas circulated unbothered, and maybe having a guide besides Kahlberg made Chris confine himself to quiet asides for his brothers and sisters. Or maybe it was that they were all still kids— still prey to Museum Awe.

The statues on the first floor were incomplete, one way or another. Most lacked an arm or a nose, but the male figures were the worst off. None of them had a penis. The castration looked deliberate, in fact, as if someone had lopped off the cock with a chisel. The scar beneath their bronze or marble pubic curls, to Barbara's way of thinking, made these men more alive. She could imagine them hurting. But then again, when it came to hurting, nobody could match the woman under the Farnese Bull. A tragedy depicted in full, big enough for a monument at Gettysburg, the Farnese piece erupted in crosscut spirals. Two nude wranglers fought with the maddened animal, men who appeared all the more reckless because they still had their male equipment, and five or six inches beneath the bull's raised hooves there coiled a woman: bare-breasted, soft-bellied, shriek-wracked, raising an arm still pudgy with baby fat.

Eventually the family climbed to the next story. The clutter of kitchen shelves and bedside vanities, up there, was laid out in racks arranged by size. At one end you had an ear-stud for a girl, at the other a serving platter to go under a boar, so from a distance the display suggested open scrolls covered with writing that grew larger, louder, more demanding. Come closer and you might see the blunt end of a pin fashioned into the pouting face of a nymph head. There was copper, silver, jade, gold.

Barbara heard Romy check something with Chris. *Most of the things here, they're things for a woman, right?*

The boy concurred, with a gesture that took in combs, jewels, vials of perfume.

Okay, for sure. Naples is a woman.

Naples was a metaphor, sure, an extrapolation—all the more diverting because the choice of comparison made no difference. Barbara could waste the whole day on such stuff; she could lose herself in another fairy tale. For wasn't today the old story of her first descent into the city? Into the speaking grid, where the mother was forever rediscovering herself? Today the downtown had a more formal layout, the scroll effect, compared to which she and the children looked doughy and amorphous, like a lower order of being. The most exquisite of the household items was a blue wine jug embroidered with white coral. An amphora brought out for good company, its cameo decoration hugged the darker glass like vines of bone. Indeed many of the scrimshaw-style carvings were vines, grapevines, among which nuzzled goats and birds and babies. Human or beast, they went happily for the fruit, in a never-ending snack time that sprouted in coils from the plump drunk head of Dionysius. The god had a sloppy smile and greedy eyes, and he was antenna'd with the vineyard's rootstock.

Compared to a thing like that, what did her squabbling amount to? The people who'd used the jug had been gone since Christ was a carpenter.

Barbara straightened up. "We need to talk," she said.

The announcement came out with surprising firmness. She saw that the two girls remained close by, and she got a hand on each.

"I'm saying, just me and the kids." With a glance she took in John Junior and Romy, facing her, plus Chris putting a word in Paul's ear. "Me and the kids and nobody else. Guys, listen. There's something I've been meaning to tell you."

The first to take her seriously was Kahlberg's Umberto. The museum guide pouted beneath his mustache, sizing the mother up. She claimed that after all they'd been through, her and the kids, they needed to take stock right here and now in the middle of the daytrip. They needed time alone to make sure that the morning's excitement wasn't too much for anyone. When the Lieutenant Major touched his lapel and reminded Barbara that she'd just had almost a week of "family-style R&R," she responded that Nazionale visit had come too soon. She hadn't realized how badly it might shake up her and the children to get back out into something resembling real life.

Downstairs we had that awful Bull business, the mother declared, *the worlds in collision, and up here we've got this impossible House Beautiful stuff.*

"Mom," Chris put in, "this is nothing. You should see what they've got—"

"Chris, this is our life, not a museum. I'm telling you, we've got to *talk*."

A few of the strangers in the gallery stared openly at the give and take, and others checked their waist-packs or watches in order to avoid staring. John Junior made a wisecrack, don't mess with Mother Nature, and Barb fixed him with the same glare as she'd given Chris. In the process she noticed that the blue of the spectacular amphora, beneath the bleached coral, recalled the color of the sea in Jay's wide and complicated map. The city in that map had been going upside her head with its tufa-stone verities for weeks now, and still she hadn't torn through the paper, she hadn't revealed what was really going on between her and Jay. Any longer and she would de-evolve further, she'd become nothing but talk. Already she was trapped in a kind of test pattern, wasn't she? Hadn't she already grappled for a moral advantage on her husband, a couple of times, only to fall back exhausted once she achieved it? Now, here and now, she needed to let the kids know. She needed privacy, a room at the end of the world.

The Lieutenant Major handled Barbara's outburst with his usual affability, but he didn't fool her. After last week's cloak and dagger, she knew he had to worry about what she might say. Sorry, S.K., but she wasn't going to hold anything back. The children needed the whole truth, the divorce and its reasons. Barb shook her head at the officer's reminder that he'd have the Lulucitas back home in no time, a couple of hours. She tugged at a seam of her dress and, noticing Umberto's wormy pout, scowled with still greater determination. Kahlberg made what sounded like a joke, something about the Stendhal syndrome, but he turned from the mother. He fell into a triangular staring contest with Romy and the loose-hipped Umberto. The bad blood between the gypsy and the other two was obvious, and the museum guide, or whoever he was, let his Neapolitan mask slip enough to show her the same in return. Smoke and mirrors—Mary, mother of God—Barbara had gotten sick of it.

The NATO man turned to her again. "It's got to be blood relatives only, one. Anything like that, that's how it has to be. You and the kids only."

Umberto had his mask back in place. He mentioned a storage area nearby.

"All I need," she said, "is a place where a person can let her hair down."

The Italian pinched his mustache, unfamiliar with the expression, and Kahlberg took him aside. The two men stepped into a corner, no end to their smoke and mirrors, and Barbara got her hands out for Dora and Syl. They deserved a last good squeeze from the Mom they thought they knew.

"Mrs. Lulucita?"

Kahlberg, a hand on her arm, had colder fingers than she'd expected. The man was a Georgia peach after all, thin-blooded and quick to burn in the sun.

"They've got a secure space," the PR man said, "at the back of the gallery." He wore a smirk, trying to keep things light. "Umberto says, they've got a surprise for you in there. Says you won't believe what they're keeping in there."

He even winked. But Barbara wouldn't soften, and after a moment the liaison showed her something new. New and startling, a face she'd never imagined on Lieutenant Major Kahlberg, one without pretense or stagecraft. For a long moment, in the museum hush, the liaison kept his hand on the mother and let her see something close to honesty.

"Let me ask you something," he said.

She wouldn't avert her eyes.

"Let me ask you, do you know what all this museum shit, this upstairs and downstairs—do you know what it's about, this shit?"

Barbara wished Chris could hear; he'd have an answer. But the fifteen-year-old was reading to Paul out of the Blue Guide, over a display of tomb jewelry. JJ of course had ducked into a conference with his girl.

"This shit has accumulated for thousands of years. So what's it all about?"

She'd seen worse, she told herself. Fond the recovered hunger striker, for instance, on the news. That man could stare.

"It's about, nothing matters except coming out on top. That's today, and that's everyday. *Si, signora.*"

The authentic Silky. Barb wondered if even Romy had gotten this close, a week ago outside of San Lorenzo.

"All this shit in here, that's all it's ever about, come out on top. Win today, one. Then win the next day and the next. Anything else is shit."

The liaison toughened of his jaw-line, nothing like a smile, then turned his back. He turned his white twill back, bisected slantwise by the strap of his bag of papers, and as the mother gestured for her children to come along she believed she understood. Not that she felt sympathy for the man—no way—but she'd gotten a handle on the Lieutenant Major, maybe as old as thirty-five, and unmarried. His search was for some challenge equal to his God-given talent for the Corporate Shuck'n'Jive. The young tyro had a genuine flair in that arena, and it had allowed him to ace the entire treacherous repertoire of the military-industrial decision-makers. Yet all that must've seemed like nothing special. It was nothing more than he'd expected, going back perhaps to his freshman days at Virginia Tech or wherever, when he'd first come to know how easy it was for him to pick up the language of power. So more recently, locally, Silky must've enjoyed a deeper satisfaction. Working through the tangle of old hegemonies around the Bay, he'd at last found a place to go native. He'd mastered the Dance of the Sirens and a whole new selection of partners (didn't he even refer to the region as a "theater of operations?"). It must've felt wonderful, as if the city was his to manipulate any way that he liked, now Pompeiian, now Borbon. And he was maybe as young as thirty. Unmarried.

Umberto had to unlock the storage space. The officer stood close, finger-combing his long hair, chin lifted, genteel.

The space held shelves and stacking chairs, a porthole window and also a trunk. The trunk looked impressive, squat and thick-ribbed, but the mother went for the chairs. As she set these up, the twins pitched in.

"What good girls," she singsonged, "my good girls."

She had the chairs in a circle before she noticed the boys weren't helping. They'd gathered over the trunk, of all things. Umberto held open the lid and JJ, Chris, and Paul all crowded in beside his skinny frame, sniggering. Sniggering. Indeed the guide wore a leer, and Barbara got a hand on JJ, nudging in for a look while the big boy made a quip she didn't catch. At first glance the stash seemed nothing special, more carbonized vegetables. The Nazionale had a lot of that, dinners baked and preserved by volcanic ash, another variety of domestic items. But why would the museum keep a big box of cucumbers? The mother blinked, she looked again, she got the picture. These little blimps and sausages were the parts lopped off the statues downstairs. In gray marble, in green bronze—they were the gathered cocks of Herculaneum and Pompeii.

"Oh, *boys*." She grabbed the trunk-lid and slammed it. "Little, little boys."

Before the sound of the slam died—the slam and the rattle— Umberto was rushing away.

"*Disgrazia!*" Barb shouted after him. She got a last glimpse of Kahlberg out in the gallery, grinning, before his sidekick yanked the door shut.

"Boys," she repeated, growling at the door. "All my life, nothing but boys."

"Mom, hey." JJ didn't like the suggestion that he was less than adult. "You've got to admit that was pretty cool—"

"Oh, don't. *Don't!* We've had enough, more than enough."

But Barb noticed she was frightening the girls. Her two youngest had slid far back into their chairs, their legs flat on the seats. The mother closed her eyes and got a breath, never mind that the dark behind her lids had been imprinted by the box of penises, a netlike pattern of oblongs. Worse, their space was little more than a closet, already close with sweat. When Barbara reopened her eyes she saw, in the porthole's sun-shaft, that their arrival had kicked up months of dust.

Talk, Mom. Another five minutes and they'll either start whining or sneezing.

John Junior and Chris perched on the trunk top, frowning, puzzled. Paul found a chair and dropped his head into his hands, massaging his face. Barb had to blink at that, too, her fey *miracolino* looking so much like the burly Jaybird. Anyway the boy appeared in better shape than the girls, almost an illustration out of the literature back at Samaritan Center: typical postures of abused children. When the mother took a seat the plastic made a lot of noise. Every creak seemed another stab at where she might start. Years needs . . . Grandma unhappy . . . Silky Papa lying deal-making . . .

"Why did we come to Naples?" she blurted out. "What are we doing here?"

John Junior snorted, crossing his muscular legs. "Come on, Mom. You feeling guilty, hey?"

"Guilty? What? Are you saying. . . ?"

"Come on. You know it was you."

Barbara had thought she'd get further than this before things got difficult.

"Mom, I mean. You didn't bring us in here to lie to us. Even the girls know what's been going on."

"What? They know?"

"Hey Dora, Syl." JJ lowered his head into the shaft of sun. "Didn't Pop take this job in order to make Mama happy?"

Dora's lips hardly seemed to move, in the dimness. "Mama was unhappy," she said, "because Papa wasn't doing good like her."

"You used to yell at him." The other twin's face seemed larger, her eyes on her mother. "You used to say, 'Don't you care about suh, about suffering—'"

"Guys, guys." Chris gestured open-handed. "I mean, everybody knows there's another side here, right? Right? Everybody knows, Mom, this isn't all on you."

Barbara managed half a smile.

"Sure, you've got Pop jumping through hoops," continued the second-oldest, smiling back. "Like, for months now. Maybe a little longer, come to think of it. Pop's been jumping through hoops, and that means all the rest of us too."

"Duh, gee, Chris-tuh-fuh. Gee, really?"

"Gee-ee. You know, Mom and Pop really should've checked the expiration date before they picked up your brains at Wal-Mart. We're trying to talk serious, here, JJ."

"Oh, serious? Tell me about it, bro. Seems to me it's pretty serious when, every time my girl and I try to go on a date, they're some guy with a semi-automatic."

"Well like, your love life, I mean. That's been referred to the Institute for the Paranormal anyway."

John Junior appeared to have a comeback ready, but he caught his mother staring. He shifted against the trunk. "Mom. Hey."

"You're all saying, it's because of me?"

"Well, I guess—not everything."

"Like Paul," Chris put in, "like Romy and all that. That's not your fault."

Either Dora or Syl began to repeat that their mother was a very good person, and Barbara's gaze dropped to the floor, the circle of sun through the porthole. "It was because of me," she said. "Because I took in Maria Elena."

"Maria Elena was hard, Mom." JJ spoke with surprising restraint. "I mean, you didn't bring us in here to lie. A girl like that, she needed a miracle."

"Aw, you got that from Pop."

"Well maybe Pop's right. Chris, hey. You saw yourself, even Pop couldn't handle Maria Elena."

"I found her through the church," Barb said. "Through the Holy Name. I told myself, this is what I'm called to do. This is what a mother can do."

"Mom." Chris may have bent nearer. "She's got to be better off now."

"They kept telling me, she was the worst case the Center ever gave out for adoption. She'd just turned up one day in a cathedral in Mexico City, naked and rubbing a crucifix, umm . . . rubbing."

Barbara swallowed thickly; no need to give the kids every gory detail. John Junior was right about why she'd brought them in here, and she had to admit that Maria Elena was, for this family, the first Beast of the Apocalypse. She had to confess to it all, the girl too. But there was no need for every gory detail.

JJ: "She wasn't much older than Dora and Sylvia."

"They never could get her exact age," Barbara said. "The way she'd been kept, you know, it affects your growth." When she closed her eyes again, the image in the dark was Maria Elena. The girl could hardly have looked less like Barbara's two, coarse-haired and mocha-skinned, with crooked teeth and an Aztec-hatchet nose.

"She was kept in a cage, right?" Dora asked. "Some bad man kept her locked up in a cage."

"H-hey." This was Paul. "Do we, do we have to talk, to t-talk ab-bout . . ."

"Some bad man," Sylvia said.

"The markings indicated she'd been in a cage. The pattern on her buttocks, I'm saying. At the Center, they showed me photos. And

Nettie and Sister Trudy warned me to think it over." Barbara gave an airless laugh.

"Sister Trudy," Chris said. "Mom, you want someone to blame, look no further."

"Brought to you by Sis-ter Tru-dy," JJ said.

"That's who's to blame. Her and the brain trust over there at the Sam Center."

"I mean, as if this was ever their decision to make! Jesus, Mom. You volunteered over there, okay. But what gives those people the right to—"

"Boys." Barb raised her eyes. "If I could work there again I would. In a minute I would. I'd work like Nettie, I'd get a real job there."

The older brothers shared a look.

"But that's not what God sent me. I didn't have a job there, I was a mother, that's all. And listen, Sister Trudy didn't have to tell me anything. Anyone with half a brain could figure out that as soon as that girl found herself back in a family situation, there'd be—repercussions."

"G-guys, guys. I don't l-like it when you, when we t-talk ab, ab-b-b . . ."

"Paul." Barb couldn't quite see him, some trick of the sun on the dust.

"Listen to me, Mr. Paul. It's Mama's fault. Mama's fault, everybody, I'm owning that." She didn't know how to avoid the jargon. "Sister Trudy and Nettie, over at the Center, you think they would lie to me? You think I would lie to them? I knew what I was risking, bringing a girl like that into a family situation. But I wanted something so simple, so simple. Basic socialization, that's all."

"Mom," Chris said, "nobody's saying you're lying."

"Socialization? Mom, I mean. The girl was only with us, what? Ten days?"

"We never even ascertained specifics about the abuse. Sometimes she talked about an uncle, sometimes it was a stepmother."

"Talked?" John Junior caught her eye. "That girl didn't talk, she screamed. Mom, she screamed all the time. And when she didn't have something she could hurt you with, hey. She's got her pants down."

Paul stood up, his chair clattering backwards.

"JJ, come on," Chris said. "You know you got all that from Pop."

"Well Pop is *right*. Mom, you know what he told me, out at the Refugee Center? He said, 'Your mother's not the easiest person in the world to live with.' Hey. You know he's talking about Maria Elena."

Barb was aware of her middle child, his white sleeves aglow. But she couldn't take her eyes off John Junior.

"Yeah, Pop tells me things. You can't keep him under your thumb all the time. The day after that girl came to our house, he pulled me aside and he told me to make sure the twins were never alone with her. Good call."

The mother had intended the Magic Kingdom, but the girl saw Gotham City. The first morning Maria Elena woke up in the Lulucita house, she'd crawled into the master bathroom while Jay was shaving and, after checking his befuddled grin, flipped his thick penis out of his boxers and kissed it. The father had lost control of the razor, slashing a half-circle across his cheek. His bellowing set Dora and Sylvia running for the stairs, forgetting even the cat; thank God John Junior had stopped them. Then after the father had banged back into the bedroom, bleeding, accusing, the little refugee had come after him with the scissors Barb used to trim the children's hair.

Had the girl been feeling scorned? Maria Elena had worse secrets than Silky Kahlberg. She shrieked in languages no one knew.

"Mom told us to stay away too," Chris was saying. "Like, Mom the same as Pop, JJ. She realized that we weren't equipped to deal, just ordinary American kids."

"Okay, but how long did it take? How many incidents?"

How long had it gone on? Had it really taken Barbara ten days to concede that for Maria Elena, home and family would always seethe, cutthroat, bloody? When Jehovah's Witnesses came to the door, Barb had been down in the laundry room, and by the time she'd rushed upstairs there were copies of *The Watchtower* scattered across her stoop and her camellias. Two women in white gloves hustled away, screeching promises of hellfire while, cackling spread-legged in the open doorway, Maria Elena masturbated with the remote for the front room's stereo. Just getting the girl inside left Barbara with a serious black eye. The bruise took longer to disappear than the scar she'd gotten from the bathroom scissors.

She and her husband managed to protect the twins from excesses like that—she and her husband and JJ and Chris, the full security team. But twice during the brief adoption Dora and Sylvia watched this older child squat on one of the better rugs in the house and drop a quick twist of shit, a demon challenge to her step-sisters. During dinner another day Maria Elena had fondled both the older boys at once, dipping in her chair to extend her reach, so that the only thing the others could see above the tabletop were her feral eyes. She'd muttered the English words she knew best, the filthiest in the language, and JJ had startled away, whipping up a full plate and breaking it across her head. In response Maria Elena, her pockmarked face like a sea-creature's draped with weeds and clams, had bared her gap-full shark-like teeth in prolonged malevolent laughter, interspersed with more of her badlands jabber. Finally she'd come up with a bit of un-obscene English: *You don wan it? You liars. Liars. What you got all those fine big soft beds for upstairs if you don wan it?*

"How many times," JJ went on, "does she have to pull down her pants or hold a knife to somebody's neck?"

"I can't, I can't," Paul said. "I n-n-need to get out, get out of here . . ."

"Mom, really. Pop called it. He told me, 'This family is going to be dealing with the damage she did for a long time.'"

Paul was trying to find a way out of the circle of chairs, but Barb kept her eyes on John Junior until she caught a whiff of the younger boy's sweat. She'd come to know it so well, her middle child's sweat; she could pick it out even in this dusty sauna. In a moment she too was on her feet, her arm around Paul. He had her mother's body, Barb recalled: the light bones of a family that sculpted shells.

"Mr. Paul," she said. "Big guy. You need a break?"

The boy slumped into her embrace, and she was stung to think how much she'd talked about the girl as he'd sat listening. How could she have let it go on so long?

"Sure you can have a break," she said. "Paulie, sure. Let's get you some air."

She glanced at the others, keeping them in their seats, and the sight brought back the notion that she'd wound up raising an abused child after all. After Connecticut Children's Services had taken the Mexican girl away—well, what would you call this boy's daily getup, the black and white, if not obsessive compulsive?

The mother felt relieved about getting out of the museum's upstairs closet. Relieved for herself, as well as for Paul: to step back into the gallery felt like going to the beach. Paul noticed the air too, his curly hair shifting against her breast, and Barbara left the door open for the others. The last thing she needed was one of them getting dizzy. She still had a dirty job to do.

Checking round the gallery, the first person she noticed was the NATO trooper. The Lieutenant Major must've figured he needed extra security, though just now the liaison was dawdling over the tomb jewelry, without so much as a glance at the mother and boy. The guy with the semi-automatic, left to his own devices, was trying out his English on Romy. To see the gypsy chatting across the bright room in an outfit that was, after all, only what all the girls were wearing—you could tell at once she was no Maria Elena.

When Umberto approached her, the mother's determination resurged, blackly. Silky didn't even bother to look, he sent his flunky, and once again she was sick of living this way. Had it up to here with this double dealer and the husband who played along.

Meantime her middle child pulled away. Paul regained his composure, smoothing his shirtfront. "I guess I j-just need to use the bathroom," he said.

"*Servizio?*" asked the Neapolitan. "*Bagno?*"

"Really?" Barbara asked. "That's all, Mr. Paul?"

"It's oh, oh, okay. And you can, you can g-go ahead a talk about, about wh-wh-whatever you need to, in there."

Behind the boy, a staring contest got underway. The loaded looks were limited this time to Umberto and the Lieutenant Major, a call and response. Barb couldn't miss it, but she kept her own eyes on her boy. She gave his collar a straightening.

"It's *okay*, Mama. It's, it's ancient hist, history."

"I don't know how I let it go on so long."

"Talking, like, talking, that's p-part of the, the, the p-process." He'd worked one hand into a pocket, the knuckles visible under the cloth. "Everyb-body's got to find their o, own way to m-m-m . . . we've all got to find a way to m-move on."

He'd picked up a few catch-phrases himself, during his therapy after the girl had been taken away. Not that Barbara could see any reason not to believe what the boy had to say. And meanwhile Umberto's smile hadn't improved any, and the liaison officer's nod was more of the same, a Power Nod. Mother of God, was she sick of these shadow soldiers and their antique charade.

So she let Paul go, once more accompanied by a bureaucrat in a blazer.

Back in Bridgeport, of course, he would've been heading for therapy. The man at Paul's elbow would've been one of the people with Children's Services.

As she returned to the storage space, Barbara kept her eyes down, avoiding everyone's look. Back at the Samaritan Center, Paul had seen—how many counselors was it? Four, five? Enough to keep Barbara from seeking more here in Naples, anyway. Here DiPio had been doctor enough for her, and Paul clearly preferred the reading therapy, the tales of witches and beauties and magic boots or hats. But back in Connecticut, he'd had to start on treatment the very day that Barbara had discovered him and Maria Elena tangled together across the Monopoly board.

The naked girl had howled, she'd jabbered in her witless tongue and leapt to her feet. She'd bent over and shown the mother her ass, her branded child's ass, with today's fresh markings, the indents of the game's plastic houses and hotels. Then English, shouting around one scarred buttock: *You liar, what you got all this for? Liar!* When Barb had looked to Paul, he'd tried, moaning, to roll out of sight. His Reading Rainbow t-shirt had been up around his neck and his blue jeans down around his ankles; his belly, compared to Maria Elena's, looked pale as the moon—pale as sperm. He couldn't hide that, the fluid that dribbled across the colors of an imitation Atlantic City. He couldn't roll over, he was still so erect.

Barb and Jay and their oldest had protected Dora and Sylvia, and JJ and Chris had protected themselves. But that morning Barbara had allowed the middle child to stay home from school, at breakfast he'd been stuttering worse than usual, and over the next couple of hours, between grunting over the garden's compost heap and scowling over Ann Landers, the mother had fallen again into that bottomless delusion, her own goodness. What you got all this for, if you not good? She'd fallen dizzily, convinced for an hour or so that her own happy family ("good as bread" was how her runaway mother would've put it) might from their own safe and comfortable corner exemplify a fix-it for whole riven and lambasted world.

By noon that same day, while Paul was still in the bath, a squad car had swung by the house. Two officers and a woman in plainclothes together managed to round up Maria Elena, after no more than a minute or two of spine-flaying screams. The screams of a baby, really. One last time the little girl tore around the downstairs, quick for her age but no match for the grownups, yanking off her soaked clothing and offering her disfigured crotch.

Nettie and Trudy, over the weeks that followed, had called in every favor they'd been owed. The Sisters felt responsible, to be sure; they had their own consciences to clear. More than that, it became apparent that they genuinely cared about their lay colleague. They didn't want to lose what Barbara Lulucita contributed to the Center. A sweet discovery, that was: proof that the Sisters hadn't just lobbed the mother a few softball duties in order to keep those monthly checks rolling in. A silver lining, that was, maybe. Nonetheless Barbara wouldn't say she ever got over the final glimpses, the final ear-splitting pleas, of her temporary additional child. Nor could she forget how troubled Paul had looked, that first afternoon in Samaritan Center. The first of Trudy's and Nettie's good turns had been getting Children's Services to shuttle their people over to Holy Name. The Sisters arranged for the boy to work in a familiar setting.

As for Jay, he'd contacted the UN earthquake-relief agencies after his and Barb's initial session. Springtime grew busy. The family threw together the move across the Atlantic. Something like twenty-five days in a row, the mother went to confession, and with that and with Nettie making so much time for her, she could begin to sound like Chris, saying that Maria Elena was better off thanks to Barbara Lulucita. Or she could sound like some honor-haunted Sicilian, insisting without the least chill of hypocrisy that Jay's mother should never know. Or she could echo Paul's CS counselor, who proposed that the boy's trauma might actually result in long-term psychosexual health. Given the right treatment, the counselor suggested, Paul might develop an exceptional comprehension of physical affection. He might grow up into one of those men who was good at intimacy; he might "achieve"—Barb repeated the expression though she never understood it—"all manner of sympathetic anomalies."

After Maria Elena had been taken away, Barbara had found comfort in the words others gave her. The difference here in Naples, as she allowed Paul the sort of bathroom break he might need for the rest of his life, was that the mother had worked out something of her own to say. She'd forged her own absolution.

Back in the closet, Barbara shut the door. The chair's plastic seat was as warm as the last time. "Your father and I," she began, "you guys must've noticed."

She looked at the shelves, the scraps of homes destroyed a thousand years ago.

"Pop's told me all about it," John Junior said.

Barb figured that if she lost control before Paul returned, if she told the others everything, maybe that would be for the best. Maybe Paul should hear it one on one.

"Mom," her oldest went on, "he says you've been way hard to live with. After Maria Elena, what choice did he have except, I mean, something totally drastic?"

"Aw," Chris said. "He talks to me too, JJ. I've heard all this stuff. And Pop also says, like, two-way street."

"Yeah, but he says *Mom* won't say that. Whatever Mom wants, she gets, but she'll never admit it."

"He says he isn't perfect either. He says that's why he was at Castel dell'Ovo, because he'd sinned."

"Guys," Dora piped up, "what are you talking about?"

"We're talking," Barbara said, "about me and your father. About how things have been going between us."

Say it, Owl Girl. See Naples and die.

"Till now," she said, "I've been holding off because, because—"

The closet door slammed open. The shelves rattled, a terrible racket, and there stood Kahlberg with his gun out.

"The girl," he said. "She's got Paul."

The weapon was in one hand and from the other dangled some kind of clothing, hard to see with the way he was blocking the gallery light. He gestured with the gun.

"The *girl*," Silky repeated. "The goddamn gypsy. She went after Paul and the guide and now Umberto's down and we don't know where she took the boy."

Barb's two oldest were off the trunk already, sneakers squeaking. The mother's thinking split in wild directions, confession and memory and Mafia movies. She asked, "He's—Umberto, he's down?"

Silky frowned and hoisted the other hand, which turned out to hold a gray blazer. "Got him right upside the head." He rotated the jacket to reveal, sketched along one lapel, a slant hieroglyph of blood.

With the coat, the gun, and the carrying case still slung across his chest, the officer blocked Chris and John Junior from getting past. "I tried to tell y'all," he said. "Tried to warn you about that girl."

JJ stepped closer, inside the man's gun-hand. "Yeah well, she says *you're* crooked. Says you've been making deals."

Across the liaison's expression flickered something close to the honest contempt that Barbara had glimpsed earlier.

"My girl says she's going to catch you any day now. You're going to be making some crooked deal and she'll *nail* you."

"Big shooter," Kahlberg said, "right now all I know is, I've got your brother missing and a man down."

Yet if Silky wasn't about making deals, why did the next ten minutes or so—it couldn't have gone on long, before the gunshots—feel to Barbara like nothing but *arrangiarsi*? She seemed to spend the entire time striking interior deals, each bargain more one-sided than the last. First she jumped to her feet beside her remaining boys. Do something, blared her nervous system, *do something*: a need so fierce it might've been what she'd wanted all along. She leapt up ready to knock over the Farnese Bull. Yet immediately she had to settle for less. The liaison officer kept his iron between them and the rest of the museum. He declared that there was no way in hell that he could allow a bunch of overexcited civilians to run around loose after an armed kidnapping.

"Listen," he repeated, "that girl took Umberto right upside the *head*. Like back when Jay was hit."

Kahlberg wouldn't hear any objections. John Junior started to shove and get loud, but he wasn't nearly so loud as the click of the safety on the Lieutenant Major's pistol.

The family wound up in the museum gift shop. On the way downstairs the galleries threw their footsteps back at them, stony reverberations that widened the time since Barbara had last seen her middle child. Overhead the PA system ordered everyone else out of the building, repeating the command in—was it five languages? Was it ten? Then down in the shop her dealing grew more desperate. She tried to get Kahlberg to stay with them, the "non-essential personnel." The mother wanted him where she could keep an eye on him. But again she didn't get what she wanted. The liaison hadn't taken out his gun just so he could play babysitter, he had the troopers for that. He told the biggest of the powder-blues to stand in the shop door.

"Wait, but, *wait*." Barbara put an elbow in the guard's ribs, reaching past him to hook the strap of Kahlberg's carryall. "Last I saw, the girl was with you."

Silky actually bared his teeth. "She went after them before Umberto and Paul got ten steps. I'm surprised you didn't notice."

Barbara remembered only bureaucrat and boy.

"Seems to me," the Lieutenant Major said, "I should've taken precautionary measures right then."

"This is *so bogus!*" John Junior shouted.

"Listen," Barb said, "listen, be careful."

"Hey! If my girl went after Paul, she was trying to *protect* him!"

"Please, be careful."

The PR man wriggled free, loping away into the first-floor galleries. He was loping, eager, and the mother was left to seek another arrangement, still less favorable. She backed away from the door, away from her shouting oldest and the other three clustered about him, and ducked between two standing racks of postcards. Perhaps that itself was the bargain Barbara hoped to strike, simply to be left alone among those glossy reproductions of museum pieces—every picture now somehow the same, a slant hieroglyph of blood—so that she could pray. Perhaps prayer had become the only negotiation she had left. Certainly nobody else appeared likely to help. Even the tourists were leaving. Barbara could see them beyond the shop's glass wall, filing out of the Nazionale one a time, presenting their I.D. to a pair of cops at the door. A backup Silky must've called in. Barbara, watching, with her rosary beads dangling from her fist, believed that she herself was trying to do the same: to expose the image of her inmost heart and have it approved.

She never had a doubt about the gunshots. Onetwo-threefourfive, they came, a rushed and untrained cluster.

JJ got loud again: "What was *that?*" But Barbara was already into her first stride, her rosary looped around her knuckles. She never had a doubt.

In Brooklyn, as she'd grown older and her neighborhood had gotten worse, she'd heard shots once or twice. At night the traffic petered out in a way it didn't over in Manhattan (and anyway she'd seen less and less of her mother's family, as she'd grown older), but other noises came on that much more distinctly. The next morning neighbors would claim, *I thought it was a truck backfiring*, but that didn't fool the teenage Barbara Cantasola. She'd always known a gunshot at once, and at once her organs of hearing had seemed to relocate to the rabbitty center of her chest. Today, the same. Today in the Nazionale, she understood at first shot and she counted all five, meanwhile bristling with fresh capacity and muscles in new places. The mother calculated where the shots had come from and she had a plan for the soldier at the door. In another moment she hit the trooper just right, using her beaded fist to catch him on his exposed jaw while he was speaking into the walkie-talkie on the other shoulder. She busted past him and shrugged off the children.

A different sort of policeman ran by, a Naples cop, with a revolver in one hand. Barb broke into a run herself, never mind the last-moment swipe by the NATO trooper, so rough that it clawed the bra strap off one shoulder and briefly recalled the pummeling she'd taken from Maria Elena. She knew the trooper couldn't leave his post. Anyway there was John Junior yelling behind her, and Chris and the girls too, a handful for any soldier. It took a moment to recognize the heat where the man had pawed her, the bruising. And if Paul went down, who would be her healer? Who would be his, who? Not Barbara, certainly—not this mother with her eyes on the stars, or on the Good Samaritan, or on another Hail Mary Full of Crap—with her eyes forever on anything but her own stuttering balsa-wood boy.

Her lungs grew hot too, as she raced alongside racing policemen, three or four uniforms and plainclothes making it clear that she'd been right about where the shots came from. Though she remained a stranger here; the cops believed she was one of them. In their boot-falls she kept hearing a pattern, onetwo-threefourfive.

Then Barb and the others were into some backstage area, a space for deliveries. Her eye was drawn first to the sunlight, the loading dock and its half-open rollaway door. Only after that, within the brightness, did she see the body. Face down, knees up, a man's body. She'd visited enough Catholic charity homes to know at first sight. This was a full-grown man, no preteen.

The guy's arms were spread wide across the dock's concrete floor, stretched out unbent towards the street. With his knees beneath him and his head towards the sulfur-scented glare he looked like a worshipper before an urban sun-god, the Sacred Light in the Alley. Prostrating himself, salaam. Barbara didn't see his gun, either. He'd been carrying a gun, Kahlberg, him with his Botticelli hair, ruffling now in the traffic winds through the door's partial opening. She had to look for the thing, the iron handful, and when she found it the pistol looked harmless enough, though it lay well within reach, just beyond one unmoving arm. Its skid across the dock floor had been halted by the spill from his open bag, the loose papers. Also Barbara lost a few shredded seconds frowning over the liaison's clothes, their uncharacteristic sloppy fit, bunching along the shoulders and around the shoulder strap. The wrinkles poked up, snowdrifts, almost, out of a widening bloodstain. It appeared that all five shots had hit the Lieutenant Major between chest and groin. Barbara detected no movement across the upper body, there where the heart and lungs are, no stirring out of the man at all except for the occasional ruffle of his hair. That hair again, the limit of the mother's ability to think. Otherwise the kneeling remains, the wrinkled bleeding spill for whom prayer had been the last negotiation, only left her low and sorry and afraid. Her shoulder and breast burned, burned and ached, and Barbara couldn't come any closer to the man but couldn't back away either. Some unknown cop had to touch her before she turned and saw Paul.

The boy stood in a corner, in the arms of a policewoman. His narrow shoulders quivering, his head was cradled in the woman's chest. Again, in a woman's chest.

The cop knew enough to keep him turned from the corpse. Over the top of the boy's small head, over the half-combed hair, there ran a blue scarf thickly knotted at the back. A blindfold? Barbara couldn't handle the question. She couldn't say how long it took to move his way. At last she got a hand on Paul and realized that his shoulders were shaking because he was crying, only crying, and he had no injury, no further abuse, he was all right—and Mother of God, the *sunshine* under that delivery door! The *racket* of cars and trucks beyond!

There was a racket in here, too, someone shouting. "*Dottore! Un dottore!*" The mother, in so far as she could think at all, could only think this was a fantasy. The word had to come straight out of her celebrating unconscious. Yes, the *dottore* was in. The doctor, healer, *miracolino*.

"*Un dottore! Signora*—you, please."

Barb lifted her other hand, the one with the rosary round it. The beads seemed to hoist her right mind into place too; she knew where she was and what she heard. But to find out who was shouting, that had to wait, yet. First she had to pull her boy out of the policewoman's embrace and into her own. She had to plant a kiss on his forehead, over the blindfold, and give the cop a calming word or two.

"*Hanno 'mazzatto! Hanno 'maz-zaa'!*"

Now that phrase got her attention, no matter who was doing the shouting,. *They've murdered him*—Barbara couldn't help but give that some thought. They, not she. Not Romy. Taking care that Mr. Paul saw nothing of the carnage on the loading dock, the mother tried to size up the scene more sensibly.

"Signora Lulucita!"

The speaker was Umberto. Wounded, weakened, the museum guide scuttled out of an unlit corner on his bony knees. "You, please, you see the *tenente*. They have killed him. I am—I must have a doctor."

Whoever this guy was, he didn't look like a useful witness. He cradled one arm, a mess, the elbow shattered and pumping blood. Then as Barbara's eyes adjusted, she realized the elbow was his only wound. Umberto's head was fine.

"Signora, please. You see, yes? You understand, yes?"

No, she didn't. The man's head didn't have a scratch. Then what was that story about getting hit, and the blood on his blazer? What—Silky's last Shuck'n'Jive?

Chapter Eight

Barbara began to have doubts as soon as she met Mrs. Roebuck, Attaché to the American Consulate and the family's unasked-for "new liaison to the overseas community." The introduction took place hardly twenty-five hours after the mother had stumbled onto Silky Kahlberg's final salaam. Fast work, and either NATO or the Consulate set limits on the police investigation as well. After the city cops had finished their first round of questions, at the loading dock and in the gift shop, they hadn't been allowed anywhere near the Lulucitas. Nor was there media access. A work crew set up sawhorses around the stoop of the Vomero palazzo, and the Attaché rushed out faxes and e-mails. The American citizen volunteers would have no statement for the press until they'd had a chance to review their rights and obligations with representatives of American authority. The very next afternoon, Barbara and Jay were whisked up to the third floor of the Consulate, a cube of sober granite from the turn of the previous century. And five minutes into the conversation, the mother began to think she could no more trust this woman Roebuck than she had the Lieutenant Major. It made no difference that the Consular official had put together a very different look from that of the NATO PR man. A woman of about sixty, without military rank, Roebuck welcomed them to her office in a skirt-suit of wintry and unremarkable gray. Nevertheless, before the three of them had worked through the small talk, Barbara found herself reaching for her husband, pinching the waistband of his underwear through his shirt.

"And the boy?" the Attaché asked. "Paul? How's he holding up?"

The Jaybird allowed himself a word or two, around a glance at Barb.

"You know," Roebuck said, "it's a blessing he was blindfolded."

Barbara's touch remained out of sight, since the three of them were still on their feet and Jay had worn a jacket. She kept her knuckles at her husband's hip a moment longer. This woman with the Consulate proved unsettling, for starters, in how powerfully she suggested the Alpha Moms of greater Catholic metro New York. Women like this had come strutting across her path from time to time, for instance when the kids kept Barbara waiting in the Holy Name parking lot. But even the Alphas with names like Deltino or Sorrenillo offered her little more than a smile of strictly molded corporate plastic. They had two-children homes and husbands in banking or law.

Here in the Consulate over the waterfront, meanwhile, Mrs. Roebuck was saying she'd found time to consult with Dr. DiPio. The old *medico* had stressed how good it was ("a blessing, honestly") that Paul hadn't actually witnessed the murder. "A boy that age," the Attaché went on. "Well. He's had a difficult time of it already. If he's exposed to some sort of major trauma . . ."

"He's all right," Barbara said. "Cesare's talking with him. My priest."

"But no counseling, have I got that right? You've requested there be no . . ."

"There's my Mom," Jay said. "You know she flew in yesterday."

When Roebuck nodded, Barb caught sight of her own reflection, upside-down in the older woman's bifocals. She must've seemed topsy-turvy to the Alpha Moms as well. She must've looked as if she ran a baby factory. Then there was her husband, practically coming home with grease under his nails, working with food and trucks and warehouse dollies. Their family had no diplomas on the wall. One grandmother was a runaway and the other might as well have been, she was such a scandal.

Roebuck was asking about the other children.

"They're all fine," Barbara said. "They have the priest, the doctor. And like Jay's saying, now there's his mother."

"I guess they're kind of worried about this meeting," Jay said. "The kids."

Barb's reflection disappeared as the older woman turned to the husband.

"Roebuck, you've got to admit this is pretty quick. Everybody's still reeling."

"Well. Reeling. Certainly we intend to help."

Certainly the woman's office felt a world away from the kinds of places where Silky had done most of his talking, or double-talking.

No guns, no dust. Someone had arranged the chairs so that, now as they all took a seat, they shared the same semi-oval around a low glass table. The Attaché would do without her desk, executive-weight, set up before an office window that wrapped around its corner. The segmented turret of thick glass showed 180 degrees of the Bay and the islands, but Barbara turned her back. She'd agreed to come, to give this a chance. Across the knee-high table she faced an empty fourth chair, and before it a laptop computer, so sleek it must've been designed by an Italian. The keyboard unfolded like a pair of hands in a linked gesture.

Jay ignored the hardware, still eyeing the woman who'd invited them downtown. He reiterated that yesterday's uproar had left the family shaken.

"Certainly," Roebuck said. "That's why, well. A meeting seems called for. Now if you'll just be patient a moment . . ."

There was a knock, but the man came in without being invited. He wore a suit as unseasonable as the Attaché's, a three-piece. His Arabian nose and skin, the color of the walls of dell'Ovo, set Barbara staring. She knew this guy—the representative from the UN, the one who'd shared the ride to the Vomero the night after the attack on Jay. The one who'd handed out the Earthquake I.D. This Roebuck woman had the same friends as the late Officer Kahlberg, and Barbara had to wonder if today were another cranking haul back up to the peak at the start of the roller-coaster.

She missed the introductions, but Roebuck kept smiling. "I believe you'll like," she said, "what this fellow's brought for you."

Heard that before, too, and Barbara believed she knew what the UN man had in his hand, a clutch of blue-backed papers. He wasted no time about it, anyway, wordlessly dropping the passports onto the glass oval before them. Fresh and glossy passports, midnight indigo, they seemed of a piece with the shapely computer.

"There," declared the Consulate woman. "Isn't that a piece of better news."

Barb had come downtown with some idea of what to expect— she and Jay had talked—but neither of them had thought of this. Bending over the skinny blue booklets, she lingered over the kids'. Those were the faces she remembered, yes. They refused to budge under the lamination no matter how often she ran her fingers over the photo. In time Barbara fanned them out before her, a poker hand she needed to think about.

"It can be an emotional moment," Roebuck was saying, more quietly. "For an American, certainly. Emotional."

Jay's chin was in his chest. Wetly he caught his breath, trembling, squeaking. Barbara blinked up at the big man, slow about it, her mind's eye full of passport photos. Jay was supposed to the one with self-control. He'd worked out a strategy five minutes after the call from the Consulate. Barb touched the man's hip again, his hefty and shuddering trunk.

"Then there's Silky," Jay croaked. "Hey. Never. Never so close like that."

Barb took her hand off him.

"Never had it happen to anyone so close. Never anything like *that*. Jesus. All I ever did was sell pasta."

Barbara wondered if her husband would've broken down like this before his mother had arrived. "Sorry," he snuffled, "I'm sorry." The rep from UN tugged at the tops of his vest, his British disdain showing as clearly it had that first night. Roebuck, though she kept a hand on her laptop, looked a bit dewy.

"I feel your pain," the woman said.

"Oh, give me a *break*." Her Jaybird was sitting there crying, and the rep had his lip curled. "Officer Roebuck, officer or whatever you are. Give me a goddamn break. What do you know about pain?"

Jay shifted her way, his fingers starting at her ribcage.

"I'm saying, the pain Jay and I have to deal with, what do you know about it?" Around the Alpha Moms, Barbara had never allowed herself an outburst like this. "You and this messenger boy here, both." She faced the UN man, giving him sneer for sneer.

"I'll tell you what you two know about," she went on, "you know about *Silky and Jay*. I wouldn't be surprised if you were the guys who signed off on the arrangement." She leaned away from her husband, another grownup who hadn't bothered to control himself. "You put us in danger, you put my kids in danger."

"Mrs. Lulucita." Roebuck stabbed at the keyboard. "Really, well. Where do I begin? Do I even dignify your allegations with—"

"Allegations? I know everything."

"Barbara." Jay was sober again. "We talked about this."

"What we talked about was, no more secrets. No more lying." The machinery of Barbara's anger included a ticking clock: hardly twenty-five hours since the shooting. "With your mother standing there, we said, no more."

Jay scrubbed his face and looked to Roebuck. "Barbara knows everything," he said. "Whatever arrangement we make today, I mean. Got to be on a different basis."

The rep was sitting at attention, his eyes on the wall. The Consulate woman tapped the keyboard. You noticed her nails, a sticky red, surprisingly flashy. "You must understand," she said finally. "No one on our end expected anything like this."

Why shouldn't Barbara grin at that? Why shouldn't she feel proud of her counterespionage?

"No one expected gunplay and a media circus. Certainly."

In fact, since yesterday people like Roebuck had been getting more attention than the family. Naturally a knot of media types had continued to come and go under Barb's and Jay's Vomero balcony, even with the sawhorses in place. But the press wasn't wasting time trying to turn up a murderer among the Lulucitas. The mother had managed only a distracted sampling of the TV and the morning paper, distracted and second-hand, but she could understand that much. The press was looking elsewhere, for the dishy angle. They were far more interested in *Tenente* Kahlberg and whatever he'd had going.

"Honestly," the Attaché was saying. "In every other instance I can think of, when one of our people was asked to gather information, well."

But when it came to the late Lieutenant Major, Barbara knew more than any of the talking heads on Berlusconi's news shows. She knew more than anyone writing for the *Mattino* as well. Now why shouldn't she grin about that?

"They gathered information, thank you. Thank you, and goodbye."

Basking a bit seemed a much better use for Barbara's energy than shouting at these two bureaucrats. She recalled the way JJ and Romy used to strut and preen, after a kiss and a cuddle. Why shouldn't Barbara enjoy a little of that, and take hold of her husband's hand while she was at it? She and the Jaybird twined their fingers so easily, you would think the two of them did it in front of strangers every day.

Roebuck never stopped talking . . . *heightened potential for terrorist activity . . . American interests have a right* . . . "But you do realize, both of you, that our country has a considerable presence in Naples? A considerable strategic stake, yes indeed. So you mustn't think that everyone in NATO, the Consulate and the UN relief agencies, are tarred by the same brush as our late colleague in Public Relations."

When Jay squeezed Barbara's hand, it wasn't about romance. Rather he had a question: are you hearing what I'm hearing?

"Myself," the Attaché went on, "well, I knew Louis Kahlberg. Certainly. And I knew that some people thought very highly of him. Some people thought of him as one of the rising stars in our community. But what we do—" she waved her nails at the suit from the UN—"and what he did, it's entirely separate. Two very different operations."

Jay's squeeze was sign language: These people are frightened. When Barbara met the older woman's eyes, again she found her own reflection, and at this angle she looked, in fact, like an owl. A carnivore, Barb recalled, a bird of prey.

"So," she said, "you knew old *Silky*."

"I did." Tap, tap. "I did, and I don't mind admitting that I liked the man. I felt as though he spoke my language."

Jay had changed the sign: Stay cool, honey.

"But Mrs. Lulucita, do calm yourself. You mustn't go seeing wrack and ruin everywhere. That's the reason we invited you here today, or one of them. We wanted to reassure you, we are your Consulate, your countrymen. We're not the Camorra."

Jay gave it moment. "And on our side, Roebuck, I mean. Let's put it this way. Barb and me, we're not about to join the Shell of the Hermit Crab."

Roebuck dismissed the idea with an Italian gesture, waggling thumb and index finger. "We never had you two under surveillance, certainly." She went on to promise that the murder would get a thorough investigation. "You have my word, you two. Full cooperation, absolutely, between this community and the local authorities."

"Okay." The husband gave a dismissive wave himself, letting go of Barbara. "One time or another, we all saw Silky with his gun out. A guy like that, we all saw it coming. Sooner or later, you're talking the last scene in *Scarface*."

The Attaché worked up a regretful smile. Barbara tried not to grind her back teeth.

"But that's in the past," Jay said. "That's, we're all to blame, there. Whatever. But the problem now isn't that Silky was dirty. That's not what Barb and I need to know now." As if he did it all the time, he retook his wife's hand. "What we need to know is, what was the man into?"

This, she'd been expecting. "That's what we need to know," Barbara said. "Why did someone have to shoot him?"

"Why, hey? What kind of mess was he into?"

The way the Attaché picked at the lip of her keyboard, with a sound like trying to strike a wet match, made it plain that the woman had some degree of discretion, in this office anyway. Here Roebuck had room to improvise.

"We don't think you're the Mafia," her husband said.

"Certainly."

"We don't think it was Romy either," Barb said. "Romy couldn't kill anyone."

"Well I wish I shared your confidence, Mrs. Lulucita." Roebuck found it a relief to be talking about someone other than her former colleague in Public Relations. "You have to admit it doesn't look good for the girl. She did flee the scene."

"But, wouldn't you? Wouldn't you, with bullets flying?"

Jay let go of her again, instead signaling out of the corner of his eye. Go, Owl.

"Since when does that make her a criminal mastermind," Barbara went on, "fleeing the scene?"

"Well, a criminal mastermind . . ."

"Roebuck, we don't even know if she was on that loading dock."

Jay nodded with his entire upper body. "Barb's right. Hey, our Paul, he got that girl out of that wheelchair. The last thing she'd want is to put him in harm's way."

The way Roebuck shook her head was just the opposite, restrained, a ticking. "I can't see why you two are so quick to defend the girl. You especially, Mrs. Lulucita. The way she feels about John Junior, I would think you'd find it a threat."

"But that's what I'm saying. That's what Jay and I both are saying. With John Junior in her life, the last thing the girl would do is pick up a gun."

"There's an eyewitness who puts her at the scene."

"Eyewitness." Barbara gave her the same sour face she'd used on the liaison man. "That Umberto, or whatever his name is. Roebuck, you talk about the Camorra—even before I left the loading dock, the guy admitted he was a crook."

"Well. I can't say what was in his statement to the police, Mrs. Lulucita. But I believe all he told you was, he wasn't on the staff of the Nazionale."

"Hey. Okay. Say the girl was on the dock. Say we trust this guy, impersonating a security guard and carrying an unregistered handgun. Okay. But, I mean. Romy would've known what would happen next. The cops would come after the gypsy."

"And they'd be doing their job. The girl has known criminal associates."

"Mary, Mother of God! You people are just full of things we already know. You're saying, Silky bent the rules and Romy used to turn a trick or two? Is that what you brought us down here to tell us?"

"What I'm trying to tell you," Roebuck said, "is that at this point, your great friend Romy is as much of an unknown as the late Lieutenant Major."

"Unknown?" Jay leaned the woman's way again, a move that put the two of them practically nose to nose. "He's an unknown, Silky? No way, Roebuck. No way, not to you people. You and this cigar-store Indian here. You know what old Silky was into."

The Attaché didn't shrink, squaresville. Barb recalled that Kahlberg, on the other hand, always had another move. He'd been all dart and flutter.

"You know," Jay went on, "the way we used to do it at Viccieco and Sons, we used to share what we had." The man had resigned as Vice President of Sales, in charge of New York and New England. "The way it worked, in order to get something, we would give up something. Sound good to you?"

"In principle, Mr. Lulucita. Though I'd prefer to keep the tenor of this—"

"In principle, exactly. You'd prefer, you'd prefer to deal. Better that than a lawsuit." Jay's gestures kept everyone else back from the table. "I mean, that's your worst case, right? You hauled us in here before they've even finished mopping up the bloodstains because, worst case, Barb and I would call a lawyer."

The UN rep appeared to have lost his disdain, one eye narrowing. "Hey. Barb and I and the kids, that's an innocent family, there."

The mother wanted to follow up, to agree, but she was too tight in the chest.

"Well," Roebuck said. "No one in this office put your children in harm's way."

"Yeah. Okay. But it looks bad anyway, Roebuck. Looks like a mess."

Five minutes after the Consulate had called, yesterday evening, the man had worked out a strategy. He'd asked Barbara out onto the balcony, and she'd asked Aurora to keep the kids inside—maybe the one time Barb had managed to look her mother-in-law in the eye. Out there above the cameras, husband and wife had shared a bottle of pale Italian beer. At a couple of the Jaybird's suggestions, she'd actually broken into a grin and raised a toast.

Upstairs in the Consulate, today, he kept on. "But, I mean. You people wouldn't bring us all the way down here just to beg. You know, to beg? 'Please, you guys, please don't make a bad thing worse.'"

"Mr. Lulucita, really. No one in this office has it in mind to beg."

"Sure. Nobody wants that. Barb and me, coming down here, we didn't want that. What we wanted to hear was, what've you got for us? I mean. There's got to be something else on the table. Hey? Something in return for our cooperation."

The Attaché showed the suit beside her an unsubtle look, something else you'd never see from Officer Kahlberg.

"Think about it. What we offer, Barb and me, our family." Jay spoke more slowly. "It's not just, you don't want us to hurt you. It's also how we can help you. Think about the way this family can *represent*."

Roebuck turned back to her laptop, some sort of decision obvious in how she gathered her fingers over the keyboard. Barbara waited out the black thought of slamming the screen down on the woman's knuckles.

"And all we ask, hey. It's got to be on a different basis, this time."

"Tell me something," Roebuck said. "Have you two seen your web site?"

Now there was a bit of Silky, sleight of hand, and they had to wait a moment or two while the wireless hookup came on. But Barbara's husband, the Cool-bird, shifted his weight so smoothly that the leather beneath him didn't creak.

"I suppose you have," Roebuck went on. "It sounds like you've thought this through pretty thoroughly."

The laptop screen, its back to Barbara, spilled colors over Roebuck's hand. You would've thought the woman had pulled a curtain back from a stained-glass window. Then the machine turned out to sit on a Lazy Susan swivel, wouldn't you know it. When the Attaché spun the thing around, the display appeared to be all saints and angels.

"I'm sure you already realize," Roebuck said, "what people make of this family."

Saints and angels, that's what. Across the small screen sprawled a radiant media collage with the Lulucitas at its center. Around a colorized newspaper photo of parents and children, themselves arranged around a twice-his-size Paul, there spiraled scanned-in headlines and smaller photos, plus catch-phrases and clip-art taken out of other web toolboxes. There were even a few words in a vaguely Cyrillic lettering.

Barb had never taken a good look at the site before. At most she'd had a glance at this home page, their "internet presence." Of course Chris and JJ got on the site a couple of times a day, and they visited all the links to which Roebuck was now taking Barbara and Jay. But whenever her two oldest had called Mama to the computer, either she'd been in no mood to see something that made her marriage look good or she hadn't wanted to find Paul looking any stranger than he did already. This business on the web was only another media *spettacolo*, after all, more of the same circus as beneath her balcony. Today, however, as Roebuck lingered now at this page and now at that, Barbara had to acknowledge that the site's designers came to the circus with a supernatural new menagerie. Even when Barbara spotted an image she recognized, from the papers or TV, it was so altered by electronic surgery as to suggest another animal entirely.

The reconfigurations appeared far trickier than the portraits mounted out at the Refugee Center, the effects the Lieutenant Major had pulled off in the NATO print shop. On every page, to begin with, there snaked a scrap of that Cyrillic-looking font. The lettering called to mind old cartoons, Disney, the sign swinging over the door to the shop of the fortune-teller from Transylvania. The text fit into the screen every which way, an eerie shadow. But then the rest of whatever was on the page, the doctored photographs, were eerie to begin with. In one, their middle child had been enlarged and given a full-body halo. That much was a no-brainer, an obvious touch, but the divine aura had been rendered so brightly that Mom and Pop and the siblings were reduced to ghosts by comparison. Also the heads and shoulders of the rest of the family, against the lower curves of the Paul's overheated corona, had been sculpted so that they composed the local skyline. Barbara herself served as Vesuvius, her head jammed into her chest, further down than any owl's. Nor was this page the strangest, the most baroque.

Another portrayed Paul with one hand up in the Pope's two-finger wave, while a wild range of photo-images and cartoon figures knelt around him in prayer. Barb couldn't tell if the assorted worshippers had been derived from pictures of the family or not. She saw a satanic Mafioso with horns, a tail, a black suit, and a sawed-off shotgun (an accessorized Jaybird, perhaps?); a woman in a skirt suit much tighter and shorter than Roebuck's, her stockings showing garters (could this be Barb herself, slimmed down?), her head framed by headphones and a mike; a Brit-looking pair in old-style knickers and caps, possibly Tweedledum and Tweedledee, except these two would turn and exchange a deep kiss every few seconds (God knows who the designer had in mind); a big decaying leper or zombie (maybe JJ) with a lover's rose between all-but-lipless teeth; a bearded guerilla-scholar (in glasses more or less like Chris's), one arm bent around a camo-colored Uzi and the other around a stack of books; Uncle Sam in his striped top hat and tails (might've been old Aurora, in drag); a pizza cook in an apron (Dora?), her head bent over a pie on a massive oven-spatula; and a mermaid with wings, fluttering just enough to keep herself perched on her coiled fishtail (Sylvia?).

"Quality graphics," declared Roebuck.

A fascinating design, the day after a murder. Jay looked it over with a small, canny smile, the same as he'd shown the family whenever he brought home some new, shelf-ready sauce or entrée. The ingredients on today's box, however, were peppered with local slang. The site had been developed in Naples. Also most pages again called to mind the Nativity scenes, the *presepi*, sold on the nearby saint-streets. The Christmas-morning figurines might be sculpted in three dimensions, out of old-fashioned terra-cotta, but they too were sometimes adapted from the news. Come to think of it, statuettes of the American *miracolino*, adapted for a crèche, might already be on sale in the city. For years now Italian politicians had provided the face for the Good Shepherd or the malignant Herod. The dark-skinned refugees from across the Mediterranean had become shepherds, or gypsies.

And on the web the most pervasive foreign touch was that Cyrillic weirdness. Barbara bent closer to the screen, narrowing her eyes.

As for Jay, he wouldn't be put off. Raising his eyes, he reiterated how the family could "represent," gesturing at the busy screen. Then he brought up the cost.

"When you think of what the taxpayers spend on foreign aid, I mean. And then you see all this goodwill, here." He gestured at the laptop again, his hand brushing Barbara's lowered head. "Goodwill towards Americans, for once. All over the worldwide web. Think what that's worth."

Hard to believe this was the same man who'd burst into tears over getting his passport back. Yet yesterday, five minutes after the phone call from the Consulate, he'd taken Barb out on the balcony to explain the quid pro quo. While Jay had talked the sun had finished setting, but the balcony railings still held the heat of midday—and so did Barbara, apparently, so distracted by the rough and tumble at the museum she hadn't realized the opportunity presented by tonight's call. It hadn't even occurred to her that if the Lulucitas stayed in town, that would amount to chocolate and champagne, in terms of public relations. The family offered a ready-for-prime-time validation of the American presence abroad.

And you thought MTV put a sweet deal on the table? the husband had asked her. *Compared to these people, forget about it.*

Out on the balcony, for an air-headed moment, Barbara had believed that the Consulate's offer was the primary consideration in whether or not the family stayed in town. Her former VP of Sales had turned her head around; she'd seen what he was getting at. To see through it, she'd needed another pull of beer. The Jaybird's strategy had another goal, too, much as he might be right about this meeting at the Consulate. The conference with the Attaché, if it went the way the husband wanted, would also keep his wife in place. Barbara saw that too, after another swallow of summer-light Peroni. But she'd gone along with the man nonetheless; she'd told him what he needed to hear. Glancing through the balcony doors into the dining room, checking on Aurora and the girls playing ponies and birds under the table, Barbara had assured her husband that she hardly intended to hop a flight for New York right this minute. She could hardly abandon Paul and the other kids when they'd strayed this close to the line of fire. It wasn't the kids' fault that Aurora had chosen such a moment to breeze into town.

Button-mouthed, slow to take back the beer, Jay had eyed her. He'd revealed something like softness that had overcome him at seeing the passports.

Owl Girl, he'd said finally, *it's your call.*

After that, while he'd roughed up an estimate of how much they might ask for at the Consulate, the husband had sounded clipped, reined in. Nothing like the Jaybird who held forth in Roebuck's office, this afternoon, his voice ringing off the wraparound block glass in the far corner. So far he'd been right about everything except the passports. All business, he laid out "the kind of help my family could use," and fended off Roebuck's objections ("I mean, it's not just about tuition, when a guy like JJ or Chris gets an internship"). Barb was let alone, free to concentrate on the screen. On this page the Cyrillic lettering was wedged above Paul's upraised blessing. The s's were like snakes, the t's like fangs. Most people, seeing that, would think of gypsies.

Yet the language, Barb came to see, was more or less English. *The saint of fire whistles while he burns*, she read, *tu too tu.*

But Roebuck was tapping again, the tabletop this time. "Our organizations can guarantee absolute security," the Attaché said. "Nobody could reach you. That's twenty-four hours a day, seven days a week. Nobody whatsoever."

Oh, another guarantee. Barbara looked back at the black, contorted words. Today, as it happened, was Tuesday, and the meeting had started at two.

"Now you know," Jay said, "we're talking a bigger crew, at home these days. We're talking my mother, too."

"Certainly. Your mother can count on the same protection."

Barbara extended a finger and dragged the cursor to another link.

"Yes, do take a look, Mrs. Lulucita," Roebuck said. "By all means, do. You've been an inspiration to these people."

"Then there's the Center," Jay said. "I don't know what they know, out there . . ."

Every Lulucita link, just as the mother had suspected, carried the same cryptic sentence. The words stretched or fattened in different directions, but there was always the saint of fire and the echoing

Tuesday-you-two. It made Barbara think of the dreams some of her visitors at the Sam Center had described, while she'd worked screening potential clients. Nettie had helped her with more pages from the copy room, guides to interpretation, material she called "Cliff Notes to Jung and Von Franz." In this dream on the Lulucita website, posted to every page, the greatest enigma was the saint. The mother, grinding her teeth again, stuffing pillows over her inner alarms—the mother believed the line referred to an actual figure. She couldn't think who it was, she'd never gotten much past Chiara and Francis and Teresa herself. Still it rang a bell, the saint of fire. And she knew that two in the afternoon was a very American time for a meeting. Neapolitans tended to get together a lot later on, after dark.

"Hey Barb, you with us?" Jay gave her a touch at a rib. "You hear that, what Roebuck's put on the table? 'Sdecent."

Barbara was bent over tightly, her purse digging into her lap.

"Not that anything's written in stone, I mean. Not yet. First we talk to the kids."

The mother nodded closemouthed.

"These are preliminary figures, ballpark. But still. Decent, hey?"

Sitting up, she felt as if she had to pull her entire head out of the splashy rectangle with the secret script. But Barbara could see what Roebuck and her friend had to offer just by once more taking in the Consulate space around her. Those greenhouse windows, that muscular desk. This was a castle keep for an Alpha princess, with round-the-clock security and junior-year internships.

"And we can walk away," Jay went on, "any time we want."

Barbara still felt something at the spot where he'd touched her. "There's a lot we don't know," she said finally. "As soon as we step back out that door, we could end up knocked off our feet."

Jay took this to be his wife's way of bringing the subject back to their late NATO liaison. Vigorously he agreed, glowering at the two bureaucrats. Before he and Barbara presented this latest offer to the kids, Jay insisted, they needed to know precisely what the Lieutenant Major had been into. After a minute Barb began to say the same, spinning the laptop away from her, throwing its colors back in Roebuck's face. Barbara told the woman to skip the euphemisms, the language of diplomacy or PR. "Just tell us about Silky." The mother was aware she was distracting herself, allowing herself to enjoy the way the Jaybird swung his handsome head. But better that than to ask these three what they knew about saints. If what Barb had seen on the website was in fact a message from Romy, well, the Attaché had already made clear what she thought of the gypsy.

Roebuck didn't look too happy now, either. She was taking her nails to her hair, raking back a few loose strands. "You must realize," she was saying, "even if I had all the facts about the officer's case, I couldn't risk compromising the NATO investigation."

"NATO?" Jay asked. "It's a NATO investigation?"

The older woman fussed at her glasses, first a corner and then the bridge.

"In the food business, I mean. When we needed somebody to go over the books, we got someone from the *outside*."

"Mr. Lulucita, I must say. If you believe anyone even remotely affiliated with this office is some sort of criminal, then what are you doing here?"

"Roebuck, hey. You want to know what I believe? I believe that yesterday my son almost stopped a bullet."

"Well. Nobody in this office fired it."

Barbara withdrew once more into code-cracking. She recalled that her own name-saint was no longer on the church calendar, but had once been associated with thunderstorms and artillery. The more disturbing question, though, was what Romy had wanted, today at two. A secret meeting, set up in private code, had to be about more than a hug and a kiss. No sooner had the mother checked out of the squabble in the office than she started to worry. The fresh static between her ears rose up so noisily, at first she didn't notice when Roebuck switched the subject to her marriage.

"Yes, your *marriage*." And when had the Attaché gotten so loud? "I must ask. After all, it's you who insist we lay our cards on the table."

Jay had his head in his hand, and he fingered the spot alongside his ear where the *scippatori* had hit him. "You—you want to know about—"

"We need to know, in this office. Certainly. Your marriage is a critical consideration for any arrangement we make today."

"You've got no right. That's personal."

"We've got every right. The overseas community is a family too."

To Barbara it looked as if the Jaybird had been cracked again. He shrank and avoided both women's eyes, seeming to seek his reflection in the tabletop glass. Roebuck was the one angling forward now. She declared that, after the way Jay and Barb had marched in here making demands, the least could expect was a personal question or two. But the Attaché didn't aggravate Barbara like the man from the UN. He'd tightened up his hauteur, his mouth shrinking into a satisfied nub.

"Now there are rumors," Roebuck went on. "Disturbing rumors."

"What," Barbara said, or growled, "in the *streets*?"

"In the streets, precisely. We have our contacts."

The best Jay could manage was shaking his head.

"We have every right," the Attaché said, "to maintain an active network of contacts. Our interests here in Naples have a direct bearing on security at home."

"And you're saying, everybody's been talking about our marriage."

"We're saying that it seems you two intend to divorce. There's talk of you whispering, well. Whispering vicious things, in places less private than you supposed."

"Vicious? Vicious, like—'Jay, *fuck*! Our fucking children might get *shot*!'"

"Mrs. Lulucita. We're not impressed by gutter talk, in this office. Especially when it comes from a woman who needs to spend a half an hour every day with a priest."

Barbara tugged at an armpit. "So what does that prove? A priest should be the least you'd expect, with what I've had to deal with."

"Perhaps. But then why should you husband have to sneak off to confession too? And why should that come as a complete surprise to you?"

Barb raised the other arm too, crossing them tightly, elbows up.

"Your first week in the city," Roebuck went on, "you inquired about a solo plane ticket back to New York."

Jay glanced up. "What?"

"Yes. A solo booking. So, then. What do you have to say, you two? Is this the end, for the family?"

The UN rep hoisted his long nose. "Is it the end?" he asked.

The husband collapsed again while these strangers teetered closer. Barbara looked elsewhere, first at the smooth gray shoulders of the laptop's shell, concealing the rococo excess on the screen, and then away towards wraparound void of the office window. Both that and the little machine on the table could've been fragments of a single vast and multifaceted eye, a cosmopolitan organ that missed nothing. Which made them also—could've been—props for another reiteration of Barbara's change-of-life first encounter with the city. This afternoon again presented the familiar moment: her big man going down amid a throng of gossips, observers who been listening in on other people's conversations for three thousand years.

"It's not true," Barbara said.

Around her the leather got noisy. People turned whole-body, their feet shifting.

"It's not true," she repeated. "There's no divorce. Jay and I, we're still good."

Roebuck brought her nails together under her chin, unexpectedly rabbitty.

"Mrs. Lulucita, well. Our contacts are claiming you're the one who—"

"I know, I know." Barbara's chair was noisy too, given her effort to think. "I've been pretty crabby, a couple of times. Vicious, okay, maybe. It's embarrassing to admit it, but I guess I'm saying, I know what these people talking about."

She worked up the right sort of smile, Oprah-sweet. There had to be evidence behind the rumors, and Barbara hadn't spent this long dealing with children and their suppositions without learning to put evidence in different light. In this case the light she needed was right outside, the hot and aggravating sun, almost at solstice intensity. She had the vocabulary, too, the way to put her explanation across, thanks to her work at the Sam Center.

"Jay can validate these feelings. He'd be the first to acknowledge, a lot of stress."

Though she couldn't look at her Jaybird just yet. The mechanical box of colors on the table (for Roebuck, on edge, trying to take this in, had spun the laptop back Barbara's way) was likewise too much. City Baroque. The wife found what she needed, rather, among the diplomas on Roebuck's walls. The neutral squares of sun-glazed glass allowed her patter to continue. Still it wasn't until her husband began to speak, coming in with firm and canny support—"Hey, I mean, *stress*? Let me tell you. . . " (support talky and taking up space, allowing

Barb to breathe *Mother of God* in gratitude)—it wasn't until the wife heard him back up her desperate play that she could so much as take his hand. Even after that Barbara kept avoiding his eyes, sensing only via the pressure on fingers and palm how the man regained conversational momentum. Her gaze remained elsewhere. She frowned again at the family website, its black could-be love-letter.

"Roebuck," Jay asked, "you married?"

The husband regained full momentum . . . *'sbeen a pressure-cooker . . . we've all gone a little crazy . . . living in the volcano with no place to vent.* A minute or two of this and Jay actually had Roebuck following his lead.

"Certainly," the Alpha Wife said, "my husband and I have our days. I can think of moments when it's as if I've just met my husband for the first time."

Barbara could let her husband have the floor again, him and the other executive, while she herself put in only the occasional nod or phrase: "Aurora's no problem, no." With her free hand, the one not gripping Jay's, she could first take time for an underwire that bit her ribs and then probe the outside of her purse until she found the nubbled shape of her rosary. Prayer would feel good, even silent prayer, punctuating her uncertainty with the names of God. It would feel as if she had a handle on what she'd just done, her screeching one-eighty. Beneath her fingers, however, Barbara's purse-leather remained silent, no match for the squeaking chairs around her, nor even the muffled thrum and bleat of day-traffic out along the Bayfront. She didn't have a handle. It was as if she'd stumbled on herself in this position, back to front and facing a new landscape. Just now the only motives she dared to identify for denying the trouble in her marriage were low ones, like anger or a general contrariness. As for the possibility that she'd actually told these people what she felt—that she remained committed to this man— no way she could think about that. She needed to tie it up in four or five decades of her rosary before she approached it. But her lower motives, her desire to smack down a woman like Roebuck, that Barbara could understand. Even on the far side of the Atlantic, she couldn't allow the Attaché any further advantage.

But what was "advantage" here? Barbara's announcement meant that Roebuck and her friends would get what they wanted, a PR windfall. And what would the mother and her family get? On the glass tabletop the five passports remained fanned out like a poker hand. What, did Barbara want to gamble? Stay in town?

And now Jay too had started to flag, no longer sounding so game and chummy. He'd lost enough steam for Barb to notice, at least. The more his off-again, on-again wife avoided looking him in the eye, the more his rally faltered. He never let go of Barbara's hand.

"So," he said, fumbling for another line of talk. "So . . ."

The Attaché was adjusting her jacket. Barb didn't like to see her touch her lapel.

"Well," Roebuck said. "I believe that's everything."

"Everything . . ." Jay ran a thumb over Barbara's knuckle.

"Certainly you'll need to speak with your children. There's no one in this office who would object to that."

Jay's thumb was tentative, never completing a circle.

"No," said Barbara. "No way we're finished here yet."

The two across the table gave her such a frown that she could compare eyes, Roebuck's round Anglo periwinkle to the other guy's leaf-shaped Arabian chocolate. After a few seconds of that, facing her husband came easy.

"There's still Silky," she reminded the Jaybird. "We're not leaving here until we know what was up with that guy."

Her husband the Jaybird. Nobody but Barbara would've seen the fresh energy coming into his looks. But Roebuck noticed soon enough, the way he followed up Barbara's lead, letting go of her to lend his attack body English. He lay his stubby hand across the spread passports, vowing that before he and his wife went to the children with today's offer, they would know everything they needed to know about the late Lieutenant Major. Jay had Attaché dropping her head, studying her nails. For a while the longest response she managed was a couple of frustrated words: *You two*.

"Roebuck. I mean. All Barb and I know is, his killer's still out there."

"Well, surely you realize that with an investigation in progress—"

"Sure sure, police procedure. Hey. Roebuck. You *are* the police."

The UN man crossed his legs the other way, a body-language harrumph.

"You are the police," Barbara said. "You make the rules."

"That NATO investigation, I mean. It's right here with us. It's in the computer."

"You two." The Attaché spun the laptop. "Our organizations are under no obligation to tell you anything."

Barbara put out a hand, stopping the machine in mid-spin. "Mother of God, you were spying on us."

"Majorly spying, Roebuck. You might as well've had someone on the balcony."

"I'm sorry you feel that way. It was your security at stake, may I remind you."

"My security? Mine and Barb's and the kids? If that's the case, hey. How come you can't tell me anything except how my sex life is going?"

"Well. We've turned up nothing that indicates your family would be a target."

"Oh, so you *can* tell us something about your investigation?"

Nobody but Barbara would notice the born-again feistiness in her husband's face, in the corners of his mouth and his upraised brows.

"Jay's right," she said. "You called this meeting, you wanted our help. So if you'd thought it would cinch the deal, you'd've told us about Silky already."

"Barb's right. You'd've told us whatever it took."

"You always had that card to play. That's all we're saying."

The Attaché had shrunk back as far as her chair would allow. She shared another look with the UN rep and then set off on a tour of her outfit's accessories, touching glasses and brooch and watchband. Barbara, watching, bit her tongue. When Roebuck let out a long exhale, to Barb it sounded like her Jaybird's cry after he'd gotten hit.

"You two. One would think you'd been married to the man."

"No," said Barbara. "You still don't get it. Wrong connection. It's that Silky could've been one of our kids."

"Well." The woman gave a tiny shrug, nothing Italian. "The evidence thus far points clearly towards trafficking in false documentation. False papers."

The UN rep looked more disapproving than ever.

"Earthquake I.D.," Jay said.

"Counterfeit, yes. Certainly there's a market."

Barbara found herself imagining that it was she who'd left the Arab so disappointed. She'd let this man down, and a lot of other people too, because she should have guessed this weeks ago.

"The evidence appears pretty convincing," the Attaché went on. Kahlberg appeared to have gotten hold of a template for the new documents of identification.

"He did it himself," Barbara put in, loud and exasperated. "He did it himself, he ran the things off in the print shop. How could we not have *guessed*?"

"Well, it's not that simple, Mrs. Lulucita."

"Jay, you remember, he even bragged about it. He told us, the public relations officer has access to the facilities for—"

"It's not that simple. These are official documentation, watermarked and notarized. You can't simply run them off."

Barbara heard Jay sighing, struggling the same as she, unable to fathom how he'd failed to notice the giveaways. His wife had told him often enough about the Lieutenant Major's sheaf of "authorizations," coming out of his bag each time the family arrived at another tourist site. The Attaché meantime acknowledged that, "in keeping with his position," Kahlberg had already been issued a notary stamp. The template for the new I.D., in the same way, would've been a simple enough business for an officer who wore two hats, or was it five? "All he needed was a single key and a four-digit combination." The Lieutenant Major could pick up the template when he needed, and no one in the Organization would be the wiser.

"But the stock, the paper," Roebuck went on, "well. That was another matter. It wasn't as if the man could simply open a cabinet, thank you and goodbye. All the investigation has turned up so far is, the officer somehow got his hands on something like a ream. With that, he could run off the counterfeits as they were needed."

"You're saying, he didn't keep a stash around?" Barbara kept her tone conversational. "He waited till, till someone asked, and then he printed off—?"

"Well, I'm not 'saying.' We don't have all the facts, Mrs. Lulucita. I can only tell you what the evidence suggests."

Jay raised his chin. "At the museum, he had the bag with him."

"Yes. He'd come prepared to make a deal, it would appear. But as your wife will recall, the papers were left lying on the dock."

Barb remembered: paper that rustled more noisily than the hair on the corpse.

Jay stuck to the subject, pointing out that Kahlberg "always had an angle," and he wouldn't have left home with his entire stash in his bag. "Bag like that, hey. Easy pickings." Instead the liaison man had probably set aside a number of the counterfeits, somewhere safe, all signed and ready to go. "Like guys who keep four or five hundred in the sock drawer."

Roebuck shook her head. "It's not my place to speculate."

"But, I mean. Chances are. There's more of them out there somewhere."

Barbara returned to her recollections of the crooked soldier-boy at work. He'd met his contacts right under her nose, and more often than not, that very evening the mother had told Jay all about it. She'd wondered aloud, in particular, about the men who'd looked over the so-called authorizations. Some of Kahlberg's inspectors had hardly looked official, and she'd never understood why they'd always needed a gunman standing by (in plainclothes, but a gunman, anyone could see). Then yesterday there'd been that Umberto. He hadn't been Silky's buyer, Barb would guess, but rather the middleman, the gofer. Either way, it was one more reason you couldn't trust the "museum guide" as a witness. Besides, the killers hadn't been in the business; they'd ignored Umberto once he was down and they'd left the fake I.D.—for just one of which 500 Euros would be a bargain rate— scattered across the loading dock. All this came to Barbara so quickly, so transparently, here in the Consulate. Here a long way from her bed up in the Vomero, or her walks around the ancient *centro*.

"Now, I must reiterate," Roebuck was saying. "I must make it quite perfectly clear, this man operated on his own. Entirely autonomous."

"Autonomous, hey." Jay broke into a smirk. "I think I like what they call them in the movies, a rogue agent."

"I'm quite serious, Mr. Lulucita. It's as you said, this man always had an angle."

So many angles that Barb began to wish she could get another look at the coded message on the computer screen, now facing away. She thought of Saint Joan of Arc. Joan had died in a fire. But so had a lot of others, and the mother knew what it would look like if she spun the computer and studied the website again. Meanwhile Jay was conceding the Attaché's point—Silky had run a one-man shop. His documents business had nothing to do with NATO, the UN, or the Consulate.

"*Well*. Thank you for saying so at last. And for my part, let me once more offer the sincerest apology, from everyone in our community . . ."

"It's okay, Roebuck. I mean, nobody's perfect. Barb and me, you heard about our ups and downs, here. We're not saints."

Roebuck allowed herself a tepid joke: if the Lulucitas hadn't been saints when they'd arrived in Naples, then dealing with a Tempter like the late Lieutenant Major had made them holy. Certainly.

"Oh, look," Barbara said. "What matters is, whoever Silky's connections were, they won't come after us."

The older woman nodded firmly, bending over the keyboard. As she logged off and shut down, Roebuck assured her visitors that any criminal interest in their family was now "moot." It had died with officer Kahlberg.

"You merely served as the front for the officer. The cover story."

"Not a player, not a target," Jay said. "I hear that. But, while we're talking about safety, I mean, also. Three weeks ago somebody tried to kidnap me."

"Ah, that was a separate matter, Mr. Lulucita." Kahlberg's under-the-table operations had taken place at economic levels far above those of the desperate *clandestini* who'd briefly manhandled Jay.

"But, I mean. Now you offer a guarantee. Everywhere we go, we're safe."

Roebuck gave a small smile, then made a remark about "acts of God." She reminded Barbara and Jay that they lived in a land of earthquakes. "Vesuvius, well. She's listed as an active volcano." Her eyes, even behind bifocals, revealed a sharpening glitter. "But Mr. Lulucita, since you bring this business up, I must add. Your near-kidnapping would seem to have justified returning at once to New York. Three weeks ago, just as you say. You had a tailor-made excuse for breaking your contract, and yet you remained in Naples. You and your wife both."

Barbara didn't realize she was reaching for her husband, for the elastic under his shirt, till her fingers touched his waistline.

"You come in here," the Attaché said, "and you question *our* motives."

To see Roebuck lash back was a help, actually. Barbara left off fretting about Romy and JJ, keeping her hand at the Jaybird's hip while he ignored the other woman's implication, once more bringing up yesterday's murder. "That investigation of yours, I mean. You've still got a lot of holes."

"Certainly. We've got a thousand questions."

"And as for the girl, Romy. I'm with Barb on her." The man was still full of beans. He mentioned that DiPio had given the gypsy a clean bill of health.

"Jay," Barbara said.

"But Silky, I mean. Anybody know anything about his sex life? Something for the autopsy, you ask me."

He'd even broken into a grin. But when faced his wife, she could see the playfulness drain from him. He fell silent, staring, until the woman across the table repeated what she'd said about a thousand questions.

Chapter Nine

They had a bigger crew these days, with Jay's mother. They had more on their hands than ever, really. Not that they didn't go through another spell of cocooning, sticking close to home throughout most of the first four or five days after Mom and Pop came home from downtown. Immediately after the meeting, Jay and Barbara had themselves a long walk along the waterfront, a long walk and a talk, trailed at a crawl by a black sedan with Consular plates. But after that everyone tended to hole up in thir ten rooms above the Vomero, sorting out new responsibilities and shoving around the heavy furniture. The apartment could feel as if the Lulucitas had moved into the van they used to share with Kahlberg. But with that guy out of the picture, and with Roebuck keeping hands off, they were no longer at a tourist's distance, staring one day at a four-poster bed draped in silk brocade, the next at a pair of household gods with oversized clay erections. Rather Barbara and the others got their hands dirty, working with more durable ore, creating a presentation with unmistakable message: This Is A Family. Their renewed commitment played a part in every decision, whether it was Jay accepting a new position at DiPio's downtown clinic or the two girls agreeing to share their room with Grandma.

Aurora would've set herself up in a hotel, ordinarily. A suite was more her style. But the new security team argued that their job would be a good deal easier if the old playgirl stayed home with the others. Then too, when it came to getting constructive—to getting rid of the wheelchair and pulling out the hammer—the primary banger was the grandmother. She loomed at the edge of everything, a brassy laugh in the next room or a painted face over somebody's shoulder. Not that Barbara was talking to her. After the Consulate she gave her mother-in-law a wide berth, or wide as the place allowed. As for the jagged edges inside, Barbara couldn't do anything about those.

First thing, back from the meeting Tuesday at two, she and Jay went to the kids.

But once she'd handed out their passports, and once she'd let them see her resting her hand on her husband's knee, how much more could Barbara reveal? What'd happened down in the Museo Nazionale, the last time she'd try to pull out her internal whipsaw? Anyway, the children had already arrived at the same conclusion as Mom and Pop and Attaché Roebuck. They wanted to stay. JJ and Chris were the first to say so, making arguments the parents had heard before. The oldest boy however kept glancing towards the balcony, where his grandmother was waiting, at Jay's request. Aurora had shut the double-glass door, something else Jay had asked for, and settled into a lounge chair wearing a two-piece with a knotted bra. One look at that and the daughter-in-law understood what her children must've imagined about staying on in Naples. The kids saw this city as Adventureland and MTV, their own version of the Italian Romance. Barb understood, and her anger started banging around her ribcage— but what could she say to her nearly-grown boy? What warning could she give any of these kids about the yearnings of the flesh and their more psychotic manifestations, especially around this corner of the urban world? After all, Barbara herself had just given in to romance. Just like that, she was playing the sappiest makeup ballad in the jukebox.

Eventually JJ and Chris finished their say. They looked to Dora and Syl, and the girls looked to Paul. The older boys too, after a moment: it was all on Paul.

But the middle child agreed. He might've been the one who'd actually gotten burnt, while the others were still poking a finger or two into the fire, but he preferred to stay in Naples. Though the way he put it did sound awfully spooky: "There's, there's so m-much g-g-going on, we, we couldn't get o-out even if we w-w-wanted to."

Jay and Barbara also sat down with the doctor, that first afternoon, but the report on their boy with the healing hands was the same as ever. No abnormalities, no signs of serious dissociation, nothing to indicate he wouldn't benefit from the sort of everyday interaction he seemed to be asking for. The parents found it almost a relief to turn to their new security team, a squad of Italian *carabinieri* and Interpol detectives. The Jaybird's primary concern was that these four men and one woman were all getting a bump in salary for the assignment. "We want guys're on the ball," he said. "None of those farm-boys Silky used." Then there was Barbara's Padre Superiore. The evening after the meeting at the Consulate, Cesare surprised them with a house call. Aurora, wouldn't you know it, was the one who met the priest at the door, Aurora in full evening makeup and Balinese head-scarf. Yet in the days that followed, too, the old Jesuit Dominican would work his slow and angular way down the Vomero staircases. During two of the priest's visits, Jay made confession, in a corner of the kitchen. The husband urged Barbara, as well, to unburden herself to Cesare.

"Get it all out," the husband said. "Get to where you can start over."

To hear the Jaybird talk, once he and his Owl Girl finished their talk among the tethered fishing boats on the waterfront, a quiet talk but to the point, their marital woes were history. Ancient history— that very evening he started referring to their trouble as "the thing." No more than that, and the wife agreed. She did agree. Still Barbara found it necessary to pray, daily, intensely, in the privacy of the utilities closet. She prayed that some middle-aged Mother, some Saint of a certain age, might intercede with her God in order to let her know just what the thing had been about. She begged that she might be shown how keep this thing from afflicting her ever again. Over the rosary she at least enjoyed the blood-rush to an alternative muscle-system, alternative and invisible, and in time she felt strong enough to send another e-mail to Nettie. The following morning, dinnertime in Bridgeport, the two women managed a real-time cyber-chat. Barbara got nothing new out of the exchange, really. Her Sam Center mentor reiterated that it would be best for Paul to stay put while he worked through *this developmental stage*, and she assured the mother that mood swings in the parents were only to be expected. *You might look at the work on marital disorders*, she advised, *in Rudolph or Bloom*.

Nothing new, from her bookworm friend, nothing Barbara felt she should copy to her personal files. Nonetheless the electronic conversation left her feeling better. She made sure to delete the chat (Aurora knew how to check the browser History, of course), but she felt bucked up even by Nettie's mystical sign-off:

Remember, she wrote, *it's always yourself you're meeting out there, day after day. We're always meeting ourselves.*

The woman sounded a bit like Paul, that time. But these days Barbara was seeing messages a lot more troublesome. There was the pseudo-Cyrillic on the website, Number One, and then there was the conversation she overheard outside the door to the girls', while she stood holding the sheets for the room's new, third bed.

"Do we still think," Dora was asking, "Mama and Papa are going to divorce?"

Now what would Nettie say about a mother standing breathless outside her children's door?

"I thought we said we don't, any more," Sylvia said. "No, I want the bird."

"I know what we said. Come on, you know it's not a bird."

"Our family is very good. Like, when Paul does a miracle, that shows Jesus is with the family. It reveals the Word of Jesus."

"Maybe." After a moment, Dora sighed.

"Dor-ra. I know it's not a bird. I know we said it's a singing Siren."

The other remained quiet so long, Barbara gathered herself to walk in. Then: "That was pretty weird, in the museum."

"Yeah." The mother pictured Sylvia frowning, trying out a new complexity. "But, since because Paul wasn't hurt, that just shows like, Jesus is still there—"

"I wasn't talking about Paul. What happened with Paul was an adventure, like in the movies. What I was talking about was Mom."

"Oh, Mom. You mean when she took us in the room."

"Now that was weird."

"That was very weird. It was like hide and seek."

"It was hide and seek and telling stories, but they didn't go anywhere."

There was a rap of plastic on linoleum. "Paul saved us. He got us out of there."

"Right, he did but then since—that means, the people he's saving, it's us. We used to think Mama and Papa were getting a divorce."

"Look. It was weird, but it wasn't that weird."

Barbara cleared her throat, shuffled her slippers, oldest tricks in the book. She walked in and at once began tucking both the linens and "the three girls" back into their more crowded arrangement. A little high-energy group activity, as they called it around the Connecticut Children's Services. Anyway, even CCS couldn't say for certain whether it was best if Mama talked with the girls about what she'd heard. The guidelines for good parenting were full of that word "boundaries." Barbara wound up letting Dora and Syl work out their own solutions, in this case. Herself, she heard something else, in the conversation. She realized that if the twins had been talking about divorce, they would've been overheard. Even Kahlberg's drivers had spoken enough English to understand that. Then there'd been the boys, a lot louder than the girls.

Talk in the streets. That night, in bed, Barbara shared her conclusions with the Jaybird, a born-again wife whispering with her recuperating husband. *I'm saying, they got it off the kid-wide-web.*

Such was the soundtrack by which Barbara pledged allegiance to her renewed commitment: whispers in bed, the putt-putt of a keyboard, and rosaries beside the washer and dryer. She couldn't speak of the thing more openly—not with the other woman in the house. Yet the very fact that she and Aurora never exchanged a significant word seemed to make the gaudy seventy-something all the more haunting. Aurora, for instance, turned out to have made it possible for John Junior to duck out of the apartment, Tuesday afternoon while the parents had been down on the Bayfront.

On the spur of the moment, that afternoon, the oldest and second-oldest had taken a jaunt over to Castel Sant'Elmo. Elmo— an Italian corruption of Erasmus, the patron saint of sailors, in honor of whom seafarers had come up with the expression "St. Elmo's fire." The stuff wasn't really fire, rather a kind of static electricity, just as Erasmus wasn't truly Elmo, or the saint of fire. But the counterfeit had stuck. If an American thought of St. Elmo, he thought of fire, because of *Moby Dick* or a dumb movie. Or perhaps the American was a bookish teenager fascinated by invisible forces like an electro-magnetic pulse. Chris would make the connection, yes. He'd know where to find the castle, too. Sant'Elmo was a brooding heap almost as old as dell'Ovo and the same dirt-yellow. It stood on the heights of the Lulucitas' neighborhood, ten minutes' walk from the apartment.

Nonetheless JJ would never have gotten to the castle, while the parents were out of the house, if his grandmother hadn't gone to bat for him. Aurora had accompanied the boy down to the piazza, and she'd made sure to keep the policemen she'd spoken with out where the TV cameras could get a clean shot.

My good-looking young grandson here, she'd told the officer in charge, *is withering away, positively withering away, from sitting around the house all day.*

JJ used the same argument on Barb: Mom, I'm sick of this. When she pressed him, the boy upped the stakes. "You're telling me I have to stay home all day, every day? *Forget* about it. Book me a flight to La Guardia."

John Junior defended Aurora too, saying she'd made him laugh. *Think of the benefit to your womenfolk*, the grandmother had told the cops. *The girls in this city have been pining away, absolutely pining away, for lack of their eye-candy.*

On top of that, JJ pointed out, Aurora had known better than to bring Paul downstairs. She'd understood that Paul and the girls had to stay in the apartment, and she'd made sure that the two older boys had a plainclothesman bodyguard, too, while they enjoyed a bit of sulfur-dusted air and sun. As for Sant'Elmo, JJ claimed, it was handy. "I mean, Mom, do you think you could remember we're the same as anybody else? We're just normal young Americans." If you asked him, the folks around the Vomero were doing a better job of that than his own mother. During his time outside, John Junior got the distinct impression that the local miracle-frenzy had started to fade. The believers in the streets had been content with a wave or a nod, and none of the media had bothered to follow the brothers out of the piazza. JJ could swear he'd heard a newsstand owner shout *lascia li stare*, leave them alone.

Really, the boys' little "prison-break" was nothing that Mom should worry about. "We had a good time, over there. Sant'Elmo, it's got all these neat places to hide."

The mother's voice tightened, though with the grandmother in the apartment she couldn't shout. Had JJ forgotten how, just the day before. . . ?

The boy rolled his eyes. "Nobody's gunning for *us*, Mom. That was all about Our Man in NATO."

Barbara's husband had given her the same assurances, or reassurances, during their walk along the waterfront. Of course the couple had their protection inching along the boulevard behind them, a Consular sedan, bulletproof. Roebuck had arranged the car, the driver, and the armed guard. But Barbara and Jay got the time alone that the husband had announced they "could use," following "a meeting like this, a roller coaster." The two of them strolled close by the small boats tethered to the rocks, wooden craft many of them, hand-painted. With the rumble of the other traffic, with the breeze and the sea, husband and wife could speak from the heart. The Jaybird had pointed out that up at the Refugee Center, during the near-month since his near-kidnap, the American Boss had often spent as much as an hour out of sight of his flak-jacketed protectors. If Silky's crooks had wanted a piece of him, they'd had plenty of opportunity.

Barbara had nodded but frowned. Even as she and her husband talked, she'd noticed a refugee African on their tail. When they'd gone out along the breakwater, she'd called Jay's attention to the man, an obvious *clandestino*. The poor guy hung back behind the Consulate's Audi, in a torn t-shirt bearing a broken pillar.

The Jaybird had rolled his eyes—the expression that John Junior would imitate a few hours later. He'd asked if his Owl Girl was frightened of beggars all of a sudden. Frightened of the homeless, in this city? The husband could understand she'd been shaken up; her change of heart made everything more vulnerable, more precious . . .

Barbara had cut the man off, letting him know what she'd seen on the website.

Jay had taken the news calmly, looking over their skinny tag-along. The African stared back over their freshly-polished ride, no doubt trying to assess whether they might give him a Euro. Barb at first hadn't felt her husband's touch at her hip.

Today, he'd told her, we start over. It's all going to be on another basis. No lying and no doubletalk.

They confronted their two oldest that evening, as soon as the boys revealed how they'd gone waltzing off to Sant'Elmo. Once more the parents asked the grandmother to step out onto the balcony, and Barbara allowed herself to bark a bit. Yet all she and Jay got for their efforts was another wild pixel chase through the Lulucita pages on the 'net. She wound up reading not only the saint-of-fire business again, but also a number of messages she hadn't picked up before. JJ and Chris knew where all the secrets were, a link that played a song about the Camorra, and another that called up a movie clip, or was it two clips? One moment you saw Jack Lemmon and Sophia Loren, the next Lemmon and Mastroanni. The two teenagers knew about them all, and they argued that every piece of input, in every format, was intended as a message for the family. Every word was meant for Jay and Barb and the kids. Whenever the people who'd followed Paul's story got together to chat, not a line of agate type went by without some private high sign to the Lulucitas, a compliment or a warning or a nudge. Every posting was intended to close the gap between the person at the keyboard and the American *santa famiglia*, a wireless laying-on of hands.

"It's like," JJ said, "say we're the Talking Heads. I mean, we're one of the guys who used to be the Talking Heads. Say, then we visit a Talking Heads site. Hey, everybody on the site believes he's our best friend. Everybody's the Unknown Head."

"Everybody thinks," Chris said, "they've got some special private connection to us. Like, they're saying their prayers, and they believe we're listening."

"Yeah. Like when Nerdly here prays to the girls from Victoria's Secret."

Jay glowered; he wouldn't let them get started. Barbara, meantime, understood that what her sons had shown her in no way constituted a straight answer.

"All right," Chris said, "think of it like—what Paul said earlier about staying in Naples. There's a lot going on. There's a whole lot out there."

"A *lot*. And Chris and me, all of us, we're just this one small part."

The boys' line of talk fell well short of convincing Barbara, they didn't change how she read the message on the site or the trip to Sant'Elmo, but they did leave her impressed. John Junior especially, showing backbone and maturity. Before Naples, before so challenging a girlfriend (if you could call Romy a girlfriend), he would've told Mom and Pop everything. He couldn't have stood up to their grilling. And both these teenagers, Barb had to admit, had learned to handle their parents a lot better than even so recently as during their Memorial Day excursion to Mystic seaport. The boys had figured out that today Mom and Pop would back off—without admitting anything of the sort, to be sure—so long as they could tell there'd been nothing too serious about the tryst at Sant'Elmo. The 'rents just needed some assurance that the get-together had been quick, clean, and free of burdensome consequences. And that's as much as they got, Jay and Barb: they could see that whatever had happened in the castle, it hadn't left a mark. JJ and his girl hadn't even found a place to lie down.

What Mom and Pop needed, in effect, was to post their own message, on their carefully encrypted site. *Good parents*, that was the message. *We're good parents.*

"Yeah, think of Paul," JJ said, following his brother's lead. "He's feeling pretty cooped up around here too. And then, I mean, his episodes."

"He's acting out," Chris put in. "Like, with the onset of puberty, the hormone thing. It's got to be some form of acting out"

"Hey, Paul wasn't a saint to start with. Our brother was a normal young American. And you guys are good parents, you can see."

"It's Hormones 101. JJ and me, we've got to get him out, do something normal."

The boys were getting so shrewd, they were practically Neapolitan.

"It could've been a lot worse, hey? All he's been through."

"Could've been a lot worse, and crazy. Like, when you think of some of the old saint stuff. The stigmata, the visions. Could've been hormones, you think."

The onus fell back on Barb and Jay—how much did they need to know? How ugly did they want the evening to get? Chris shut down the browser, so the family's Christmas-shot screen saver replaced the site's tormented pictography, and the mother moved to the balcony doors. Vesuvius had stained the sunset a sallow white, like a t-shirt handed down from brother to brother.

Then the door slid open. The mother-in-law stood before her, smiling and half naked. She'd recognized the end of private time.

Aurora was forever nearby, just off-screen. Barbara could see the old woman in the very face of the grandson who might now be planning something dubious with his gypsy girlfriend. Jay's mother was the Irish one in the family, the one who'd gifted her first grandchild with puckish black eyes and laugh-ready dimples. She was a beauty, Aurora. At seventy-something her build remained catlike and her wrinkles suited the shape of her face. She'd helped herself to a bit of cosmetic surgery, to be sure, and she freely owned up to these "repairs." Also her long widowhood had included seminars on wardrobe and yoga and toners and proteins. Barbara's notions of old Italian women, of crones in black with faces like bark—the kind of aging she imagined for her own mother—these were the opposite of Aurora. Jay's mother even knew which events showed her off to best advantage. She was a familiar face at high-profile benefits around New York, dolling herself up for the sake of homeless shelters or free medical clinics. Two or three times, when her dress or her companion had been right, Aurora's picture had run in the *Times* Sunday Styles. Even the two-piece she wore out on the Vomero balcony provided a camera-friendly complement to her hair, a richly flowing red. Silky.

A lucky woman, she was, and getting the most out of a long widowhood. Jay's father had suffered a freak accident for which some of the wealthiest people on earth were liable. Paul Lulucita (Jay had put off passing along the name) had strayed into a mid-Manhattan movie set, some epic about a monster loose in the city. The director had loved the look of broken power lines showering sparks over standing water. So young Jay had been gifted with an exceptional trust fund, Hollywood blood-money, and even from overseas Barbara had made sure to check the remaining investments. The retirement account had grown nicely, and it looked like they wouldn't have to worry about the college fund any more either—not since they accepted the offer from Roebuck. More than that, some years ago now the wife had grasped the emotional impact of Jay's tragedy, the way the sudden loss of his Dad had helped prompt the son into marriage at an earlier age than might've been wise. Barb understood even, thanks to the Samaritan Center, how her husband's vaporized father matched up with her own runaway mother. The absent parents provided a relationship balance, a set of ghost parallel bars.

Or you could put it another way: you could say the relationship had been trouble from Day One. Trouble was where Aurora came in. The death of her husband had scarred her differently, very, from how it had marked her son. In the widow's case, flirtation had been raised to the level of a credo: I seduce, therefore I am. So long as I remain more flesh than bone, I'll go on seeking fleshy pleasures. Barb recalled when they'd first met, a high-breasted Barbara Cantasola shaking hands with the mother of her hard-bellied new boyfriend. This had been barely a year after the accident, and already the widow had a man at the kitchen table, his head slick with Grecian Formula, looking over a brochure for a spa in midtown. The movie studio responsible for her husband's death had abandoned its project, but Aurora had no qualms about stepping in where they'd left off, the monster loose in the city. Nor was the mother shamed by her son's quick retrenchment in family life. As an in-law, too, she flaunted her "capering." She'd shown up at Barbara's house with men-friends as young as thirty-three (granted, no one saw his I.D.) and as old as something close to eighty. Her one rule for the children was that she never be called "Grandma." If the kids didn't forget she would delight them with gifts for their saints' days, or for Easter or Pentecost or Advent or Epiphany. It might've been the woman's idea of yin and yang, getting lots of men and giving lots of toys.

During every visit, Barbara would study that weekend's date. In the man's eyes, she always saw the same questions: This isn't going to get much crazier, is it? It isn't going to get much scarier? Not much, brother. The affairs never lasted. The men would slingshot around the grandmother for a month or two, then whistle away with their tails on fire. And here on this side of the Atlantic the air-time wasn't likely to get any less turbulent. Aurora had arrived for the visit without a boy-toy, and Barbara would bet—what? the cost of a remodel for Roebuck's office?—she would just bet that her mother-in-law was going to score some local talent. The woman claimed she lived in Greenwich Village because she found it "romantic," and Naples might've been the city that had given Greenwich Village the idea. Her most likely victim in town, in fact, began to seem obvious by the fourth or fifth day after the grandmother's arrival. *Dottore* DiPio, sure. The doctor was a bit of a dandy himself, and during these housebound days, his beard-plucking grew ever more agitated around the grandmother.

When Aurora spoke to the priest, on the other hand, the man went quiet. He stopped shuffling his knobby joints. Barbara assumed the old playgirl offended him, but when she asked Cesare about her in-law, she didn't like his answers.

"Our Savior," he said, "condemns hypocrisy. The whited sepulcher, don't you know, that hides our rot. But your Aurora accepts her decay. She honors it."

Barb figured Cesare was impressed by the widow's charities. Barb had told him how, at the Samaritan Center, the donors' plaque listed Jay's mother as an "Angel."

"She'll be useful to you," the priest went on. "Italians respect a woman like Aurora. With her around, they'll tend more to steer clear."

Barbara had noticed as much already. When she did get out, these days, she experienced the same falloff in local attentions as John Junior. The day Jay began his duties at DiPio's downtown clinic, she took everyone else back to the sports facility, the soccer field. Everyone, including Aurora and the security. But this time, there and back, even *Paulo miracolo* went pretty much un-harassed. The boy was asked to bless a saint's medallion or two, naturally, and Barbara as well. Also the group had another *clandestino* keeping an eye on them, trailing the crew for a few blocks, while never daring to approach, to panhandle. But the guy was another harmless stick of a sub-Saharan. He disappeared as soon as Barb pointed him out to one of the security. The only significant interruption, really, came from the energetic Maddalena.

The celebrity girlfriend no longer needed to carry a camera, but that day she'd settled in with the other media, behind the sawhorses in the piazza. She stuck around, too, after Jay hiked off to the funiculare and the clinic downtown. By the time Barbara and the others appeared on the stoop, Maddalena might've been the only journalist waiting. Then she hurdled the sawhorse, with an eye-catching flip of her tight-jeaned legs. The security didn't faze the girl. Two of the squad had to brace Maddalena in a way that made Barbara think of the scene out in the tent-chapel at the Refugee Center. But even then the young woman kept asking, just this side of screaming, that Paul meet with her boyfriend Fond. Ten minutes was all the former hunger striker asked for, *ten minutes*.

One of the men from Interpol reached under his lapel, but the mother put out a hand. There'd been enough of that.

Maddalena didn't fail to notice. "Signora," she cried, "you know my Fondo! You know he has good heart!"

JJ bent towards his mother's ear. "I'm so sure," he said, "this girl knows all about a good heart. That's why she was in such a rush to get her face on the news."

"He will give you new meaning!" Maddalena called, as the family started away. "Your prayers and your miracles, they will have new meaning! A new life!"

But to judge from the rest of the excursion, free of stop and go and hassle that had always been part of the package with Kahlberg, the Lulucitas already had a new life. The pretty reporter and her Hermit Crab contact were behind the curve. Rather Barb now had to figure out where, in this renewal, could she fit all her old guilt? Whoever she'd become here in Naples, a good witch who guided her family to the greater truth or a banshee who wailed the end of everything—whoever, she wasn't the woman she'd been before these lengthening June days, in this reeking city layered like the decades of a rosary, or like a long marriage.

And Aurora, new in town, was something else again. The priest wasn't alone in saying that the septuagenarian prankster, always ready for a quick game of cards or Monopoly, Nerf-ball or birds-&-ponies, did the kids some good. She offered a healthy alternative, after a month when their Mama had come across as ever more fire-&-brimstone. Dr. DiPio had told Barbara the same. Of course the old *medico* was already under Aurora's spell, the black widow had put him on the menu, but when it came to the children he could still be trusted. He'd fingered his Christopher medal and claimed that the grandmother "increased total sympathy levels." Nor could Barb fail to notice that, with the mother-in-law around, everyone under twenty-one acted more goofball and agreeable. A couple of times the kids even mounted impromptu performances on the balcony, doing their bit for whoever might still have a camera, down in the piazza. They pretended to be a rock band, and Paul was the surprise star of the performance. The middle child threw in loose-hipped dance moves while his brothers wailed away on air guitar, rather Broadway in his black and white, almost like that choreographer with the Italian name—was it Fosse?

A day or so after Jay started his job at DiPio's clinic, Barbara announced that the older boys could go down to the *centro* with their father, if they cared to pitch in. A "situation" that hadn't been "compromised," according to Attaché Roebuck, the clinic was a psychiatric facility for disorders resulting from the earthquake. It was the same jerry-rigged baronial home, its closets made over as offices, to which the doctor had taken the family on the first day after the assault. The place was tailor-made for sneaking off. Boys like Chris and JJ would have no trouble showing up to "pitch in," and then gallivanting all over the original city. They could set up any assignations they liked. Then there was Jay's job, another word that belonged in quotes, though Roebuck and the former VP had worked out a position title that wouldn't damage the resume. Nevertheless, not quite a week after Jay had worked out the deal, the mother announced that Chris and JJ were free to join their father downtown. She used the news to kick off the dinner conversation, while setting out a hefty platter of octopus sautéed with garlic. More than that, declared the newly-fledged Owl, she'd come up with something fun for Paul and the girls to do.

With that, Barbara wound up in her first direct exchange with Aurora.

"Why, bravo," the old playgirl told her. "Ever since I'd heard about our Junior here and that girl, I've thought there was no point pretending, simply hiding our heads in the sand and pretending. Of course they were going to try to see each other."

Barb put her clean hand, the one untouched by olive oil, in Dora's hair.

"Nothing so inflames love's sensibility," Aurora said, "as being forcibly kept apart. Why, it goes back to the myths, Hero and Leander. It goes back to the Kama Sutra. 'Once the wheel of love has turned,' you know."

From where Barbara stood, she had a good view of Aurora's favorite studio portrait. The merry widow never traveled without it. The photographer had posed her facing a fan, a silk scarf trailing from her silky hair. Aurora Isadora.

JJ and Chris were speaking up already, falling all over each other to make it clear that they had no idea where Romy had gone. "I mean," said John Junior, "the Kama Sutra? Aurora, get real." But both boys also insisted that the gypsy couldn't have had anything to do with the murder.

"Mom," Chris reminded Barbara, "you don't think so, either, right? You know that Romy's like, the least of our troubles."

John Junior added: "You know the real trouble we've had over here, it's been between you and Pop. I mean, whatever."

But that had been the old Barbara, the one who'd struggled with "whatever," setting off all kinds of speculation among the kids. Tonight she worked up a smile and pointed out that, anyway, the next morning Chris and JJ needed to be ready when their father was, if they wanted to go downtown. She reiterated that she'd figure out something for the others as well. She sat and enjoyed her octopus, she arranged a fair distribution of the KP duties off the top of her head, and then she stepped out for a limoncello on the balcony. Only out there was the wife forced to admit again, silently, that she lacked the deep tranquility she wished for when it came to her new commitments. She hadn't yet wrapped the inner whipsaw in canvas and put it in the shed. To her the sunset appeared to have left a bloodstain out on the Bay, and the smell of diesel recalled the museum loading dock. Here it was five days after Silky's murder, and Barbara's clearest impression of his death was that the white-suited rule-breaker had fallen to his knees before Aurora. He'd made his final bloody salaam to the home-wrecking prototype, the Siren who'd been, at just that moment, winging towards him over the dark Atlantic. Yet hadn't Barb herself been preparing for an even nastier Coming? And how could she be certain that she knew better now? Whatever Romy might threaten, whatever other trouble might be lurking around the city, Barbara had to deal with it from a new wholeness. She had to be like something you might see on the family website, a bad bird-woman who'd morphed into the Phoenix.

By the time she came in off the balcony the kids had settled down to a game of Clue with Aurora. They were into it, laughing; they didn't notice Mama. She found Jay at the other end of the apartment, in their bedroom, going over his checkbook with an old-fashioned calculator. Right there the wife settled into nuzzling and sweet nothings, with the same bewildering relief such puppy love had afforded her over the last few days. She wouldn't have thought she'd missed it so much, or that it could feel so good to cuddle. She sank more deeply into the man, and shifted to a more serious kiss. Her husband's fingers trailed over her breasts, her ribs, the waistband of her underwear.

"Let's try again," she murmured. "Let's please."

"Right here right now," he said. "Like two kids."

Should they have talked about who'd murdered the Lieutenant Major, or what papers he might've left behind, instead of stretching out on the bed he'd provided for them? Barbara had the sense that the answers would help a little, just as the stroking Jay gave her as he pulled away her clothes seemed to ease her closer to a genuine peace. Should they have talked about all they were risking, in this search for a fresh, shared self that was hardly half-defined? Yes, no, maybe; the answers might do some good, just as for a while it seemed to be working as Barbara shifted her pelvis into a better angle against Jay's, as she yielded to the man's plying. They appeared to be making progress as she gave him back three, four, five kisses. But in time the answers proved not to be here with them, or not enough for Barb at least, and she held back. In the few seconds between one kiss and another their touch cooled. Not that Barbara resisted her man—she would've worked out some variety of pleasure if he'd needed it badly enough—but Jay too relented when he understood that his wife was short of real arousal. She wasn't herself, dry between the legs. There remained something else she needed, and she'd been this way every time since, in front of the entire overseas community, Barbara was forced to recognize how badly she'd misunderstood what she'd thought she'd needed up to that point. Since the meeting at the Consulate, in their moments alone, she and Jay had gone no further than tears and whispers and unfinished business. Tonight, after a cry from down the hall about Mrs. Peacock, Barbara again told her husband that she wanted him inside her, she knew it would help. She left her legs open long after he lost his erection, and she wondered aloud how she might find a decent Naples gynecologist. Also she mentioned the jelly and oil in the nightstand drawer. But the man's touch turned conventional, he'd rarely been selfish or needy anyway, and settling back against the pillows he whispered, "Soon. Soon."

Chapter Ten

But Jay's and Barb's whispering in their dim bedroom, loving yet ascetic—what did it amount to out in the bright Mezzogiorno? Soon— *what*? The damages heaped around them remained the same. Barbara might claim that these days constituted a "change of life," a play on words she used a time or two with her husband or priest. But the big news in her family, once Jay and the boys started spending their days downtown, was that the teenagers were making a documentary.

In order to concentrate on the film, Chris and John Junior more or less bunked up together. Barbara helped them arrange the extension cords necessary for the computer, in there, but she let Chris drag the mattress across the hall by himself. The mother could hardly believe it the first morning she saw the fifteen-year-old stumbling out of his older brother's bedroom. They hadn't shared a room since fifth grade. Nonetheless, there in John Junior's with the family desktop, and with the door shut, the teenagers stayed up so late they risked missing their morning funiculare. Once or twice the boys barely had time to haul the computer tower and monitor back out to the front room.

During these early stages of their "project," Chris and JJ relied on text, voice, collage, and still photos. Even with all the craziness of the last three weeks, it turned out, the boys hadn't forgotten about the digital camera. Barbara couldn't remember taking so much as a single picture herself, in Naples. She could hardly recall anyone snapping a shot, come to think of it, but then the boys hadn't been wound so tightly, so blindly. They had photos, they had materials off the web, and they worked up text and voiceovers as well. Meanwhile, like everyone else in the apartment, the two oldest did some thinking about Papa's latest windfall. Chris and JJ knew the very day when their father would receive his first bank transfer, a "reimbursement for transitional expenses." That night, the two teenagers sat the parents down and asked for video equipment. The brothers needed cameras and up-to-date software. And while they were at it, the family should get some zippy new hardware too.

"It's not just about JJ and me getting the tools we need," Chris said. "The tools to like, realize our vision. Also, a laptop, that would benefit the whole family."

The younger boy claimed that the documentary had been his idea, and the older one sat back and let him say so. After a moment JJ added that, as soon as Chris had brought up the project, it seemed like a good one for him.

"I mean," said the seventeen-year-old, "he's been taking all this stuff *in*, right? So now, this movie, it gives him a way to let it out."

Chris grinned. "What can I say? I've found my city. Like, my home ground."

Barb and Jay shared a look.

"And me," John Junior said, "I'm thinking, hey. Chris's idea, it means we're all going to come out of this with *something*. I mean, a document. Solid."

"A documentary. About like, my odyssey, but not only mine. We're all wanderers, the whole family. We're all returning to home ground."

Barbara had to smile. It sounded almost noble when the boy put it that way, these weeks of wandering. And it did appear she'd finally gotten somewhere; she'd come to feel comfortable about allowing her two oldest free rein—still more free rein. Barb turned back to Jay with a calm that would've been out of reach a week ago. Since her husband seemed to have developed a golden thumb, she told him, a new laptop struck her as a useful way to spend the money. Or part of the money. That little machine down in Roebuck's office, Barb went on, was enough to make a girl jealous. Then the mother tried out her new serenity on Chris, suggesting a connection between how greedily he'd devoured his *Blue Guide* and how badly he wanted to make this movie.

"I'm saying, this would be history too. Even *The Real World*, shows like that, these days they show the early episodes in college classes."

"Exactly. History, like, it used to be on stone, it used to be on vellum. Now . . ."

"Oh right," JJ said, "vellum. "The vorld vide vellum."

Chris shook his head. "Slipping bro, slipping. A line like that, it could be Talent Night at the Heart of the Poconos."

If the mother stared hard enough she could almost see the puppet-strings of the younger brother's thinking, the lines that stretched from head to wrist and made him poke the bridge of his glasses. But the actual puppet-master would be JJ, sure. He was Geppetto to all the children, and without a doubt the one who'd come up with the idea of the documentary. His shadow girlfriend must've asked what they could do, how they could meet. Her love-note on the website had managed to slip her barefoot life into his bulging Nikes, yes, a miracle shoehorn. But after that they'd needed something better. If they relied on the website, soon enough Roebuck or one of the *carabinieri* would spot it. John Junior must've come up with the movie.

Not that Chris was lying about his own motives. The way he saw the project, its benefit to his older brother's love life was secondary. Chris believed in the film, a good parent could see that at once. The boy brought up the *Odyssey* again, claiming there was a narrative to the Lulucita's experience in Naples, "a total narrative arc." That shaping curve gave the documentary its larger purpose, a record of where the family might eventually touch down. "Like, maybe in some scary places, the arc comes down."

"What?" Barbara asked.

"Mom, it's like a myth. We're confronting monsters."

"Monsters?" The mother's hand strayed to her husband's beltline. "Are you saying, this would be about the problems between Jay and me?"

Now Chris and JJ were sharing a look.

"You guys told me in the museum," she went on, "what you thought was happening. You told me Naples was all about me and Jay."

"Barb's right," Jay put in. "No way I'm paying for a movie that says your parents are monsters."

Time for JJ Geppetto. The puppet-master reiterated that the way he was thinking about the project, it was for all of them. It gave them something tangible they could look at and talk about for years to come, something they all took away from this experience. "When Chris brought up this project, Pop, he never said it was all about you and Mom." And the younger son followed suit, saying that the entire metropolitan area had a part in this picture. "Millions of people in motion, day and night." His mother needed to see the greater arc, in which everyone in the city risked ending up in a scary place.

"It's a journey," JJ said. "Hey? A journey, it could go anywhere."

"It's a myth, but for all of us. The project has to include Paul, too."

Barbara had rather liked the business about millions of people in motion, but she hadn't counted on Mr. Paul getting shuttled around. The Jaybird, likewise unsettled, turned for a look at the middle child. Paul was on his knees, in the front room with Aurora and the other kids. A card game tonight. Meanwhile John Junior made it clear that he'd come to this discussion with all his strings in hand. The big teenager declared, four or five different ways, that his youngest brother would be handled carefully and kept safe. JJ mentioned the new security team, "those guys're on the ball," and speculated aloud that there were more where they came from. One phone call to the Consulate and they could have double the police protection. "Plus, speaking of phone calls, we've got the extra cell phones now, with the emergency numbers on speed-dial." They'd seen that the Naples cops could move pretty fast when they had to.

Chris was nodding along, but he preferred to keep the emphasis on the documentary. He pointed out how useless and "touristy" he and his older brother would start to feel if their project was limited to just the two of them. "I mean, at that clinic downtown, what can we do, really? Take out the trash?"

And John Junior assured the parents that they wouldn't need Paul everyday. Chris had "storyboards," JJ explained. The boards laid it all out, the whole narrative to date, and Paul would only have to tag along for a couple of "sequences." Also the oldest was smart enough to bring up, yet again, the change in local attitudes now that the Lulucitas were rid of their former liaison officer. "These days," JJ said, "hey. Everywhere we go in this city, there's an angel looking out for us."

Barbara was trying to see past his sweet-faced Irish blarney. But the Jaybird beside her knew the way she was leaning. The husband heaved a sigh, okay okay, and asked if the boys had a figure, "ballpark," for what this stuff would cost.

"I know this," Chris said. "With the situation we've got here, the PX discounts, we can forget about the sticker price."

"Figure back in New York," JJ said, "the best deal on the street. Then take off another, hmm, twenty percent."

Jay couldn't be sure what Roebuck would be willing to do for him. There were a lot of Americans over here . . .

"Hey," JJ said. "Aren't we still Americans?"

"Pop," Chris said. "Haven't you heard what I've been saying? This project, it's something for any American. We all want to return to home ground."

Barbara used to be the one pulling the strings around here. Straightening the front of her dress, she suggested that the boys might not need so much high-tech equipment. Didn't Chris keep saying this was all a myth? Maybe he would be better off trying to write a novel. . . .

The younger boy was shaking his head. Had Mom even been listening? What good would it do to write a novel? "In the first place, everybody knows how to write a novel by like, age ten. JJ and me, we need to learn something. Like, to *get* somewhere."

"Word," said John Junior.

And in the second place, the younger brother went on, their project involved real outreach; "it's big, Mom." It wasn't about one person sitting alone writing, and then one other person sitting alone reading.

Again the mother heard the nick of authentic ambition, in the boy. She figured JJ had something similar working at his nervous system, the rough grain of desire for a greater impact from his "on-location footage," a greater reward than sneaking another kiss or two. Barbara shared a different sort of look with Jay, the okay-look. The husband was perhaps the lone remaining family member who still would wait for her approval. And even after as the Jaybird turned back to the boys, admitting for starters that he'd been thinking they could use a laptop, Barb sat thinking it over.

"One day at a time," Jay was saying. "This is on a provisional basis."

The boys weren't about to quibble. Looking very young all of a sudden, they erupted in a loud high-five. With that the mother sat up formally and made another stipulation. Barbara insisted that, on the days when Paul joined them on the shoots, Dora and Syl would have to go along too.

"Uhh," John Junior said.

"You said this was about everybody taking part," Barbara said.

What else can a mother do, when her children go through the change? What option did she have except another touch of underhandedness, using the boys' new freedom against them? While her seventeen-year-old had been developing additional clout around the home, he must've also been brought up short by the dawning sense of what he owed his brothers and sisters. Dawning complication and guilt—Barbara knew all about it. And these days, if the younger sibs were around, the oldest would rein in whatever else he might be up to. If the sibs were on hand (plus some of the new security team), and if the police too cruised the shoot (the cops would be given the boys' schedule), that should keep any clandestine make out sessions from going too far (and also put the kibosh on any other illegal activity).

All this had come to mind in the time it took the boys to raise their spread hands and slap them together. Anyway, what else could Barbara do?

Also she handled the call to Roebuck. If the mother was still working the angles, still speaking in codes, she might as well use them on an Alpha. With no more than a well-placed silence or two, the next morning she scored a laptop of the coming generation. Chris and JJ got fifty-hour batteries, beefed-up wireless reach, and well-nigh bottomless storage, plus a couple of scan-disk sticks as a throw-in. The software came straight out of Industrial Light & Magic. On top of that, the boys had the stuff in their hands by lunchtime. It arrived in a fortified Hummer, maybe one of Kahlberg's old vehicles, and the brothers had the driver wait in the piazza while they whipped through their installations.

Naturally Barbara tried talking to her priest. A couple of days later, in the kitchen with the old man, she had to ask: "Is that all this is? You know what I'm saying?"

Cesare met her look, something he hadn't done much since he'd arrived.

"Think about it, Father. Cesare. This family goes through six time zones, three miracles, three thousand years of history, and one walloping, super-size self-delusion. That's the short list, you know? But then, what's the big diff? I lose a little and the kids gain a little. Is that all this is, the same as would've happened anyway?"

The priest was barely with it. He made a faltering mention of things she couldn't have expected to happen, like living with twenty-four hour security.

"But even that—today when the boys went out, all they had was the driver."

"Well, one can see the logic in that. There's little threat of kidnap."

"So it's just like I'm saying. We might as well be back in Bridgeport."

His crumpled eyelids drooped again, and he glanced away again, looking out the kitchen door. The man might've been some fleshy-faced animal, sniffing round an unfamiliar space. Between them she had out the garlic and onion, the cans of crushed tomatoes and tomato paste.

"I was thinking, signora." Now he was addressing the crimson show-biz lettering across the larger can. "About your boy's idea for his film, don't you know. I was thinking about the wanderer's return, to the—the home ground."

Barbara began with the garlic. If the old man wasn't going to pay attention, she didn't want to be working on the onion and maybe breaking into tears.

"What your boy seems to be up to, it strikes me as peculiarly Italian. Italian-American, I would say. The very idea of 'home ground,' don't you know, of keeping the old country close. As if a person needed to take communion at the ancestors' table."

"Cesare." Barbara left off peeling the first clove. "Did you bring the handout for this lecture?"

"I do realize, it's irresponsible to generalize." The way that beak of his shifted directions, the priest looked like he was trying to screen out the makings for the sauce, to catch a subtler scent. "But I must say, I've seen it a good deal of this by now. Seen my share of the families, asking how they might find where *nonna* was born. Or they tiptoe into the rectory and request all the birth records between 1914 and 1921."

"Huh. Do you remember what happened when I had a chance to visit where my mother came from?"

"It's got me thinking, don't you know. Do immigrants from the Punjab need this sort of thing? Some *nan* out of the old ovens? Or let us say some transplanted Dubliner, some man now happily producing memorial videos for a mortuary in Texas . . ."

Barbara slapped down the knife. "Memorial videos? A mortuary?"

The old man's chin dropped into his robe, and he crossed his legs the other way. He offered a mumbling apology and a scrap of justification: only thinking of the boys. Didn't want the boys to waste time reinventing the wheel.

"Father, Cesare. So what if they are? So what if Chris and John Junior are out there doing the same thing as everyone else?" Barb got her hands back on the garlic. "It's still new to them, isn't it? Everyone they run into, everyone who's just like them, they've still got something to teach the boys.

"Listen," she went on, "Chris and JJ showed us rushes last night. They actually used that word, 'rushes.'"

At a noise outside the apartment, on the stairway landing, the priest put his back to her. The walk from the church, Barbara saw, had soaked him through the robe.

"Not that they showed us anything," Barb went on. "They were out all day and all they showed us was five minutes. Another lecture, Chris at the Sibyl's Cave. Now, what do you think, Cesare? You think, it's time Jay and me asked a direct question?"

The noise in the hall had disappeared. Cesare swung round again, slumping, eyes on the floor. If he was so unhappy here, Barb thought, she could easily have made the trip to the church. These days she could climb the Vomero stairs without risk, taking along the guard assigned to her. And Barbara's man was the least impressive on the crew. He was the youngest, with curls that hung in his eyes. He liked to read a comic books, her bodyguard, and he liked to pile on the gelato. But why not let the boy eat? Anyone could see that *Mama Santa* was no longer at risk. So what if some underfed *clandestino* trailed her a while, seeking a long-distance blessing? So what if some white churchgoer held up a crucifix? Barbara took care of them with a nod and a word. Even Maddalena had backed off, lately. The morning before last, Barbara had allowed the girl ten minutes with the family, a Q-&-A down on the stoop. The priest had shown up that day too, and the pretty young media climber had also caught Barb and Cesare bent together over the rosary. Good TV, that prayer—Barb and Cesare were getting wider play than Barb and the interviewer. Latest word on Maddalena was that she'd been offered a position on a national digest.

All around her, people were going through changes. But here in Barbara's kitchen, this afternoon, she was getting nowhere even with her priest. Likewise the old man looked as if nothing short of another earthquake could move him.

Once more the mother banged on the table. "She isn't here," she said.

That brought his eyes up.

"Aurora. She thought today she'd help JJ and Chris."

Apparently the Jesuits hadn't taught him how to handle getting caught. The priest blushed with such heat that for a moment he might've been a stranger, a blistered stranger, here at her table. But then Barb had never known him, had she? She'd been clueless, hadn't she, when it came to his cranky old heart? She'd completely misread the stillness that had fallen over the man during his first meetings with Aurora.

She didn't understand his first words either, some bitter dialect. Then: "Oh, my." The priest appeared to test his joints, his legs toggling around beneath the robe. "There's, there's a cliché, don't you know," he stammered. "'No fool like an old fool.'"

She went to the fridge, yanking the handle and the drawer, pulling out a bell pepper. "Father—Mother of God! Of all the women in the world."

"I, I realize how you feel about her, signora. What am I to say?"

A good big bell pepper, she could use the chopping.

"What would you like, Mrs. Lulucita? Shall we put an end to our talks?"

"Oh sure." She couldn't sit yet. "That's just what I need, more sneaking around."

The man's wrinkles multiplied around an uncertain squint.

"If I say you can't visit"—Barb pointed at him with the pepper—"then I'll have two pairs of lovebirds sneaking around."

Cesare didn't quite nod.

"Do you know what that's *like*, Cesare? Do you know what it's like, living with *doubletalk*? If I say you can't visit, I'll never be able to think straight again. If it's not JJ and Romy sending signals, it'll be you and Aurora."

The old man plucked at his sweat-stuck shirt, and the gesture unexpectedly softened her. With that Barbara could see how he lonely he'd gotten, caught between a comfortable parish and radical dreaming. For years and years, his own heavy-knuckled hand must've been the only touch he'd known.

"Plus," she said more evenly, "I won't even have a priest to tell about it."

"Perhaps then we should do as the Romans do." He too was regaining control. "We should say *Dio boia*, 'hangman God,' don't you know. An apt blasphemy."

She sat and attacked the garlic again.

"Apt," he went on, "when everyone's got their neck in a—"

"Cesare, don't. Don't give me that Irish wit, pseudo Irish, can you imagine how it sounds? Your lying pretend Irish? I mean, I *am* trying to understand. I'm trying to tell myself, a priest is as human as the rest of us. That's sort of the point, isn't it?"

"The point, oh my. The point."

"Please." Her wrist was burning; she set down the knife. "Cesare."

"Signora Lulucita, it's high time we stopped this charade. You call me your chosen priest, as if I were some boy at a dance."

"Can I help you here, Father? Can I try? Aurora, you know, she didn't—"

"Fa-ther, oh my. Really, signora, this has to stop. You're more than bright enough to have realized, long since, just what a miserable excuse for a proper Catholic father I've become."

Barbara's turn to pluck at her clothes. Whatever she hoped to accomplish by staying in town, she'd counted on her priest to help. When the guard downstairs had announced the man's arrival, she'd taken a moment with her hair and exchanged her frayed slippers for her best flats. Jesuit, Dominican, whatever, he still carried a communion kit. He still conducted the Mass. The old man even held a weekly service for the head cases, down at DiPio's clinic.

"Cesare," she tried, "you said yourself, it's Christ who calls you."

"But what if I no longer hear him, signora? What if my faith has become, as you say, mere lying and wit? I daresay you could see the truth the moment we met."

The garlic had been reduced to crumbs, and the onion and pepper looked overwhelming, far too much to start on.

"Signora, my faith—it's dwindled to nothing. A heap of offal."

Barbara shook her head. "Cesare, please. Can you understand, Aurora's not worth it? You know how many men have fallen for the merry widow?"

The man flushed again. This time the red-and-white contrast, cheeks and hair, suggested one of the local cameos.

"Sorry," she said. "You understand, I'm angry? I'm still angry."

She could've avoided this, she thought. Five minutes ago she could've made believe that she hadn't guessed who it was that Cesare had been hoping to find, on this visit. She could've avoided any mention of the grandmother.

"Signora," the old man was saying, "I've come to think I'm eavesdropping on a life in Christ. I've been at it for years really. One long evening after another, I've stood up at the front of the sanctuary and I've eavesdropped on the liturgy. It's my own liturgy, yet it's chatter from another room, don't you know. It's nothing but bits and pieces. Whoever designed that awful business above the altar, it's awful indeed, oh my yes. But he knew what he was doing, with his broken bits and pieces."

Barbara could've let the time pass harmlessly, here in her kitchen.

The priest, if you could still call him a priest, went on to explain how he'd tried to sustain his faith by his work with the homeless and the illegals. "I believed that among the lost sheep, the least of His children, I'd hear Him plainly again, my Christ. I hoped and prayed that out in the streets, I'd hear it again. Clear as a shout."

If this man knew how he got to Barbara, how raw he scraped her, he wouldn't have these doubts. "Father . . ."

"And it's not as if the Christ has gone anywhere, don't you know. He's still out there, isn't he, calling for our hands and hearts. If anything, these days—"

"Cesare, please. You talk as if you've turned into Silky Kahlberg."

Something of his former tartness returned. "Well, signora. If you don't see how the Holy Roman Church can seem as perverse and greedy as NATO, you're something less than the bright woman I've taken you for."

"Did I say Church wasn't—wasn't perverse? Sometimes? The Church and NATO, they're both of them the Mafia, sometimes. I know that. You should've gone to some of the fundraisers back in Brooklyn, Cesare."

"No, I shouldn't have. I've seen too many abuses of Christ's teaching as it is."

Barbara's hand had dropped from the table, the fight gone out of her. Quietly, she admitted she'd always wondered about the priest. "But still, whatever we talked about—we always talked about Jesus."

"Witchcraft. Incantations. One speaks the name hopefully."

When the man turned a phrase like that, his look displayed something a lot like righteousness, and Barbara told him so. "Really, Cesare, what does it matter if you sound like Che Guevara? Better that than Kahlberg's thing, playing the saint to line his pockets."

The old man, too, appeared to be softening. He revealed that the last vestiges of belief had left him only a day or so before Barb had first stopped into his church. "It was that pair of refugees, don't you know, the *clandestini* down in my cellar." A day or two before the mother showed up, these two young men had come banging on the door, off-hours. "Banging, yes, quite literally. The bruises on one of them, bruises all over his knuckles. I found him some ibuprofen."

For Cesare, to have a couple of shadow-citizens come begging for help was nothing new. "They know how to find me, to be sure. Word of mouth, word of the insatiable Neapolitan mouth. Do you realize there are miracle stories about me?"

His smile was like the vein in a dead leaf. "Stores about your 'chosen priest,' yes. A woman comes to the *prete coi Settebelli*—the priest with the condoms, don't you know—and then her brother in the Ogaden eludes the search-dogs. That sort of thing. Some of their stories, you'd think I walked the streets draped with *ojetti*."

But Cesare supposed that there must also be talk that was closer to the truth. "Some of them must have some idea what I'm doing in there. Or should I say, what I'm not doing. There must be some who've noticed how I avoid saying prayers."

Barbara figured it was time to risk slicing up the onion. She had the thought that the man might reveal some way to keep him out of Aurora's clutches, and so return to God. The priest meanwhile explained that, though he'd wound up allowing these two *clandestini* to bed down in the church, they hadn't come to him looking for a roof over their heads. They hadn't come for food or some other kind of handout, either. "Signora, they were there seeking Christ."

Again Cesare rearranged his knees and elbows. "They were seeking absolution, no less. These two actually believed that a few words, words alone, and out of my own unclean mouth . . ." The old man needed a moment, his baggy fingers extended towards his face. "That I could wash them clean."

She waited, her knife in the middle of the white bulb on the cutting board.

Cesare firmed up his expression. "They'd committed a crime, you see. Nothing so terrible really, not in this city. Your classic *scippo*, come up behind someone and hit him. Take his money. In this case, it did sound as if they'd hit the man rather hard."

"But you're saying, these two had faith? And that's when you knew, you didn't?"

"You understand, signora, there are things about these two I can't reveal. I no longer believe in the sacraments, but I daresay you know better than most, I still have—"

Barbara didn't want to hear any more posturing. "Cesare, what? What's the big secret? They got a little rough on their latest victim, okay. So, what, were they hustlers too? Hustlers, I mean, the sex trade? One of them had AIDS or something?"

His face screwed up in a wizened and approving pout.

"So, okay. There they were, dying and ashamed. Hey." She shouldn't talk like Jay, it made her sound shrewish. "And once you heard that, everything you'd lived by was gone. These two were the thing in the street, not Christ, not your call, but just a pair of crooks. They were full of disease and, and looking for a saint to kiss them."

He'd never heard about her vision of Naples either.

"You could even say this killed your faith. Just another hit in the street, and for you, it killed Christ. Am I right?" She sounded far too much like Jay. "Okay, Cesare. Okay, for the sake of argument. But, I mean. What has all this got to do with Aurora?"

The man's hands startled up. "Signora! Surely you can see." He sketched coils in mid-air. "I'm a man losing every least thread of light and meaning, and then your mother laid her hand on mine."

"She's not my mother."

"Boh. My apologies, I'm sure." His hands dropped back across his knee. "Signora, are you a woman of faith or aren't you? A woman of faith should have no trouble at all understanding what I feel for your Aurora.

"Now, let us say, my church had collapsed around me," Cesare went on, "and an angel reached down through the rubble. It's a radiant energy your Aurora has, nothing short of numinous. And don't you go getting all shifty and uncomfortable on me, Mrs. Lulucita. Don't you go fishing out some expression you learned in therapy. That woman laughs at our puny ideas of personality, don't you know. We fish out a word like 'neediness,' so threadbare in its concept of the soul, and she laughs. She puts her fingers to her neck, the base of her lovely neck—I do love to see her touch it, signora. She touches her neck and she lets loose that chuckle. A dart of purest joy."

"Cesare, give me a break. You talk as if she was Paul."

He shrugged. "About the boy, as ever, I refuse to speculate. But that woman, her laying-on of hands, it's a power beyond any cheap attempt at psychoanalysis."

"Cesare, how can you say that? Whatever power Aurora's got, it's *money*."

"Signora! Surely you can see, money isn't the point, for this woman. Money and the comforts, that's not it at all. Rather she herself is the comfort, the cup that runneth over. She's the very embodiment of *abbondanza*."

Barbara got back to work on the onion, noisily.

"Signora, I've never met anyone like her."

"Maybe not, but you've read about them. Caligula, Nero."

The priest gave his first real smile of the visit. "I believe I know better . . ."

"Cesare, don't. Father. How can you fail to see that Aurora is the worst kind of bourgeois? How can you fail to get it, she's one of the ones who's keeping down the two poor creeps you've got stashed in the church?"

The man's joints were quiet. The way he stared, thoughtful under a white shock of hair, unexpectedly called to mind Barbara's mentor Nettie.

"I'm angry," the mother said. "I'm still angry."

The movies got it wrong, she thought. What happened to foreigners in Italy wasn't a mere hotting-up of the love life. It was crazier than that, a roiling makeover, the ingredients chopped and cooked into another kind of pasta altogether. The movies got it wrong, the mythology got it right: everybody turned into something else.

"I think," she said, "I'm the one who needs to get out of the house."

When Cesare nodded, she wasn't watching. She only heard the scraping, his hard-to-shave neck against the confining collar.

She had alternatives to working at DiPio's clinic. A number of alternatives, in fact, including a couple that Barbara and Jay had rejected as soon as they'd left the meeting with Roebuck. The family could've moved, for instance, taking a place more under American protection. NATO housed most of its people at a base in Aversa, an old mozzarella town north and inland, not far from the old Borbon playground at Caserta. According to Cesare, according to Silky, the base was a transplanted California suburb. San Fernando Mediterraneo. The Lulucitas could've transferred to one of those ranch-style prefabs, walking distance from a PX with ten movie screens. Or they could've moved down into the Consulate compound. The Attaché herself kept some sort of executive apartment in one of the attached palazzi, with a gun-toting doorman and steel-shuttered windows. Telecommunications hookups linked the houses with both land bases and carriers, the Sixth Fleet, and the nuclear presence beyond the Suez was just fifty minutes away. Down in the Consulate or out at Aversa, the family could've holed up like Crusader princes in Castel dell'Ovo. The new monsters imitating the old monsters.

But they'd all gotten enough of that with the late Lieutenant-Major. Nor did the parents waste time with Aurora's loose talk about "the Grand Tour." The in-law suggested that the family jaunt all over the NATO-lands. They could take in *Hamlet* at the Stratford-on-Avon; they could visit the grave of Jim Morrison. "Quite the spree," so the grandmother put it. And all the family would need to do in return was make the occasional stop for Public Relations. A hospital here, an orphanage there.

Aurora, however, surprised Barbara with the restraint she showed about raising the possibility. The old playgirl never suggested the Capitals-of-Europe business directly to the kids, she wasn't so nefarious as that, and so the daughter-in-law had kept her head as well. She'd dismissed the grandmother's proposal out of hand, but she'd been polite about it. Besides, Barb figured the children wouldn't have wanted to leave town. Hadn't they asked to stay? Hadn't JJ announced that here, he and his brothers and sisters had found fresh ground for the spirit, an inner *Nea Polis*?

Barbara, on the other hand, couldn't get unstuck. That's what she'd intended to talk about with the fallen priest, today, before the old man had let her know just how fallen he was. So ten minutes after Cesare left the apartment Barb found herself ranting again. She upbraided the old man in the sort of fury that, a few short days before, would've been reserved for the Jaybird and her marriage.

"You're a wolf in priest's clothing!" she cried. "This is just another oily *Latin-lover* thing, another . . ."

The empty room had an echo; that stopped her. She'd been railing at the blue-bordered map of Naples, open on the family table. What had triggered her outburst, the mother realized, was that she couldn't find DiPio's clinic on the map.

She tugged at an armpit and turned to the door. Her bodyguard was across the piazza at the gelateria, but once she caught up with the overgrown boy, he assured her he knew "the asylum." In half an hour Barb was down in DiPio's office, and in another half an hour the place began to feel like just the change she'd been seeking.

Though a stopgap measure with Byzantine funding, the clinic meant business. The disaster had left behind a considerable spectrum of situational disorders. Even as the goatee'd *medico* finger-walked Barbara through the building directory, it sounded as if she'd stumbled on a transatlantic annex to the Samaritan Center. Here was a counselor who handled phobias, there a pair did group work on socialization, and a third specialized in dissociative episodes. Barbara saw post-traumatic stress, family-of-origin issues, and dual diagnoses. The tune was so familiar that she could sing the harmony right there across DiPio's desk. Between what she'd learned over the winter and what he needed this summer, Barb had no trouble arranging another of those jobs-in-quotes. She didn't have to mention reimbursement from the Consulate either, not with her husband already at work in the kitchen. For the next four or five days, until one of the doctors called Mrs. Lulucita into his office for a chat, she arrived at the clinic each morning at ten, with Jay and the boys.

Chris and JJ, though, never hung around the downtown *studio* for long. The boys were good for a chore or two, and if DiPio could think of some drug or other supply that didn't need to be rushed back to the clinic ASAP, the two teenagers were glad to handle the pickup. But for the few days that Barbara played at having a Master's in Social Work, or the Italian equivalent, John Junior and Chris didn't linger at the old palazzo much past the time Mama was assigned a client. As soon as DiPio had someone for her, JJ would throw the camera bag over his shoulder. He'd hook the canvas pouch to his belt as well, an extra precaution against *scippatori*, and the later some staff member would let Barbara know which of the security team had gone off with the boys. She and the Jaybird wouldn't lay eyes on their two filmmakers again till dinner.

This was as she'd expected, really. She counted herself lucky just to get the brothers to stop calling DiPio's place a "booby hatch." She knew better than to take them seriously, too, when the teens suggested that the patients' psychosis might "rub off."

"That's always the danger," Chris said, "when you're exposed to another culture. Like, it rubs off." The boy kept a remarkably straight face. "Next thing you know, JJ and me will go out and be crazy."

"Hey," said the older brother, "why go out?"

Wise guys. Barb had to admit, though, that the clinic hardly conveyed a sense of order. DiPio's palazzo, like many in the *centro storico*, was a multi-generation treehouse. Five stories of unmatched heights, with porches in different places, teetered around a small courtyard that, at the time when some baron had tacked on the first of the upper floors, had served as the stable. Apartments burrowed from one converted space to another, from a Borbon widening to a Fascist subdivision. There were rooms that could only be reached by first stepping out onto a balcony. The doctor himself had made changes, setting up therapy-cubicles in a couple of street-floor parlors. When Cesare spoke about the place, he fell back on antique vocabulary: *a veritable Bedlam*.

So far as husband and wife were concerned, actually, Bedlam felt like a healthy work environment. Around the clinic Barb and Jay encountered fewer hot buttons, fewer issues that came back to sex. They might've been a couple of expats going partners on a B&B. The Jaybird never gave the least indication of hurt feelings, for instance, about having his wife outrank him. She was playing doctor, around DiPio's *studio*, whereas Jay's position might've been chief cook and bottle-washer.

Not that Barbara didn't experience a worse shiver, now and again. There were times when she pulled open a door to discover something she hadn't expected, a closet instead of an exit or a dormer instead of an office, and there came the shiver . . . not déjà vu, say rather *gia visto.* The chilling sense that, once more, she'd tumbled back into her first day in the old city. In the corner of one of the ground-floor wards, where the wall might've gone up over a medieval oven, where there might've lingered a tang of ash, Barbara discovered the standing cross from the Refugee Center. She had to touch the thing, jammed in at an angle. The corners of the wood remained furred here and there, no better sanded than the day Silky and Paul had carried it into the fluttering chapel. That hadn't been so long ago, that visit to the Center. Yet how many reiterations of Day One had the mother suffered, since?

Now in the clinic Barbara stood staring at the cross until, behind her, one of the patients started to laugh. Or rather this guy pretended to laugh, his hilarity an imitation, too wicked to believe. A parody of a villain out of James Bond, and maybe he was right to poke fun. The mother couldn't be certain this soft-pine cross was the one her middle child had helped slap together. A lot of accessories around here were makeshift. Cesare used to handle the Mass, but never on a regular schedule. Lately the Vomero priest had declined to drop by at all, claiming he was too busy (and when DiPio told Barbara that, she had almost broken into a wicked laugh herself). The old *medico* responded by bringing in Jay's former colleague from the Refugee Center—what was his name? Interstate? In any case the hairless German with the Franciscan T at first seemed uncomfortable around Barbara. His Midwestern greeting sounded pinched. But the wife had no interest in raking through the garbage about Jay's initial UN contract.

What difference did it make to her if, here at the clinic, a deal had been struck between the chaplain and his former American Boss, and a bit of cash had changed hands? What mattered was, the Jaybird would tell Barbara if she wanted to know. The husband would do as he'd promised; between him and his Owl Girl things were on a fresh basis. As for the Missouri-trained chaplain, Jay had gone so far as to show him a piece of paperwork from early June, a notice of a bank transfer Silky had arranged.

And as for the people under DiPio's care, they found the German's freewheeling religious services just the ticket. The cases here, like those out at the Center, had seen their worlds destroyed in more than a single, simple sense. Barbara could see why most of the clinic staff needed a couple of degrees and three or four languages. Her first morning downtown, she found herself shuttling between the kind of decision-making for which she was trained and considerably greater challenges. She took a hand in one-on-one counseling, in groups and role-playing sessions. Once or twice she even suggested her own therapeutic variation, since despite their education the counselors here remained Neapolitan, willing to improvise. And she liked it—hail Mary full of grace, she did. When Barbara got to try one of her improvisations (a "trial methodology"), she enjoyed a sober exhilaration that fired up all her daytime energies and yet never lost the sense she was in control. Whatever other alternatives she'd had to staying up in the Vomero apartment, none could've offered so sweet a fit to the nervous system.

And come bedtime, while she and Jay exchanged mumbles about the ups and downs of the workplace, these worked like a relaxation massage composed entirely of words. The Jaybird sometimes broke into a snore before he finished an anecdote. Even to discuss the politics of the clinic had a gentling effect, strange when Barbara thought about it. In this same bed, after all, she'd lost hours of sleep fretting over who was calling the shots within the family.

Yet Barbara's visits to the inner lives of the *terremotati* could also leave her troubled and let down. There was a distressed afternoon or two when she picked up her bodyguard outside the clinic and, before getting into the car, shook off anyone who approached her for a handout or a prayer. She wasn't able to do much for a lot of these cases, no more than for Maria Elena back in Bridgeport. Rather she was forced to see as well the stubbornness, the grip of pattern and loop, that had made those syndromes so familiar in the first place. It hardly mattered when Barbara didn't understand a victim's fevered Italian, peppered with dialect. She couldn't mistake the old story of their night sweats. During such difficult nights, the vision of a visiting saint only distracted these *terramotati* from the real problem. Worse, it was usually the same saint, Padre Pio. Pio was a recent addition to the canon, a Capuchin who'd worked his miracles in the 1950s and 1960s, and mediagenic in his way. Nowadays, when Fond came on the tube to pester the family, he earned his camera time by a sleek hint of hard living. The refugee Lazarus. Pio had been the opposite, Yoda, squat and wrinkled yet aglow within his robes. He was said to have convinced a movie producer, via telepathy, to bankroll *La Dolce Vita*. And so long as

Barbara worked downtown, it seemed that some of the sorry creatures she tried to help would've gotten more out of watching Fellini than going on their knees to Padre Pio. Fellini would at least have showed them outrageous faces not unlike what had hurt them. But the figure out of their Catholic faith, Barbara's own faith, got in the way of their trauma, of coming to know it, as if they'd hung some hollow gold knickknack over the pain—another *ojetto* for the city's tormented walls. She hated to see it. Her church had brought her better than that, palpable comfort, honest strength.

But the clinic's population couldn't risk depths like that. They preferred the saints, the stand-ins. None of these patients claimed to have seen the Devil, or none that Barbara talked to, though a couple suffered nightmares in which some troublesome relative figured as a witch. She knew all about that one. She understood the kind of people she was dealing with, Cesare's "bourgeois." These were card-carrying citizens, the professional class, all registered with the national health program. Yet while DiPio's cases had little in common with the desperate strays out at the *Centro Rifugiati*, they were by no means untouched by tragedy. More than once Barbara was left looking for a place to pull herself together, trying unknown doors with a dripping face. There was a man who couldn't get beyond a thoughtless curse he'd growled at his mother, an angry word that he believed had attracted the Evil Eye. There was a woman who spoke obsessively, in halting half-English, of the extension cords she'd run into a child's bedroom, overloading the circuit behind the wall.

And there was one neurosis Barbara had never come across in the textbooks, nor on the internet either: a man who claimed he couldn't be living in Naples because he wasn't old enough. This was a guy of about sixty who styled his remaining hair in a frowsy Mohawk and claimed he was still at work on his name. Every stage of life, so Mohawk believed, was a city. He himself had only recently reached the minimum entry requirement for elementary cities, like the fresh and exotic Portland, Oregon. In another ten years, if he kept up his research and steered clear of the wrong crowd, he might grow into Houston or Tokyo. The last thing you wanted, he explained, was to try and jump a level—to claim a more complex citizenship before you'd worked up the orientation. The last thing you wanted was to have the avenues around you all at once changing direction, thrusting out fresh lampposts like fingers through the holes of an afghan, the lampposts plastered with notices in God knows what language and your own frail body God knows how far from the sidewalk. Or you might discover yourself at the wheel of a new SmartFiat, engineered to millennial environmental standards, careening head-on towards a knight on horseback toppling from his pedestal. Repeatedly the old-timer insisted he wasn't ready for the next move, and not nearly prepared for the adult dose that was Naples, or say Damascus. Those sank their underground agora and raised their satellite dishes only for the most mature.

Delusionary, indeed. The guy could've taught Barbara something. If she'd spent more time with this "unripened metropolis," him and his frayed toothbrush of a hairdo, she too might've achieved a more profound shakeup and understanding. So she told herself at week's end, anyway, after one of the ranking psychologists asked her into his cubicle.

This doctor had done two years at UCLA, and she could hear it in his voice, relaxed, beach-y. Nonetheless he was firm with her. The man made it clear that he and the rest of the medical staff could no longer trust the fragile personalities around here to an amateur. No longer, Mrs. Lulucita. She didn't have so much as a certificate for social work, let alone medical credentials.

After a while—after he saw how calmly she took the news—the psychologist began to sound more Californian. He assured Barbara that everyone in the clinic had nothing but affection for her, personally. She'd brought a fresh perspective to the work, and that was always useful. She was certainly welcome to help in some other capacity, some sort of work like her husband did . . .

"Like my husband?" Barb tugged at her shirtfront. "What? Take out the trash?"

The doctor ran the entire length of his tie between thumb and forefinger. When he spoke, the edge had returned to his voice. "I realize that you and your husband have powerful friends."

He realized, too, that *dottore* DiPio himself was among those friends. But Mrs. Lulucita needed to understand, should she have it in mind to contest the staff's decision, that DiPio didn't oppose it. He might be a bit of a maverick, the old man, but he would never go against the consensus of the people he depended on to run his clinic. And (at this the young therapist fingered his tie again) additional funding from the Consulate wouldn't change anyone's mind either.

"*Ci sono limite*," he concluded, his first sentence in Italian. "There are limits."

Her driver and bodyguard, the big curly-head, hadn't expected *l'Americana* to knock off early. Now as Barbara waited for him, on the bench inside the clinic's iron gateway, she figured that what she felt was something like her Vomero priest in his church: she was disgusted with herself for all the time she'd spent eavesdropping, her whole working week vicarious. Yet even this afternoon, in Naples she couldn't remain entirely a sourpuss, not as the downtown emerged from *riposo*, as it set up a fresh display of the pedestrian baroque. Barbara discovered, or rediscovered, that this must've been part of the reason she'd chosen to work down here in the original city. She'd never grown indifferent its stagy mash of hustle and museum effects. There was still the echo, the gesturing, the whole-body Neapolitan shrug. Then too, one or two downtowners recognized the mother of the *miracolino*; they came close enough to extend a medallion or crucifix through the bars. A man who looked to be at least eighty, his hand like the brown husk of an insect, went into a staggering bow as he held out a silver-plated heart.

She allowed the man her word, her prayer. But the visitor who mattered was her middle child Paul.

Today the Consulate had assigned the kids a wide and factory-fresh Audi, a ride that didn't fit down the last half-block before the palazzo entryway. Paul had to walk from the intersection. And he didn't go unnoticed, his walk so full of beans, his black-and-white so crisp. By the time Barbara heaved herself off the bench the eleven-year-old was sandwiched between a pair of housewives, each with her net bag of vegetables. When the women fished out their bric-a-brac, the silver flashed in the late-afternoon sun. At this hour the light poked into these man-made canyons at odd angles.

The mother couldn't help but notice again how the excitement over her *miracolino* had settled down. The scrawniest *clandestino* on the street, a young man with a filthy bandanna, gazed at the boy mildly. Around the clinic too, when it came to Paul, DiPio alone remained a true believer. Barbara's middle child had visited once during her week, and everyone except the old *dottore* had confined themselves to brisk courtesies. The therapists here were on soft money, like most of the people in quake relief; they couldn't waste time with a disorder that was beyond diagnosis. As for the patients, they hadn't been paying much attention to the news.

Paul finished with the housewives. "Hi, h-hi Mom."

The boy could just show up? Like any other eleven-year-old? (More or less—Barb shouldn't forget the armed escort and private limo).

"It was, it was b-*boring*, with Chris and, and JJ," he went on. "All they do is tell us wh-where, wh-where we have to stand."

Barbara found herself angry, upset with the security team or the housewives or DiPio or somebody for leaving her child so exposed. There had to be *somebody*! Maybe that Doctor L.A., yanking the clinic's rug out from under her! But Paul was showing Mama a smile with adult overtones, fleshy, almost flirty, and in another moment Barb's anger had swung round on her. She was swamped by fresh recriminations. How well did she know this boy, any more? How much had she helped him, in fact? She recalled that she'd seen, for instance, inklings of sexual ambiguity, but she'd offered Mr. Paul nothing like an invitation to talk about it. Yes, she knew it might help him to "assert" his "identity" in that way. Nettie herself, still dealing with her own long years in denial, had brought up the idea of such a talk. But since returning Maria Elena to Children's Services, when it came her pubescent boy, the mother had let the professionals handle any talk about the facts of life.

She hadn't wanted the other kids bothering Paul about it either. Romy and JJ could kiss all they liked, that was different thing, almost a political transaction. Anyway the eleven-year-old had already seen his brother kissing a girl or two, back in Bridgeport. But just the other evening, Barbara had come down hard on Chris after he'd walked into the kitchen with a fresh printout and announced that Paul had five of the early indicators of homosexuality.

The fifteen-year-old had just walked in and announced it, while Dora and Syl were helping Mama make popovers. She'd ordered the girls out and then read the riot act to her second-oldest.

"Do you want to live your whole life like this?" she'd asked. "An IQ of 150 in the classroom and zero everywhere else?" His sisters were still in elementary school, she'd reminded him, and Mother of God, this was his *brother* he was talking about.

Chris couldn't stop touching his glasses. "Mom like, come on, like, what are you? Like, homophobic?"

"Chris, don't. I'm saying, you leave that *alone*. Paul is his own man."

She'd grounded the teenager from a day's work on the documentary. She'd made him give Dora and Syl a tutorial on the camera and software.

Now her miracle child was asking something, from the other side of the clinic gate. Barbara couldn't understand, given the traffic. Where was her driver, anyway? To judge from the noise, everyone else was in a car, on a Vespa, or pulling up to a street stall in a three-wheeled truck. The din seemed to rise as uncontrollably as the sulfur smell from under the paving-stones. Then amid that cacophony, with her boy's pretty mouth shaping unheard words before her and, in her ribcage somewhere, a sore spot lingering from losing her job—in there, Barb got the idea of an interview.

Chapter Eleven

PAUL (*adjusting his belt, squinting away*): It's like a, a tunnel or, or more like, something *making* a tunnel. It's like something h-h-hollows out a tunnel, through the trouble. Like maybe a tentacle pokes its way through the trouble and at, tat, attack . . . a tentacle attaches. You can just feel it.
BARBARA (*off-screen*): A tentacle?
(*PAUL laughs, shakes head.*)
BARBARA: Just friends talking, Paulie. No judgments, no bad words.
PAUL: You feel a flow, and it's a wet flow, like this flowing wet that w-w-worms its way through and then at, tack, attaches. That's where you can get hold of the trouble.

"Check it out," the editor said, freezing the image before them. "Check it *out*, the boy just eats the screen."

Barbara crossed her arms, seeing Paul as a movie star, the computer's flat screen making more of his lips and eyelashes. She hadn't known that this was how the editing would work. She hadn't understood that she would watch it happening, rewinds and cuts and freeze-frames, all handled with a wireless mouse and biomorphic keyboard and taking shape on a screen perhaps a foot from her face. But then, there was nowhere else to sit. The editing room might've been a utility closet. The entire "studio headquarters" (according to DiPio, their films had won awards) fit in a single five-room walkup. The only air-conditioning was a unit in one wall of this same cramped space.

The editor himself seemed to prefer things tight. His striped sleeveless t-shirt hugged his torso so closely that it rode up his midsection, exposing a deeply indented waistline. His hip-hugging sailor's pants, white, looked more snug still. Yet while he sat grinning up at Paul's image, he appeared hardly older than Barbara's middle child.

"That stutter is right on, too," the editor added. "Total authenticity."

PAUL (*looking left of camera*): You feel, you feel so much when it at, attaches, like so much a-all at once. I, I mean whatever the trouble is, a-all at wuh-wuh-wuh . . . all at once you know you can fix it.

BARBARA (*off-screen*): Do you hear anything? Voices or anything?

PAUL (*frowning*): Mo-om. (*hesitates, fingers to cheek*) It's not, it's never in words. There m-might be n-n-*noises*. There might like a single n-noise c-coming on, like a r-rising, a r-rumbling rising that's a-also lots of, of noises a-at once.

BARBARA: Like traffic noise? Traffic and street noise?

PAUL: Whatever. A-anyway it's never w-words. Words, you know, they a-add up, they, they line up a-and go somewhere. This, it just comes on, buh-buh, behemoth, you know? It's shapeless and, and e-everywhere at once. That's also, it's a-also how I know this, it can't, it can't—this won't last.

BARBARA (*sharply*): What? This won't last?

PAUL: It's, it isn't, the h-healing, it won't go on forever.

BARBARA: Are you saying, these episodes—

PAUL: It comes on so aw, aw, awesome, w-with the rumble a-and the flow through the trouble. It's, it's such a force when it at, attaches. You just feel it. And, and that's got to mean, there's o-only going to be so many. There can only b-be so many.

BARBARA: The episodes are a temporary condition? You won't always . . .

(*PAUL plucks at pants-legs, pinching the crease*).

BARBARA: Sorry, Paul. You tell it. Your story.

PAUL: Well, come on. This can't keep, keep h-happening the rest of my life. Even when it, when it d-does happen, you can feel the thing has like, it's licked out its, its one and o-only tunnel. One soul, solo tunnel, one ten, tentacle. Then it's done.

(*BARBARA moves onscreen, beside the boy. Focus widens around them: a balcony over a piazza. He's in a chair and she squats beside him, against railing.*)

DR. DIPIO (*off-screen*): Si. Phenomenon is situational.

PAUL (*hands clasped but fingers extended, Italian*): You know what i-it
  feels like when, when something can't last.
(*BARBARA nods slowly.*)

"Look at him," the sailor-boy said, "like the camera isn't even there.
Do it do it *do* it. Superstar authenticity."

Spare me, Hollywood. The editor was Neapolitan, born and raised
not far from Barbara's upscale palazzo, but he'd gotten a film degree
from NYU and he'd asked the mother to call him Whitman. If you
asked her, the way he darted between mouse and keyboard called to
mind a dancer rather than a poet. A ballet dancer, nothing but muscle
and bone. And every time he made a pirouette, the video became
more interesting. Whitman created emphasis; he made Paul's gesturing
hands fill the screen.

As for the young man's gayness, flaming, *l'Americana* couldn't say
she was surprised. Naples was famous for its queers, a sailors' town.
Even her father had told her a story about the local demi-monde—or
part of a story. Dad had managed only a halting effort at sharing such
stuff with his Barbie, sweet but halting. He'd done what he could to
increase his daughter's sophistication while, at the same time, striving
to comprehend his own failed foray into love. But she hadn't needed
her Babo's help. The drag queens of Naples actually rated mention in
the guidebooks. An American could find a photo or two, since a
number of the male hookers found the pictures good for business.
The poses made Barbara think of her mother-in-law, her man-catching
sashay.

Silky Kahlberg of course had known all about such creatures of
the shadow. Once when he and Barbara had been away from the
children, he'd pointed out a couple of the more flagrant cross-dressers.
As if the mother could've missed them in the first place. Dr. DiPio
however, forever needing the consolation of his Mr. Christopher, had
surprised her. She would never have expected the old *medico* would
know someone like Whitman. Nor would Barbara have thought that
an editor of this young man's rank and accomplishment would bother
with her material, the roughest kind of point-&-shoot. In the States
only someone on the fringes of the business, say a student strapped
for cash, would've accepted such an assignment. The keyboard
Baryshnikov beside her, on the other hand, boasted openly about a
short he'd just completed. It had been picked up for an anthology of

"the Naples new wave," he announced, and what's more, his first full-length feature would be rebroadcast next week on cable-access. You could buy that earlier movie off the web too, Whitman told her. A five-minute trailer was available without subscription. Just watching the man sent Barbara into another dizzying carom between believing she had a handle on this city and thinking she knew nothing.

Whitman also insisted they speak English. "I need the practice," he said.

The man worked Christopher Street into the conversation, "Christopher east," as if the distinction mattered. What Barbara was finding significant, however, was something close by—the man's hair. Above his nipple-notched top, Whitman affected the look of a young King David, with luxuriant black curls that hung to his shoulders. As he sat working the computer, in that shifting and indirect light, he called to mind the late Lieutenant-Major. Barbara couldn't help noticing: Silky had worn his the same length. He'd tossed it back with the same vanity, the same flair, and with an almost identical twist of the neck. Now what did that mean?

PAUL: S-Situational, yeah, that's the way it, it comes. Like, so situational. Something, something hollows ow, out the tunnel, and then it a-all, it all whacks you a-at once. A-all at once, it's there in front and, and it's there in back, and if there a-are words, they're a-all at once. It's, it's in your fingers, or it's, it's right at your fingers, you, you can just reach it, and, and, it's between your, your legs too, it's buh, buh . . .
BARBARA: That's okay, Paulie. I understand.
DIPIO (*off-screen*): But why the tongue, please? Why the tongue?

Whitman's hands kept accelerating: first ballet, then jazz. To watch him go, snipping out the overlap in the two interviews Barbara had brought him, you'd think anyone could do this. Anyone could make it interesting. But the young pro had an idea behind every cut and paste, and he shared a lot of his thinking, while also getting off snide remarks about "movies that should go on a diet." Barb was left feeling like a hayseed, a dumbo American, because she'd never heard of most of the films he was complaining about.

But then, she'd asked for this. Naturally, when she'd told Chris and John Junior she needed the equipment for a couple of afternoons—she too needed to make a document, a picture about Paul—once again the teenagers had sworn up and down that their younger brother was a big part of their own project.

"Hey. This isn't just another teen movie."

"Mom like, think of *Casablanca*. 'The problems of three little people don't amount to a hill of beans in this world.'"

But Barb had never cared for that movie, to her it played as if the whole point of the Second World War had been to make Humphrey Bogart's love life more interesting, and she'd been under no illusions about what her two oldest would do with raw footage of the middle child talking. They'd tear it apart. They'd warp their younger brother's hard-won articulations in whatever way might serve their own purposes. What could she expect, from teenage boys? If Barbara let them handle the interviews, or if she gave them the interviews unedited, Paul would get lost in translation. Once more he'd go neglected, in the name of some greater, foggier good.

PAUL (*squinting off*): Their tongue, wow. But it's, it's like I say, this never hap, happens in words, or, or never words lined up a-and getting somewhere. It's never like a, it never adds up to a, a, a story.

(*BARBARA nods, upright, propped on railing*)

PAUL: The tongue is like the tentacle. Wh-when that feeling is row, is rolling, it comes, it comes o-out at the tongue. (*eyes shift to BARBARA*)

BARBARA: This is what we're here for, Paulie. It's nothing bad or crazy.

PAUL: Can't, can't you understand, that's where I catch it? The tongue. It's, it's the place where I, I get hold of the trouble. Can't you, why can't you j-just feel it?

"You know after I edit," Whitman said, "I can download straight to the web."

He made an acrobat of the cursor, swinging it from icon to icon along the top of the screen. He assured Barb she'd leave here with the edited file in her scan-disk stick, and a DVD as well if she wanted. "But streaming video, that's instant gratification."

The mother didn't respond, thinking differently. What her youngest boy had felt, during his episodes, no longer sounded so strange. This time around the mother noticed how his descriptions fit the testimonies that had turned up in the reading she'd done, ten days ago now. She saw what the boy had to say carpentered into a single fifteen- or twenty-minute burst, stinging but confined, and as she watched, Barbara understood better than before how Mr. Paul had been living with an invisible talent like her own, the talent to link up, now and again, with the Universal Horsepower. She understood that the absence of healthier exercise for the boy's spirit-muscle had forced up these recent eruptions; the miracles had worked as a safety valve, an overflow. And while Barb got the picture, all at once like this, she suffered its wallop, sure. But then the picture was over—the cry from Paul's heart shrank into an icon on the monitor. Soon enough that icon would disappear inside another, and neither would appear larger than the tip of her pinkie. Likewise the entire family's transoceanic event, in which an untreatable sickness on one side of the Atlantic had turned into an unknowable medicine on the other, would be reduced to a moment's chatter between satellites.

Barbara's footage, in other words, was only another item for the local closets. After all, what city in the world was so full of discards? She remembered the trunk in the Nazionale, and she wondered just which shelf or cellar would wind up storing the business on Whitman's screen. This longhaired *artiste* had composed another storytelling platter, on which was depicted a slender hero who, despite his frail youth and stark robes, possessed the touch that could restore life. He was the Anti-Siren, this creature. But after he dropped in, after he sent the shock of recovery through a few broken bodies, he went away. Paul would go away, him and his well-intentioned family, and Barb couldn't have found a more powerful proof than this: his face collapsing to fit into a file within a file. Lively as their Neapolitan crisis might've seemed, in the end it was only another scrap for the display case, catalogued and wired to an alarm.

A storytelling platter, Barbara thought, or another version of the movie cliché. Another couple of Anglos felt a bit better about themselves, thanks to their trip to Italy.

PAUL: The only one, really, the only wuh, one I've really been a-able to talk to, uhh, talk to about it is Ruh, Ruh. (*swallows*) It's Romy.
BARBARA (*straightening*): She talks to you?
PAUL: I used to, used to talk to her. (*twitches*) She knows a-about the lick, the licking and flowing and all. I, I used to, a-and she said

219

when she, when she st-still had her broken back, she could sit in her wheelchair and feel the rest of her, really, like flowing. She sat there, and she said it was like she was a, a s-seabird, a seabird who'd gone over the land a-and tried to dive for food in a, in a well. She was a seabird in a well, can't you just feel it? A well isn't for seabirds, it's too, she can't—

BARBARA: She's been tricked. The things she trusted, now they hurt her.

PAUL: Oh, oh, okay.

BARBARA: The things she trusted, suddenly they left her useless. She felt like she was no good to anyone, I'm saying. Just baggage, garbage.

PAUL: But she, Mom—that's not, not it. No. She wasn't g-garbage, she was, she was still a bird. R-Romy I mean. Garbage? She w-was still a, a bird, she could feel it, she could even, even h-hear it. She heard her like feathers, the, the rustling. The wind.

DIPIO (*off-screen*): The body remembers. *Come si dice*, the limb like a ghost?

PAUL: Romy, Romy understands. She was a-always flying. And we, we've a-always got that, I'm saying, we've all got that ex, ex, extra rustle a-and flowing.

(*Blinks at BARBARA, at camera, lowers head. BARBARA touches boy's shoulder. Inaudible murmur.*)

PAUL: We've all got them, ah, always, really. Alter, alter, like feathers and wings, a-alternative body parts. You know? Alter, alter . . . they're flowing a-and it's all this life, a-always. (*head comes up, eyes enlarged*) It's never gar, garbage. Never you, useless. It's always w-whispering and a-alive and coming on, like a, a thousand words a-at once. If you tried you, you could feel it. You could a-all feel it.

(*to BARBARA*) You said, you said there've been o-others, p-people like me. (*waves arm*) There been lots of others, y-you said. Which means, which means, we l-live with the crowds, all, all the time. Why, why don't you feel it?

DIPIO: (*sound of scratching*)

"A masterpiece," Whitman announced. "*81/2*."

How much had he left for the older boys? Fifteen minutes? She almost dropped the DVD Whitman handed her, then let the scan-disk stick slip through her fingers.

The filmmaker picked it up, then spoke her name with maximum musicality. "Honey," he asked, "what about streaming the video?" The young man tossed his hair. "You wouldn't be able to drop the footage if we posted it directly to your sons' site."

His hair was lovely, the curls classic, the DNA out of Africa. Barb had to wonder again about the late Lieutenant-Major, whether he'd gone for men. And so what if he had? *Silky's Secrets*—if that were a book, it would've been a doorstop. Plus when it came to this particular secret, around his Organization, the rule was don't ask, don't tell. On top of that, if there'd ever been a man who preferred life in the closet, it was Officer Kahlberg. He would've savored every irony in playing it straight.

The mother turned the scan-disk between her fingers. Chris and JJ had their secrets too, tucked away in their "project."

"Those boys of yours," Whitman went on, "haven't they got something set up for visitors? A guestbook or a blog or something?"

If they had a guestbook, they were hiding something under it. When Aurora had asked what the boys wanted for a present, recently—she always made a big, romantic deal about summer solstice—Chris and JJ had requested a standing screen to set up around their desk. They'd wanted to make sure they weren't surprised by anyone who neglected to knock. Aurora had come through with a typically extravagant gewgaw, a triptych of young love, set against a background of a fire-breathing Vesuvius and adorable broken temple columns. The girls showed a lot of petticoat, the men wore buckled shoes, and the old playgirl, in choosing such a screen, gave the boys a nudge and a wink. She let them know she was all for love amid the ruins.

Not that JJ and Chris, in accepting the garish piece, had revealed that they got the message. They'd offered nothing beyond the usual teenage grumbles of thanks. Whatever they were up to, it mattered more than returning their grandmother's secret OK. Just as, Barb would bet, their documentary mattered more than finding Romy and John Junior a room with a bed. So far as she could tell, the gypsy and her oldest were still drawing the line at a kiss and a cuddle. That's what the mother concluded from a close study of her boy, from the tightness in his long legs and the sparkle in his one-liners. The evidence might be circumstantial, but many a parent had built a winning case on far less. Barbara would bet that her two goodhearted young Americans had a nobler purpose than helping one of them get laid. More than likely they had a notion that they could clear the girl of Silky's murder, in some public forum . . .

She shifted to face Whitman, their knees knocking.

"It's all on the web." Barbara ignored his shuffling beneath the table. "They've got everything right there on the web."

When the skinny auteur narrowed his eyes, his thick-lashed eyes, he looked more like King David than ever. He looked so haughty and aware that for a moment Barb thought he knew what she wanted. Of course he didn't know, he was only swayed by the reverberant waves of her intensity, but no sooner had Barbara put it into words—they should crack into her sons' materials—than Whitman agreed. She didn't have to come up with an excuse.

"Oh, honey." He gave a lippy grin. "This is going to be *sweet*."

She'd offered an extra fifty, when she'd asked, but Barbara got the impression that her companion would've done this for nothing. The way Whitman faced the screen, grinning and flexing his striped chest, you'd think he got a kick out of poking through the heteros' dirty laundry. Or did he merely enjoy the challenge? In any case he was whiz enough to at once isolate that part of the boys' site labeled "Under Construction." As Whitman had done with his own film, Chris and JJ had made five minutes of footage available as a sampler. Also they'd set up additional "rushes" in a file for which they'd given the rest of the family the password. A dummy file—look Ma no secrets.

But what was under "Under Construction?" Seeking a way in, the mother gave the campy wonk birth-dates and middle names. He pecked in variations, the digits in European order instead of American, the words abbreviated or syllables reversed. After the first five or six suggestions Barbara detected a throb in the same intangible space where a meaningful Communion usually touched her. Of all the unlikely . . . but didn't she know the sensation when she felt it? Hadn't she just realized that Paul had the same perplexing talent? She wondered if those thoughts about her middle child, about the here-and-gone fragility of the whole Naples experience, had brought this on. Or it might've been this bitty production room, this kitchen-sink Warner Brothers; the set-up wasn't much different from a confession booth. Barbara frowned and stayed on-task, sharing her maiden name with the stranger beside her. She told him her wedding anniversary. When those didn't work she drew a breath.

"Try divorce," she said. "Or Naples divorce."

After variations in Italian and English, handled without once meeting Whitman's eyes, she added "Angry Mama." Next, "Crazy Mama."

She could see that the boho was glancing at her, his long hair shifting in the corner of her eye. Still he never hesitated to sling a new set of letters and digits across the screen. They worked like skipping stones, setting off the ripple of windows popping open. The central box always read the same, *Invalid*, and Barbara came to think that some of her excitement was entirely ordinary. What mother doesn't get a little thrill out of checking her kids' pockets? As each potential password came to mind, however, she kept sensing that deeper release. What would you call this, if not confession in code? She rose and paced, wheeling between the worktable and the air conditioner, and Whitman had to ask that she speak more slowly. His English couldn't keep up.

When they hit on the password, she was facing the air conditioner, and for a while she stayed there, letting the freon tickle her neck. The Open Sesame to the boys' private footage had nothing to do with her. The choice must've been John Junior's.

"My ro," Whitman said, drawing out the pronunciation as the unedited files appeared on the screen. "From Romy."

Children grow, they grow away. How many reminders did she need?

"Looks like there aren't too many files." When the young man pointed at the screen, his silver snake-ring turned blue. "One two, three four five."

Not many yet, Barb thought. Not when the children were only starting out. She returned to her chair, still savoring traces of exhilaration. Maybe she should consider today another trial methodology. Onscreen she saw four files whose labels included either "Npls" or "hstry," and one more, with the simple name "INNOCENT."

"Innocent," Barbara said.

Whitman set up the link to the video player. The window on the software opened, and at its bottom a set of concentric circles shrank and grew, shrank and grew, a visual cue for establishing the connection—or perhaps the blinking and thickly outlined eye of the gypsy girl, one of those Mongol-goddess eyes, never so fierce and burning as when they suddenly took over the player's window. Romy had got a tan, some impossible tan that lent her skin a lush hint of violet. Her gypsy trimmings worked as well, the earrings full of shadows and the scarf electric with tinsel. She was made for this, precisely the sort of dark and voluptuous fairy the technology needed to open its box of secrets, and John Junior stuck with the talking-head arrangement for the first few minutes. He and his girl had found some privacy in a grove of trees off a highland roadway. From time to time you could hear the whine of a *motorino*, and see that Romy delivered this appeal from well above city and Bay. The faraway water behind her glimmered a chromium blue that picked up the hints in her face. The trees were umbrella pine and the gray shreds in one corner of the sky must've come from the volcano.

The gypsy began: "I am innocent of Silky Kahlberg's murder. Like, it was almost the other way around."

John Junior interrupted, in a voice the mother couldn't make out, more restrained than she was used to from him. Romy shifted places in a blink, reappearing framed between tree trunks. Her hair had been tied back too.

"I did not shoot Lieutenant-Major L-Loius Kahlberg," she repeated. "I am innocent, and for sure, it could've been the other way around. Could've been him still running around and me . . ."

The gypsy lowered her head, trailing a fingernail down her glittering scarf.

"I knew that he was dealing in fake ID's," she went on finally. "In counterfeits, officer Kahlberg. Also he knew that I knew. For sure, we both knew the signs, like—"

JJ interrupted again, and Romy reappeared in better posture. With this third take she got across that, at the Museo Nazionale, the liaison officer had planned to kill her.

"I warn the Lieutenant-Major that I will expose him. On the streets there are ways." Her smile was bitter, the shape of the noise of another passing bike. "The normies never know, the signs we use. Like the SMS, the message on the *telefonino*. Only better, because Kahlberg, he got it right away, and he knew he had to get rid of me."

Her stare gathered force. "The man played me, at the Museo. He *played* me."

Girl, thought Barbara, join the club.

"Officer Kahlberg," Romy was saying, "he set it up, he will get rid of me and like, he will look like a hero same time." Her chin lifted, her confidence growing. "The way the man played it, he will be on top both ways. On top out on the streets, so nobody could take him down, and on top in old Babylon too, in NATO."

So far as the "play" was concerned, the Lieutenant Major's plan to get this girl out of his silky hair, Barbara had heard all she needed. The museum visit had always struck her as a dubious trip. And when she'd asked for time alone with the kids, that afternoon, the liaison and his Umberto had run through their bebop repertoire, all those significant looks. What they'd needed was the opportunity to get the gypsy alone. The mother's request had given them the chance to improvise.

"He was looking forward to it," said the girl onscreen. "That gun of his, he couldn't wait to use that."

Barb was nodding, getting it. She even believed she understood why the liaison had thrown in the tall tale about Romy getting violent: *she went right upside his head.*

"I knew the man, for sure. But I never expected trouble at the museum."

Neither the gypsy nor anyone else had cracked Umberto's head, before the Lieutenant Major went down. But Silky must've had it in mind to smack his flunky a good one. Umberto would need a wound to match the story told by his boss. Being boss mattered a lot to the Lieutenant Major, Barbara could see that now. So the liaison must've intended first to put a bullet or two in JJ's girlfriend—or five or ten. Then to top off his afternoon, and to make a point for his colleagues in the Camorra, he'd have given Umberto a pistol-whipping. The NATO man might also have thrown in a bit of groping, a bit of grinding, letting the so-called museum guide know what an American officer kept beneath his Palm Beach whites. He would've enjoyed that.

The charade became transparent to Barbara, like a Christmas crèche in which the terra cotta melted away to reveal frames of barbed wire. Meanwhile the fruitiness of Whitman's shampoo grew stronger, and the girl onscreen, recalling that morning at the Nazionale, looked ever more frightened. The lone stabilizing influence was John Junior, running his set like a pro. Like an adult, leaving the choice of time and place to Romy (the gypsy knew the good hiding places), but meantime taking charge of the larger project. The password, the

purpose of the interview—that must've been all JJ. And every time
you heard Barb's oldest, through the speakers mounted on the walls,
you heard genuine caring, but also restraint. A good deal less histrionic
than his mother, lately. JJ's sweet sanity might in fact make as much
of a difference for the former cripple, over time, as his younger
brother's healing hands. Before the picture onscreen jumped again,
Romy had broken into a more open smile.

Then JJ went to a whole-body shot, and you could see that the girl
had toned down her look. Her jeans fit more loosely, and she toyed
with what looked like a childish prop, a thin, smooth length of wood.
Was it a sawed-off broomstick? Where had she found that?

She flipped the stick from hand to hand, her tone of voice playful.
"I have to show you this. Pinocchio."

The boy's off-screen murmur remained unsexy.

"No, get this," the girl said. "Like, the *real* Pinocchio."

She slipped the abbreviated pole between her legs. Like that the
mood changed, the girl's pose appeared obscene, and Romy threw in
an orgasmic gasp or two besides. She held the stick so the end just
poked from her crotch.

"Pinocchio says," Romy said, "I got no diseases."

The wood grew longer, emerging from the vee of her jeans.

"Pinocchio says I love you, always I love you. Since Christ was a
carpenter!" The gypsy worked still more of the stick's length out
before her.

"And always I will love you!" Now she needed both hands in front,
to hold its full length. "I will be a good *father!*"

The soundtrack turned to laughter, and the stick fell from Romy's
hands while she wobbled down into a crouch. Or was that the camera
wobbling, in JJ's hands? So much for any sexy mood. Whitman too
chuckled over his keyboard, hitting Pause. The filmmaker, the way
he laughed, sounded thoughtful; he sounded as though he wanted to
work the bit into his next feature. And Barbara remained quiet, though
she was grinning, not wanting to make her editor self-conscious. A
joke like that could only make her wonder again about this girl and
John Junior, how much had gone on between them. When Whitman
restarted the video, the mother was glad to see Romy jump-cut back
to seriousness. The gypsy was in close-up once more, and frowning.

226

ROMY: I used to believe in the power of the street, the greatest power. No one can beat (*nodding, in rhythm*) the power of the street. (*starts to smile, stops*) I used to believe this, it was history. What does Chris always say about history?

OFFSCREEN: History moves to the left.

ROMY: To the left, yes, like, which means to the street. You know? I used to scrabble around living for no money and, at the same time, I live for this. I believe that, in history, maybe next year or maybe the year after, I will have the power. I believe, old Babylon and the cops, and the suits, they will fall. (*shakes index finger*) I believe will come a better day, and the suits will sell their blood for money. For sure. We take the sticks from the police and . . . (*throws a punch; hair comes loose from ponytail*).

We will make them stand and smile while we run our disgusting hands all over—

(*inaudible word, o.s.; jump-cut, ROMY with hair off her face*)

Revolution from the streets, this I live for. I am, I was, a soldier, a revolution woman. I am never scared of the officer Kahlberg. (*lowers head; touches scarf*) But I think, better I been scared. I knew the man, another dealer. But better I knew more.

(*chin comes up; small smile*)

Paul, your brother, he shows me first, a different power in the streets. Paul breaks through the like, the stones surrounding me. He shows me, I never understand. Never understood. For sure, I never even dreamed about it, a life like—like your brother shows me. He has the revolution in his hands, the better life in the streets, for all the punks and thieves, the revolution and the life. All the soldiers, we're in his hand.

(*Looks away*) I been in the life ever since I left the camps, since Lapusului, and your little brother like, one touch and in that touch . . . (*faces camera*) it's all my life, and it's new forever, it will never drop into the dark again, never again beneath the stones. Your Paul picks me up, he has me in his fingers, all my life, and all the other soldiers too. It's another power, in the streets. It's so strong, your brother, in his fingers, it picks up the rich neighborhoods too. He even picks up Babylon.

(*nodding in rhythm*) Old Baby-lon, your po-wer's gone. (*smiles*) He picks up the cops too, all the cops, no matter what their uniform . . .

(*frowns, starts to speak, frowns again. CUT to three-quarter profile.*)

Lieutenant-Major Kahlberg, I knew him, but—better if I knew more. He moves between NATO and the street, very smooth. Better if I understand, if I understood, he has, he had people. Kahlberg had like, some of the same people I did. At the Nazionale, the Museum, if your brother isn't there . . . (*touches scarf*) your Paul saved my life again. I am so sure. Paul is, he was there, he was at the museum back door, and because of him these two strangers jump up off the street. Your brother is the revolution, the noise forever in the streets. He calls two soldiers up off the street. There is the old story, you know, the old fairytale, the stones turned to soldiers.

(*CUT to waist-up shot*) I was saved by two men with—like in masks. Over their mouths, over their faces, half their faces (*waves hands before her*), a bandanna? Give me a break, my J-Bud, how can I, how did I see their faces? Like, I was paying attention? The clothes, okay. The clothes, the same as on the punks all over the world. I mean like, jeans. Shirts, t-shirts, maybe a blue shirt, or maybe a blue bandanna. One man is maybe a little, he has something tight and sexy in the clothes, you know? A little gay, kind of, one of these men, maybe. Femme, maybe. J-Bud, I thought I was going to die!

O.S.: Height or weight? Race?

ROMY: Height, okay. Taller than me, but not much. Not much weight either, for sure. I know what they been eating. And the race, to me, I don't, I don't think twice. Like, what's my race? (*frowns*) What, JJ—white, am I white? In the States, am I?

O.S: Ro. It's just evidence.

ROMY: Maybe one was more white and the other more black.

O.S.: Then there's the timing. Hey. Majorly convenient timing.

ROMY (*closer, angrier*): But that's what I'm saying! We have power too, we soldiers, the punks like me, like these two. (*shakes head*) I mean, your brother—I learned some things, because of your brother. I learned better, the love, the better life, so definitely better. But I'm saying, these two, the ones who shot Kahlberg, Paul pulled them off the street—but they weren't like, it wasn't magic! (*rakes hair off face*) It wasn't Disney. They had a gun, does that sound like magic? They are buying a gun in the street. These two, they love your brother. For sure, like I love your brother. But they also know the word in the street. They pay attention, the talk, there was some scary talk, that morning. And I'm saying, better if I paid attention. Better if I really listen, that morning. Because that's how they knew, that's how they wind up hanging around.

(*murmur O.S.; CUT to close-up*)

ROMY: The two men who shot Lieutenant-Major Kahlberg were shouting at him. They were saying, and this is as they are shooting "Don't touch him! Don't hurt him!" It was all about Paul, for sure. They were hanging around for Paul.

O.S.: They'd heard rumors there might be trouble, and they came to protect him.

ROMY (*tucks hair behind ear*): In this city, there was always the internet . . .

O.S.: My Ro. I think we have enough

ROMY: What, my J-Bud? No way we have enough. I'm thinking—the two shooters came out of nowhere and then disappeared? That's majorly convenient.

O.S.: We've got enough for now. The principle facts of the case.

ROMY: But we don't know when we can do this again. JJ, one thing I know, the police are stupid once, but not twice.

O.S.: Tell me about it. I'm the one saying we should keep our clothes on.

ROMY: (*smiles*) We keep our clothes on. When we kiss is the hottest thing in Europe, is Vesuvius. But we keep our clothes on.

(*O.S., inaudible*)

ROMY: Okay, this—we are needing this, for the case. The thing about the Earthquake I.D., the counterfeits, the question is, where did Kahlberg get the paper?

O.S.: The paper? What's the big deal with that?

(*ROMY frowns*)

O.S: I mean, Silky was in the NATO shop. He had high-level access—

ROMY: No, my J-bud. Listen to yourself, how you are talking, just another American, you don't know the street. Another American who thinks the Sixth Fleet has some kind of super magic machines. You think only NATO has the access. JJ, for sure, I could go downtown right now, and I could buy a printing machine.

(*shrugs*) They come in every day. They come from Japan, and they go to the trucks. You think we can't get into those trucks? You think we can't like, do the printing in a basement somewhere? (*shades eyes, squints past camera*)

O.S.: Okay, okay. You're saying what Silky had, that no one else had, was the paper stock. So maybe if he left any of the counterfeits behind, if we find those—

ROMY: How long has that *clandestino* been up there? (*points away, but looks into camera*) Honey, why can't you be more like your brother? (*CUT*)

As her driver ferried her back through the city, Barbara was thinking about love and romance. About men and women, keeping their clothes on and otherwise—she had time. She was picking up Jay at DiPio's clinic, and she'd made sure to have the older boys stay out of the apartment, out where they wouldn't open their laptop and doctor the evidence. She'd arranged it with a single call to the security who'd gone out with the older boys today; she set up a meeting down in the Vomero piazza. At the *gelateria*, Barbara had said. She'd asked that Aurora join them, as well, if anyone knew where to find the old playgirl. The whole family would gather at the tables clustered alongside the piazza, where Chris and JJ wouldn't dare to get into their film files.

What was on those files was no small accomplishment, the mother had to admit. Just getting around the security team had taken some doing. Barbara especially respected the older boy, keeping his Vesuvius in his pants. But things had reached a point that called to mind the message Romy had posted, ten days ago, on the family site: too, too, too. Barbara wasn't going to waste time with her bodyguard, either, though she found him sitting over pictures of half-clad women. Out in the studio's front room, the plump young security man had found a set of promotional 8x10's, glossies of Italian starlets. The mother didn't say a word, holding out a hand for his phone. As for Whitman, he got twice the extra payment they'd agreed to, and Barbara counted off the bills slowly, making sure the sailor-suited blade didn't miss her look. He was an artist; he knew how to keep his mouth shut. She left the production company feeling as if her hilltop surprise would come off. She began thinking about love and romance.

This might be the subject about which Barb had learned the most, during the afternoon's private screening. The mother had no more than half a notion of just what she would say to her seventeen-year-old, once she got him back into the apartment, but she understood, through and through, the dynamics between him and Romy. She saw how the crush suffered strains beyond the obvious, the skin color and the socio-economico what-have-you. Also Barbara's big American wasn't so stupid after all. He hadn't failed to notice the way the gypsy's hands were forever double-checking something or other, compulsively, and he hadn't failed to make the connection to his youngest brother. The manhandling that Romy had suffered must've saddled her with the same sort of unease, and JJ had been smart enough to realize coming too close might leave him likewise bruised. Then there was the girl's end of the dynamics: she'd never had a John like John Junior. She'd never had to deal tender for tender. The gypsy too, Barbara would bet, had gotten skittish whenever the hugging and kissing went on too long.

As her driver poked through the gathering afternoon traffic, Barbara could extrapolate. She could apply the teenagers' problems to a far older pair, Aurora and Cesare. Barb could practically pick up of the vibrations of Merry Widow and Gloomy Cleric, two rhythms woefully out of synch. Yet she doubted Aurora would prove as smart as her oldest grandson, should she and the priest ever share that first kiss.

Barbara could hear, as well, how Cesare would speak of such differences. The guerilla Jesuit would sound a little like Romy, calling for revolution in the streets, raging about skin color and the socio-economic. And Barbara knew what she'd say in reply, too. She'd say that Franz Fanon and Karl Marx didn't know JJ and Romy. Fanon and Marx couldn't tear their eyes from their own pet projects, worked to death on their private screens, but if they did, they'd make out the new freedoms available at this cracked and upended moment in history. Border-crossing hooking up, Barbara would say, was the inevitable future. Border-crossing, skin-blurring, bank-account-tangling—all of that was coming on at digital speed, a message texted to the entire phone book, wireless and instantaneous. Plus this was Naples, where it wasn't just the Twenty-first Century of Our Lord, but something like the thirty-first century of multi-culti barter. In this theater of operations, more than in most, the young and hormonal were free to try on any role they felt like. When Barbara's priest started dithering over which lover had the fatter wallet or the kinkier hair, he sounded as if he still thinking Montagues and Capulets.

Now if a person wanted to talk about relationships as business, as politics, the case in point was Silky Kahlberg. The late Lieutenant Major, too, had a place in Barbara's meditations on her way back into the city. According to today's news flash, the White Shadow had preferred his sex man-on-man, and Barb had figured out already that he must've been just the opposite of someone like Whitman. Kahlberg would've preferred the kind of dynamics you found in prison, where every man's forehead was stamped either Boss or Bitch. After all, even when he'd been dealing with Jay, a quintessential Kinsey Zero, the NATO officer had manipulated the situation in order to achieve all the additional clout he could. Therefore whenever the liaison man had found a more ambivalent business partner, he must've gleefully gone for every advantage, private as well as public. He must've run roughshod over the guy.

Now Barbara was into some roughness herself, as the Fiat jostled onto the stones of downtown. They swung around the San Carlo opera house, where the backstage wall used to open onto the Royal Gardens. The singers had performed love songs by Mozart out among the birds and the bees.

Barbara didn't want to think about it. Love songs, *basta*—because she still lacked a strategy, a way to begin, once the family got back to the apartment. All things considered, she'd prefer it if Aurora weren't home. After picking up Jay, it was easy enough to fill him in, though with the driver in mind the wife stripped her explanation down to shorthand. Still, it wasn't difficult to share the information, thanks to the code of the long-married. In words of one syllable, Jay had agreed they needed the meeting, and in the Vomero gelateria there was no sign of Aurora.

Better yet, the kids were behaving themselves. Nobody appeared all sugared up, though Dora and Sylvia had each gotten a free scoop, the usual treat for the "American dolls." So Jay and the boys went into the palazzo before Barb and the girls, best to leave any gelato mess out on the stoop, and the mother could use a stretch anyway. In the elevator Barbara laid her hands on her girls' heads, with a silent prayer for help.

But as soon as she reached her landing, even before the cage clanked open, Chris showed her worse trouble.

His look showed something more childish than could be blamed on his nerd's glasses, and he took the girls' hands. He might've said that his sisters should wait with him outside the apartment, or Barb might've inferred it, picking up yet another code, reading it first in his gaze and posture and then in the spasmodic moaning and gulping that came from the apartment. The mother got the same message from the wide middle-aged back of her husband, in the doorway.

Keep the little ones away, was the message. Keep Dora and Syl from seeing Mama's priest stretched out naked and fighting a heart attack.

Cesare lay on the couch, his arms and legs splayed up along the wall and down onto the floor, splayed and flailing, as if trying with all four limbs to grab some fat and invisible balloon lifting away from his midsection. Never mind if he exposed his distended cock and iron-gray pubic hair. Never mind if he fell off the couch, though Aurora held him in place, kneeling with one kimono-clad arm across his chest. Nothing mattered except to get hold of that escaping balloon, that ghost of a parade blimp, and the skinny old man pawed after the swollen impalpable thing even with the foot that was still in its black nylon sock. Indeed his drowning reach, his cold feet, all appeared more human than his face: a mottle of brick and chalk, with wrinkles like seismic fissures.

Here was another first morning in midtown, a cityscape so vivid as to suggest that her husband had melted out of Barbara's way. Here again she needed to sort out the hard surfaces on which she'd stubbed her bones earlier from those against which she was banging for the first time. Banging, to see her priest in cardiac arrest and her mother-in-law beside him, an old couple discovered in the act—and yet Barbara also thought of the Latin, the dead language: *in flagrante delicto.* Banging and up-to-the-minute, the undone belt on Aurora's kimono, the small nipples a brighter pink than Barb's own—and yet what could be more basic, more timeless, than nakedness? What language was simpler than the Braille of the erogenous zones? Barbara could see that she sent the priest into worse convulsions, his eyes leaking tears and his gasps growing louder. His arms and legs trembled, all but losing hold of whatever it was they clung to, his nails scratching the wall and floor. But she couldn't move, neither to spare Cesare the sight of her nor to help John Junior, on the phone in the corner, gabbling away like a frightened tourist: *Aiuto! Aiuto!* Barb couldn't budge from between old hurts and new, like what she'd seen on Whitman's computer, a boy's heart and nerves tucked into a file. Only Paul could defeat the paralysis, getting round his mom, his outstretched hands electric. Only Paul could keep on surprising them, laying one of his hands across the priest's spasmodic chest, above the grandmother's, while with the other going to the cracked wall of a face, to the mouth already open around a wordless but fluttering language-muscle . . .

Chapter Twelve

"What kind of a woman are you?"

"Barbara, I apologize again. I'm so sorry you had to see this. But you must realize, you absolutely must, that Chezzo and I would never have— "

"Chezzo? What kind of a woman *are* you?"

"Oh, here we go."

"Here we go? Are you saying, this is some kind of *dance*?"

"A dance indeed. Patently a dance. We've all known from Day One that it was only a matter of time before you cleared the floor and called me out for the big finale."

"The finale? Aurora, a finale would be the answer to my prayers. Don't you know how you stick in my craw? Can't you imagine how many times I've wanted to tell you off once and for all?"

Aurora heaved a showy sigh, a movement that called attention to how small she was. Barefoot, in a flimsy kimono, the old playgirl barely came to Barbara's chin. She wouldn't get into a staring contest either. Instead the grandmother looked to Cesare, still flat on the sofa. One of the boys had covered the priest with a summer bedspread. Light cotton, powder blue, the blanket set off the man's long face, its flush of color showing the good that Paul had done.

"That's right," Barbara said, "look at the poor guy. And he's only the latest victim. He's practically got holes in his neck."

"Barb," Jay said.

The in-law's painted face seemed smaller, doll-like. Her hair might've been a kid's, rumpled and glossy, jittering under the ceiling fan. She must've turned the thing on to help her and Cesare get comfortable.

"This isn't the time," the husband said.

"Oh, Jay. Are you saying there is a good time? There's some better time for our kids, for instance? The father was *dying*, here, till Paul stepped in! So Jaybird, tell me. When's a good time for them to at last understand what a, what a *monster* they've got living in their own—"

"Barbara, excuse me. If I may interrupt." Aurora finger-combed one of her unruly patches of hair. "Am I correct in assuming that you had some reason for rushing everyone home like this?"

"Mother of God." Barb suffered the whipsaw too, jam and recoil across the ribcage. "You've got no respect, no—no *limits*. Now you want to tell me how I should run my family?"

"Owl, hey. Think about it."

"Your family, precisely. Would one be correct in assuming that it was some pressing new crisis for the family, that had you so suddenly rushing home?"

"Mom, you too. Easy."

Barb looked to her husband, but he was checking down the hallway—the older boys and the twins had scurried off into the girls' room. When the Jaybird swung round again, he glowered at his mother. "Look at you. Hardly any bigger than Paul, here. Plus, what, seventy-five years old, now? Hey. It's lucky we didn't find you and the father both having heart attacks."

"Oh, John." The grandmother fingered her kimono together at the throat, drawing in her bantam frame. "Really now, do I seem so frail?"

"You," Barbara began, "you're seventy-five years old. You're a *mother*!"

"Easy there, Owl Girl. Think about it."

Barbara dropped her head and tugged at an armpit. She hadn't been wrenched around so badly since the museum.

"John has a point, Barbara. Think about the things I've learned, living under your roof these last ten days or so."

What the mother thought of, seeing Aurora square her flinty shoulders, was of Roebuck and all the Alpha Moms before her.

"I mean to say, the children have been talking to me. They've told me a thing or two, you know. For that matter, so has Cesare here."

"Him? Cesare?" The words came out quietly, surprising her. "What kind of a woman are you, getting a priest to talk?"

"Oh, here we go—you're calling me a witch. It was inevitable, I suppose."

"When I visited with the father, it was a sacrament."

"I suppose I'm that witch Ulysses had the problem with. The woman who turned men into swine." Her bright mouth crooked up smartly. "You know, Barbara, whenever I was lucky enough to enjoy a private moment with my Chezzo, the last thing I was interested in talking about was you and your secrets."

Barbara tried to get her bearings. The space around her might still have been that first morning downtown. She might've come across Cesare in the niche of a catacomb, the tunnels of *Napoli Sotterraneo*, The only person who'd taken a chair, normal living-room activity, was the miraculous eleven-year-old. Meantime the grandmother was pressing her point, arguing that if she'd wanted "to start playing the bull in the china shop, around here, I could've found a far less humiliating way than this." Today, the last thing Aurora and the fallen priest had expected was to have the rest of the family burst in on them.

"On the contrary, we had a more than reasonable expectation of privacy. And do you mean to tell me that you and Jay have never made love on a couch?"

Barb didn't trust herself to respond.

"Really, I've been the soul of discretion, around here. It's hardly as if I've gone looking for dirt about you and Jay. It's hardly as if, in order to learn that you two have been squabbling, I needed to bewitch a priest."

Behind Barbara, from the room down the hall, came the small sounds of sneakers and toys. "Aurora," she asked, "what do you know about it?" She kept her voice under control. "What goes on in a family, what commitment even means, what do you know? Twenty years ago I took a vow in front of God—"

"Hey," Jay said. "Both of you. Down off the high horse."

"Precisely, John. How many apologies does your wife require? Why won't she admit the least responsibility? Rushing everyone home without so much as a phone call."

"Mother of God! You monster, weren't you just saying you don't want some kind of big, apocalyptic dance?"

"All I've ever said to you, Barbara, is stop pretending you're a saint. Telling me you stood up in front of God, now really. The truth is, you're blundering around having emotions like the rest of us."

"I'm—I'm a wife and a mother. I took a vow."

"And I was there, in case you've forgotten. Then more recently I was out on Capri, and even my carriage-driver was talking about trouble between you and my son."

At some point the grandmother had slipped on pants. Balloony Arabian velveteen, she'd pulled them on while Paul was still over Cesare, a hand at each of the old man's breaking points. In those same swarming moments—while Barb had stood dumbstruck, unable to manage more than a silent prayer for her priest—Chris and JJ had hustled the twins down the hall to their room. Jay had done what he could, using his upper body as a screen. As near as Mama could tell, the girls hadn't seen anything.

But even now with Cesare breathing normally under his blanket, with the girls out of harm's way and Mr. Paul parked in a chair, she had so much turning over within her that she might still have been praying. Turning over like the beads on a rosary. She grabbed the mother-in-law by the lapels.

"What kind of a woman *are* you?"

"*Barb!*" Jay said. "We've got enough trouble."

"Jaybird, I swear, if you don't back me up on this, if you don't . . ."

"Then what, Barbara dear? What do you intend to do, to your husband?"

As soon as Barbara let go, the in-law fisted her kimono back together. Its bright threads sparkled against the shadows of her wrinkled neck.

"*Both* of you. Last thing we need is this kind of playground stuff."

"Jay, how can you let her turn it around like this? How can you let her talk as if today, as if everything were *wide open* to any kind of way she—"

"But Barbara, you're the one who's left something open. First you announce that this man is your husband, eternally, before God. And then you tell us that should he neglect to 'back you up,' well—what? What's the truth?"

"Mom, Mom and, Aw, Aw . . . Mom and Grandma," said Paul. "I'm tired of this."

Jay had gotten a hand on each of the women, under the murmuring fan. He'd taken his mother by her shoulder and Barbara by a hip.

"I'm tired o-of it. It's, it's like—I can see this o-on any street corner."

The Jaybird, with the hand on Barb, lightly aligned a finger with the top of his wife's panties. Between that familiar tickle and what her middle child had to say, his exasperation, she found herself cooling improbably. She blinked and saw how silly she and her in-law looked.

Silly, a whipsaw *a deux*, choreography for the end of everything. As if they could! As if either she or Aurora, with no more than a harsh word or two, could erase a way of life this long in place and thick with sediment.

Paul spoke, Jay touched her, and with that Barb pictured the opposite. She saw herself and this woman knocking off the Siren song and instead brokering a whole series of practical solutions. She blinked again and her imagination kept on like this, so sizeable a shift in her thinking that Barbara looked to Cesare. Was this something for confession? The old man hadn't moved from the couch but he was watching closely, from that angle he could see how Jay was stroking his wife's hip, and chagrin rose hotly up Barbara's neck even as she couldn't stop thinking that she and this old woman had now spit up the filthiest business between them. Now, with that out of the way, they might find what they had in common. They had the city, for starters. No one else in the family had made such intimate connections here as Aurora and Barb.

"You got it now?" Jay was asking. "The big picture?"

Anyway, Barbara asked herself, wasn't the older Lulucita a natural for this chameleonic town? Couldn't she stand in for a Neapolitan mother?

"Goodness," Aurora said. "I thought for a moment there we were going to end up like something from a bad movie."

"Yeah, yeah like a, a movie I've seen a, a thousand times."

Barbara looked to Paul, square-eyed, refusing to blink again. She thought of the jump-cuts back on Whitman's screen, the faces altered in an instant. Could she trust this latest edit?

"Owl?" her husband was asking. "We all on the same page, now?"

Then there was Aurora, her little *nonna*. The in-law's smile no longer looked so jagged; Barb couldn't help thinking it looked like an olive branch. A lipstick-red olive branch, a strange image but one Jay seemed to see as well, since he eased back and took his hands off the women. The big son and husband gave himself a breather, while Barbara found herself smiling back at the old woman, guarded about about it but nevertheless finding words for what she'd just been imagining.

Needed to get some things off my chest . . . get it out in the open . . . some on both sides, sounded like.

Aurora made the same noises, give or take. In her voice, conciliation took on a greater refinement, the melody of the Alpha. The younger woman didn't lose her smile, but she cast around for a place to sit. Both the sofa and the nearest chair, however, remained spaces for the handicapped. Cesare's color was back, but the lines around his eyes had deepened. He looked as if he'd fallen into thoughts as intense and surprising as Barbara's. And while Paul too was himself again, what did that mean? What, really? The boy had lowered his teeming head, holding his belt in one hand while with the other he poked between pants and shirt, tightening the tuck. The mother went to him, sidling past the displaced coffee table.

"Remember, Mr. Paul." She squatted before the boy. "It could be any of us."

Over the child's shoulder, she saw the priest kick the blanket off his black-stockinged feet.

"That's what you said, right?" she continued. "These episodes, whatever's in them, it's there all around us all the time. It could be any one of us, laying on hands, if we could only feel it."

The buzzer for the palazzo's front door sounded, a racket under the high ceilings. The priest sat up, revealing shoulders tufted with shocking white hair.

"I'm saying," Barbara went on, "you're not so strange. We're the strange ones, the ones who don't ever feel it."

She stroked his cheek, its hint of hair. Meantime the buzzer kept coming on—the police of course. Police and paramedics both had rushed to the Vomero in response to the American family's *pronto soccorso*. But in the ten or fifteen minutes since the older boy had gotten off the phone, a big public to-do had become the last thing anyone wanted. Even Cesare, at the word *polizia* crackling over the intercom, shook his beaky head. Jay was the first to think of the balcony. He stepped outside, the room's overhead fan sucking in a fresh dose of the sulfur air. Barbara, hearing her husband call down to the cops, was surprised at how good his Italian had become. The Jaybird reeled off four or five different kinds of reassurance, even working up a laugh as he shouted that the family was fine. Nevertheless he seemed to need reinforcements. He poked back inside and asked Barbara to join him.

Out over the piazza, the sun surprised her, still noon-bright. The wife had to squint, and though she made nice, though she tried to sound trouble-free, her act was out of synch with Jay's. When the Jaybird said the call was a big mistake, false alarm, she shook her head, and when he asked her whether anyone was hurt she nodded. Below, a camera or two went off, with a scratch and fizz like faulty matches. Against the high railing, the s-curved childproof bars, Barb realized she was the wrong person for this job; she was still too raw from thrashing things out with Aurora. She hadn't gotten back on her feet, or gotten her head back on its feet. Then there were "the symptoms that generally follow the healing event," according to Nettie's recommended reading. Fatigue, disorientation—pretty ordinary symptoms, when you thought about it. In any case Barbara wasn't much help. She frowned, reminding herself why she'd come back home in the first place; she still needed to sit down with Chris and JJ. But when she waved to the cluster of folks below, she felt like she was doing a high-school version of *Evita*. She was Evita next to Mussolini, and the act didn't appear to be working. Down on the spirals of paving-stones, the police and the medics wouldn't leave. The lights on both vehicles kept flashing, and now they'd attracted additional onlookers, maybe as many as twenty-five. The biggest crowd for the family in days.

Then Cesare joined them, back in uniform. Out in the volcanic breeze, with the Bay visible behind him, the man's collar suggested some fresh-scrubbed temple on the horizon. He hadn't yet pulled on his shoes, but the people in the piazza couldn't see that, and when he spoke he came across in terrific voice. A voice Barbara had never heard from him, it turned out: the local accent and slang. She couldn't translate the bawling, the abbreviations, but neither of the American's could miss the old Jesuit's point.

"*O' cane arragia' ne reste 'e pille!*"

Cesare put a lot across without a word, with body-Neapolitan, the shaping hands and shifting hips. He quickly had the cops and medics grinning.

"*O' puorco!*" Cesare shrugged, whole-body. "'*Na sbaglia!*"

Before the men in whites and blues headed back to their vehicles, the priest even threw in an exhortation that they come to Mass.

How long's it been, homeys? Words to that effect, anyway.

"Cesare," Jay put in quietly. "I owe you one."

The rest of the crowd dispersed while the ambulance and the police car were still circling the piazza, but the old man carried on until the last one had found some shade. He turned a last head or two, bellowing in more straightforward Italian that he held a service every evening. Meantime the cops paused again, at the edge of the piazza, pulling up beside a couple of tobacco-brown beggars. The police asked to see I.D.

"Okay," Jay said. "Party's over."

He brushed past the priest and headed inside. While the others followed, he spoke up again. "Father, Cesare, thanks. Thanks, okay? Okay. But now, it is *over*."

Barbara hoped her husband wasn't about to launch into the same thing she'd gone through with Aurora, this time with testosterone flavor. The mother looked for Paul. In the absence of the other adults, it turned out, the grandmother had gotten the boy to help straighten up the room. Now the two of them were bent over either end of the coffee table, lining it up in front of the sofa. The blanket was folded and lamp and chairs were back in their places.

"Enough," Jay went on. "Know what I mean?"

From down the hallway came a cry, one of the girls: *That's it*! The priest nodded and reverted to schoolbook English, saying he understood.

"Time for you to leave my family alone. You know?"

"John!" Aurora straightened up.

"I'm talking Barb, me, and the kids. My family. What you do with my mother, that's your business. Hey, been there. Been there, and good luck. But so far as the rest of us are concerned, it's got to be on a different basis."

"John, honestly. What on earth makes you think you've got the right—"

"I couldn't agree more," Cesare said.

"This isn't about you and the Church, either. Like I say, that's your business."

"Well, the Church and I, as for that. I'd say the worst strain on my relationship with the church is the harm that I've done your family."

Paul settled on the sofa, one stovepipe leg over the other, and Barb sat beside him. From that angle, looking up, she noticed the two men stood eye-to-eye. Jay cocked his head, and after a moment Cesare went on.

"I've done worse than you know, signore. I stand before you the worst of all."

"Oh, now, really." Aurora might've put an elbow into Jay's ribs, though gently, as she stepped between him and the priest. "Chezzo, we've been through this a hundred times. Nowhere in the Gospels does Christ suggest that it's a sin to have sex."

Cesare backed away from her, glaring. "You dare speak for Christ, woman?"

"Wo-man?" Aurora put a hand to her neck, so slowly the arm might've been developing an exoskeleton as it moved.

"You know," she said, "what Our Savior condemns, actually, is *hypocrisy*."

The old man's look lost something.

"Really, Chez-zo. You ought to look at yourself, you absolutely ought to see the torment in you face. Now, dear man. Talk to me."

He managed a sputter. Jay too backed off a step, glancing at Barbara and Paul.

"Your Aura, you called me—less than an hour ago, was it? Then tell me, do. What madness are you proposing now?"

"*Cesso*," the priest said finally, shaking his head. "*Cesso*. Woman, do you know what this pet name of yours means, in this country?"

Aurora's smile had become a spiked extension of her vivid nails. "I hope this isn't another of your lectures, Chezzo. I cannot abide a man who lectures."

"It means 'toilet,' this name. You call me your toilet."

"What's this," Jay said, "Round Two? No way, guys."

Barbara figured her job was the eleven-year-old. She bent to Paul's ear and whispered that she'd like him to join the other kids. The boy narrowed his thick-lashed eyes, about to make some objection, but then Cesare swept round to face him. Swept round, his robes lifting, and Barbara figured that only she and Aurora noticed the exaggeration in the move, the message for the grandmother in the way he turned his back.

"*Miracolino*." The priest spread a hand across his chest, lowering his head.

"Hey," Jay said. "We had a deal. Enough with this."

"Holy child, I thank you. I must thank you. You've ripped me out of . . ."

For the next long moment, as Barbara took in the transformation of her guerilla priest—Cesare seemed about to prostrate himself across the coffee table—mostly she went on thinking about Aurora. Now the old playgirl rolled her eyes, now she looked sympathetic and called his actual name, in good accent: "Oh, *Cesare*." As for Jay, he'd gone slack; his mother had just gotten jilted: his mother. Barbara in fact had half a mind to snatch the blanket off the sofa and fling it once more over the old Dominican's face. But that face appeared ecstatic, nothing less, like something off the family website. Then too, she recalled her own recent convulsions, regarding this same mother-in-law.

"Cesare, come on." She kept her voice level. "What were we just saying?"

"My daughter-in-law's right." Aurora found a chair. "She's entirely right."

Paul huddled against his Mom, the still-damp hairs at his neck tickling along her collar. "I can't," the boy was saying, "I can't really say it's ah, a-about God. What hap, what ha-happens with me . . ."

The priest waved a soft hand, eyes closed, quieting them both. He appeared to have come out of his fervor, his bare feet whispering against the marble floors as he shuffled back from the table. Jay closed the distance between them again, glaring, taking hold of the man's skinny arm. But Cesare kept his eyes shut, shaking his head as if the Jaybird weren't there. Quietly he declared that his worst sinning, "the very blackest mark" against him, concerned the boy.

"What?" Jay asked. "You sinned against Paul?"

Barb put an arm around her boy, getting set to haul him out of the room.

"The worst I did," Cesare went on, "was to hurt this consecrated brood."

"Hey. How many times do I have to say it?"

"Now Cesare, please." The old woman leaned over velveteen legs, her hands between her knees. "This isn't the man I fell in love with."

"Just, I mean, speak English. Hey? Plain English."

"I fell in love," Aurora said, "with a beautiful Black Irishman who used to say the Holy Spirit dwelt in our desires. 'Dwelt,' oh my Chez-ah-ray. The only proof of God you could take seriously, you used to say, was the sheer variety of human yearning."

Jay remained at the man's arm, frowning. For the first time in a while Barbara noticed that her husband was wearing a uniform too: his hospital whites.

"Oh my Cesare," Aurora repeated, then at a glance from her son fell silent. Her doctored looks hardened.

"You and Mom," Jay said, "that's your business. But what's this about Paul?"

Cesare had fallen so still that Barb could spot a wet streak along his jaw-line, a mark left by her child. The boy himself was worming in closer, under her arm, and so when the old man began to speak, to murmur, a priest at confession, at first she could only pick out the words in Italian. Or was it Neapolitan, that drawl, those dying final syllables? Even when Cesare said a word she knew well, *clandestini*, Barbara couldn't be sure she'd heard him right till he put it together with another one she recognized: *scippatori*.

She shifted her grip on Paul, blocking his body if they shared a car seat and were skidding towards a collision. "Mother of God," she said.

Jay let go of the priest and gave her a look. He asked something she didn't catch. Aurora too faced around, pant-legs flopping, looking glad for the distraction. Meanwhile Cesare continued his explanations, the murmur of troubling thoughts, and Barbara began to regret how easily she understood them. She regretted everything she'd learned during this last clue-spattered month. For her there could be no mistaking this old man, her lone Vomero friend, with whom she'd spent hours in a church otherwise deserted—except, that is, for a couple of fugitives in the basement. And those two, there could be no mistaking, had been something more than lost sheep.

"It's the *scippatori*," she said at the priest's first decent pause. "Our *scippatori*, that's what you're saying. The two you've been hiding are the guys who hit Jay."

Cesare may have raised his eyes, Barb couldn't be sure. His back was to the balcony doors, and in the shadows, his face was another map of disease. In any case he hardly had a chance to nod before Jay erupted. The wife didn't catch every word, as she studied the new plague-map above her, but she knew what her husband was saying. *Hey, how long, how could you—what* is *this?* The former lineman took hold of Cesare's arm again. He shook the old priest and looked about to do worse before, good Papa, he shot a glance at Paul. Not that this made him any less threatening. The Jaybird went for a height advantage, firing questions with his heels off the ground.

"You had the guys? In your church, you had them? You had both those guys, and I mean. You just sat there."

You could see kitchen grease under Jay's fingernails. And for all the priest's experience with unhappy wives, he didn't know what to do about a husband. He flinched and responded in single syllables.

"How could you?" Jay asked. "How can a man just sit there?"

Barbara might've seen Cesare on his deathbed, but she'd never seen him so at loose ends, the fractured Jesuit Dominican. He stuttered as he tried to get into details. The two clandestini had showed up at his door the night of the mugging. Scrawny, in cheap jeans and T's, and one of them bruised deeply under his eye, both clandestini nonetheless brimmed with a naïve certainty that the Church could wash them clean. At each word they spoke, Cesare had heard the echo of his own emptiness. He'd heard how his soul had become a husk, pitted by years of neglect and baked in the *Mezzogirno*. After that it had taken the priest a couple of days, talking further with these two, before he was convinced that they had in fact . . . they had, in fact . . .

"Hey," Jay said. "Don't stop now, buster. What'd they tell you?"

"Quite," said Cesare. "They told me, yes, that's it, quite."

Scowling, Jay once more seized the old man's arm.

"They *told* me," the priest repeated. "It was confession."

The Jaybird rocked back, hands at his sides. He and Barbara got it at once, how deeply the sacrament mattered to Cesare, fractured and in need of a splint. Confession must've been the man's primary mode of communication with the two refugees, and now when his faith was still trembling from the effort of resurrection, the sanctity of his priestly rituals meant everything. How could he violate the *clandestini*'s trust? Cesare bit his tongue, making a show of it, so that even with the shadow you couldn't miss the wet red muscle bulging between his teeth. Barbara didn't see why he had to do that, especially not staring down at Paul the way he was, but she admired the man's backbone. Aurora too grinned a bit, something more than polite.

"Come on." Jay reined in his tone. "Cesare, all due respect. I mean."

Then there was the eleven-year-old, all eyes, drawing his knees to his chin as he stared at the priest's tongue.

"Hey, Mr. Paul," said Jay. "Hey guy. You know. What you did was good."

The priest startled and turned, dropping his face into his hands.

"Everything else, it's mixed up. It's for grownups, it's mixed up. But Mr. Paul, big guy, what you did—you know. That was good."

The next breath of out Cesare sounded choked, a sob. At that, Aurora spoke up. "Cesare," she said, "honestly. You must realize that the only person in this room who was ever interested in your soul, absolutely and truly interested, was myself."

Barbara looked up from Paul, then on second thought let the woman talk.

"Your Aura was the only one who cared," she went on. "I did, absolutely. 'To live to err, to fall, to triumph'—that's Stephen Dedalus, as I'm sure you know. And had anyone asked, I'd have said old Stephen was talking about you and me."

Jay and Paul had turned to the old woman as well.

"Now, honestly, Cesare. In the name of my caring, quite genuine while it lasted, I have to ask whether there isn't something you can do."

The priest, his fingers slipping beneath his eyes, gave the beginning of a nod.

Paul had the heightened sympathy levels; he began nodding too, waving a hand at the old man. "He, the priest, he, it w-wasn't so bad, what he, he did. Help, helping those guys, h-hiding them. It wasn't so bad, because if, if h-he, he, if he helped them, he, he knew, then w-we weren't in a-any danger. The family."

The boy pointed out that the *scippatori* had been ashamed of what they'd done. They'd been frightened "a-about going to Heh, Heh, Heh, to H-Heh—"

"Okay," Jay put in. "Maybe they weren't such a threat, those two. But at this point, that's all I'll give the guy."

"See but, see but they a-already got rid of the papers. Like, the pass, passports."

"Paulie," Barbara said, "this is very nice of you, but can you see—"

"Hey. Look at it the other way around. Those two took our stuff, they took it and they made some money off it."

"A-and they, they got h-h-hit, for it. One, one of them w-was banged up."

"Cesare?" Aurora asked. "Have you come up with something, after all? Some nice piece of Jesuitical logic?"

The black figure at the center of the room had pulled himself together. He extended an arm in blessing for the boy on the sofa, beaming with uncomplicated gratitude for another long moment. But then Cesare asked if anyone had noticed where he'd left his shoes.

"I believe you'll find then beneath one of the dining-room chairs." Aurora drew her lips into a hard red knob. "Are you going somewhere?"

"I am," the priest said, "and I hope your son and his wife will come with me, don't you know. I hope they'll accompany me up to the church."

Jay whipped round, frowning, but Cesare went on unruffled. "I know more than I can say, but I believe I don't have to say it, in order for you to know it."

As the old man turned towards the dining room, you could see his face better, its color. Barbara looked first to him, then to the Jaybird, and what could she show her husband except the prickly understanding that they had no choice? What, when the priest was prey to such wild moods? They couldn't be sure what Cesare would feel like in another hour, whereas they could be sure about the kids. They'd stay put—for Paul's sake if not for the parents'—and they'd have the grandmother with them. Barb could see at once how it would work, how it had to work, the lesser of two evils. The risk in the teenagers' work with the gypsy was outweighed by the threat from the two outlaws who'd nearly killed the boys' father.

Jay however looked dubious. He returned to Cesare, bent over in one of the head-of-table chairs, on the other side of the open double-doors to the dining area.

"If you've got something at the church, I guess I want to see it." The husband kept his voice businesslike. "I mean, that's the plan, right? Something at the church?"

The old man nodded without straightening up.

"Okay." Jay lifted his chin, impressed. "Okay, we look at that, and you've still got your sacrament. Good plan." The Vice President of Sales. "But after that, it's like I say. Everything's got to be on a new basis."

The priest's head came up while one foot waggled into its loafer. He declared that parents needed to see what he had for them; they needed to "understand the forces arrayed against them from the start, here."

Jay frowned again, puzzled, grumbling. Barb wondered about the police. That was the last thing she needed, today, another visit to the precinct station.

"But beyond that," Cesare said, "I don't see that I'd need to have any more dealings with your family whatsoever."

Aurora clucked her tongue and put her back to the man. It took her a moment to notice Paul, but when she did, the woman cocked an eyebrow, playfully.

In fact the eleven-year-old seemed the main concern, at the moment. Barbara bent to his ear, whispering a word or two. Best if the boy joined the others without additional rumpus; best if, after the things he'd seen already, he didn't have to deal with either of the evils, lesser or greater, now facing his Mom and Pop. The middle child didn't move, however, until Aurora made him an offer.

"You know, Paulie," the grandmother said, "we don't usually have all you kids together. We so rarely get an afternoon like this one, with everyone in one place. What do you say if we round up the others and put on a show?"

Just like that, the boy was ordinary again. Ordinary for a Broadway Baby, anyway: "With, with songs?" Paul asked, eyes shining.

"Oh, with songs, certainly." The way Aurora nodded, she and Paul must've discussed the possibility before. "Songs and dances too, for the fairy-folk."

"Well, well m-maybe not Chris. Chris, h-he can handle the music. H-he can, h-he can download the music, w-whatever we need."

At the mention of the computer, the computer and her teens, Barbara tightened her hold on the middle child's arm. Couldn't let him go yet. Aurora didn't fail to notice, and she caught the mother's eye—was it the first time since they'd been yelling at each other? Quietly, so the men wouldn't hear, she told Barb not to worry.

"Really now," Aurora said, "we're not so different, you and I. The children's safety, and life of decent abundance—honestly, isn't that all we're hoping to achieve?"

"See," Barbara said, "it's hard to hear someone like you talking about 'decent abundance.' That's a hard word to take, from a woman in golden velvet."

"Oh, now." Aurora was smiling again, but gently. "And this from a woman with five finished rooms in her basement."

"What? Are you saying my utilities room is finished?"

The grandmother put a hand to throat, chuckling.

"As for Jay's workshop, the kids were getting in there. Once that started, we had to put down carpet."

"Barbara, indulge me. We're not so utterly different. Let us say, neither one of us has so much in common with an abandoned child from Mexico."

Barbara dropped her gaze. "I would say, when it comes to abandoned children, there's no one who has a clue."

Which seemed to take care of their business at home. Barbara let go of Paul, meanwhile telling the mother-in-law what she needed to know regarding Chris and JJ. "Just keep those two from sneaking away with the laptop, okay?" She didn't have to get into the details, though she didn't want to think about how much Aurora knew already. But there was no point doing something drastic either, like taking the machine with her when she left for the church. The boys could hardly erase Romy from their files. Soon enough the mother was running her fingers one last time through Paul's hair, telling him to have fun. She caught a few words between Jay and the priest, and they too were finishing up. *So long as you understand, Father, we can't take long . . . like I say, some family business here . . .*

As Paul picked his way around the coffee table to his grandmother, Barbara saw again how she might coexist peacefully with this woman. Peacefully, usefully—but before Barb could work out something for back in Bridgeport, maybe some help with the Saturday driving (the girls at one soccer field, the boys at another), here in Naples she had to allow the old playgirl one last dig at her momentary boyfriend.

"Oh, and Cesare." Aurora paused between the two men, with Paul under one bright kimono-arm. "Always remember, this great revival of yours began with me."

The old man's prominent nose seemed to droop still lower.

"Do remember. The journey back to God began with your Aura."

Naturally Jay and Barbara needed to check on the others, too. The girls and the teens had just finished a game of Life, and as the mother looked over the setup, it seemed like the most American thing she'd ever seen. At the center of the game board rose a plastic mountain ringed by a highway. Around it coiled suburban-style loops of road, decorated with futures so bright and various that just to look at them was like surfing through a 100-channel cable lineup. And somehow Aurora couldn't have fit in more neatly, though it was Hindu yoga that kept her so spry, and though her shimmering clothes came from Persia and Japan. The widow settled down beside the board, tossing off a quick joke in a Noo Yawk bray. She assured the kids that their "nice old priest" was feeling much better, and breezily explained he going to "run a quick errand now with Mom and Pop." Meantime the woman was picking up the game, she hadn't forgotten her promise to Paul, sorting swiftly through the cards for good luck and bad.

A couple of scruffy types, perhaps clandestini, idled in the shade of the stoop as the Lulucitas emerged with their priest. But these were European, or as Euro as the golden-brown Romy. Perhaps a couple of Khazars, they might've been the beggars the police had stopped to check, earlier. In any case Barb knew what to do. She raised an open hand and, as she spoke her blessing, made sure they saw her lips move.

Also she dealt with her bodyguard. The young chowhound would've preferred to take the car, though it meant a roundabout of one-ways. Barbara had to insist, glancing up the stairs and thinking again of her mother-in-law, her trim flexibility. Here's Neapolitan yoga, Aurora: the stairs. The security officer sighed mightily, combing the curls from his eyes with pudgy fingers. But the air on the hilltop wasn't so heavy, so sulfur-rich, as down by DiPio's clinic or Whitman's studio. Besides, the gunman had Cesare to inspire him, a man in his seventies all but jogging uphill. The priest would wait for the other three at the top of each flight, his long face blazing with revival.

Barbara's own face must've gone purple, because she kept talking. She filled Jay in on everything she'd learned that morning about the gypsy and the late Lieutenant Major; earlier, during the ride from DiPio's to the Vomero, the husband had only gotten the shorthand. And more than that, the mother came to think she'd filled in a quake-wide gap in her own grasp on what had happened. As she climbed, she put it together, the news from her boys and the news from her priest. The two who'd come out of nowhere to gun down Silky Kahlberg—they must've been the two *scippatori* from the first day downtown.

"Romy was saying," she huffed. "Guys from off the street."

As the Jaybird took it in, he started climbing two stairs at a time.

"And a bandanna," she went on. "Blue like the first day."

"Guys felt guilty."

"Felt contrition. Seeking absolution."

"Plus Paul, hey. A holy child. To those two"

"Plus one was queer."

This was only a guess based on a guess: the gypsy's surmise about one of Silky's killers. Nonetheless a gay clandestino would fit the scheme of things, as it was emerging there on the Vomero stairs. The aerobics hadn't made Barb and Jay that dizzy. The husband got the connection, having sussed out the liaison's sexual preference in his first week up at the Refugee Center. "See what he wanted. Nice boy-toy. Price of a pizza." Jay understood that, for the former *scippatori*, the gaydar would've been part of the surveillance system. Part of tracking the family, seeking an opportunity to atone for what they'd done to the family, since the NATO man would've bragged to his sex partners (while of course giving away nothing they could use against him) about the systems he was jerking around.

"Silky's boys," Jay said. "They could've said something. Talked to our two guys."

"This city. Always somebody talking."

At last they reached the church, another Naples church with a cellar full of surprises. A person didn't need to go downtown to find a *Sotterraneo*. The priest rushed on to the rectory but Jay and Barbara allowed themselves a breather in the narthex. Wonderful, the cool, the dim. The wife tugged at her armpits and the husband swabbed his neck as they eyed each other in a wheezing double-check of their sudden detective work. You think, Jaybird? Does it add up, Owl? Two homeless illegals had somehow first gotten a bike, then gotten lucky. Yet after that they'd suffered such pangs of remorse that eventually, in a perverted attempt to make amends, they'd committed murder. Their victim had been more of an inveterate bad guy than either of them, but nevertheless a figure of daunting status, an American officer.

The husky bodyguard came in off the church steps, with a melodramatic exhale. That and the petulant look he shot his two charges was enough to stop Barbara's second-guessing. How far off the truth could she and her husband be? Anyway less than a month ago, outside these same weighty blonde doors, the police had snatched her. They'd snatched her and the children, and they'd taken their sweet time about letting her know what had happened to Jay. But neither then nor now had the authorities came anywhere near the real danger to the Lulucitas. Strangers had been privy to the moves they were making and the ways they were hurting, since the first blow to Jay's head. For all Barbara knew, the blessing she'd given five minutes ago, the vagrants outside the palazzo, could've been another source of information for the family's addled *scippatori*.

The mother turned and headed into the sanctuary. As soon as they reached the pews the bodyguard took a seat, sinking down and spreading out.

"Jay," Barb growled as she marched on, "I'm angry. I'm still angry."

"I hear that. Fucking can't get past that first day. 'Scuse me."

Barbara, slowing down, gave him half a smile. She suggested, more gently, that they appeared to have figured out most of what had been going on.

The Jaybird nodded. "Next couple cases of pasta should about fill the truck."

Beside the splintered altarpiece, the rectory door, they passed a crucifix. When Barbara paused to genuflect, the husband did the same, then ventured to guess that Cesare had some of the late Lieutenant Major's counterfeits.

"The Earthquake I.D. He must've had some left over."

The wife didn't respond, surprised by the priest's rooms. In Brooklyn and Bridgeport, the spaces behind the altar wall had looked more churchy, deep brown, a lot of oak. Cesare's was mostly fungus-gray, steel-drab, as modern as the rest of the building. The old man stood at the desk, pulling open a drawer he hadn't bothered to lock. First he brought out four or five vials of communion wine, the kind used for bedside visits, and these gave Barb a unexpected pang. Out of the blue she recalled the last time she'd seen her father. The grown Barbarella had spent an evening with fumble-mouthed old Dad, on his condo's tiny deck in Vero Beach. They'd drunk the wine she'd picked up during the flight, the little bottles of red.

Then the priest brought out something else. Paper, that's all: a sheaf of blank paper hardly pinkie-thick.

"The *scippatori*," he croaked, at last showing the effort of getting here.

Jay frowned. "What? I wasn't carrying anything like this."

For Cesare, raising his eyes seemed suddenly an enormous effort. His forehead crumpled; his grimace deepened. Barbara tried to look encouraging, she fingered her Madonna out from under her neckline, but she didn't have a clue so far as the papers were concerned. The priest tapped a finger against the stuff, then as husband and wife bent over the desktop, he collapsed into his chair. The mother turned, worried; never mind the papers. She noticed how heavily the old man was sweating, the stains showing through his black cotton. He sprawled across the chair almost as feebly as he had (was it only an hour ago?) across Barbara's sofa. By the time she could be sure that Cesare was breathing decently, Jay had begun to speak.

"It's about the paper," her husband was saying. "The paper *itself*."

Barb felt crowded again, there between one man's rickety splay and the other's barrel build. The Jaybird held up two sheets of the stationery, a heavyweight bond. A specialty bond, with the roughage of an old scar, in which faint blue threads came together in a watermark.

"Are you saying. . . ." Barb looked from the husband to the priest and back again. "Jay, those aren't the I.D. There's nothing—"

"They aren't the *I.D.*," Jay said. "There's nothing there. This is about the paper."

"Are you saying, the actual stuff? The stock, the, the bond?"

"Look at it. Think about it. Kahlberg, I mean, this is what the guy *needed*."

Barbara settled a hand on her husband's shoulder, thumbing the strap of his undershirt as she began to understand. Why, Jaybird. Look what we found. Roebuck couldn't find them, not even with the F-16s just a touch of a button away. But now all the facts were in, they were here on a desk belonging to Barbara's priest, and while they added up to nothing you'd call good news, they were easy enough to understand. Another folder came open, onscreen, and a dead man popped up with a grin.

Jay looked pained, dripping sweat as he fingered the paper—like the last guy who must've handled the stuff. There were smudges across the bond's watermark and wrinkles in several sheets, and this damage must've been done by the first day's *scippatori*, the two Cesare had been hiding. The NATO liaison would've kept his materials pristine. This was his I.D. stock, the most valuable stuff in his over-the-shoulder bag. The clandestini, on the other hand, had been strictly smash-&-grab.

"Kahlberg," Jay repeated. "Hey, he was already in the shop. The print facility."

"He told us," Barbara said. "He bragged about his access."

"The forms, the logo, he didn't need that. The NATO logo, the UN, forget about it. Hey. If that guy kept forms around, the whole forms, ready for signature?"

Jay's eyes grew large, and Barb was already nodding. Everybody had it wrong, both in the offices of the Consulate and in the dens of the Camorra. Everybody was trying to find where Kahlberg had hidden his forms. But a stash like that, lying around waiting for someone to fill in the blanks, would've constituted too much of a tangle for the Silk-Man. One more thing to worry about. Rather, whenever he had five minutes alone in the printing facility, he could dummy up an I.D. template.

"This is about the paper," Barbara said.

"Plus one of the hitters was queer."

Puzzled, she met her husband's eyes a moment, then suffered a chill she couldn't place. She turned to the priest, but he still looked useless, sprawling like an injured crow in a box. Or was the rectory the box, too small for its complications?

"Outside, Owl, hey? You told me. One of our guys swung to the left."

Barb found no clue to her husband's thinking in his look, but once again she couldn't face him for long.

"See, Silky, I mean. He knew what he needed. Time we got to Naples, he knew."

Her hand came away from Jay's shoulder, in a zero-G drift. Barbara found her purse, then through the skin of the purse the vertebra of her rosary.

"That guy. Lord of the Underworld. Any angle he could play—"

"Holy Mary," Barbara said, "Mother of God."

The Jaybird's stare offered little comfort. What she mostly detected was willpower, a determination not unlike what she'd picked up in his expression in their bedroom, during these recent nights when she'd been too dry for loving.

"You're saying," she said "this is about Kahlberg, what he needed. And by the time we got to Naples, he had it all worked out."

"Barb, it's got to be. He had the plan, he had the guys. The right guys, a couple of poor sad creeps, plus one who Silky could really do a number on—"

"All by the time we got to Naples."

He eyes fell again on the I.D. bond, flesh-colored: flesh once dead but now erupting in fresh sweat and goose-bumps. If she could've said more she would've agreed with Jay, *it had to be*. Only one explanation had room for all the folders now open onscreen, and this was that the late Lieutenant Major Player had known the Lulucitas were coming downtown with all the documents required for a family overseas. He'd arranged for the necessary sort of emergency, the kind that would allow him into the high-security cabinet where they kept the watermark bond for the Earthquake I.D. He'd set it up: Americans down, white folks, executive class, and he'd selected the timeframe and street corner—plus the right sort of accomplices.

"One of those guys anyway." Jay kept his voice low, not wanting to interrupt a prayer. "Kahlberg, I mean. He had one of them wrapped around his finger."

Now came the sound of the wheels beneath Cesare's chair. The old man toed closer, first eyeing the papers, then looking up to Barb. How long had he had these things? His destitute guests must've brought him this veiny ragstock the way a cat would bring its owner a dead mouse. But that was about as far as she could take her thinking, otherwise tripped up by mounting anger. In her mind's eye Barbara pictured the Lieutenant Major during his lone moment of sincerity, back in the museum. He must've worn the same honest sneer the night he'd shown these million-dollar blanks to his nigger-bitch *scippatoro*.

"Signora," Cesare said, "I was bound by the Church, by the Order, don't you—"

"The church?" she snapped. "You mean, like a sanctuary? A home?"

Jay spread his hands and motioned as if pressing down the air.

"Are you saying," she went on, "this is a home, here? A place where a person can count on hearing the truth?"

When her husband touched her, Barbara jerked away so hard that the back of her head slammed against a bookshelf.

"Oh, pleas-s-se." Hissing, wincing, she lifted a hand to her head. "Jay, you're just as bad."

"Owl Girl. Hey. Me and you, we were both part of—"

"Oh, don't, don't! Are you saying, that first day, it wasn't all about you and him and the itinerary? Or are you just stupid, Jay? Are you so stupid, you've *forgotten* about the itinerary? That pervert knew exactly where we were going."

On a bookshelf over one shoulder, on the side where her head hurt, a clock and Bible blurred into figures. They looked the terra-cotta imposters of a Neapolitan crèche, a shepherd and a Moorish king. It was yet another first encounter with the city, the instant version, to go with yet another abortive spell of echolalia: . . . *hey, all I ever did . . . how else was I going to get around . . .*

"You did what he told you!" she barked. "You went where he told you!"

Then there was the priest, him who had care of her soul. Cesare had laid a long middle finger over puckered lips—and wasn't that an obscene revision of the crucifix? A depravity, like his endless talk about doing something for the helpless and the clandestine? Mother of God, these men in charge.

"No more," Barbara said. "No more of this ever. I was right in the first place."

These men were all the same, their startled heads cocking in synch.

"I'm saying, I want a *divorce.*"

"Owl Girl, I mean. Not again, babe. We've been there."

"Been there, where? A house full of lies? I had no idea!"

The priest dropped his hand to the chair-arm, readying himself to stand.

"Don't bother, Cesare. Father. When I think of all the yadda-yadda I had to sit through, that meandering Dublin yadda-yadda. It's over, Fa-ther. The End."

Jay tried for her waist and she wound up whacking her head again.

"Don't," she groaned, "don't. What are you going to say, we'll work on this? We'll rebuild trust? Listen, from now on, there's nothing to rebuild, ever. You, all you *men*, you're gone, so far as I'm concerned. You're history."

"Owl," Jay said. "Think about it. I mean, the day you've had."

"This isn't about today." She found the door. "It's about *forever!*"

She turned and bolted. The dash down the long sanctuary felt wonderful, the blood singing in her ears as she plunged into the big room's cool. She couldn't hear whatever was behind her. Anyway after the first few strides all that mattered was the goal ahead, where she was going—the kids. The kids needed the truth. They had to learn about her and Jay, about Silky and his paper chase, about Cesare and the night visitors. Even the older boys and Romy, the others had to hear about that as well, another working piece in the whole truth.

And Barbara was the one to lay all the pieces out, because at last she'd come to see how to live in the truth. Before she'd gotten halfway through the church she understood where safety began, perfect safety and freedom from any confusion whatsoever. It was squatters' rights, simple as that. Just hunker down and refuse to budge.

The back pew sat empty. Her bodyguard had wandered off, leaving behind a dirty comic book. Barbara couldn't miss the page to which the book had fallen open, a man and woman in a naked embrace. But she'd hit her stride now, heading for home. She had to gather herself for the door to the street. Jay and the priest couldn't be far behind, so she had to get ready to grab the thing and yank. Barbara whipped out into the city air, the stone and salt, the volcano and diesel and sun.

Three men fell on her. Three guys who'd been waiting on the stoop, one black and two white—she got that much from a single dumbfounded look before one of them slapped a cloth over her mouth. The rag had an awful taste and a chemical odor, yet another tang in the air, searing and new. Barbara might've smelled something like it in one of DiPio's hospital wards.

There was a blinding moment when her arm felt ripped out of her socket, and the stranger's head against hers proved more heated and sweat-soaked than her own. Only one of the men had hold of her, the African, but his fingers were tough as bridge cables. He had no trouble keeping the cloth over her face and pinning her wrist between her shoulder blades. It hurt in spite of whatever they'd poured into the cloth, and she wanted to scream, especially when one of the other attackers stopped the hard-charging Jay by putting a gun to her head. The Jaybird, seeing that as soon as he was out the church door, tripped and fell and wound up with a gun on him too. Swiftly the two Americans were wrestled into a car, the husband getting his own taste of chloroformed cloth. When the priest loomed on the steps behind them, his shouts were nebulous, no more substantial than the local or two who'd stopped to watch.

It was broad daylight, the end of *riposo*. But the car stood close, on the same spot where the police had pulled up on the day when Jay had been kidnapped.

Chapter Thirteen

From the church to the waterfront seemed a single downward acceleration. The whining transmission and the lumpish embrace—she was pinned against Jay, head down, sinuses burning from the kidnappers' crude anesthetics—all this took Barbara back to her mother's cousin's, in lower Manhattan. The cramp recalled the sofa-bed above Lafayette Street. That thump against her hip might've been the cousin, trying to cheer up little Barbarella, a woman with a touch clumsier than Mama's. But no. That was a gun, nudging Barbara's love-handle, and she remained in a fog even after she was freed from the Fiat's back seat. Jay didn't appear any better off, staggering, groaning. Husband and wife were prodded under a low opening into a dank hatchway. There was another whine, wood on metal maybe, and Barb may have seen a crowbar at work, planks coming off. The smell was rust and mold, a reek that after a moment woke her enough to discover she still carried her purse. Her cash was where she'd put it, and her new passport too. She wondered about Jay's wallet.

Once husband and wife stamped the life back into their legs and cleared the fuzz from their sight, they discovered themselves in a low cellar. A few leaky barrels of wine remained racked against one wall. An eatery in the *centro storico*, condemned after the quake—Barb struggled with the logic, working against a headache and pinpricks and the renewed aggravation of her interior whipsaw. Up in Cesare's she'd been screaming again. Again it was all about the end of everything. Meanwhile, two of her captors came up with flashlights. Nobody let go of his gun, but they got the lights switched on and began to nudge the shambling Americans towards the darkest part of the basement, behind the racked barrels. The Jaybird put up a muddled resistance, shoving, wobbling, the wine-softened earth noisy underfoot. Then however came the distinct *click* of a pistol's safety switch. After that the five began another descent, difficult, backwards. They clambered down a narrow tunnel hacked into the city bedrock.

The Jaybird had to move on all fours, his groggy eyes on his wife above him. His shoulders scraped the walls of the passageway, and the scattershot beams of the flashlights caught white crumbles of stone in the chest-hairs that poked out of his collar. Years ago the kids had splashed him like that, leaving dribbles of spit-up after a feeding . . .

But what was Barb dreaming about now? What, how good this guy had been when the kids were babies? Strangers were forcing her at gunpoint down into a hole. They had her on a sloping mole-run. The temperature kept dropping, the stink of Vesuvius was replaced by the prickle of limestone, and the walls were toothy with pick-and-shovel work. Barbara knew where they were headed, the *Sotterraneo*. Just the place for kidnappers' hideout. The Late Lieutenant Major, now, he hadn't needed to get his hands dirty. He'd had the printers, the NATO facility, and he'd had his *clandestini*. No doubt he'd laid out the cash for their motorcycle too.

Yet as the mother found one toehold after another (the tunnel was roughly laddered), she came to believe that the liaison man had nonetheless kept some lair down in the vaults and warrens beneath the city. He would've liked that, a stony and hurtful love-nest. Come to think of it, the exercise was proving good for her too. As Barbara felt her way into the cold, her head kept clearing. She recalled a nasty tale of Italian revenge, one that featured a cellar like this. Some poor bastard was lured underground, then clapped in chains and walled up, still wearing his clown's cap and bells. The story was one of those she'd read to the boys, only; the girls weren't old enough. She herself wasn't old enough, not in a skirt and pumps like this, the clothes she'd worn to meet a movie director. Still she knew something about the Sotterraneo, and not just from reading Edgar Allen Poe. Chris said that the first quarries had been cut by the Greeks. The tufa was perfect for building, cool in summer and holding the heat in winter. The work had been done by slaves, of course, a lot of them children.

At length the Americans and their captors emerged from of the tunnel. Barb straightened up to see a flashlight beam playing along high and strictly cornered walls. She recalled more of the history, the secret churches carved out by the early Christians, the bomb shelters built by the Fascists.

But today wasn't that kind of excursion. One of the kidnappers put his gun against Barbara's shoulder, almost resting it there. A slant automatic like Kahlberg's. Meantime the African, the one who'd first laid hands on her, sent two or three echoing shouts into the black.

The word sounded familiar, a name perhaps, short with a long vowel. Barb might've recognized their language too, a pidgin French. But once her captors realized that they were alone, someone they'd expected hadn't yet arrived, they confined their talk to whispers. The African appeared to call the shots, he did most of the talking, and he directed the others when they turned and herded the Lulucitas across the dark. The floor, Barbara discovered, was cut in herringbone. Then ahead, along one side of the cubicle vault, the flashlights picked out what looked like the entrance to another shrunken tunnel. But this proved to be no more than a hole in the wall, a step-down storage area or sleeping compartment. Even before the flashlights illuminated the space, the redoubled lime odor suggested how small it was. The mother's head bumped the jagged ceiling. Then before she could get a look around she was yanked to the floor, her purse stripped away, her arms forced together behind her back.

So that's how it would be, tied up in a stone burrow, *tied up*. One of the white guys had a ponytail, she remembered after a moment; his leather hair-band secured her wrists. As for Jay, with him the crooks used his own sturdy belt, $50 at Bridgeport Leathers, and the big man didn't make it easy. He swore and kicked until he was stilled by a couple of swats with a sound like an Atlas slapping shut. A pistol-whipping? Anywhere near the temple? Barbara saw nothing but shadows, though there was no mistaking how her husband went limp, sagging against the wall with a groan.

"Jay?" She swung his way, in the crowded hole. "Jaybird?"

"We don' need him," one of the kidnappers said, out of the cell's backlit opening.

"What?" she asked. "What are you saying?"

"*You* the one, Missus. Him, man, we don' need."

"What—what are you thinking?" The flashlight beam shifted and she noticed the purse at her hip, still shut, snaps fastened. "What do you want?

"Oh, listen," she went on, "anyway, really, whatever it is you want, forget about it. This will get you nowhere. You'll be lucky if they don't send you to Abu Ghraib."

Tough talk. Barbarian talk, surging up anew after the discovery in Cesare's back room. "Maybe," she went on, "maybe Abu Ghraib is what you're scared of? You're facing prison, deportation?" This seemed the likeliest possibility. "You're facing deportation and you think, with Jay and me, you can negotiate a deal. You think, the Americans can make a difference for you. Mother of God, do you really believe . . ."

The kidnappers moved away without responding. The lights cast a wan back-glow, and the sandal-shuffle echoed a bit longer. Barb was left in a dark so thick that her staring had a lozenge pattern, a ripple of snakeskin. She sneezed, chilled. Still she couldn't shake the clarifying anger that had sprouted in her, a sense that she had the nerve to handle this. Until a year ago she wouldn't have dared to take on a challenge like Maria Elena, and since then Barbara had grown that much stronger.

Beside her Jay stirred, finding his voice with another obscenity or two. She tried to imagine an escape. They would sit back to back, pick off each other's . . .

"Barb?" Jay asked. "Hey?"

"Right here, Jaybird." Was he talking into a wall? "I guess," she went on, "I'm more angry than anything else. I'm not hurt."

She had to wait for his response, ". . . angry. . . ," then wait again.

"Well I'm hurt," he said finally. "The fucks whacked me in the head. I've got to wonder, where's Paul when I need him?"

The best she could manage was a smile he couldn't see. "Try a few deep breaths," she said. "The air's supposed to be good for you."

"Smells like lemon." He seemed to be extending his legs. "Lime and lemon."

"The rock's supposed to have this great stuff in it, the vitamins and minerals for the whole region. It's in the fruits and vegetables, it's in the mozzarella."

"The waters. The healing spa waters."

It would do no good to look concerned. "Jaybird, really. They hit you."

"I'm okay, Owl Girl. Between a headache and a broken head, hey. I guess I know the difference."

No good to nod, either. She nudged backwards with one shoulder, and there he was, his heaving ribcage. He spoke again: "Just, what would be nice, about now? I mean. Would be nice if we had a clue, here."

He gave a sigh, her elbow lifting against his chest.

"You notice they didn't bother to tie our feet," he said.

Barbara wanted to talk about something else. "Jay, have you noticed how, in this city, everywhere you go triggers another round of starting over?" She sat up, losing touch of him. She explained that where they found themselves now was a case in point; they were back at the beginning of things, for Naples.

Jay took his time responding. "At least," he said, "the money's no problem."

"Huh? Jay, look at where we are." She almost laughed at the expression: *look*. "It's the Sotterraneo. It's back to the raw materials."

"The ransom, forget about it. Roebuck, I mean. She's got it in petty cash."

"Jay, would you listen? Anyway, can't you see this isn't about money?"

He sighed in a way she'd always hated, as if she was ten years old.

"Jay, haven't you still got your wallet? Don't you see what they're doing? They've gone off to get somebody, and he's going to tell us what this is about. Now, for once, stop this, the tough guy. Stop and think about what I'm telling you. Ever since the first morning in town, this family's had to stop, step back, and start over."

She'd never brought the idea up to him, not even at bedtime. "I'm not saying we're not at the age. Middle age, aren't you always getting turned around? Isn't there always something that takes you back twenty years? Always something makes you think you have to start over. But around here, it's not just about our age.

"Around here, also we're tripped up by this incredible Naples past." She'd never told him, between the urges to obliterate and the efforts to repair. "The city goes back three thousand years. And it triggers a kind of syndrome, it takes us back too, so that . . ."

"Jesus, Owl. Are you telling me how you *feel*?"

The contempt she heard—that might've been the echo.

"Telling me how you feel. Let's see if I got it. We're all getting nowhere."

"Jay, don't." She had the nerve for him too, now. "I'm talking about emotions."

"I mean, it's beautiful. We'll just sit here talking emotions, since whatever we try, hey. We'll get nowhere."

"It's better than sitting here babbling about money. If you'd done half the work I did at the Sam Center—"

"Aw, not again. Sam Center, Holy of Holies. Give me a break."

EARTHQUAKE I.D.

"If you'd done half the work I did, you'd realize there's nothing more dangerous than a personality that's stuck in old patterns."

"Okay, Doctor. How about this, okay? If we're all the time winding up back at Square One, think of it this way." He might've sat up. "Doesn't have to mean we're stuck. Maybe it means just the opposite. Hey, how about that?"

She flexed her bound wrists till they burned.

"How about, we might go anywhere? We're back to Day One, this godforsaken hole, okay. But then, how about, somebody does some actual *work*?"

"Mother of God."

"Barb, I mean. It comes to work, you haven't got a clue. The sacrifices."

"Listen Jay, here's a clue. You talk about sacrifice, but you love it. Your work, all the politics and the deal-making, you love it. Swapping favors—"

"Oh, here it comes. Everybody's dirty except Barbara." She heard a scrape, and his knee bumped hers. "Everybody else is some kind of bottom feeder."

"You're saying, *I* play the saint? Jay, if it were up to you, the kids and me, we'd have built you a shrine by now."

"Hey. All I ever did was sell pasta. That's your—your *husband*."

"We'd have a shrine, Saint of the Holy Paycheck. Martyr of the working man."

"Angry Barb. Angry, angry, angry Barb."

She jerked herself around, banging her fists against a wall. "Well it gets old, it gets very old, when every day, it's all about money." She might've cut her hand against a spur in the rock. "All you ever want is money and a good car—"

"Hey, what do you know about it? Never earned a nickel in your life. We had to come here to Naples to help the poor, holy of holies, and still you weren't willing to earn a *nickel* to make it happen. Didn't matter who you hurt, didn't matter even if you hurt your own *children*, because—"

Barbara began to scream. She had to scream, her cuts burning and full of grit, and she heaved herself across the scaly floor towards the man's growl. She had to get her hands on him. Seizing Jay by his soaked jacket, getting a fistful of chest-hair too, she set him bellowing. The man struggled to throw her off, his hips bucking

264

and his midsection twisting, humped over still-bound hands. Now grunting, now louder. With the harsh words the two of them spat out, *liar*, *witch*, with their choking and hissing amplified around the hollow, *what? your hands?*, she would've thought that the kidnappers could hear. The din seemed enormous, a monster in an alley. At least one of their captors should've heard, the man who'd tied her up. He should've kept an ear cocked, after using such a cheap scrap of leather on her. One good spur in the tufa had been all she needed in order to tear free. Yet the crooks didn't show, while Barbara and Jay scuffled around the hole, two arms against none. The two of them might've been having this blowout in a bedroom a few hundred feet overhead.

They went unheard and they fought unfairly. Jay couldn't lift a finger. But then again, Barb had spent most of her day in a carnival Scrambler, flung from one side of the car to another. In no time she wore out. She went limp so soon, she wondered what would've happened if her husband been able to get a hand on her when she'd attacked, a hand for instance at her panty-line. As it was the wife lost the heart for fighting halfway into a fresh insult. She swallowed what she was saying and slumped against his cook's uniform, her cheek to its slick synthetic weave. With that, Jay too quit the struggle. His next word slackened into a moan. And the wife couldn't pull herself off him. Instead, she found the Jaybird a useful prop, a loosely-packed duffel on which she could rest. Then this blinking and cooling, curled into him and herself both, rewarded Barbara with a terrific relief: a sense that she'd heaved off years of something or other weighing her down. She'd flung it off either just now in this semi-crypt or over the tussling course of the last five weeks. With that she spread her hands against him, believing they could bring healing. She could offer them both an ultimate healing, with no recurrence of this particular pain at least.

Also Barbara lay her overheated ear in the center of her husband's chest. The thudding behind his ribs seemed the loudest thing in the hole, audible through even the groans and chuckling that followed. A patchwork laughter erupted from them both, ragged and short of breath.

Jay was the first to bring off actual words. "How'd you do that?"

Barb had to sneeze again, drenched in sweat and powdered with rock-dust. Eventually she explained, concluding that the man must've bought the thong on the street. "You know the kind of thing," she said, "leather and beads."

"Leather and beads," the Jaybird said.

Barb ran her itching hands through the man's chest hair, then risked a lick of her cuts. Nothing special, salt and chalk, but she'd skinned herself badly. She'd let herself go. The wounds could use another lick, and this time she let her tongue stray to Jay as well, his skin a more familiar taste. Then the next lick was just for him.

"Another time for that," he said. "Owl Grr-irl. Another day."

The big man needed Barbara's help to sit up. Scooting behind him, she felt her way to Jay's wrists, the belt wrapped together round them.

"Hey," he said, "I'm sorry. It wasn't about you. I felt helpless."

Her own voice caught at the first syllable of a reply. The way her hands closed around his bindings, as he kept up the apologies, she might've been at prayer.

"Jaybird." She coughed and snuffled. "If anyone should say they're sorry—"

"But you were right, up there. Up at Cesare's, you called it. I did tell the man. Kahlberg. We talked about that first day. I gave him the whole itinerary."

"I know. Honey, I know."

"The errands we needed to run. The first errand, the second. He got it all."

"But there's no way it's your fault. All this, no way."

"Fucking guy. He even told me the street. Of historical interest, he told me."

"Jay, please. There's something else, listen. I'm the one. I should apologize." She fingered his bindings but couldn't find where to begin. "Listen, Jay, I'll just say it, I need to get a job."

She felt him start to speak, then check himself.

"The work at the Samaritan Center," she went on, "that's been great. At DiPio's too, just great while it lasted. But otherwise I—this is nuts, what I've been putting us through. I need to get a life, an adult life."

And when she did undo the belt, she didn't know it until Jay's rump started scuffing the floor as he turned to face her. "You want a job," he said.

"Maybe I had something to prove by being a Mom. Maybe I did, once upon a time. But I'm saying, I've done that. Five times now, been there done that."

He rubbed his wrists noisily. "Talking a degree, you know. Hey? A Master's."

That took her by surprise. She'd had all these explanations lined up ready to go.

"Talking an MSW. The program in Danbury. Then there's certification."

"I think I'm talking a green card." Barbara settled against a wall. "It's like I've got to immigrate into my own adult life."

"Got to be on a new basis."

"All I need to do is get over the water and become a citizen. But meanwhile, I've been driving us all crazy because I've been scared to get on the boat."

"That's okay, Barb. We've done the apologies. A little on both sides, okay."

"You called it, the program in Danbury. That's the one, that's the future, and now I'm thinking of child care, it's not a problem. We have the boys. We have Aurora."

Neither of them was trying to find the exit.

"I hear that. With this, starting fresh, you'll be a better mother anyway. Happier person. Plus Mom, yeah. I mean, a weekend now and then. It's a plan."

The Jaybird gave another groan, different, relieved, and maybe he got a good stretch. Barb was reminded of their scuffle. It felt as if the punching and name-calling had taken place in another life, already a long-ago life, and yet the thought gave her a shiver. What could it do, such craziness, except make her shiver?

"You know," she said, "speaking of middle age. There's menopause."

"Barb, hey. Problems, I can think of a million problems. But now we've talked, we've got it on the table, a good plan."

She squinted, trying to make him out. The dark showed her nothing but the lozenge pattern.

"Good plan," she said.

It wasn't much longer before they picked up the noise from the outer room. There was talk, there was movement, and after that came the faint unfolding petals of electric light. Jay and Barbara discovered they sat opposite the hole's egg-shaped opening. As they put up their empty hands, Barb had to fight down another shiver at the blood on her wrists and hands. She'd marked up Jay's uniform too.

The first man in carried no light, and when he stooped to enter, the beam behind him blinded her. Barb glimpsed only a shaved brown head and another pair of stringy sandals. The same flimsy footwear as the others—the same as you'd have found on the slaves who'd hacked out these cellars. Then the one with the light squatted at the opening, the space grew bright and hot, and after more blinking and squinting Barb recognized the man these crooks had gone to get. Fond.

If that was the name he still went by, this handsome and moon-scarred beneficiary of Paul's most dramatic healing. The guy was so reed-like and flexible he had no trouble slipping into the cave, but his smell carried something different, a hint of wildflowers. And whatever you chose to call the man, refugee Lazarus or yippie guerilla, postcolonial hiccup or the last free-standing exponent of non-violence—whatever, it hadn't lowered his status with his crew. Fond carried no weapon, yet with a single raised hand he held back the men outside the chamber. The closest might've been the African again, though she couldn't make out his face. Not that she had any trouble understanding the way he shifted his light from hand to hand. He didn't like finding the Americans untied.

"Easy," Jay said. "I mean, look at us. We're not going anywhere."

"Fond," Barbara said, pronouncing it English-style. "Great, oh, *Fond*! What a load that is off our minds."

The clandestino leader, folded mantis-style, crooked his narrow head.

"If it's you," Barb said, "we know we can talk."

"Barb's right," Jay said. "Guy like you, no problem. We can work it out."

Lazarus gave a snort, not too encouraging. But he allowed them out of the cell, and in the process he made sure of everyone's accessories: Jay's wallet, the mother's purse, his own *telefonino*. Out in the larger room, as Barbara came upright, she smiled at the blood-rush. A rush of revival—the same ferocity as she'd rediscovered up in Cesare's plus, after that last round of talking in the dark, a renewed faith in what she and the Jaybird could accomplish.

She took a moment to reacquaint herself with the high square walls, the herringbone floor. She looked over Fond's two backups, whaddyacallem, henchmen, subalterns. In any case they'd left one of their number behind, a lookout at the next exit perhaps. Now as she studied these two, she came to think that the white one, the lighter one, had been one of the beggars in the shade of her apartment stoop, this afternoon. Seemed more than possible, a couple of feelers out from under the Shell of Hermit Crab, poking around the Vomero. They'd been tailing the family for a couple of weeks now, hadn't they? By the time today's opportunity came up, they'd learned how easy it was to lure away her bodyguard.

She had a clue, as Jay would say. But the Girl Detective wasn't much help here, not with those two guns in plain view, one raised and tacking slowly between her and Jay, the other jammed in a henchman's belt. Then there was the equipment Fond carried, a digital videocamera, state-of-the-web.

The camera was the Hermit Crab's next concern, as soon as it was obvious that the two captives weren't going to try anything. Fond and his soldiers bent over the technology, grumbling in French, in Italian, in English. Barb picked out enough to understand that the kidnappers hadn't found the boss waiting for them, when they'd first arrived at the hideout, because he'd never counted on rounding up his own equipment. He'd expected Maddalena to take care of that. But the girlfriend had realized that today's caper would get her in far worse trouble than leaping a police sawhorse. That business in the piazza a week ago, leaping and pleading with *la Mama* while somewhere a camera rolled, that had been another step up the media ladder. But when Fond had suggested the woman pose for a scarier picture, a violation of international law, he couldn't get a callback. The celebrity renegade had been reduced to haggling on the black market.

They think I'm rich, Fond may have muttered now. *They don't understand, our movement isn't about money.*

The guy had been sending mixed signals since back in dell'Ovo, when Barb had squeezed his hand. The hand itself, she'd thought then, had meant he would die young. But she knew today's code better.

Still, when Fond took up the camera and punched it on, his movements so loose and easy you thought of a dancer, the obliterating white of the spot had her turning away. The gun was worse, its barrel a hole in the brightness.

"Ow," said the Jaybird. "Can't we wait a minute on that? Can't we talk first?"

Barb gathered herself and faced around again. She put a hand to her throat, showing the worst of her wounds. "Fond," she said, "be sure to get the blood in the picture. Everyone needs to see how you've hurt us."

When Jay glanced at her, his look showed more than reflected light.

"Everyone needs to see," the wife went on.

"That Maddalena, hey," Jay said. "She knows what people want to see. She'll put the blood front and center."

Barb couldn't suppress another smile. "You understand, Fond? We're saying, what do you want to tell people, when you put your pictures on the web?"

She was quiet, speaking without an echo. Jay was the better negotiator when it came to the office, or a maneuverer like Roebuck. But Fond was another matter.

"We know you don't want money." She hoisted her purse, its leather freshly scuffed. "You, your movement, we understand, you want something better."

"Barb's right," Jay said, a bit too hearty.

"You want to change the world. You want to do that with this video, and with us two, right here, and in the next ten minutes."

By the time she'd finished, Fond had lowered the camera. He spoke with his black second-in-command, using yet another language, something from the far side of the Mediterranean. Barbara couldn't let that go, not with the fresh audacity she'd come to. After the first exchange between the clandestini she stepped up to stick a finger in Fond's face. She ignored the other man's pistol, at the corner of her eye.

"You talk to *us*," she snapped. "The people you grabbed off the street."

Fond's smell remained wildly out of place, a perfume from a five-star hotel.

Jay closed in too, touching her shoulder. "Owl."

"I said a rosary over this guy. I said a Hail Mary for his soul."

This tall and mediagenic blade, this hint of *la dolce vita*—he'd come a long way from stinking up the security ward in dell'Ovo. And that was his problem, Barbara realized. The man was struggling to get fresh bearings, after spending too long in a scented Jacuzzi, with mint tea and crème brioche by the tub. Fond had become a soul-brother to old Cesare, the priest driven mad in the presence of sybaritic Aurora. But today Cesare had gotten his head on straight again.

"Fond, listen. I'm just saying, this kind of strong-arm business was unnecessary."

"Playground stuff! All it does it cause a lot of hard feeling."

She turned to her husband.

"Plus," Jay added, "remember how you found us here. Hey. Our hands were free."

Turning back: "Fond, you've got our attention. Now what are you trying to say?"

"Except first you've got to lose the guns. I mean, guns? Forget about it."

"I can see," Barb tried, "how you thought we'd never talk to you. I can see how that was for you. You kept showing up on TV, you kept asking. And, nothing."

"Talking about emotion, Fond. We feel your pain. We can see you were getting desperate. But guns, forget about it. I mean, today, this, what you're trying to say, it's not just for you, it's for all the brothers out there—"

"*Assez, assez,*" said Fond.

He set his arms akimbo, calling attention to his rap-star clothing, the plaid boxers bagged over low-slung jeans. He wore his cell phone clipped above his crotch. "Enough, for pity's sake," he said.

His eyes were on Barbara. "I want to bring you and your Paul to the *Republique du Mali.* To the Sahel."

Once the former hunger striker went into his appeal, the parents confined their responses to a word here or there. Anyway Fond began by telling them things they knew already. He assured Barb and Jay that he hadn't ordered the kidnapping in order to hurt anybody or "acquire personal gain of any kind." Rather all he wanted, today, was a brief statement on-camera. In this the parents would agree to bring Paul and the rest of the family down to equatorial Africa, and then the mother would recite the rosary, as she had when Fond could barely hear her or see her, lying in what he'd believed would be his deathbed. Since then the *clandestino* leader had been unable to shake his faith in her prayers, even as he'd enjoyed five nights in the penthouse at Hotel Parthenope, the guest of the rock star Sting. How could he forget the Hail Mary of Signora Lulucita, shaky but determined? He believed "the sorrows in the homeland" would begin to heal as soon as Barbara's recitation was put on the web and streamed worldwide.

At least Fond spared them more than a thumbnail description of how bad things had gotten in his part of Mali. The widening drought and the Saharan gang-war were all over the news. Rather he emphasized that, as soon as Barbara appeared on the first screen down at the desert's edge, her and her "quite awesome prayer," his home country "will take a turn towards a betterment."

Barbara remembered plenty of people around Naples who'd come a lot closer to her praying than that, lately, with no discernible betterment. But she figured she'd soon enough get the opportunity to wipe the stars from this boy's eyes. Soon enough she'd go to work, especially, on the man's well-nigh infantile belief in the power of television. For Fond also believed that once he got the agreement on video—plus the prayer, he reiterated—he'd have no trouble with the authorities. Once he got the material onto the internet, multimedia proof of his good intentions, he and the other Shell members could return to street level without consequences. Everything, declared the young West African, would be perfectly fine.

By now Barbara and Jay had settled on the floor at the edge of the flashlight's halo. Fond remained up and stalking about, from time to time spreading both arms and all ten fingers for emphasis. The rap star, he even had stage lighting, a flashlight on its end at his feet. He assured them he didn't intend the family's visit to the South to go on very long. He hoped the trip would save a few lives, to be sure, but more than that he intended to help his country claim "a better place in the Imperial feast." Nothing could accomplish this, he felt certain, more quickly than decent exposure on television. Once the Republic and its suffering began to play across the dinner tables and living rooms of the United States, not to mention the web broadcasts in their children's bedrooms, everything would swiftly "take a turn towards a betterment." Fond was confident that their work would be done by the start of the American school year.

"Your children," he said then, "they begin school, mm, *a Settembre, non*?"

Barb nodded, less than enthusiastic. She hoped he was wrapping this up.

"You do intend to return to America, *non*?" Again his eyes were on her. "You have always intended this, this goodwill visit—it was always to be brief?"

That got her angry. She'd already had this glum epiphany, watching Paul's face zip into its files, on the oversized screen in the editing booth. The mother had seen the whole Naples trip looking pointless, zipped into a box and deleted. The recollection must've started her frowning, because Jay sharply cut off whatever she had in mind to say. Again he brought up the guns.

"I mean, before you go calling us *tourists*, let's talk about those guns. Before you go getting insulting. 'Goodwill visit,' give me a break."

The backup with his pistol in his pants, the white man more or less, noticed Jay's tone and put his hand on the handle of his weapon.

"You walk around packing iron, hey. You're the tourists. Anyone carrying a gun, he's in and out fast."

The leader of the crew dropped his arms, looking hurt, struggling to understand. Jay pressed ahead, arguing that so long as Fond kept threatening to "put a bullet" in the two Americans, any statement they made wouldn't be worth a thing. "I mean, 'Hail Mary, full of grace?' How's that going to come off? Just, for starters, think how it's going to sound to the cops."

"But, *sans blague*, I cannot foresee any significant charge against me."

Fond smiled, a slim ebony Buddha. "Once the authorities are witness that video, I cannot see how my brothers or I will have any legal charge that will, will stand."

Jay looked to Barb, his question so obvious that the lanky radical went on at once, assuring them he wasn't crazy. The police knew him, he argued; they understood he was no Bin Laden. He apologized again, "*de tout mon coeur*," for the extreme measures he'd been forced to take today. And did the Lulucitas realize that before coming to Naples he'd held a fellowship in Philosophy of Cinema at the university in Bamako? Did they understand that the actions of his Shell amounted to a natural extension of his research into the socio-political ramifications of Spectacle?

"I know you're a smart guy," Jay said. "And movies, hey, I'll sit and talk about the movies all night. Just as soon as you lose the guns."

"But you must understand, today is never been an act of violence. Today is a performance and a, a credo."

During the fifteen months he'd been able to afford at the university, Fond explained, he'd developed a thesis on "the politicization inherent in representations of the Foreign," as it occurred in the work out of Hollywood. Then later still, after his mother had died of the guinea worm and he'd paid to for a passage to Salerno in a shipping crate—he and a Nigerian who never recovered from the dehydration—Fond had come to see greater metropolitan Naples as a rare opportunity for applied learning. "For are you seeing how the American cinema treats the experience of Italy?"

Jay looked like he was about to erupt, to bark an order like the American Boss, but Barbara held up a finger. There had to be a thread here, glimmering on the labyrinth floor, something she and her husband could pick up and follow.

"Are you seeing what happens to you Americans, their signification in the cinema, whenever a representative character comes to Italy?"

"I've—seen the movies," she tried.

"You Americans," the young man continued, "you are fascinated with Italy, and cinema provides the signifier for this fascination. The cinema makes spectacle of the secret dreaming, to *l'anime* of a society at large. Thus what appears as spectacle should be understood as confession. The culture presents its case to God."

Now there was a possible thread. "Are you saying you believe in God?" she asked. "Because if you believe it's God at work in our Paul, you don't understand—"

"Ah, Signora. If you would only have responded to my initial request on the MTV, we could've spoken comfortably of everything. Of this God as well."

"Well, on MTV, in front of fifty million viewers, I would've said the same thing. You don't *understand* about Paul. You want to talk about a spectacle? I would've looked straight into the camera and said, our Paul, when he, when he has an episode—he can't do it on demand."

"Barb's right."

"Dr. DiPio," she went on, "he already tried this kind of thing, you know. As much as I let him, he tried it. He put Paul together with a couple of the *terremotati*."

"I mean, you must've seen it," Jay said. "Even in dell'Ovo they had a TV. We could take Paul down to the desert and, hey, you'd still get nothing."

Barbara, meantime, let her gaze shift away from their keeper's sleek face. One of the other *clandestini* was acting as if he'd heard something, throwing the flashlight beam around the room, but Barb stared elsewhere, into the dark. She didn't want to think about asking more of her eleven-year-old.

"Ah *oui*." The outlaw was saying. "This I do understand, the boy's visit may come to nothing." Nevertheless, he went on, he believed he'd detected something about Barbara's prayers that had eluded everyone else.

"It is been the spectacle, in every case," he declared.

Barbara faced him, frowning. "Prayers—it's private. It's you and God."

"But when there is the betterment, it is been on the video, in every case. The miracle with the boy, with your Paul, it is beginning on the TV, *toujours*. His mother is saying her rosary on the TV."

And Fond squeezed her shoulder. Barbara startled, drawing in a leg. At least he kept it brief, correct, French.

"Are you saying, every healing episode is on account of me?"

The refugee *philosophe* stepped back again, his subalterns nodding to either side of him. "I am saying, it is beginning with you. You, the spectacular image."

The man's perfume had faded; maybe that's why she hadn't noticed him bending closer.

Fond waved a hand at the ceiling and walls, his smile the same gleaming business that had worked so well between hip-hop videos. "The prayer on television, what shall we say, it is the image on the walls of the caveman? The painting and the dance, which is bringing good fortune in the hunt?"

Mother of God, who was this guy, to talk crazy one minute and then the next . . .

"Fond," Jay said, "hey, maybe you got something there."

"*Seulement le logique.*"

The next minute, the guy came up with an idea no one else had thought of. Barbara, looking for a hole in Fond's theory, realized the clandestino leader couldn't have known about Cesare—but then again, she and her rosary had gone on-camera with the old Jesuit Dominican, too. Her last favor for Maddalena.

Jay appeared to be going through the same thought process, taking a while before speaking again. "It's like we said before: with you, we know we can talk."

But why shouldn't this hand-to-mouth intellectual have come up with a decent idea? Above his bright smile his eyes were wedges, as they'd been a couple of weeks ago, packed in cotton. He'd seen a lot worse than either of the Americans, no denying. And when Barbara pictured her and her priest bent over a string of beads, their camel-backed shadow cast across thousands of screens, she realized that she couldn't begin to say what her prayers might be capable of. Hadn't they gone jaywalking, those prayers? Darting about in heavy traffic?

"Fond, I mean, I'm impressed. Me and Barbara both. It's a plan."

The husband eased forward as he spoke, leaning into the inverted cone of light. You couldn't help but notice how he'd begun to bruise.

"You're a smart guy," the Jaybird said, "that's obvious, very smart."

The worst, purple already, was under the eyes. Fond couldn't help but notice. As he stared he went from the head of the class to boy who always got picked on.

"You, you get it. Smart guy like you. Talk about making a spectacle . . ."

Fond used a local gesture, nothing like a rap star, pressing together his flat hands and waggling them before his chest. A pleading gesture.

"Lose the guns, Fond. This isn't you. I mean, whacking people around."

The young skin-and-bones looked to his African sub-commander, then dropped his eyes. In a different voice, halting, he admitted that ("just as *le père* is saying") lately he hadn't been himself. "After your son is made me well, for some several days, I am thinking I am signed onto another social contract altogether." He'd soaked in two separate bathtubs, both in a single suite; he'd stroked the endless silken hair of a blonde. "I am thinking I am moved into this new paradise, to which all the hetero-glottic world is coming." In the hotel penthouse, with every pleasure of the North at his fingertips, the former clandestino had seemed to vanquish divisions of faith, skin color, or "the nation-state." So long as the expense account held up, he'd lost his bearings.

"Yet there came a morning I came down from this paradise," he went on. "When I did, I found my brothers and sisters living still in the inferno. An inferno where we are sleeping still in the boxes, the boxes of durable paper. Like the hermit crab, we live. Always we must be finding another *shell!*"

He stamped the floor, setting off an echo. "What God is it that excludes my brothers, when He is so sweetly embracing me?"

Barbara wobbled in an undertow of Samaritan impulse. Maria Elena came again to mind, shrieking to split the roof the day that Children's Services took her away. The mother tugged at an armpit, glad for the Jaybird beside her, refusing to go soft and distracted. He argued that any man who could set up today's kidnapping knew perfectly well what God watched over Naples these days.

"Hey, this city, it's still about the nation-state. Nation-state even with the United Nations in town. They've all got laws, the UN too, and you broke the laws."

When Fond met the father's look, Barbara could see that she wasn't the only one wobbling. "Today is a performance," said the Hermit Crab leader. "An enactment of violence, only, today will bring into being, down in the South, a turn towards—"

"Yeah, yeah, that's nice." The way Jay shook his head, you'd think he was showing off his bruises. "'Turn to the better,' very nice, except it's a broken record. Broken record, Fond, you know—repeating and repeating and getting nowhere."

"I mean," Jay went on, "you're way too smart to go on kidding yourself, about what's going to happen upstairs."

Briskly the former VP summarized what was in store for the remaining Shell of the Hermit Crab. It wouldn't matter what their captured Americans said on the video. When Jay mentioned "deportation," the eyes of the other African grew bigger than they'd been all afternoon. He scowled up at his boss. The Jaybird didn't miss it, and he switched to simpler English.

"A case like this, Fond, you know. They come in with very good shooters. Case like this, NATO gets involved, they come in with the Elite Forces."

The clandestino leader tried to ease his man's concern, putting on a rickety smile.

"Don't, Fond," said Barbara. "Don't. Lying to your friends, that's not you. Or are you saying, these two didn't realize the danger?"

Jay let the question sink in a moment, then pointed out that if one of the NATO Elites saw an illegal alien carrying a gun, he wasn't going to wait and watch a video.

"Plus, ask yourself, ask your buddy there too." When Jay gestured at the nameless African, he backed Fond away a step. "Do you really believe this place is so secret? Do you really believe nobody can find you?"

All three kidnappers eased back. Now the light at their feet only caught the brighter bits: the undone buttons, the lowered gun.

The Jaybird was more interested in Fond's cell phone. He said that the signal might not reach this far underground, but then again, NATO had the best tracking technology in the world. "Anyway, could be, they don't need the technology. We've been down here, what, an hour now? Hey, the story's got to be all over the street."

Another noise sounded beyond the quarry-room, a tumble of scree. The African spun round, his weapon raised, but Barbara thought of earthquakes. She pictured the walls collapsing; she got her fingers on her purse, the outline of her beads.

"It's got to be all over the street," Jay repeated, "and Fond, think about this." He brought up the wine cellar overhead, where he and Barbara had first been wrestled underground. "I mean, place like that, how long did it take you guys to find it? Place used to be a restaurant, right, lots of business. How long'd it take?"

She picked up on Jay's charisma, too. The husband could've been the one onstage, in the spotlight.

"Fond, hey, you know what you're going to be facing up there. You know they're going to have the kids with them. They want the kids for the negotiation."

Off in the shadow, the man in charge and his next in command put their heads together. They reverted to whatever homeland tongue they'd spoken before.

"That's right, talk it over. Whatever we do down here, Fond, you and your guys are going to be facing the same thing up there. The kids and the very good shooters."

"Listen," the mother put in loudly, "you already beat one suicide."

Fond looked angry when he stepped back into the light. "The starvation is nothing so bad," he told her.

The subterranean air itself sent mixed messages, cool as October and yet full of odors, like high summer. "And a bullet," the man went on, "this is even easier. You should be seeing what happens when the guinea worm took Maman."

Barbara wanted to ask about the virus, she thought it'd been wiped out in a recent World Health initiative, but then Fond gave an order. Another word Barb didn't know, but plainly an order, echoing round the stony cube. The darker henchman had been expecting it; in the next moment he stepped past his commander and turned his gun butt-end out. He handed the weapon to Jay—handed it over, a sleek gray Italic of a pistol, the kind of iron Silky Kahlberg might've carried. Barbara's husband, too, looked as if he'd known what would happen. He hardly missed a beat in taking the thing, his movement so smooth that his kidnapper's caramel-colored hand remained extended, empty, long enough for the Jaybird to put his own into it for a confirming shake.

The lanky radical over Barbara meantime had more to say about dying. Fond declared that he was willing to risk a lot worse than standing in the crosshairs of some Marine with an infrared scope. Barb didn't catch it all, nor what Jay was telling the sidekick, either. She noticed her husband's tone, reassuring, even fatherly. It sent a pang of remorse through her, since even today she hadn't quite believed in his pitch. To her, for years now, Jay had always come across as a bit of a con, wheedling, angling. She had to get over that, but just now Barbara couldn't catch everything he said, not with all this elation ruffling up, so intense it made her drop the purse. She seemed to forget to breathe; the air burst from her heavy chest with half a laugh, half a shout. Hey there, Mr. Paul—what do say to these healing hands? Her husband had one gun, and now the Albanian or whatever, the whiter Shell, was about to offer the mother his. The man was slower about it than the African, taking more time than he needed to yank the pistol from under his belt. He needed to double-check the order, looking up at Fond narrowly. Anyway Barbara wasn't ready to take the thing. If she couldn't manage her heart and lungs, how could know what to do with her hands? She tried smiling at the guy, and she hoped she had a finger raised.

She still hadn't touched the weapon when the two *scippatori* rushed in, and one of them had a gun too, the nose up and pointed at Fond.

Chapter Fourteen

If she'd thought for a moment that these two were anything other than the *scippatori* from their first morning in town, if it so much as crossed her mind that they were cops or Camorra, Barbara couldn't remember. It seemed as if at once she'd put together the clues, if you could call them clues. She'd picked out the blue bandanna before the two scrawny creatures came entirely into the light. She'd seen the unmatched skin, one brown and the other butter. She'd noticed the eyeliner and gloss that one was wearing, the darker one, and the sashay in his approach. He was the one with the gun, and that too branded them as the original *scippatori*. The queer would've been the one to work with the late liaison man, and Silky would've loved to teach his boys about guns.

Quickly she was on her feet. "Don't," she said, her arms coming up with hands open, one extended towards Jay and the other towards the two men who'd split his head. "Don't, no shooting. *Non sparate*."

Back in Brooklyn, she remembered, she'd never thought that gunplay sounded like a truck backfiring.

"Everything's all right," she said. "*Tutt'a posto*." The scippatoro was pointing his pistol at Fond, the lighter-skinned soldier was pointing his back, and Jay shifted his from one to the other. "I'm saying, we're all safe. *Non sparate, nessuno*."

In Brooklyn, as a girl, she'd learned her Italian. She'd learned to recognize a revolver like the one this queen was carrying, a .38, the kind they issued the police.

"Nobody shoot," she said. "Nobody, it's safe."

As a girl she'd wondered how it felt, pointing a gun and then hesitating. You saw it often enough in the movies, they took aim and then—they hesitated.

"*Sans blague*," murmured Fond. "Quentin Tarantino, *sans blague*."

"Shut up, Fond." The American Boss. "Hey. Trying to save your life here."

"It's all good, all safe, listen, *tutto sicuro*." Barb's legs and arms were tingling, she'd been down on the floor so long. "Don't shoot, nobody shoot."

"We shoot or we don't shoot," said the darker scippatoro, "it is as you desire. *Miracolosa, santissima*, it is only as you want."

Barbara risked a look at Jay. Had he understood? Her husband appeared to be working on the translation, the connection, frowning and up on one knee. He kept his automatic leveled on Fond's man.

"*Mama santissima*, our entire life, its is as you desire."

The Jaybird eased up onto his feet, giving a groan that may have been an act, a pretense of normalcy, as if he were getting out of the living-room sofa. Once he was standing again, once he could be sure that all the nearby bullets remained in their chambers, he looked to Barbara. "Owl Girl, these guys, are they who I think they are?"

"Our soul," said the queen with the gun, "is in your hands. Tell us as you desire."

"Buddy boy," Jay said. "I mean. Why don't you tell *us* something?"

"*Papa santissima, Mama santissima*. Restore our souls."

"Okay, okay, I get it." His voice gone gravelly, his gun now trained on the scippatoro, Barb's husband swiftly confirmed with her who these two were. "Hey, who else? Got the Monsters' Ball down here." He mentioned the Vomero church—it sounded like a distant constellation—then turned again to the painted wisp before him. "Except, hey, asshole." Jay scowled, his bruises stretching like the skin of spoiled fruit. "I don't believe we've been *introduced*."

The Shell member closest to Barbara, the one from the Balkans, shifted position. That got her attention, even as Jay went into a one-of-a-kind tantrum, his body stock-still while he said things like, "you fucking fuck, I mean, fuck you!" His gun hand never wavered so much as half an inch, and the weapon was pointed at the gut rather than the heart or head. After a moment Barbara extended one of her own hands in front of the next-nearest pistol, the white kidnapper's. She found she could curl her palm over the open end of the barrel. When the man looked to his moon-scarred commander, Barb did the same, and once more she put a stern finger in Fond's hairless face. She still had the nerve she'd discovered earlier; coolly she thought through how this must look to him. The former film major would

281

grasp easily enough that the new arrivals weren't cops, nor mobsters either, and it was likewise obvious they had some history with the Lulucitas. Now the tarty scippatoro, his gel-curls dropping as he dipped his head, was telling Jay that he and his "fellow sinner" would do whatever it took to "resurrect our soul."

At this the other one spoke up. "We sin against the *miracolosi*, only the *miracolosi* wash us clean."

"Give me a break. You came in here ready to kill somebody." The Jaybird looked pointedly at the .38, still trained on Fond's henchman. Otherwise however the husband remained motionless, a manner of speaking that Barbara wouldn't have believed he was capable of. "Same as when you jumped up and popped old Silky."

The darker sciapptoro raised his overgrown head, perplexed.

"You two shot the NATO man." Jay moved at last, raising a hand to indicate the late Lieutenant Major's long hair. "You caught him by surprise in the Museo Nazionale and, bang bang, goodbye."

The farther of the two, lighter-skinned and unarmed, was the one to groan agreement. He admitted to the shooting and then went into a whispering prayer, his head down. The one with the gun, however, must've come here knowing the news was out. He played it tough, baring his teeth at Fond and his soldiers.

"So you murdered him," the husband said. "And today, I mean, you come here ready to kill a few more. This is how you save your soul?"

The wife broke into the staring match. "Fond," she asked, "what about you? "What do you think you look like, holding a gun on you own brothers?"

Balefully the clandestino leader met her gaze, saying nothing. His head tottered above Barbara like a weight about to drop. Nonetheless she let her irritation show, lifting her hand from the kidnapper's gun-barrel, spelling out her point: what Jay was telling his two muggers applied equally to Fond and his crew. "You talk about spectacle, think about this one. Think about what it would look like, if you put a bullet in another poor boy from the South."

Actually she couldn't say where the whiter scippatoro came from. In New York she would've guessed he was Puerto Rican, with zits like those, with that single wooly eyebrow over a sleepless stare.

"We shoot or we don't shoot," the darker one repeated. "As you desire."

The mother began to give her dress a tug, then dropped her hand, frowning. Enough with fretting over the clothes she wore, the dreary old bindings. "Fond," she went on, "just relax and let me handle this."

She faced the femmy of the two and extended her hand, palm up. "As I desire?" she said. "All right, give me the gun."

Taken aback, looking to his companion, the man showed her an elaborate earring. Wavy silver strands in a jellyfish design, too delicate for such a hole in the wall.

"You want to wash your soul clean?" She stepped closer.

"Barb," said Jay.

"Let me handle this."

The queen was looking over Fond and his backups, his glance nervous and the others likewise twitchy.

"Absolution," Barbara said, "isn't that what you want?" She ventured a smile. "You want to wash away the bad old past, so your soul can be renewed, you can be born again—isn't that it? Okay, let's start. Why don't you tell me your name?"

Over his revolver, the lithe young man began to blink back tears. He choked out, "Men say I am The Moll."

"The Moll?" Barbara's smile changed shape. "Where did you learn gangster slang from a hundred years ago?"

"It's the cinema," said Fond, "the gigantic prayer that crosses every border."

"The Moll has committed great *sin*," said the scippatoro with the gun. "Sin against the *miracolosi*."

"Only the *miracolosi*," said the other, "wash clean our—"

"You guys," Barbara said. "Think about it. Look at this family, and think about that 'great sin.' You've been stalking us all this time. You know we're doing fine."

"But you are to divorce!"

The little guy was quite the package, wasn't he? A whore with a bleeding heart, a trembling gun, and all their secrets. "*Mama santa, Papa santa*, you divorce."

The Jaybird was the first to object—"Forget about it!"—and the mother began to say the same, making the sort of denials that her husband had back in Roebuck's office. Well . . . there'd been strains, between she and Jay, a lot of stress . . . But this felt like the wrong tack to take, a smear of hypocrisy across a conversation that should be entirely frank and aboveboard. Barbara fell silent and once more took in the whole group, jittery, dusty, the crossed beams of their flashlights looking like they'd lost juice. Fond's Albanian appeared the most dangerous, both arms raised, both hands on his gun. He paid no mind to Jay's weapon at his head. And the other two were ready to jump in wherever they'd do the most damage. Barbara looked away, finding the deepest dark she could beyond everyone's scowling heads, then hefted chest and shoulders in a Neapolitan shrug. She admitted that for some time she'd believed that she and Jay had to divorce.

"I'm saying, I wanted to end everything. How long did it go on, a month?"

Jay could recognize the right move when he heard it, though Barb couldn't think of what she was saying, unvarnished and from the heart, as a "move." Anyway the big man held his peace. Barb kept her eyes on The Moll but noticed that the Albanian had slackened a bit; his aim was lower. "But those hard feelings between my Jay and me," she went on, "it's history. It's ancient history, the divorce."

Waving towards her husband—her hand open, slow, harmless—she asserted that the renewed connection between them was obvious. "If we were still at each other's throats," Barbara said, "wouldn't that come out now?" She worked to keep her English free of therapy-speak, telling the former stickup man to think about the anger in this hole. "The tension, Moll. Tension like this, now, I'm saying if Jay and I still wanted to divorce, you'd be hearing it."

The scippatori appeared to get the point, their shared glances crackling, their appraisals of the Jaybird easy to read. The husband reached out to Barbara, the fingers of his free hand finding her panties' waistband at first touch and lingering there, another good move that wasn't a move. When Barb asked if Jay's attackers believed her, she wouldn't take a simple nod for an answer. She figured everyone in the three-thousand-year-old quarry needed to hear one of these two say yes, out loud, to the preservation of the marriage. Indeed, as soon as The Moll acknowledged that *la Mama* was right, his words halting but unmistakable, the Shell member still holding a gun relaxed visibly. His aim sagged another notch. The other Crab soldier meantime went back on his heels, and Barbara knew what to do next.

She started by asking the same thing her husband had asked Fond—whether the scippatori realized the kind of firepower likely be waiting upstairs.

The Moll looked a little offended. "For sure. The cavalry to the rescue."

The cavalry? Where did he get this stuff? "Yes, that's right."

"But we have a gat. We will defend you, everywhere, down here and—"

"Stop, don't. Wait." Barbara ran another check around the group, making sure of Fond in particular. She declared that she was going to get something from her purse. "And you all know," she said, "I don't carry a weapon." The clandestino leader waggled his head, perhaps giving her the go-ahead. Barb bent and pulled out her passport.

"Here you go." She held the blue booklet out to The Moll. "You take the passport, and I get your weapon."

The mugger's stare was so bewildered, and his friend bubbled so excitedly (*"Mille Euro, mille!"*), that at first Barbara didn't notice Jay speaking up behind her. The husband grew noisy, he even jerked his gun-hand a time or two, and he didn't bother with simple English. The first words Barbara heard had to do with debts. "Any tourist off a cruise ship," Jay was saying, "could tell you:" the scippatori carried the debt; they'd struck the first blow. At this Barb started to object, but Jay kept on, talking over her—he knew his Owl Girl. He knew she wasn't on a cruise. "For you, I mean, this is all about the lost sheep." For her, what these two outcasts had done back at the beginning of June didn't matter. "It's, hey, we *forgive* our debtors."

Barb heard him, the need in him. She didn't interrupt as the husband went on more quietly, acknowledging that one way or another, a passport with a woman's name would be useful for The Moll. Jay could see that. He'd had his eyes opened here in Naples, and he could see as well that the scippatori had been victims themselves. "Must've gotten a pretty bad smacking around, these two, working with old Silky.

"Owl, I mean, I'm with you that far. I guess I can go along with you. It's a plan."

The Jaybird's tone was conversational again. His gun-hand had settled. He got a slow breath and asked if Barbara had thought about the possible legal issues. "You realize, a document like that, it could get complicated?"

"Come on, Jay." Sure as she was of herself, Barbara nonetheless hadn't expected to sound so easy-going. "Are you saying, Roebuck can't cut through the paperwork? She can't have two new passports by the end of the week?"

"Hey, Roebuck can do all kinds of—what? What? *Two* passports?"

"I give mine to The Moll and you give yours to Fond's guy, here."

Her arm still extended towards the scippatoro, she nodded towards the remaining gunman. Meantime she couldn't miss the possibility of relief, of safety, that flooded her husband's looks. The deal wasn't one for one but two for two, and then all the weapons would be in friendly hands.

"We'll be back in the Consulate anyway," murmured the former VP for Sales,

"Back in the Consulate," Barbara said, letting him think. Letting him fill in the blanks: "A day like today, hey, there's a million ways we could've lost them." But more than that, she could see how he needed this to end. When he'd left the house this morning, he'd believed that come dinnertime he'd be riding back home on the funiculare.

The Albanian had something to say, his first words since they were up outside Cesare's. "A pass-port? American pass-port, is mine?"

Then The Moll: "We, how can we take from you? We, our lives, are for *you*."

Fond got a hand on his second-in-command, the unarmed African, and they murmured in their shared tongue as they watched Jay pull the pamphlet from his wallet pocket. Like Barbara, the husband had wanted it with him every day, so already the thing was curled and wrinkled. Barb however had to check Fond again; she needed him speaking in English. "Fond," she said, "look at it. Look at how beat up it is. Hard to believe, isn't it? Hard to believe something like that could save your man's life."

The deep-thinking renegade frowned down at her, so close he might believe that he and his friend had a decent chance of jumping in and snatching away both Jay's automatic and The Moll's revolver.

"This morning, you know," Barbara went on, "I saw my son on a screen, and I saw him fold up just like that passport. I watched my boy fold up and disappear."

"The Shell of the Hermit Crab," Fond said, "is not a criminal organization."

"Well, Jay and I aren't criminals either." He was the one to worry about, all right. "And like Jay says, giving away our I.D., we're taking a risk, it could be trouble."

But whatever came of this underground exchange, iron for paper, sooner or later that story too going to fold up and be finished. "It's going to be put on the shelf," Barbara said, "the Jaybird and I, all our drama, plus you and your Hermit Crab too. Isn't that Naples, where you're always running into some old drama? Old prayers, mashed flat and stuck to a wall? Down in Pompeii they were flattened in the middle of dinner."

"The past in all its folly. *La comédie humaine.*"

She watched him, not the passports. "And one day, isn't someone going to run into our leftovers, on the shelf, on the wall? Isn't that Naples?"

"*Assez, assez,*" Fond said. He dipped his chin, this scarred and lanky visitor from the fringes of the desert, he gave the least sign of assent, and with that the exchange took place too quick for Barb to see it. By the time she spotted Jay again, he had guns in both hands. Once more her elation ruffled up, an interior match for the thrill that played across the face of the white Shell member. The folder in his hand was worth *mille Euro*; the sensation in Barbara's heart had her grinning wildly up at Fond.

But he was looking over her shoulder. The Moll still hadn't gone for it.

"We are prepared," the scippatoro was saying, "to lay down our *life.*"

"Lay down your life?" Barb tried to rein in her smile. "Isn't that the opposite of a miracle?"

But her reasoning got nowhere, it choked her, because the femme with the memorable bandanna slipped the paper from her hand. She hadn't realized how stiffly she'd been holding her arm. It didn't drop at all, at the weight of the revolver.

Chapter Fifteen

The Refugee Lazarus had come back to his idea about a video. "Our arrangement, madame?" Barbara couldn't follow him at first, instead staring at his long-toed feet, before which Jay had turtled down over the automatics, indulging himself in a one-man Demolition Derby. The husband sent black bits and pieces sailing through the flashlight's dwindling glow, the magazines in one direction and the bodies in another. Barb understood, she approved, but when the metal landed it clattered like tin, as if somehow she'd wound up in a space without dimension. When Barbara once more took in the outlaws around her, keeping her own gun cradled against her hip, the five young men appeared like sketches on a clay vase. The two scippatori, huddled over her passport, might've been heroes of Troy consulting a map. She was back on the second floor in the Nazionale, cruising the display cases of kitchenware. Then on one of the kraters or serving bowls, one of the figures began to speak.

"*Madame*? You recall our arrangement, the prayer on-camera?"

Barb slid the revolver behind her, tucking it against her spine. With her whipsaw turned to feathers, with her eyes and ears likewise playing tricks, she wondered about the meager word "relief." She needed some word out of a fairy tale, an incantation.

The rangy clandestino looked a bit like a celebrity again, lifting his chin, regaining his swagger. "The video, Mrs. Lulucita? You are listening, please? I will tell you now how this film will be made."

"Oh, Fond." She suffered fresh tenderness towards him even as she shook her head. "No more playacting, I just can't."

"But, *playacting*, what is the relevance? My project is never merely artistic."

"No more movies, no screens or media. From now on it's real life, face to face."

Jay was back on his feet, stepping up behind her. He put one hand on her panties' waistline, the other on the gun.

"But, face to face, just so. Just so will be our video statement, much better enabled back up on the street. Up there, it will be the NATO, yes, but also the news."

"The—news." Barbara, trying to think, became aware of the limestone in her scalp. "There'll be cameras, you're saying. You're saying you and I can talk face to face, like human beings. And the newspeople, *they'll* make the video."

"Works for me," said Jay, a bit loud. "Hey. Sooner we're back to sea level, I figure, sooner we can make this right."

Fond frowned at that, his gaze dropping. He stared at Barbara's belly as if he could see through it to Jay's busy fingers, trying to take her weapon. The leader of the Shell grumbled that, here in Naples, they couldn't make much "right"— the real problems were down in the Sahel.

"Don't go there," Jay said. "Don't go back there, squabbling, trouble. We've been there and we just saw better, a lot better, a beautiful thing."

The handsome skin-and-bones went on frowning. "*La vie est ailleurs,*" he said.

"Whatever. Pont is, I mean. We all just saw the same thing down here."

Then why was the Jaybird still trying to take Barbara's weapon? She gave him a look, over her shoulder, then told her kidnapper to speak English.

"Life is elsewhere." He perked up, sounding prideful. "From 1968."

Jay remained at Barbara's back, close enough to make the snatch, as once more he acknowledged that he liked Fond's idea. "They're the pros, up there, the newspeople. It comes to spectacle, I mean, that's what they do." Jay wasn't just telling the man what he wanted to hear, either. Also the husband reiterated that a trip to Mali didn't seem realistic. The problem wasn't only that the Lulucitas had family issues, he pointed out; on top of that, the authorities might question their security. "Hey, never mind Africa, they might not let us back into New York."

"But I will say the rosary with you," added Barbara.

The young man squinted down at her, picking at his low beltline.

"Fond, you know me. You know I'll have to get those beads out."

"I know, yes. For this reason, I am making the plan with my lieutenant."

Barbara remembered: the two Africans murmuring cheek to cheek as the exchange of weapons hung in the balance. "So, I'm saying, it'll happen the way you want, up in front of the cameras. I'll say a Hail Mary for you and you people."

No more playacting, Barbara had told him, and she wasn't playing now. She could hear the difference when Jay did the talking. She was in love with the big Jaybird, no question—tickled afresh by that love, both in a half a hundred familiar ways and in ways she'd never felt before. Nonetheless she could hear the difference, the long-ingrained dissembling of the salesman. But then Jay had a lot to handle, even without the gun, he had a wife with a goofy smile and feathers in her ribcage. Barb was a mess, to boot, as crumpled and stained as the Jaybird's bartered I.D. She began to think about the ibuprofen she carried for cramping. She began to think of Cesare, the priest she'd chosen for her work in Naples. Another university man who'd been all over the map, Cesare would've proven useful down here.

The least she could do was mention the time. Jay had called it, said Barbara: the longer they stayed in the *Sotterraneo*, the worse things were likely to be upstairs.

"Think about it," she said. "Roebuck will call in the hovercraft—" and she broke into a chuckle, though she managed to disguise it as a clearing of the throat. How could she talk so silly? Hovercraft? But Fond massaged his long neck seriously. He said there was something else the Lulucitas needed to know. Whatever else might be up outside the condemned restaurant, in the wine cellar they would find another member of the Shell.

"Perhaps you are remembering, earlier, there is another man with us—"

"I remember," said Jay.

Fond picked at his cell phone, head down, explaining that he'd posted this man in the restaurant basement as a lookout. "He has a weapon, too," said the *commandante*, "but I will reach him."

He snapped the phone off his belt-loop. "As you go up, there comes the signal."

Barbara's impulse to laugh drained away. Jay was the first to respond, looking from Fond to her, thinking aloud about what it would look like when they came out into the wine cellar. "First there's us coming out," he said, "second there's Fond, okay so far. This lookout, hey, he knows us. But do we want anyone else climbing up. . . ?"

"But, 'anyone else?' Who else, *monsieur*? Truly, you must realize, I will be the only one to return with you to the streets."

Barb let her gun-hand drop to her side. "Of course."

"Is this not the significance," Fond went on, "when you are giving away your documents? These soldiers of mine, these friends of yours, they are free to go."

"Friends of ours?" Jay put it. "These two? I don't think so."

"Of course," Barbara repeated, "yes. We knew what we were doing, when we gave away our passports."

Fond showed her a youthful smile, wide-eyed, without the lemon wedges that that she'd found so hard to take in Castel dell'Ovo. As for her husband, when he stood this close she could see how many of his chin-hairs had gone white, a white that had nothing to do with the limestone—but her aging husband too appeared comfortable with the idea.

"Hey," he told her, "didn't I just say, we don't want to go back there?"

The Jaybird must've figured out the consequences of handing over the I.D. the same time as the two Africans. "Less we have to squabble about," he said, "the fewer complications on our way out, the better."

"I must insist, I alone am returning upstairs." Fond too sounded offended. "Only in that way is my project enabled."

Barbara got a look at the others. Neither the scippatori nor the soldiers had failed to grasp the exit strategy. As they jawed over their books, one pointed off towards Germany, another towards the U.S.

"Upstairs, when I am speaking for my brothers and sisters without a roof over their heads, I am knowing that these down here have their mobility."

Barbara could think of no better way to prove that she was with the man than to squat down and, propping the purse open before her, shake the bullets from her revolver into the bag. She found the barrel release at once. Maybe a cop had shown her once, back in Carroll Gardens, or maybe an uncle in the East Village. Jay uttered a moment's objection, a garble, a yawp, but he made no move to stop her. She would swear that what she heard was the sound of a man conceding the point—the safest way out was to go unarmed. Perhaps however she only heard the soft thump of the rounds falling into in the bag. They landed against the rosary at the top of her goods. After that the iron was nothing but a paperweight, and a considerably lighter one at that. As Barbara straightened back up she had no trouble tossing the thing off into the darkness. She didn't have to check the scippatori again, or the Shell members either. Everybody held their peace.

She faced Fond and asked if there were anything else.

Fond turned to his soldiers, still practically at his shoulder, and conferred in a murmur. Barb and Jay couldn't have heard even if they'd known the language. After a moment, the husband took the opportunity for a private talk of his own. "Owl, I mean, it's a risk." His gaze showed off his deepening crow's feet. "There's, what, a hundred things? A hundred things could go wrong."

Jaybird, a thousand. Barbara touched his hip and cast a glance at the scippatori, starting to say that at least The Moll and his friend would be watching their back. But the femme of the two jumped to his feet as soon as she turned his way. He moved with a revived charisma, like Fond, though this clandestino had curls to toss.

"Yes," declared The Moll. "We go free, so that you are forever safe."

The thief blinked, long-lashed, pretty. "We go free, all over the world, and we are watching for you. Maybe we are over in New York, and we are watching."

He summoned up an unlikely smile, at once imp-like and dignified, and broke into song: "Every mo-ove you make, we be wa-atching you."

Barbara thought of JJ, his one-liners. *You learn that from Silky?* Still, the song made the wiry youngster seem more real-world, a pop reference from after 1930s. The Jaybird followed up accordingly, telling The Moll it was time he started watching out for himself. "I mean," Jay said, and hesitated. Barbara could see his problem, needing to say it without recourse to New York shorthand.

"Jay's right," she said. "You and your friend have helped us enough."

"You've helped us enough," Jay said. "Any bad stuff this family went through, because of you, it's over now." He gave the washing-hands gesture. "*Capisce?*"

"You already saved our lives. Today, you saved us." Barbara recalled the museum, too, but thought better of mentioning it.

"*Basta cosi. Capisce? Finito.*"

She was impressed by Jay's Italian, emphatic as a native's. Nonetheless she couldn't be sure how well he was getting across. The Moll went on blinking slowly, thinking it over—and then the man was back in darkness. Fond had picked up the nearest flashlight, shining it at the tunnel wall. In the stone, the ridges and shadows of the chisel-marks looked like pieces of skeleton.

"Just take care of yourself," said Barbara, to the black patch that had almost killed her husband. "Take care." By the time she turned to follow Jay's tugging, she couldn't help but wonder how it should turn out this way—that the two richest and most powerful people in this underground had wound up, when all was said and done, better off than anyone else down here. The American visitors were climbing back towards the best neighborhood in town, Jay with his wallet and Barb with her purse, while the hand-to-mouth outsiders scuttled back into the rocks and gloom, with no more to show for the encounter than an extra piece of paper. Barbara had done all she could to make that trade-off happen, a comforting one for her and her husband. And now she had to wonder about it, as first she, then Fond, then Jay bent into the laddered and sloping crawl-space. She had to ask herself, as honestly as her aching and weariness allowed, if she was any better than the others who'd simply seized what they wanted from these hardscrabble souls, whether it was the late Lieutenant Major or, way back, a kingpin out of Rhodes or Corinth with a well-disciplined phalanx of swordsmen. Barbara tried to assure herself with thoughts of the program in Danbury, the Master's in Social Work. But this prompted further questions, nagging, unsettling. Even after she got the training she needed, and she did what she could for an unwed mother in Bridgeport, or for a victim of abuse in Ansonia, would those good deeds extend via some improbable karmic reach to sore-boned and uneducated creatures like these, used and discarded in a chilly and lightless maze? Could Barbara matter, ever? Could she actually help to create better? She needed to think, and, once more, to believe.

Back before the quake, tourists who'd bought tickets for the *Sotterraneo* had visited via staircases cut in the 1990s, with rails and wide cornering. This tunnel on the other hand was fit only for slaves. It triggered shivers of claustrophobia, the limey walls too close for a day-tripper. From time to time Barbara could barely grip the steps, the toeholds, their edges so ruggedly spurred that you'd think they'd been hacked out yesterday. She recalled that, for years now, she'd made one of the older boys take on any chore that involved a stepladder. Plus today, as first in line, she carried the flashlight as well as the purse. A few minutes up into the tunnel, she tucked the heavy cylinder down the top of her dress, between her breasts. The bulb housing bumped her chin, and her head got in the way of the light, but there was only one direction to go after all. There was only the hand-over-hand, each upward move another realm of doubt. Soon everything about the return to street level started to feel likewise sketchy. The entire arrangement, from handguns to prayers, might've been a scaffold cinched with bobby pins, swaying across a deep and sudden chasm.

Barbara's hands began to itch and burn. Her breathing grew full of phlegm and the flashlight between her breasts kept thumping her jaw: *shouldadone, shouldadone*. She tried thinking of faraway business, the new doctor she would get back in the States. A woman would be best, an older woman, sixty at least. With that Aurora came to mind, no doctor but somehow, in this burrow, triggering a spasm of fellow-feeling. Nettie was more like it, with her diplomas and her no-nonsense brush-cut, and Barbara also recalled a well-weathered and sharp-tongued tutor in Language Arts, back at Sacred Heart Elementary. A former schoolteacher some ten years past retirement, the old girl had seemed such good company that Barb had volunteered in Language Arts herself. She'd read one circle of second-graders the Alice-in-Wonderland sequence twice in a row. For the life of her, she couldn't understand what these mouthy and assertive American Brownie Scouts saw in that pampered and over-polite English girly-girl.

Four or five times during the climb, Fond called a halt and juggled up his cell phone. He tried to call his man in the restaurant basement, as Barb peeked down past her hips (as soon as they'd come into the tunnel, she'd decided not to worry about what, if anything, Maddalena's former boyfriend might glimpse under her dress). From that angle the phone's number pad would turn him briefly into the Clandestino from Another Planet, casting a green speckle across his face. But Fond could never get a signal; he'd gone too far underground.

When she first picked up a shadow cast from above, a faint stippling, she thought it was only a trick of the sweat in her eyes. But then it turned up again: a cloud-over-cloud effect. After that came the stink of the ruined wine.

Coming into the basement from behind the barrels—and free, this time, of a chloroform doping—Barb could see the quake damage better. Some casks had sprung their staves, and others were cracked and leaking. Of course she still suffered a wooze, a stab, as she emerged into unlikely brightness. A surprising amount of light came in from the street, dazzling to Barbara, like sunshine after a matinee. She knew it must be late, and she could make out a loose plank or two still covering the basement hatchway, across the room from where, at last, she stood again at full height. But this was the time of year when the sun lasted into the Italian dinner hour, dawdling as it sank between the Gulf islands. Twilight went on forever.

Behind her, Fond spoke at conversational level but with a hoarse insistence. *"C'est moi, c'est moi. Ne vous derangez-vous pas."*

The space was larger than she remembered, too. As Barbara stepped around the wine rack, drawn towards the light, she realized that Fond would have headroom here. Some headroom anyway, under most of the sagging ceiling. There was air enough for the smell of sulfur to pierce the cellar mold, the fermentation. From the street descended a noise of raucous normality, the unmuffled rasp of Vespas and Suzukis. Barbara, taking a long step sideways for the sake of the two big men still unfolding out of the tunnel, pulled the flashlight from inside her dress and let it plop into a wine-puddle. She indulged herself in a terrific shake, triggering yet another sweet rush, her most intense yet, of reviving spirits. The doubts of her up-tunnel laboring fell away. At her first lung-full of air she could've sworn that the matchstick odor coughed up by Vesuvius had turned sweet, in some improbable chemical reaction with the spilled *Lacrima Christi*.

Then Jay: "Is that a blue light? Revolving blue light?"

Barbara gave herself another shake, more businesslike, getting her wits about her. The Jaybird knew the cops when he saw them. The revolving light of a police car, maybe more than one in fact, shot an intermittent darker hue between the planks over the hatchway. Hardly glaring, the blue had Barbara squinting nonetheless, thinking again of the warnings that she and Jay had raised down in the *Sotterraneo*. To her they'd all sounded bogus half the time: the cavalry to the rescue.

"Hey, Fond, you see? There it is, man, happy ending. People we can talk to."

The police weren't stupid and the system worked. The sun was shining. Barbara kept shedding her long day's burdens, the weights that had pinched every encounter, and she was slow to translate the amplified voice that began to cut through the traffic noise. A bullhorn, this was: *Pronto, pronto. Senta, senta?* Testing, testing, listen . . . and with that she spotted the man to whom the authorities were speaking. In the hatchway squatted Fond's lookout, the third of the crew who'd snatched her and Jay off the church steps. The refugee had kept himself hidden on the stairwell's bottom step.

Big guy, small guy? Skin tone, hair style? Barb couldn't remember a thing from up in the Vomero, and down here she couldn't see much besides his gun. Another sleek automatic, standard issue for the Shell of the Hermit Crab. The lookout wasted no time sizing up the situation: the cops on the doorstep and the *Commendatore* held hostage. Barbara was still feeling optimistic when the man spun in a crouch and put her in the middle of another worst-case scenario, an easy target in the middle of the room.

"Hey!" said Jay, raising his empty hands.

"*Arrête!*" shouted Fond. "*Relâche!*"

The lookout's eyes appeared hypnotically enlarged, and Barbara thought again how little sleep the Shell must've been getting. Behind him continued the amplified hollering, and she wondered how much he could hear of what was said in the cellar.

"Fond," Jay said. "Talk to him. Last thing we need, here"

Barbara knew she was scared, the light and air hadn't made her crazy, but she experienced, as well, a sustaining levelheadedness. She put out her arms as if to corral an overexcited kid at a party. Was it the guns she'd faced earlier that left her so cool now? Was it another product of her long afternoon's revival? *Well*, she'd once told Cesare, *my soul* . . . Yet she remained worn to a frazzle, flinching each time the bullhorn cut on. What she was trying to accomplish had nothing amplified about it: no playacting. Fond spoke up again, perhaps using the man's name. He sounded so gentle Barb didn't need to know the language.

The cellar's plaster dust gave a queer shiver—a sideways jerk, impossible to miss in the blue-gold air.

"Talk to him," Barbara said. "We're all going back up into the city."

The man's arm shivered too. Was he beginning to lower his weapon? Barbara hoped so, she prayed so, even as she noticed another bobble or tremor in the room's dust, slashing this way and that around his wavering fistful of iron. Also fresh cement- or mortar-powder sprinkled down from overhead. When a sudden *crack* sounded across the basement, Barb knew it was no gunshot. She'd never taken her eyes from the man's weapon, she knew his aim hadn't dropped below her gut, and anyway the crack or snap had a different feel entirely, the splintering resonance of wood. Now the noise came again; now the whole basement gave a shake, and as Barbara lurched from foot to foot she glimpsed the wine rack coming apart, the barrels that had survived the last earthquake tumbling out of their shelves. The Jaybird too tottered and spread his stance, trying to catch some prop or balance with one arm and flailing after Barb with the other. As the next tremors got to her, as the eruptive dust stung her eyes shut, she pictured a goofy day with the kids, the yelly interference that threw off every move.

You'd think the cellar itself had gotten into the wine, staggering, drooling. When Barbara opened her eyes again she found the long-boned Fond out of commission, rolling through the plaster-spotted puddles with his head cradled. He might've been some essential Naples potful, a tangle of squid, a heap of discarded *ojetti*. Then Jay got a hand on her, but it did no good, he only snagged a bra-strap and popped her breast out of its holster. Everyone in the room was undone and flopping around, now heaved towards the tunnel that led back underground and now thrown, with a bellowing red splash, towards the hatchway stairs. Everyone was shrieking and getting hurt.

Yet the worst noise came from up on the street. Somebody out there took the horn and started to shout, and one word echoed clearly across the cobblestones.

"*Terramoto! Ter-ra-mo-to!*"

The light and dust gave everyone in the basement a whole-body Afro, a ghostly weedy fringe. Barbara was half-blinded or worse and she gagged from the murk, the upheaval, the tickle inside her shirt. She couldn't see where the lookout had gone, him and his slashy weapon, but she knew she had to get herself braced somewhere. She knew the hatch lay just ahead and there was a scaffold at the top of the steps, extra reinforcement. She pitched that way, groaning a Hail Mary, *nowandatthehourof-ourdeath*, her arms wide open and hands outstretched.

The clandestino Fond had left behind turned up against one side of the stairwell, huddling against the concrete but jerked around as badly as the rest of them. As the woman loomed above him the gun went off. Just went off, it had to be an accident, or such was the scrap of a thought that passed through Barbara's head along with the tiny yet shattering pain. She couldn't even be sure she'd heard the shot, before the shock of the wound spiraled outward from her collar to yank her away into a deepening distance, ever more lightless and yet blue.

Underwater, the soft Mediterranean water, *morbido* in Italian, down in this death-soft water in the wine-dark sea that made a blind poet of anyone who plunged deep enough, down where you're blind also to whether these are poems or prayers, she knew she could find her mother. It was only a matter of the right shell. The sea floor was volcanic and crowded but her hands were alert, some people had fingers that could read the words right off the tongue, could read the braille that rolled off the tongue of the blind poet, and among the vapor leaks of the sea-bottom, the shoots of steam flecked with flame, each shell had its song. Each was another humpbacked vehicle in the night, from which arose the persistent voicings of the singers who'd fallen and drowned, a music half-birdlike, the ululations still alive amid the traffic of weeds and small fry, a song in play for thousands of years. A runaway mother might dart from shell to shell, she might duck under one high dome of a tomb after another, its calcareous edges sharp enough to pierce a side or cut open a head, to open the very dome of the brain, but once the refugee knelt under that shell the singing inside was altered, a living voice came into the ghost choir, a sinning heart sent its dissonance through the harmony of the saints. It was only a matter catching the voice out of place. Already her searching alert fingers had tuned in something like that, a rushed and unpracticed tempo, one, two, threefourfive, and either the wrong person had died or the person under the wrinkled clothes of this particular shell was a deceiver, playing games, and indeed whatever lay under the dented fenders of this oyster wasn't to be trusted, you could see that in the weeds that poked up around its hem, thrusting up long and thick and stiff *against the current*. The flame-speckled bottom waters rose and the wine-dark top waters fell, yet despite the sea's whipsaw confusion this studly erect tissue should never be confused with her mother. Nor was the diver thrown off when her discovery turned out to possess a certain viciousness. The creature shot out of its horny lodging shaped like a tomahawk and flew into her face, but she could handle this too, she understood that her little attacker was merely traumatized by its displacement, like all the living down here, and she wouldn't have made this voyage in the first place if she hadn't done her coursework in submarine vocabulary, so that the other could read her words right off her tongue, so that all she needed to do in order to begin the dialogue, to explore the issues around her mother, was get the tomahawk's clinging wet feathers out of her mouth—that was the real danger, the thing's childish need for her mouth, the feathers clogging her nose and throat—and filthy besides, after so much time under wraps amid the bottom-traffic . . .

Choking, spluttering, Barbara woke. Dust cluttered her throat, dust and something thicker. She flung herself up on her elbows.

Round her arms and waist lay a swill of wine, discolored by chunks of ceiling. Round her head burst a phenomenal outcry, a sighing and bawling that might've been scraped from the walls of the gut. A din out of the Old Testament, its first comprehensible word was *God.* "God, thank God!" Then still more sighing, tumultuous, half-vocalized, and full of joy.

She wondered about the echo in the battered underground space. The nearest support pillar stood at an unnerving tilt, angled her way above one shoulder. But down closer to her stood Jay, the first person she noticed, and he was the one who sang out the most extravagantly, wringing every last remnant of breath from his thanks. He'd been crying but he didn't wipe his face, his handsome head and face, still worth a look when it was bruised in five places. His hands were occupied with his two oldest, grown boys who were making less noise than he but appeared more out of control. JJ and Chris grimaced and wobbled from foot to foot, leaking tears, figures out of a midsummer night's drunk. As for the two girls, each stood knotted around a different brother's leg, mewling wetly and yet helping their father keep the two teens from falling on Mom.

Down at everyone's feet huddled Paul. The eleven-year-old had his head sunk on his folded arms; he peeked at her over wine-stained shirtsleeves.

Barbara, working against the uproar, tried to concentrate on the boy. Stained sleeves? Also her middle child wasn't crying Hosanna, but he was crying a bit, and now he yanked up his collar and wiped his nose on it. He might've pulled his shirt untucked. The mother of course understood what he'd done, she sat there unwounded, actually refreshed, but she wasn't sure whether she still knew this child. Paul remained her prettiest; The Moll would envy those eyelashes, and the thick and pet-able curls that covered his preteen head. He must've looked like a doll, Mr. Paul, even when he'd had his fingers in Mama's mouth. But now those fingers dripped doughy clots of plaster, steeped in juice-like blood.

Blood had caked at the corners of Barbara's mouth as well.

"Must've been like this back on Day One," her husband was saying, or singing. "Owl Girl, I mean, Jesus *God*! This is how it must've been for the rest of you guys, Day One in this city."

Sitting up straighter, Barbara got a look at herself. Not that she wanted to neglect her eleven-year-old, looking so shaken, so weakened, but she needed to know the damage. Round the neck of her dress lay a thick mud-red, more than wine and revealing her unprotected nipple. A fresh and ragged hole gaped in one lapel, and around it the sticky maroon business lay smeared the thickest. Underneath, under fabric and collarbone, a faint buzz radiated. Pins and needles, more painkiller than pain.

Barbara frowned, the last spooky shudder of her dream draining away, and she looped her bra back where it belonged. She doubted the children noticed, and anyway they'd seen their mother half-undressed plenty of times before. Many the weekend morning she'd come to with a couple-three youngsters giggling across the bed, her in a flimsy nightgown and the Jaybird in boxers and a T. The difference today was, they'd been delivered to Mama's bedside by the police.

"Paul." She reached for the boy. "I know what you did. I *know* what you did, Mother of God. Thank you."

"My ma-an." The husband's voice broke again. "My Mr. Paul. I mean, even this he can fix, even one in the *throat*."

Now Dora and Syl fell on her, they could see Mom could take it, though Barbara kept working her way towards Paul. She budged over the wet gravel of the floor, against the girls' murmurs and nuzzling. Once again, flakes of dried blood drifted down into the twins' puff-blossom hair, and noticing that, the mother also began to take in the damage done by tonight's quake. The tremors didn't appear to have had much impact. At a glance you could see that most of the ceiling and its support remained in place, what with all the light pouring down from the street. Could that be daylight, still? Or was it the combined glare of official vehicles, television crews, and the cars and bikes of gawkers trying to get a look? In any case Barbara figured that the basement had lost only a few more barrels and chunks of ceiling plaster. It didn't take much of a shock—when a man was a bundle of nerves to begin with—to jog him into firing a gun.

But never mind that guy, the clandestino who'd almost killed her. Never mind, once Barbara got hold of her middle child and pulled him into her lap. As the twins made a place for the scrawny next-oldest, the mother felt her teens hugging her too, kneeling into the muck to press their faces against her sopping back. Still she paid the most attention to Paul, taking fresh note of what a slob he'd become all of a sudden. His shirt appeared to have lost its starch, streaked with mud and wine and worse. With that she was racked by a bout of shivers and cottonmouth, and sank deeper into the fold of her children. Embraced by ten hands, she curled up and closed her eyes.

Eventually Paul's breathing calmed and dried. "Mom," he said.

She couldn't respond. She couldn't shake off one of the twins probing along her mother's collarbone. The girl ran a finger over the center of the healing, the target buzz, and Barbara became aware of a roughness, a scar. Only then did she notice that Jay had squatted beside the group. He'd hooked an arm around them all.

"Never again," he said. "Going off half-crazy, like we did, I mean. Never again for this family."

She made some room between one of daughters and one of her teens, finding the Jaybird's face.

"Barb, oh God, I mean, no way, never, forget about it. Next time this family makes some kind of move, we're *whole*, we're together on it. That's the new basis."

There might've been a reply partway up her throat, a throat full of knuckles, unstable yet from all her children's touches. Jay tried out a smile and she managed a nod. She managed a neck-stretch, bending first towards one shoulder and then the other, and the group hug began to weigh on Barbara. It began to recall the burdensome climb up from the sotterraneo, and the more suffocating heap of laws and paperwork that she and Jay faced next. She, Jay—and at least one other person in this cellar.

Barb sat up, wriggling off Paul and the girls as she extended her legs. The teenagers backed away without needing to be told.

"Listen, Jaybird." She had decent tone. "What's happened to me, I know, I realize—what's happened to me and you both, here in Naples—it's really something, but it's not the whole story. Where's Fond, I'm saying? Where's his man?"

"That's my Mama," John Junior said.

The older boys came around one shoulder. "Five minutes after a near-death experience," JJ went on, "and she's back to being the Good Samaritan."

"To put it mildly." Chris pulled off his glasses. "She's going for, like, the Guinness Book of Samaritans."

She could play catch-up. "Actually," Barbara said, "I'm just trying to nudge up above Worst Parent of the New Millennium."

"That's my Mom."

"Mom, I'm telling you. Like, Pop came out of this place screaming for help—"

"All right, I hear you, my guys, my good big guys." The rancid stuff on her tongue helped keep her sober. "And I'm saying, we'll talk. Your father's right. Wherever we go next, first we've got to all sit down and talk."

The teens' solid front remained unnerving. "What?" JJ asked, straight-faced. "Like back at the museum?"

"Bro. Cut her some slack. The museum, that's ancient history."

Now that was a surprise, Chris choosing not to talk about a museum. Had her bookish boy too moved on to new priorities? In any case the fifteen-year-old gave Barb the chance to get a better look around. At the edge of the wine-puddle in which she sat, amid the flesh-like hunks of plaster, she discovered her purse. Wasn't too far to reach, though it was heavy from the soaking, and as she got the bag, she found the man she was looking for too. Fond was part of a cluster off in the darkest part of the room. He stood against a wall, handcuffed to a cop, while a second officer kept a grip on his opposite arm. But so far as Barb could see, the clandestino rebel hardly noticed his keepers. In the nook where they held him, he could stand full height, and his doctored cheekbones caught the light from outside. Once more he looked like a star of the screen. As soon as the mother spotted him, she could tell he was staring her way.

Apres vous, madame.

Barbara nodded, but she knew that wasn't nearly enough. That was no way to keep a promise. She started to raise a hand, but this felt likewise flimsy.

Dropping her chin, tuning out the latest between Jay and her oldest, the mother again caught sight of her purse. The top was open and something glinted within—maybe a bead, maybe a bullet—

but the rosary was just the ticket, wasn't it? The rosary would do it, the sign she needed, allowing her to pass as an honest woman. She found the sculpted coral greasy, but the loop came out of the bag without snagging on the rest of Barbara's swamped clutter. When she got the swaying icon up into the light, she made the figure in custody break into a smile. Fond even hitched his hips, a touch of the rap star. With all he'd been through, the man must've pinned his hopes to far less than a string of beads. He'd never have founded the Shell of the Hermit Crab if he were scared of flying on a wing and prayer.

But the soldier who'd been posted lookout, Barbara discovered, was nowhere to be seen. Fond must've arranged that, too, ordering the guy out of harm's way as she lay dying and Jay rushed outside screaming. Now Fond was the only illegal in the room—and come to think of it, since his healing he'd gotten his papers. He had better I.D. than Barb and Jay did, just now. Otherwise the basement was full of the law, in plainclothes or in uniform. Among them loomed some sort of military doctor, in a Red Cross helmet. There were also a pair of Marine Elites, bulked up in flak jackets. Wedged behind what was left of the wine rack, one leatherneck carried a W-shaped automatic rifle and the other a gleaming boxlike lamp, and they stood looking down the entrance to the slaves' passageway.

None of these people had anything to say. For some time now, since Barbara had hoisted her rosary, the only noise had come from outside, the shouting and traffic.

Jay broke the silence. "Good call. Good one, Owl, that's what Fond needs to see. Plus, you realize, he told his man to get lost while you were—"

She nodded, keeping her beaded hand up by her face.

"Got to give it up for the Refugee Lazarus." Jay broke into a grin. "He makes sure his guy's safe, did the right thing there, and then he goes down on his knees. I mean, down flat, with his hands out where the cops can see them."

Barbara looked again at the youngsters clustered around her. The girls were still trembling, holding hands, and Paul remained a mess. Today's quake hadn't amounted to much, an aftershock, and when the Jaybird first came out from under the condemned restaurant, they must've thought for a moment that everything was all right. Then they would've heard him calling for help.

Barbara focused on John Junior. "You know your Mama," she said. "You know we'll talk."

His smile was artless, closemouthed. He settled the others with a look.

"There's lots to talk about," she went on. "There's Silky Kahlberg and your Pop, and there's you and Romy."

JJ turned to Chris, and she could read the body language; she knew her Irish Michelangelo. She wouldn't have any trouble getting them to hand over their files. There were people in this city who could do a lot more for the gypsy than they could, and there were lawyers and others who could do a lot better by Fond than Barbara could. Also DiPio could arrange for counseling, if the young man from Mali wanted.

Barbara gave a sigh of her own and got her feet beneath her. Standing, she swiped the muck off her backside. Her thighs itched from the sticky residue.

Jay had taken over with the two oldest. "Whatever you guys've been into, the main thing is, it's in the past. Hey?"

She showed the Jaybird a grateful look.

"Way I see it," Jay said, "we came out ahead, swapping Fond here for that Kahlberg. We're way ahead there. I mean, anyone see any other changes, worth coming all this way and going through all this?"

"I think I can tell you one," Paul said, evenly. "My eh, eh, episodes are over."

Their Italian boy, his hands fluttered as he went up on tiptoe in an extended stretch. As his narrow chest filled with air everyone turned to stare. Paul's top was so streaked and speckled it called to mind one of his grandmother's scarves.

"Paulie," Dora said. "Look at you."

"Look at *you*," said Sylvia.

"I, I mean it," said the middle child. "The healing, the eh, the episodes . . ."

"Laying-on of hands," Chris said.

"Whatever." Rarely had Paul sounded so ordinary. "I, I just feel it. I, I know it. With, with Mom just now, that was the eh, the end of it."

His sisters and brothers went on staring, his father too. Barbara however brushed herself off and pulled her clothing straight, preparing herself the best she could to face the cops and the media. She could handle that kind of thing, she and Jay. Her youngest boy, on the other hand, had endured enough Q-&-A for a while. Hadn't Barb spent the better part of the morning giving him the third degree, in close-up and in freeze-frame? Now this evening, if you asked her, he was right that the healings had ended; in so far as his most recent case had any sort of feeling about it, she felt the same. The boy had worked the process, she felt—through a rare quirk of recovery from trauma, a coping mechanism to help him deal with a terrifying round of Monopoly. But if that machinery had finished its cycle, then the last thing Paul needed tonight was to talk his way back through the wheels within wheels. He'd have time enough later; they'd all have time enough.

Barbara finished with her clothes, also working her tongue in her mouth, trying to clean. Enough with the kiss of disease. Around her the stipples of reflection across the wine had to be streetlamps and headlights, night traffic.

"Mr. Paul," Jay said. "You had two today. Knock anyone for a loop."

"But that's just what I'm, I'm saying." The boy turned over a limp wrist.

"Hey, big guy. Nothing to be ashamed of. I can't tell you how often your Mom and your Pop have been knocked for a loop."

"But, but, o-ordinarily I could never've done this second wuh, this second one. That's what I'm saying. I couldn't've, I couldn't've done this one if, if, if . . . I couldn't've done it if it wasn't the last."

On either side of the family, now, the Marines stood waiting. Nobody was going after any hostiles until the civilians were secure, and Barbara figured she'd find their C.O. first, the ranking officer on the scene. Also the police bided their time, though she could hear the click of the cuffs as one of them shifted his grip on Fond.

"It's not," the ex-*miracolino* was saying, "it never happens i-in words. If Romy were here, she'd uh, she'd understand. It doesn't a-add up to like, words and a story."

"I hear you," Jay was saying. "If today, these healings, if they were ordinary, hey, two of them, there's no way. I hear that."

"I could do it because this, this with Mom, it was the last."

Barbara noticed the boy's gesture, effeminate again. He stood hipshot, pouting, looking more and more like a younger Aurora.

John Junior broke in. "Hey! Hey my man, the P-man!" He raised a long finger. "I *got* it, the laws of the universe. I got how this worked."

The big teen whipped his finger around the oval of family faces. "Check it out, you completed a circle. Check it out, the first was Pop, the last was Mom. A circle, my little big man, that's how it worked."

"Or think of it this way," Chris said.

"Oh, here we go," JJ said. "Alternative theory."

"Now, *Junior*. Try to think for a minute."

"See, my brother never learned, he's the alternative theory."

"Try to think of it *this* way, okay Junior, and then we'll all get down on our hands and knees and look around for your I.Q."

"You guys," said Paul.

"Well, think of this—five children, five episodes."

"That's right!" exclaimed Dora. "Sylvia, count. One was Papa, two was that girl, that Romy, and then—"

"Five equals five." Chris poked his glasses at Paul. "Could be, Mistah P."

"Hey," Jay said. "Save it for Dr. DiPio."

The mother liked both theories, actually. Either of them made more sense than most of what she'd had in mind back when she'd come to Naples.

"Whatever," said her middle child. "It's not going to h-happen again."

John Junior was nodding. "Five children, five episodes."

"Good, bro. Good boy. Now for our next act. . ."

The girls were looking from brother to brother, spinning, delighted. Barbara had to move the other way, towards the exit, the uncertain lights of the city above.

Biographical Note

John Domini has won awards in all genres, including a fellowship from the National Endowment for the Arts and the *Meridian* Editors' Prize. He has published fiction in *Paris Review*, *Ploughshares*, and anthologies, non-fiction in *GQ*, the *New York Times*, and elsewhere, including Italian journals. Alan Cheuse, of NPR's "All Things Considered," described his second collection, *Highway Trade*, as "the way we live now... witty, biting portraits." His first novel, *Talking Heads: 77*, was praised by the Pulitzer winner Robert Olen Butler as "both cutting-edge innovative and splendidly readable." Domini is also a reviewer with *The Believer* and other publications, and has worked as a visiting writer at many universities, including Harvard, Lewis & Clark, and Northwestern. Italian publication for *Earthquake I.D.* is being arranged through a house that was the first to translate Don DeLillo.